THE PATTERN SCARS

CAITLIN SWEET

ILLUSTRATED BY MARTIN SPRINGETT

ChiZine Publications

Library and Archives Canada Cataloguing in Publication

Sweet, Caitlin, 1970-
    The pattern scars / Caitlin Sweet.

ISBN 978-1-926851-43-3

    I. Title.

PS8587.W387P38 2011   C813'.6   C2011-905031-5

CHIZINE PUBLICATIONS
Toronto, Canada
www.chizinepub.com
info@chizinepub.com

Edited and copyedited by Sandra Kasturi
Proofread by Samantha Beiko

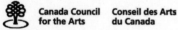

**Canada Council Conseil des Arts
for the Arts du Canada**

We acknowledge the support of the Canada Council for the Arts which last year invested $20.1 million in writing and publishing throughout Canada.

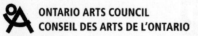

**ONTARIO ARTS COUNCIL
CONSEIL DES ARTS DE L'ONTARIO**

Published with the generous assistance of the Ontario Arts Council.

Printed in Canada

For my sister Sarah, who is unerringly, firmly, lovingly, always right.

THE
PATTERN
SCARS

BOOK
ONE

CHAPTER ONE

A tale was always told, in the lower city and in the castle (and I know, because I've lived in both places): When Teldaru, who was later seer to King Haldrin, was a boy of five, a powerful and much-hated lord ordered him to fetch a flagon of wine. The boy did the lord's bidding, for he had no choice, being a child, and the son of the tavern keeper, and of no account. The lord was already drunk, but he swallowed most of the wine in a few gulps. He set the flagon down unsteadily and it tottered and fell. "Wretch!" he cried at Teldaru, who was still standing there by the table. "You've brought me a faulty cup. And now look—such a mess—only a seer could make sense of it. . . ." The man narrowed his eyes at the dark spatter upon the wood, then shifted them back to the boy. "Make right your clumsiness," he slurred. "Entertain me. Read my future in this pattern and I will withhold the order to have you flogged."

Teldaru stood up on his tiptoes and peered across the tabletop. He frowned. "I see a breaking wave," he declared in his high, clear voice as the others around the table and in the room fell silent, "with you standing beneath it. Your face is still and purple." It is said that the midday sun, which had been spilling into the tavern, dimmed, and an owl hooted, as if it believed night had fallen. Some claim that stars shone, in the sudden dimness, and that one even fell, to signal a prophecy confirmed.

The lord gaped at the child as the darkness made way again for daylight. After a moment he rose, knocking over his stool, and all his men rose too, their mail shirts hissing and their scabbards clattering against benches. "Kill him," he said, waving a hand at Teldaru, but no one moved to obey him. He stumbled backwards and fell down unconscious. Three days later he drowned in his mistress's bath. Two days after that, the king (Haldrin's father, then) installed Teldaru by the Otherseers' pool in the castle wood.

"And how did it happen first for you?" people would ask me, thinking of the boy and the lord and the wine. I heard this question in the brothel where I spent my girlhood, and by the seers' pool where I left my girlhood behind. For a long time I answered this way: When I was eight, I came upon a woman weeping beside the fountain where I liked to soak my feet on the hottest summer days. She grasped my hands and cried, "He has left and gone—and oh, what will become of me? Tell me; tell me, child, for my own eyes are closed. . . ." As she spoke, my gaze strayed to the water, which was spraying in fat droplets from the fountain's white stone mouth. And I saw her likeness in the air—only she was laughing, holding a baby above her so that it laughed too. Such an image: golden but made of all the other colours; thin and faceted as a dragonfly's wing.

"There will be a child," I told her, and the vision rippled and fell like the water. "You will laugh together." The words were like the vision itself: heavy and light at once. There was a humming in my head.

She embraced me (her tears made a warm trail across my neck) and said, "Such a hopeful thing you've seen," as if she didn't quite believe me but wanted to be kind. A year later I saw her again by the fountain, holding a red-headed babe on her hip—and she embraced me again and gave me my first silver coin.

This was what I said to the people who asked about my first vision. A less grand tale than Teldaru's, but the gold of it shimmered every time I told it, and the red-haired baby made me smile. And it *had* happened—just not first, as I claimed. So I suppose I was a liar even before the curse.

The true answer to the question was: My mother was crying again. The newest baby was crying. "He's left," my mother sobbed, "he's gone." The same words over and over, as she chopped a potato on the scarred, stained table. "He's left—he's gone" until the potato was a collection of slivers peeling away from the knife. "Quiet!" This word was a scream. Her head was turned to the kicking, red-faced baby. The knife slipped. She made another noise, like the grunt of an animal. Blood pulsed over the table and onto the ancient, yellowed rushes on the floor. She stared, then raised her head to me and whispered, "Nola." Her eyes were wide. "Nola." I could not move from my little stool by the door. "Help me. Tell me what will become of me, for my own eyes are closed."

I was gazing at the pattern of blood and potato peelings as I heard her words. After a moment I saw a darkness seeping up around her legs, and up around the baby's cradle, and over the pallets where the other children huddled.

The darkness thickened until no one was there at all. When it began to ebb I thought I might remember to breathe again, but I couldn't, because there was still emptiness where everyone had been. The room was the same as ever, but also vast, and there was a feeling in my chest that was new, like a weight of stones.

"Nola!"

I was lying on the floor. My mother's face swam above me. She was holding her hand in the air, and I noticed from a faraway place that it was already wrapped in a piece of cloth, blood-soaked now but likely filthy even before. The baby's wails sounded louder than they had. "Child." Her eyes were sharp and narrow, now. "Did you see something? *Tell me*"—and I did somehow, in a voice that didn't sound like mine at all.

She took me to the brothel the next day, and sold me to the old seer there for a bag of copper pieces. I never saw her or my siblings again.

So I'd ask anyone: Which answer satisfies more? Gold-drenched water and a chortling baby, or darkness, and stones instead of breath? I knew as soon as that first person asked me the question. For several years I replied falsely, but by choice. My listeners believed me, also because they chose to. There was no curse, for those first few years; just innocence, and a gift I hoped might someday bring me joy.

I was filthy. I had always been filthy, but only realized it now. I was ten years old: ten years of ash and soot, and muck from the sunken patch of ground in front of my door—all of this buried in my skin and matted in my long hair.

"The hair will have to go," said the tall, clean woman who was standing in front me. The woman was wearing a gown of blue velvet belted with silver links. My fingers itched to touch the cloth (heavy and warm, I imagined, and smooth in the worn-away patches) and the metal (cool and hard), and I curled my ragged nails into my palms. "I won't have my ladies crawling with bugs because of her."

"Of course, milady," said my mother from behind me, "I thought of that, would have done it myself before I brought her here, but she made a fuss, bawled and shrieked until I left her alone—though she's usually a good girl, milady," she added breathlessly, her voice false and sweet, "a good, biddable, obedient girl, that's sure."

I never bawled or shrieked, I thought, *and you never even mentioned cutting my hair.* I longed to say this but did not, in case the blue-gowned woman should send me out of this room of curtains and carpets and back into the street.

"What is your name?" A new voice; another woman, rising from a low stool by the fireplace. This one was old and bent, her back a lump of flesh that made her look like she was carrying something—a bolt of cloth, or a baby. Her skin was very dark, and I thought that it must be even filthier than my own. "What is your name?" the woman said again, the words a low, thick lilt. Her eyes looked all black, with centres that shone like pearl (I had seen a pearl once, hanging at the throat of a rich woman). Othersighted eyes. I had encountered such eyes only in tales, and I shivered deep in my belly as these real ones gazed at me.

"Nola," I said—and then, more loudly, "*Nola*," because the baby had begun to cry again, snuffling and coughing tangled with tears.

"I am Yigranzi," said the old woman. She stepped closer and gripped my chin in her fingers, which were hard and dry. Her skin was not dirty, I saw, just dark brown with a sheen of something darker (not quite purple). I thought that maybe it had been polished by an island sun, or a future sun—some light never known in Sarsenay.

"And do you have the Othersight, Nola?" Yigranzi asked.

"She does," my mother cried, "she does, for when I asked her to tell me my future—though I wasn't asking her truly, of course, just saying, but that was enough—her eyes went very big and black, somewhat like yours, milady, and she fell to the floor and when she woke up she said—"

"Nola." Yigranzi was not looking at my mother. Her eyes were steady on me, and her voice was hard but not harsh. "Do you have the Othersight?"

"I . . . I'm not sure." The vision of night and disappearing had been yesterday; today I feared hope.

"Test her," said the tall woman. "Immediately. If she is Othersighted and you'll take her on, I need her clean—now."

"Very well," said Yigranzi, and, to me, "Come," and we left the room, though not by the door that led to the street. Another door, so low that even humpbacked Yigranzi had to stoop, and a dimness beyond it that smelled of soap and rotting meat—and after a few steps, an opening that was larger and wavering with daylight. For a moment I believed that the doorframe itself was moving in the wall, but then I stepped closer to it and saw that there was a curtain made of ribbons hanging across it. Even though they were frayed and faded and nearly as filthy as my own clothes, I thought they were very beautiful. I wanted to stand still and let them trace ticklish patterns on my skin—but instead I followed Yigranzi into the thin sunlight beyond the door.

Four walls of greyish stone with yellowed ivy clinging; two storeys, and wooden-railed balconies all around, and at the centre of this a courtyard. I saw this in a glance and turned my gaze up to the second-floor balconies. Women were leaning on the wood, staring down at me; women and girls too, who looked no older than I was. They were silent and motionless and none of them was smiling. Their dresses were reds, oranges, purples, and their arms (some as pale as mine, others as dark as Yigranzi's, and shades in between, as well) were ringed with slender bands of copper and silver. I had only ever imagined cloth in such colours, and the metal I had seen had always been grey, dented into dullness. I stared back at each of them and stood up very tall, as if this would make me clean and pretty.

"Come," Yigranzi said again, gesturing to the courtyard. It was small and empty except for a wooden walkway and the mud beneath it; a short, twisted tree with two branches and twelve dark green leaves (I counted them); and beneath the tree a low, flat stone. "Sit," Yigranzi said, and I did. The stone was cool. When I laid my hands on its sides I found that they were worn-away smooth; the paths of many other fingers, gripping or stroking in anticipation.

Yigranzi knelt by the tree. Only now did I see the hole in its trunk. Its edges and top were rounded, the wood there lighter than the rest of the bark, and lined with carvings. Zigzags and spirals, rows of waves and circles connected by marks as vague yet distinct as veins below skin. *The Pattern*, I thought, and tried to dig my fingers into the stone, which was already warm from me. The Pattern that was all lives and one, all times and one; the Pattern that only seers could glimpse. . . .

As Yigranzi reached into the hole her hands and shoulders brushed pieces of cloth that hung from nails above the carvings. Some pieces were no bigger than a thumbnail, while others fluttered—I thought—like flags that cats might carry, if cats could carry flags. I could see designs on these larger ones— stitching in gold or silver thread that still glinted, even though the cloth around it had been bleached pale by sunlight and rain. Some of the stitches held locks of hair, teeth, little pouches that bulged with things I could not see. Offerings or pleas: *Show me his future . . . show me my own. . . .*

"What was it that brought your vision on?" Yigranzi had shifted to face me and was leaning back on her heels. There was a round piece of copper in her lap; she was running her right forefinger around its rim in a way that seemed both purposeful and idle.

"My mother's blood," I said. "She was cutting potatoes."

"Her blood." Yigranzi's white-speckled eyebrows rose, which made lines in her forehead. "Ah. A dangerous pattern. There's power in it, to use or be used by. This"—she set the copper on my knees—"is not so dangerous, but will still seem strong to you. Have you ever gazed at your own face in a pool of water, or in a piece of metal—a mirror, like this one?"

I shook my head.

"You've never seen yourself at all, then?"

I shook my head again. Suddenly, with the mirror heavy against my thighs, I thought that I did not want to see. I raised my hands to my cheeks and cupped them there.

"Then your experience of the Othersight, if you do have it, will be very pure."

I pressed my hands inward until I felt my lips purse. "I don't want to see myself," I said, my voice strange because of the pursing.

Yigranzi smiled, so faintly and quickly that I (who was not accustomed to smiles) was not sure there had been one at all. "It is not yourself you'll be looking at. Never yourself—always others, the ones whose faces will also be in the mirror. And this time," she added, getting to her feet slowly, her hump swaying—or so I imagined—"that person will be Bardrem. Bardrem!"

That's a boy's name, I thought. I just had time to look up beyond the spindly branches at the balconies and the silent girls before the boy arrived. He crossed the wooden walkway so quickly that his fair hair rose behind him and his linen leggings rippled around his shins. When he reached us his hair settled on his shoulders and over his eyes; he thrust at it until it was behind his ears. As soon as he turned to look at me the strands escaped again.

"This is Bardrem," said Yigranzi, "who, as you can see, is always lurking somewhere nearby."

"He's a boy," I blurted, and flushed—I could feel this, even though my hands were in my lap again, resting on the mirror.

"He is," Yigranzi said. Bardrem scowled at his leather boot's toe, which he was digging into a ridge of dried mud. "Though he looks as dainty and lovely as a maid, does he not? I've made him promise to cut his hair by the time he turns eleven, when his resemblance to a maid may cause him some trouble, here."

"*Yigranzi*," the boy said, throwing his head back so that I saw his rolling eyes. The old seer smiled—a broad smile this time, all yellow-white teeth and dark gaps—and he grinned back at her.

"Bardrem is the cook's boy," Yigranzi said, and held up her hand as Bardrem opened his mouth to interrupt. "Though really, he is a poet. Yes?"

"Yes." He looked serious now, though not in a way that made me think he wanted to seem older (I had already determined that boys usually wanted to seem older).

"He is a poet and a cook, tender *and* strong, and is thus able to withstand the strangeness of other people's vision. He's very useful, our Bardrem."

He shrugged, smiled again. "It helps me with my poems. And," he added, "I like it. Other people's vision."

Yigranzi put a hand on his forearm, which was covered with tiny golden hairs (like the thread, I thought, so slender but catching the daylight anyway). "You will look into the mirror with Nola until she sees, and speaks."

"If she does."

"What does he mean?" I asked Yigranzi the question but kept my narrowed eyes on Bardrem's.

"Many have come to me claiming Othersight. Many like you, who desire a different life, a life of renown like Teldaru's."

I did look at Yigranzi now. "I don't want renown. And I'm not pretending about Otherseeing." I spoke loudly but still did not believe myself.

"Very well," said Yigranzi. "Let us all see."

⁂

At first I saw only myself. I knew that I wasn't supposed to look, but I couldn't help it—there was a girl beneath me, her features blurry because of sunlight and metal and dents, but sharpening with every blink. She was pointy—her nose and chin and even, somehow, the angle of her brows. Her cheekbones jutted. Her hair was an indeterminate shade of dark, as were her eyes, though as she blinked some more the eyes seemed to grow larger, swimming up through copper toward her real ones, which could not blink any more. . . .

"Nola. *Do not look at yourself.* Look at Bardrem—now, child. Look at him."

I heard Yigranzi as if she or I were underwater (though I'd never truly been underwater—just had my hair soaked, from time to time, with drinking water too dirty for drinking).

"*Look at him*"—and I did—I shifted my reflection-eyes and found his.

15

"Speak the words, Bardrem," said Yigranzi, and I watched his lips part.

"Tell me. Tell me what will come, for me . . ."

He doesn't sound like a boy, and he doesn't look like one. His face smudges in the mirror, and then all its lines dissolve. It oozes together again, so slowly that each pore must be taking its own turn—but soon it is done, and he's back, but he's a man. His hair is darker and cropped close to his head. His lips are thinner. Even as I strain to hold his face still it recedes, so swiftly that it feels as if I am falling backward. There are stones behind him: row upon row of them, all tall, all bent into terrible, bulbous shapes. He stands among them and cries a long, raw, ragged-ended cry. Looking at me—but not at the child-me: the mirror-me, who (I see, glancing down) is wearing a cream-coloured dress. There is a thick red-brown braid hanging over my left shoulder. I wrench my gaze to him again—this isn't right; how can I be with him among these stones?—and he shouts again. Maybe it's my name? I try to turn away from him but cannot, because we are both Otherselves, in another place that doesn't exist for us but is part of our Pattern anyway. His mouth twists and he rubs tears away with his palms, viciously. Just then a bird rises from the stones: a glorious scarlet bird with a blue head and a green and yellow tail. Blood is coming from his eyes now, and from mine; I feel it on my arms, warmer and thicker than tears. If I could look down and see the pattern of the drops; if I could just do this perhaps I'd be able to find a way back through the copper-tinted sky. I try to look, but I'm frozen, watching him bleed and weep, and suddenly a scream rises in me, as quick and bright as the bird was, but even it gets trapped—

"Nola! Nola, come back. . . ."

I was lying down, but this time Yigranzi, not my mother, hovered above me. She had looped her cool, dry, hard fingers through mine and was squeezing them so tightly that the pain returned my breath to me. I gasped and coughed.

"What did you see?" Bardrem's voice—his boy's voice, awed and high. "Your eyes went black and silver: I saw them. What did you *see*?"

"Bardrem," Yigranzi began. That was all I heard her say. I stared at him (he was holding his fair hair back from his eyes, and his lips were slightly open and very red) and I turned my head and vomited, and then I saw nothing at all any more, not even darkness.

CHAPTER TWO

I woke up in a bed. A *bed*, not a thin, smelly pallet on the floor. I rolled to one side and then the other atop the mattress (rough linen stuffed with straw that prickled my bare skin) and listened to the creaking of the wooden frame beneath it.

I woke up alone, in silence. No babies wailing; no older children pressed up against my back, quivering with fear or fever. No mother. I stared at the walls, which were wood, and a deep, deep red. I had never seen a painted room before, and it made my heart race, for a moment. Perhaps I was dreaming, or dead? But when I squeezed my eyelids shut and opened them again the dark red walls were still there, as was the door in the one opposite the bed. There was a window, square and very small and set high enough up in the wall that I would have to stand on my bed to see out. I did not do this—not yet. It was enough to look at the sunlight, and the latticed pattern of a shutter I could not see, wavering like water on the red paint.

It was dark when the door opened. I had not moved—not because I was afraid of what I might find, but because I was still sure I would discover that it was all a fashioning of my mind that would vanish the moment my feet touched the rag rug on the floor. "You're awake." The woman was wearing her blue dress with the silver belt; its oval links shone in the light of the candelabra she held in one of her hands (each of her fingers had a ring, I noticed).

"Yes," I said, thinking, despite my awe, *It's obvious that I'm awake; what a silly thing to say.*

"Sit up, child. Let me look at you."

I obeyed her—and right away I could tell that I was different. My skin—all of it bare beneath the woollen blanket that I now held against my waist—was clean. I could see this, in the candle-glow, but I could also sense it: there was a lightness about me, a burnish that made me feel like a smooth piece of metal. And my hair was gone. There was no weight of it against my back, and when I lifted my hands to my head I felt only thick, dense stubble. For a moment I remembered the braid I had seen in my vision, but then I ground my fingertips against my skull and forced the memory away.

"Better," said the woman. She set the candelabra down on the low washstand that was the only other piece of furniture in the room. The little flame-lights danced on the surface of the water in the basin. Clean water, waiting for me.

"So you'll stay—which is well and good, since Yigranzi is old and ugly and men have little desire to pay money for her to look at them in her mirror. You, though . . ." She crossed her arms, leaned her head forward, thinned out her lips as she regarded me. "You're young, at least. And you may grow pretty enough to draw the coins from men's pouches. Though you'll never be one of my girls. You will not lie with men for money, and you will not mix with the girls. A seer's place is apart—and if you forget this you'll be flogged. It's not your *flesh* that matters, after all, and I won't fear you as all the others will."

She paused—for breath, I imagined. I had never heard one person speak so many words together.

"Have you anything to say before I leave you?"

I was safe: I knew this now. And flogging had never frightened me. I pulled my naked shoulders back and gazed straight up into her eyes. "I'm hungry."

Her brows rose. I was beginning to enjoy having this effect on adults. "Impudent girl," she said, almost lazily. "You will get your dinner. No doubt it will be the finest meal you've ever eaten in all your life. Was there anything more?"

"My mother." I hadn't known I was going to say these words, and this unexpectedness—and the sudden quaver in my voice—made me flush. I twisted the blanket in my hands, which were so clean—even the nails—that I hardly recognized them. "Is she gone?"

The woman nodded. "The moment the copper pieces were in her hands."

"Did she speak of me?" The quaver was gone from my words, but I could still feel it in my chest, which both confused and angered me.

"No." She picked the candelabra up again. The links of her belt made a soft, singing noise as she moved to the door. She looked back at me. "She was a horrible woman. You should be thankful that the Pattern has brought you here."

"Yes," I said, and then I was alone again, in deeper darkness than before, hugging myself as tears I did not understand fell upon my new, clean bed.

The girls *were* afraid of me. They stepped quickly aside if I was coming toward them in one of the brothel's narrow hallways. If they were alone they lowered their eyes, and if they weren't they fell silent, though they would murmur and hiss when I had passed. Many of the ones who did glance at me would put their hands to their own long hair. (Mine was cut every few weeks to keep me undesirable to the clients—though as Bardrem said once, "Some of them like boys, you know; you'd still better look behind you, especially in the dark.")

At first I didn't see many of the men. I spent most of my time with Yigranzi, either in the courtyard or—when it grew too chilly for her there—in her room, which was as small as mine but filled with wondrous things: sea shells hung on dyed string, and masks carved out of enormous leaves, and candelabras made of volcano rocks moulded into the shapes of snakes and fish. The rest of my time I spent in the kitchen, where Rudicol the thin cook shouted himself hoarse and Bardrem slipped me pieces of seasoned meat and sometimes even apples and pears: food intended for the men, not for me.

The men I did see, in those first months, were the ones who sought out Yigranzi. She always sent me away when she saw them coming, but I'd peek at them, either on the walkway or after. I'd turn, look over my shoulder, and Yigranzi would call, "Nola! Go!" even when she wasn't facing me. These men, I saw, were all different. One was tall and red-bearded, and for a moment I thought he was my father—or the person my mother had always told me was my father. But then I drew level with him and saw that he was younger, his eyes wide and darting beneath his red brows, and although I was relieved that he was not my father I was a little sorry, too, for I'd always liked his wink and the flash of his silver-capped tooth.

Another of the men was short and so fat that his belly rippled beneath the green silk tunic he wore. His breath whistled and a sour smell wafted from him. I stared at the silk, and at the gold chain that was nearly vanishing beneath one of his chins, and thought, *This is what a rich man looks like?*

"Why do rich men come to you?" I asked Yigranzi one day. It was autumn; three of the tree's leaves were scarlet, one was yellow, and the rest had already fallen.

"For the same two reasons all men come," she replied, "and women, too. Two reasons; you'll learn this. To hear what they think they already know about what the Pattern holds for them, or to be surprised."

"What if they don't like what you see?"

She smiled her smile of holes and took the mirror from my lap. (She had not let me look for a vision in it since that first day—and I had not wanted to—but she said I should get used to the feel of it.)

"Many don't. Many bluster and stamp, and some grab hold of you and shake you until you're dizzy. So you have to learn calm. To wait for their anger to pass, if it's all-of-a-sudden anger, or to speak quietly before it can grow. You have to tell them: *The Pattern is not set. I see the truth of* you, *before and now, and the maybe of your future. But nothing is set; it is only waiting.*"

I shook my head. "No—the Pattern *is* set—that's what everyone says."

Yigranzi was silent for a bit, as she folded the mirror into a square blue cloth stitched with golden spirals. When she was done she placed the bundle inside the tree, then turned back to me.

"In Sarsenay they think this, yes. Not where I come from. There we know that what seers find in men is truth, but also that it does not have to be."

I shook my head again and must have scowled, because Yigranzi laughed and said, "You'll grasp it someday, Sarsenayan or not," which only made me scowl more.

Most of the things she said to me were simple. "You must eat well before you use your Othersight—but nothing rich or heavy, because sometimes the strength of your vision will make you vomit. As you've already found out, no?" (She had never asked me to tell her about my first vision, though with Bardrem it had become a half-jest: "Tell me now. No? Very well—now? Or maybe now?")

"In times of great difficulty for all—wars or plagues or famines—people want to know about their children. At other times they mostly want to know about themselves."

"When your monthly bleeding begins, your Otherseeing will grow stronger, especially when you have visions for other women. Blood gives power."

Although she did not allow me to use her mirror again, in those first months, she did teach me different ways to Othersee. There was wax, melted and poured into a bowl of cold water, and kitchen scraps (Bardrem brought them and sulked when he was not permitted to stay): crumbled-up stale bread and chicken bones, thrown into wind. "Once someone has asked you to Othersee for them, anything that forms a pattern will help you. Each way has a different strength, and each seer reacts differently to them."

"And when will I try these ways?" I asked, wriggling on the brightly patterned hide stool by her bed.

"Later," she said, "when you have learned more."

"But I want to try now—the wax one, because it's pretty."

"No, Nola. Not yet."

"Teldaru went to the castle two days after he found out he had the Othersight! The king didn't make *him* wait. All you do is show me. You don't let me *do* anything!"

She gazed at me with her eyes that were always black-and-pearl. She had not told me what it was like to see normally, with these eyes, even though I had asked. She had told me so little—only the simple things, the ones I probably would have found out on my own anyway. I glared back at her, not fidgeting any more.

"Two months ago," she said slowly, in a strange voice that had nothing of Sarsenay in it; only depth and lilt that sounded wild and very old, "you were living in filth. Two months ago you were eight years old and likely to die of sickness or at your own mother's hand—eight years old and lucky if you saw nine. And now here you sit, forgetting your 'before' and even your 'now' because you're as tempted by your 'later' as anyone else who walks into this courtyard to find me."

I felt my lip wobbling and bit it to keep it still. I didn't want her to notice but of course she did.

"Nola. Child." Her usual voice, and a smile. "I was fifteen when I came to Sarsenay. A strange land and stranger people, and me alone. I remember what it is to want and to need, and to forget everything else." She rose from her bed and then bent to touch my cheek. She had never touched me before. I think now that no one had ever done so with any tenderness—and that was partly why I flinched away from her hand. As she went to the other side of the room, I stared at her carpets, which were small, nubbly with wool ends, and woven in every colour, even ones I couldn't name.

"Be patient," she said. I heard water pouring into a cup—probably her ceramic one, which was short and squat and had an orange background with a black crab painted on it. I liked this one because the crab's claws looked like they were lifting off the pottery; like they might pinch your lips or your nose.

"The Othersight is difficult to have, and you are still young, and there will be time to do, after you have learned. Be patient, Nola, yes?"

I lifted my eyes from the rugs and looked at her. "Yes," I said, and I believe that I meant it. I believe that I did intend to try for patience, restraint, obedience.

I was young, though, and I failed.

It began with a poem.

A girl lives here who needs your eye
To look at her and then to scry
So tell me yes and I'll tell her
No one will have to know.

It took me several minutes to read this poem, because I was simply slow (my father had taught me to read a little, years ago; my mother laughed at us and then got angry), and because it was written in tiny letters on a piece of paper that fit in my palm. Also, it was smoky in the kitchen, even though the window shutters and door were open to the autumn air.

I had just finished squinting at this scrap of paper when Bardrem dropped another one into my lap. I glared at him but he was already gone, whirling from countertop to cookpot with trays of carrots and potatoes while Rudicol yelled, "My granddam moves faster than you, boy, and I don't even have to flog her!"

The words on this second bit of paper were not a poem. They said: "My poems are usually very serious. That one was like a joke—but what it *said* was real. Wait for me after. Bardrem."

I peered again at the poem, frowning. I thought I understood it, except that it didn't seem possible. (My heart was already beating faster than usual, in a place that felt very high up, closer to my throat than to my chest.)

"Who is she?" I asked him later. It was about midnight; my room was dark except for the flickering of a single candle. I had fallen asleep waiting for him and was now trying to shake the heaviness from my head and limbs without seeming to.

He shrugged. "Just a girl. I think she's fifteen."

"Why doesn't she want to go to Yigranzi?"

Another shrug, and eyes cast toward the ceiling from beneath a swatch of fair hair. "Because . . . I don't know. I think she might not like her. Because of where she's from, what she looks like. Something like that."

"Oh." I blinked and ran the back of my hand across my eyes, trying to make it look as though I was itchy rather than tired. Bardrem had begun pacing from one end of the room to the other, whirling at each turn as if he were still in the kitchen.

"I shouldn't. Yigranzi's told me not to. I don't know enough—I haven't practised since that time with you, and the mirror was so strong—"

"So don't use the mirror. Try another way. You know some, don't you?"

My heartbeat was so close to my throat that I thought I might not be able to speak—but I did, said, "Wax on water . . ."

"Good." He was already at the door. "I'll go get some for you. And I'll get her, too."

"No—wait—" But he was already gone, and it was too late.

⚜

The wax was wine-coloured and the girl looked young. *Fifteen?* I thought, staring at her blond plaits (rows of them, all tied at the ends with blue ribbons), and at her scowl.

"Stop looking at me like that," she said. Her voice was a surprise: low and dark. "You're not Otherseeing yet, are you?"

"No." I tried to keep my own voice calm, as Yigranzi had told me to. "But I need to look at you, before. I need to see you with my own eyes first." I felt silly saying these words, because I hadn't thought of them and because I didn't really believe them. All I saw now was a girl with squinty green eyes and thinned-out lips and a sleeping gown that was too big for her.

"Ready," Bardrem said. He was at the washstand; the pitcher was on the floor, though the bowl was still where it usually was, full, waiting to serve this new purpose. I went to stand beside him. He was holding a little clay pot above the candle flame. The pot was swimming with wax.

"Stand here," I said. The girl obeyed. I was not sure whether I wanted to smile or tremble. I took the pot from Bardrem, who stepped away, out of my sight. I tipped, poured; the wax fell in slow, fat drops that darkened and spread as soon as they touched the water.

"Now," I heard Bardrem hiss, and the girl cleared her throat.

"Tell . . ." she began, then faltered. "Tell me my future"—louder, almost angrily.

Words, wax, water—and my vision staining wine at the edges.

The girl is there—her shadow in the wax-blotched water, but also her Otherself, solid and see-through. She is naked. Her nipples are very dark; I think, Wax, but then see how wet the darkness is. One drip, and another, and I think, knowing this is truth: Blood. The belly beneath her breasts is swollen in a way I recognize. Blood spatters onto flesh, making new patterns, lines like snakes. There are snakes everywhere, suddenly: crimson ones emerging scale by scale from the girl's distended bellybutton. Their tongues fork fresh blood, which sprays toward me. I hear myself cry out once, and again as I wrench my gaze away from the bowl.

I was on the floor, my legs twisted beneath me. The girl—the real one—was gaping down at me. "What?" Bardrem's voice, but I could not see him. All I saw were the girl's wide eyes and the cream-coloured, lace-trimmed cloth that had slipped off her shoulder.

"Snakes." I didn't wait to breathe or think; just spoke the words that were as thick as my tongue in my mouth. "You're having a baby but instead it's snakes and you're bleeding from everywhere, especially where the milk should be—"

The girl screamed. She screamed only once, but it was piercing and pure—almost like music—and moments later there were footsteps in the corridor outside.

Yigranzi was wearing a long, shapeless robe with splotches of rainbow colour on it. The girls gathering behind her were wearing their own night clothes: dresses cut to mid-thigh; dresses made of long strips of cloth that whispered apart to reveal kohl-patterned skin. I saw all these things with a clarity that hurt me like a headache.

"Go. All of you."

There were no more girls, after Yigranzi said this—except for the one, of course, who had wrapped her arms around herself. She was shaking so violently that her sleeping gown slipped all the way off her shoulders. I could see her nipples through the knot of her arms. They were dark but did not look anything like blood.

"I said *go*." This to Bardrem, who was still standing by the washstand. The jug on the floor by his feet had fallen over. He glanced from Yigranzi to me and

Yigranzi stepped toward him, her arm raised, her hand a fist. He left in a flurry of limbs and hair, and then there were only three of us left in the room.

"Child." Yigranzi had turned to the shivering girl. She reached out her dark, round-knuckled hand and put it gently on the girl's bare shoulder. The girl made a low, ragged, animal sound. She clawed at Yigranzi's hand with both of her own, which were white and slender, and I couldn't tell whether she was trying to clutch or to push away.

"Sit, child," Yigranzi said in a quiet voice I had never heard before. "Sit and talk to me. I will pour you some wine, and there is a blanket there—"

The girl spun and ran. A trailing bit of lace caught on the door latch and ripped away from the dress. I stared at the lace, after the girl was gone. I was desperately thirsty and very dizzy; the lace, which I had thought before was cream-coloured, now looked blue with livid yellow spots.

"Nola." How many voices did Yigranzi *have*, waiting in her throat? This one was flat and empty, as if it wasn't made of sound at all. "I will go after her to see what may be done. You will stay here. I will lock you in tonight and tomorrow, and perhaps for many days after. You will see no one and speak to no one. When I decide that there is seeing and speaking to be done, I will come for you."

I was looking at the floor when Yigranzi left, so I saw only the swirl of her sleeping robe and the tips of her soft leather shoes (which were a light green that made me thirstier). The door closed and the key turned. A few moments later, I went to the washstand and picked up the fallen jug. The rug beneath it was soaking, but there was no water left to drink. No water except what was in the bowl, thickened with wax. I stared into the bowl, and even though I was shaking now, and Yigranzi's new, cold voice was still in my ears, I felt a stirring of something that almost made me want to smile.

Yigranzi came for me three days later.

"Follow me," she said while I was struggling up off the bed, sucking in the scents of baking bread and sweat and perfumed oil that were rolling in my open door. I followed, feeling feeble and awkward. It was midday and the hallways were empty and silent. Yigranzi led me into one I'd not yet been in; it had higher ceilings and dark, rich, worm-eaten wood paneling around the doors and up the walls. She stopped before one of these doors. I heard the sobbing before she even opened it.

The girl who had come to me was lying on a bed. Three other girls sat around her, stroking her hair, her arms. *Her dress is red*, I thought, *and so are the sheets*—but then my vision-memory returned and I knew that all this darkness was blood—and as soon as I knew it I smelled it, heavy and rank-sweet. Her skin was even paler than before. Several of my mother's babies had died, and I had washed most of them, after. Their flesh had looked like this—white stone, white eggshell; something tender and hard.

"Her name was Larally," Yigranzi said from behind me. "She was from a town to the east called Nordes."

The girls stopped their noises when Yigranzi spoke. They blinked up at us as if they'd just awoken. One of them—black-haired, with a wine-coloured birthmark under her left eye—reached across the bed and gripped her friend's wrist. It was me they stared at now, their lips slightly parted, their eyes round. I had never been regarded with fear before. I had never been regarded with much of anything, before I came here.

"I saw her belly," I whispered. "In my vision. There was going to be a baby." The girl's belly was a hollowed-out space beneath her blood-wet shift. Her hipbones stuck up like knife hilts. "Where is it? Did it get born too soon? Is that what my vision was about—it coming too soon?"

Yigranzi was staring at me too. I almost expected the dead girl's eyes to pop open; this thought made me want to giggle, all of a sudden, which made no sense at all. "Where's the baby?" Yigranzi said slowly. "I wonder. On the midden heap behind the kitchen, maybe, or burned, or buried at the edge of the courtyard. It wouldn't have been very big—which is likely why she thought it would come out easily. Why she had someone take it out for her, with long hooks that probably hadn't been cleaned since the last time they were used. Because you know, Nola, that when the girls don't take the bleeding draughts the Lady mixes for them, or when the draughts don't work, they use hooks."

I didn't understand what she was talking about, but I understood her anger. "It was the Pattern," I said, the words cracking as they left my mouth. "It was meant to happen to her."

Yigranzi smiled, her lips pressed so tightly together that they seemed to disappear. "You're sure of this, even though you have no idea what your Othersight showed you. But you're sure of the Pattern. You and so many other grown seers, too. Such a perfect thing, this certainty. Lets you say things that are always right and claim that the wrong belongs to someone else." She took me by the shoulders and dug her fingertips into my skin so hard that my whole chest went numb. "You'll stop being so sure, Nola, if you stay here with me. *If you do.* Because hear me and know this for certain: if you ever do a thing like this again I will walk you back out into the street myself. I will, though it will make me sick at heart to do it."

It was her last words that finally started me crying. Her kindness, and then, belatedly but even stronger because of it, the girl on the bed—Larally of Nordes, who had been fifteen. I cried in great, gulping sobs until Yigranzi's fingers loosened and her arms came around me. "Don't make me go," I said. My head was pressed sideways against her breasts, which were very soft beneath the rough cloth of her dress.

"Hush, Nola," she said, "hush." And she rocked me, like the child I almost was.

CHAPTER THREE

A gentlewoman just came to me. It's quite late, and Sildio has gone to his room for the night. She knocked, and swept past me the moment I opened the door. The moonlight trickling through my window shone off the jewels she wore at her throat and on her fingers. She stared at the dog, the baby, the bird, and then she stared at me. There was fear and hope in her eyes, and some revulsion, too. I knew what she wanted.

"I will not Othersee for you," I said, before she could command me to. "The king has decreed that I will not Othersee for anyone."

"I know," she said. Her voice was very low. She walked up close to me, with a surge of firwater perfume that made my nostrils tingle. "But I hoped you yourself would make an exception for me. I am . . ."—and then she gave me her name, and the name of her cousin, who was some sort of lord.

I try not to listen to such details. Yigranzi taught me this. She used to say, "All you need to know, before you call the Othersight to you, is what you can see with your own vision: people's clothing, their hands, their eyes. Some of them will talk too much and others not at all—so only look, and be quiet, and this will begin to show you what they are, even before the mirror does."

I told the woman that I could make no exceptions; that, even though I was still a young woman, I was finished with the Otherworld.

She shook her head. When she spoke again her voice was louder, shriller. "But you are Mistress Nola!"

You're right! I wanted to cry. *I knew I'd forgotten something!*—but she might not have understood that my scorn had been directed mostly at myself. That it had little to do with her tightly clasped hands—with their winking gems and thick loops of gold—or her awe, or her need.

And so I'm alone again. These pages lie around me, scattered because I've written some of them so quickly that I've simply dropped them, in my haste to continue to the next ones. My hand hurts. My whole arm hurts, in fact, and my neck; they're stiffer than they are on a freezing winter's morning when I've slept in an awkward, twisted-up way. I've gone through pots and pots of ink and most of the paper Sildio brought me earlier today (at least I think it was today). I'll sleep soon. But there's more I need to write before I do.

Funny, how it's the starting-off words that come to me most easily, all in a row, as if they were waiting—like those visions that rise up from mirror or water almost as soon as you look. The ones after are more stubborn, but the beginning ones are usually so clear. These, this time:

I was very good, after Larally.

I was—truly. There were four years of quiet, which I can hardly remember. By "quiet" I do not mean tranquility. There were fights—among the girls, or between the girls and the men, or once, among several groups of men—that ended in injury or even death. Screams in mid-afternoon stillness; blood on the snow of the courtyard. I remember staring at the spirals of droplets until they blurred; the Otherworld was so close, but invisible until someone said, "Tell me." Which, thankfully, no one did.

But the blood was not mine, and it was not spilled because of me. I felt safe. This feeling, and its constancy, may be why these four years are so indistinct to me now. That, and the too-sharp horror of what came after.

I grew quickly—every part of me pointy, or long and lanky. Everything except my hair, which Yigranzi continued to crop every three weeks, with her little bronze scissors. For a few years I was much taller than Bardrem, something I mentioned as often as I could.

"Step aside, Bardrem: I'll get that tankard down for you."

"The problem is that you don't like carrots. I do, and just look how they've helped me grow!"

"Could you please get me the mirror? I'm having trouble reaching it; I think my legs are just too long now. . . ."

He never failed to flush, or mock-growl, or disappear behind the hair he still had not cut.

He would often sit on the ground near the stone and write while Yigranzi taught me. The poems usually had nothing to do with us, but I do remember one that did. It was more like a list:

Wax and water
Scattered corn
Wine in droplets
Pattern-born.

"Yigranzi would like this one," I said. I spoke lightly, even though the words had sent a shiver through me. "She says the Pattern isn't set, and it seems like that's what your poem's saying, too."

He shrugged. "I just liked the way the words sounded."

Sometimes he claimed that poetry was the most difficult thing to do ("Even more difficult than carving up a spitted pig?" "No*la* . . ."); other times, he treated it like something simple. His inconsistency annoyed me, but I envied it too.

He was scribbling by the stone on the day Chenn came.

There had been other new girls, in the years since I'd arrived. A few of them had claimed to have the Othersight, and more wanted to make their living on men and their coins. They were all brought to Yigranzi. The ones who wanted to be seers worried me, at first. I would watch them as they leaned over the mirror and raised their eyes to Bardrem (never to me; Yigranzi always insisted that seers should not submit themselves to the Othersight, whether their own or someone else's). I would tense, waiting for their eyes to wash black. Some did; more did not. Soon, though, I realized that even the ones who could Othersee were no threat to my own position.

"You see the Pattern," Yigranzi would say to them, "and this gift will maybe grant you success and joy. I know of another seer who needs an apprentice—at the brothel by the western wall, near the Deer Fountain. . . ."

"Teldaru has many apprentices," I said to her one day after she'd sent another away (this one a boy with long, thick, red hair that Bardrem stared at fixedly).

"Teldaru is a royal seer," she replied. "He serves king, castle and land—a task too big for any single person, even him. Me, I serve only the Lady and this place." She paused, smiled down at the tiny glass vials she was arranging on a board. "And anyhow," she continued, "I'm too old for more children and teaching and all that excitement. There's enough of that now, Nola-girl."

Chenn, though. Chenn. Waiting for me, gazing at me with her gold-flecked eyes.

The day was unremarkable; it was snowing, and everything was white, flat, featureless. Even the tree seemed barely solid, despite its bark and bits of hanging cloth, and its one brown, curled, clinging leaf. The girl was mostly unremarkable, too. She was wearing a dark grey cloak and a headscarf, pulled low over her forehead. But her eyes gazed out from beneath the dull cloth like jewels. They were a dark blue that was nearly black; the gold flecks were sprinkled through the darkness so thickly that they glinted, no matter which way she held her head.

"Yigranzi," the Lady said in her sharp, impatient voice. "Look. Look at her eyes. She claims she has no Othersight, but surely with eyes like that she has already looked long upon the Pattern."

I was fascinated by the girl, but I looked at the Lady, whom I had never seen in the courtyard before (usually she summoned Yigranzi and me to her chamber). The blue dress seemed more worn, in the daylight, and her belt and rings more tarnished. Her face, I saw with a start, was etched with deep lines where her white powder had gathered like snow.

"It is hard to tell," Yigranzi said. "Some people simply have strange eyes; nothing to do with peering at the Pattern."

She was peering, though, studying the girl, her cracked lips pursed.

"Test her," the Lady said. "I need to be certain of who and what she is before I'll consider taking her on."

Yigranzi's brows went up. "Taking her on?" Another pause, while the girl shifted from foot to foot and turned her beautiful eyes to the top of the tree. Bardrem, I noticed, was sitting very still, his writing stick poised, forgotten, above the paper in his lap.

"Very well," Yigranzi said briskly, "I will test her—but Bardrem must leave, as must you, Lady."

After another hard look at the girl, the Lady nodded. "Bring her back to me as soon as you are done, no matter what the result." She walked away from us. She held the front of her dress up, but the back of it dragged a new path through the snow.

"Bardrem."

He scowled. "But you might need—"

"*Bardrem.*"

He rose, tossed his hair back over his shoulder. "If you need me," he said, "I will be finishing this poem in my room."

There was a silence after his snow-scuffing footsteps faded. "So," Yigranzi said at last, making the short word very long. She was tapping her front tooth with her little finger. "What is your name?"

"Chenn." The girl's voice was soft and rough, as if she had been shouting too much. She and Yigranzi were gazing at each other with an intensity that I saw but did not understand.

"Not the name of a girl who sells herself to men," Yigranzi said. "Not nearly pretty enough. The Lady will have you change it, if you stay."

"No. I am only Chenn." Soft, steady defiance; I tried to note how this sounded, thought I might use it myself, sometime.

"You have the Othersight."

"Yes," Chenn said. "I thank you for telling the Lady what you told her. About my eyes."

"When Otherseers seek to hide their gift there is always a reason. I will not ask you yours. But *here*, girl—why hide it here?"

Chenn wrapped her arms around herself, beneath her grey cloak. Snow was gathering on her eyelashes and dissolving when she blinked. "Because I will need money, if I'm going to leave this city and stay away. And I'm a comely enough girl—someone . . . people have told me so." A tremor in her voice, a few quicker blinks.

Yigranzi shook her head. "Hmph," she said. Her shoulders were hunched, maybe because of the cold, or because she was unsettled by the girl. Her hump looked even bigger than it usually did, beneath her orange and yellow cloak. "Well. We'll stay here a few more moments; the Lady will expect the test to take longer. The test, and then the Otherseeing, which we will also spare you."

"But you look at all the other girls who come, don't you? You do. So you must look at me, too. I'll be treated no differently, if I'm to be one of them. And I've decided . . ." She paused, ran her tongue over her lips, catching snow. "I've decided that if my Pattern is dark, I will take another path."

I had never seen Yigranzi struggle for words as she was now, her mouth open and moving soundlessly. "Nola," she finally said, "get the barley, and—"

"No," Chenn interrupted, "I want the mirror. And I want both of you to look."

I sucked in my breath. Chenn had not yet glanced my way, but now she turned, and I felt pinned by blue-black and gold.

Yigranzi said, "It is never wise for Otherseers to allow the vision to be turned on themselves. It—"

"I am not a seer any more." Chenn's voice cracked again, and I thought that it sounded as new-raw as the cracks in Yigranzi's lips looked. "Please: the mirror."

Yigranzi went first. I'd watched her do this many times, over the last four years, and it still amazed me—not because she was quick and effortless about it, but because she was slow. I used to fidget while I waited, but recently I'd been watching with more care. *She* took care—but it was more than that. She was slow and careful, and she struggled.

"Why do you take so long?" I had asked her once. "It only takes me a moment to see a vision. And why do you twist up your face so much, like it's hurting you?"

She had lifted one eyebrow. She had been thrusting copper combs into her hair, which, if not contained, stood up around her head like a thick, black-and-white bush. "The visions are clearer and easier when you're a child—I've told you this—do you hear anything I say, Nola-girl? They rise up like breath—and usually only one of them for any one person. One, which you can look at and then away from. But"—another thrust, and copper tines disappearing—"then, if you're a girl, you begin your monthly bleeding, and everything changes. The one, quick vision may still come up to meet you, but now it's not as clear, and not alone. Layers, Nola. Layers of pictures, and you wondering which among them is truest."

"So do boy seers always have the easy visions, since they never bleed?"

She made a huffing sound that I knew was a chuckle. "No. It is harder for them too, as they grow. Seeing either world is never easy when childhood's gone."

When Chenn arrived I had not yet begun my monthly bleeding. My Othersight was still swift and easy; all that happened after I used it was that I felt dizzy, and colours looked different. But I was twelve, and I knew that things would soon change for me—and so I watched Yigranzi with particular attention.

She ran her fingers around the mirror's rim. Her eyes were on Chenn.

"Tell me what the Pattern holds for me," said Chenn.

Yigranzi looked down at the mirror. She began to hum: a low, formless tune that was different every time. Her fingers slowed against the copper. Moments later they stopped, and so did the humming. She was motionless. Big, round snowflakes fell on the mirror and she did not brush them off. There were only a few patches of metal showing when she lifted her head.

Usually she was smiling a small, lips-together smile at this point, no matter what she had seen. This time she was not. Her eyes were all black; the pearl centres returned as she blinked. She was quiet for a long time, which was also strange. (She had told me that seers should say something as soon as the vision had passed, something slow and quiet that might have nothing to do with the vision itself, but that would be calming to both seer and seen.)

"Well?" Chenn bit her lip as soon as the word was out.

Yigranzi did smile now, but I could tell that she was trying to; that it was weak, held on only by her will.

"The Pattern is unclear," she said. "There are many spirals, all of them twisted like—"

"Just tell me."

Yigranzi's smile vanished. "There was a wolf with the hands of a man. Its teeth were set with gems. It snarled and reached for you, and you turned to it—you knew it, but this did not matter, for it fastened its jaws around your thigh while it held you still with its hands."

I had never heard her describe a vision so starkly. Chenn did not seem as alarmed as I felt. She nodded once, as if she understood what Yigranzi had told her, and said, "And what of the other, lesser pictures?"

"Unclear," Yigranzi replied. "The twisting lines, all of them the colour of blood."

One more nod, and then Chenn turned to me. "Please," she said, "tell me your name, and take your turn."

I straightened. I noticed only now that I was taller than she was. "Nola," I said, trying not to sound too proud or too timid, and reached for the mirror. I wiped the snow off it with the hem of my cloak and sat down on the stone.

"Tell me what will come, for me," I heard Chenn say.

I see right away. I am sure, as the copper mist eddies and parts, that there will be horrors—but there are not. Just Chenn sitting on a golden chair like a throne, only smaller than I imagine a real throne would be. She is bathed in sunlight; the gold shines, as do the beads of her light green gown. Her hair is as dark as her eyes and unbound, brushed glossy-smooth. She is looking off to her right, smiling at something or someone I cannot see. She lifts her hand and her mouth makes a word—a name, I know, even though I don't hear it.

The glow begins to dim a bit, as the mirror's hue returns. Later I try to tell myself that the copper shadows confused my Othersight; the shadows, and the beauty of the girl and her dress and her smile. "I never saw anything else," I think later, or "I saw—but how could I have been expected to truly grasp what I saw? The vision was fading, after all. . . ."

It is her throat—white and smooth and utterly unremarkable except for the cloudy opal in its hollow. But as my Othersight begins to lose its strength, I see her throat open. It opens side-to-side, the two edges curling outward like lycus blossoms. There is no blood.

This is what I saw, and then I blinked, and all I saw was the shadow of my own face in the snow-dusted mirror.

"Nola?" Chenn said.

I looked up at her. A strand of long black hair had escaped from her headscarf and was looping over her shoulder.

"What did you see?"

I was already forgetting. Her eyes made me forget. "It was beautiful," I said. Her smile wobbled because of my dizziness. The falling snow was the same colour as the beaded dress had been. "You were sitting on a golden throne, wearing a rich, green gown. There was an opal necklace, and maybe some rings. Your hair was all loose and shining. You were smiling at someone, and then you reached for him—I felt it was a 'him,' even though I couldn't see. . . . You were happy," I said. And that was all. I barely knew her, and yet I needed her to smile at me as she was. I needed her to be happy.

"Thank you," she said. "That is a heartening vision."

Yigranzi was frowning. "A wolf, a throne—take care, and remember that though neither is fixed in your Pattern, both are possible. Think, girl, and make no decision now. You remember: a seer must use patience in all things."

"I am not a seer any more," Chenn said, with more steadiness this time.

She gazed around her—at the tree, the balconies and walls, the heavy grey sky. "I sense the truth of both visions, but the gold is stronger. Take me back to the Lady now, please."

The Pattern thickened around us like the snow, and only Yigranzi knew to shiver.

CHAPTER FOUR

Bardrem used to make lists. Words he thought of but could not yet make into poems; words that he needed to see together, rather than only hearing in his head. Sometimes he left these lists in strange places so that he would stumble upon them later, when the look and sound of them might seem new and surprise him. Rudicol would shout at him, when he found the little folded pieces of paper in seldom-used pots or spaces between the hearthstones. He would tear them into tiny pieces; several times he thrust them into the cookfire; once he threw one into a pot of soup, then scalded his fingers plucking it out again, and shouted until we thought his eyes would spring from his head. For a while after one of these episodes, Bardrem would write the words in or with the food itself. A boiled potato would have "belly" and "ire" carved in it; salted round beans would spell "conquered" and "moon" upon a plate.

He'd leave me notes, too—in one of my shoes, or underneath the rag carpet, or wedged into a hole in the courtyard tree. I sometimes wouldn't find the notes for days or even months. He needed to put himself onto little pieces of paper, and he needed to know that someone would find them. It's beginning to be the same for me now, though my pages are bigger and (at last, this morning) arranged in a neat stack. I write these words for myself, but I think as I do that others might read them, too. Grasni and Sildio at least, and maybe some of my old students, when they're grown—and oh, what a giddy rush of pride and selflessness and simple, yearning joy I feel, imagining this.

But for now there is only me.

Or rather: Chenn, Bardrem and me, sitting cross-legged on Chenn's bed.

Chenn was cutting my hair. Yigranzi's fingers were too swollen now to use the little bronze scissors.

"Listen," Bardrem said, smoothing his piece of paper out on the coverlet. "I think it's nearly done." He cleared his throat.

It was one of his longer poems—though they all seemed to be longer, recently, and more about battles than about the shape of rain or the songs of night birds, as they used to be. This one was, in fact, about a battle—one fought centuries ago by an ancestor of King Haldrin's, Ranior, great War Hound of Sarsenay, when there had been no peace. The poem's lines were thick with word-pictures, and there was scarcely any room for Bardrem to breathe. I closed my eyes, hoping he would think I was listening, rather than resting.

"Blood-drenched sunrise," I heard, and "the Plains of Lodrigesse, stretched like sea beneath the stars of Sarsenay." Mostly I heard the *snick snick* of the scissors, and Chenn's hands brushing the cloth where the hair was falling.

"So?"

I opened my eyes. Bardrem was standing; he sometimes leapt to his feet and paced during a recitation. His hand was on the wood of the bed across the room from Chenn's.

"So," I repeated, as if I had something to add.

"It was very grand," Chenn said in her steady, calm way. "I liked the part about the armies looking like swarming beetles on the plain. And it was very exciting when the island king's throat was torn out by Ranior's dogs—and of course Ranior himself was very strong and handsome. How did you say it? 'Hair of beaten gold and shoulders that bore up all the world.' Lovely."

Bardrem flushed a little, around his cheekbones. I wondered whether this was because of Chenn's words or because of Chenn herself.

"Good," he said. "I was happy with those parts too." He paused, gazed down at the paper. "Do you think King Haldrin would like it? After all, he's still young—surely he'd appreciate the work of someone also young. A grand work like this one."

"I don't know." Chenn was dabbing at my neck with a piece of damp cloth so that the tiny cut hairs would not cling and itch. "He's not a very grand sort of person. Several times I've heard him say that . . ."

Her words trailed and echoed. I turned. She was staring at nothing, holding the cloth in midair. She looked made of ice or stone.

"You've been to the *castle*?" Bardrem said. His voice broke on the last word, as it so often did in those days, making him sound both man and girl. "Is that where you were before—at the castle? That's good—wonderful!—you can take me there when my poem's done; you can tell the king how well I'd serve him, how many more works I'd write for him—"

"No," Chenn said.

I saw her far-gaze and heard her determination, but as a new silence fell, the words in my own head only grew louder.

"So," I said at last, my attempt at nonchalance undone by a quaver, "did you know Teldaru too?"

Chenn stood up. The scissors and cloth slipped from her hands to the floor. "I will not speak of this," she said. Her eyes leapt from Bardrem's face to mine. "Not ever. And for your own sakes, you will not ask me to."

"But why?" Bardrem's entire face was flushed now, and the paper shook a bit in his hand. "Why must we not speak of it, and why did you leave, and—"

"Chenn," a new voice said. There was a girl in the doorway—the girl who had been the newest, before Chenn came. She did not look at Bardrem or me. "The Lady bids you come to the receiving chamber."

Chenn shook her head. "I . . . I cannot. It's my bleeding week—the Lady knows this."

The girl smiled a false, quick smile. "She does. But it's the silk merchant asking for you—the one who's promised her a lower price on his wares. He knows you're bleeding, and he doesn't care."

For a moment Chenn's face seemed to tremble—her lips, her cheeks and chin—and she closed her eyes. Then she said, firmly, "Very well," and opened them again. "Tell her I am coming. And leave me—all of you."

Bardrem gripped my wrist when we were in the corridor. "Did you *hear* that?" he hissed.

"Of course," I said, but he was not listening.

"We have to find out how long she was there, and who else she knew—but did you *hear* that? She knew King Haldrin!"

"She didn't want to tell us, so we shouldn't press her." My words came out sounding priggish because my desire to agree with him was so great.

"But the castle, Nola! I would never have to chop another potato or be struck by another man who's drunk and unhappy with the girl he chose and claims the soup is what's made him angry . . . I'd learn my true craft at the feet of the king's poet, and then someday *I'd* be the king's poet."

He was still squeezing my wrist; I wrenched it free. "She left there for a reason and she doesn't want to go back. And don't talk of another life when this one is all you'll ever have."

I walked quickly so that he would not see my sudden tears, and so that I might outpace my confusion. Familiar halls, with their cracking plaster and smoke-darkened wood; my room with its rug and the bed that had seemed so luxurious, the first few times I'd awoken in it. And now this other place—only a word, but one I could see and feel, like the fire in the kitchen when a gale was blowing outside. "Castle:" a high place, closer to sunlight, where girls wore real jewels and were loved by men who did not pay them. Where a young seer could study in a real school, surrounded by safety and luxury and others like herself.

Despite my curiosity, I spoke to Chenn of the castle only once, and only by accident. We were in the courtyard. It was spring—the tree's twelve leaves were a bright, glossy yellow-green, and there was a scattering of new grass in the mud—and I had just had a lovely vision of a man sleeping with a book in the crook of his arm. The actual man had been pleased with this, and had paid me more than he'd said he would. When Chenn came to me, after he had gone, I was humming, putting the mirror away in its cloth.

The day was warm, one of those early spring days that feels like summer. She stood by the tree and watched me, and when I was done she smiled at me. I had learned that she, like almost everyone else I had ever met, had two smiles: one that she used when she did not really want to be smiling, and one that appeared when she was actually happy. That afternoon she smiled her happy smile, and the day grew even brighter.

"I just got my month's pay," she said. "I have almost enough now. One more month like this and I'll be able to leave."

"Oh." The air had darkened again, though Chenn's smile remained. "Where will you go?"

She had been as secretive about this as she had about her previous life, but today she raised her arms above her head and made a happy, stretching noise and said, "South, where it's summer all the time."

I opened my mouth to reply, but my words vanished—because I had seen the insides of her forearms, and the two long, puckered scars there.

"What are those?"

She lowered her arms and crossed them across her chest. "What?" Bardrem often pointed out that both Chenn and I were terrible liars, and said that he would be hard-pressed to choose the worse one. Now she clutched her dress sleeves over her wrists and would not meet my gaze. Her cheeks had gone very pale, which made her hair and eyes look even darker.

"The scars," I said, standing up to face her. "The lines"—from elbow crooks to wrists, the light purple of wounds only recently healed.

"An accident I had before I came here," she said quickly.

I snorted. "An accident? But there are two of them, exactly the same—did you happen to drop the same knife twice, or—"

"Nola." Yigranzi was standing at the end of the walkway closest to Chenn and me. I had not heard her come, even though she now used a walking stick that made a soft, hollow sound on the boards. She was so bent that she had to crane upward to look at us.

"Nola," she said again, her voice as strong as ever, "do not press her."

"I will!" I cried. "I *will* press her, because she was hurt—and this isn't the only secret—she used to live at the castle! That too . . ." My breath caught in my throat. I thought I had spoken too swiftly again, betrayed a confidence—but when I looked at Yigranzi I saw no surprise on her face.

"You know about the castle," I said, slowly now. "And about the scars, too?"

Yigranzi nodded. "Chenn and I have spoken a little of these things. I did not want you to know too much—I do not—for Nola-girl, there is ugliness in the world that you do not need to see. Not yet."

"Ugliness?" I was shouting, my voice cracking almost as Bardrem's did. "You think I don't already see ugliness? I see men kill each other; I see girls with sores, girls dying and bleeding—I see visions worse than these!" The shouting was hurting my ears and my throat; I lowered my voice a bit, though I kept it ablaze with anger. "Do not try to shield me from things: I need to know. I need to, because you are my friend"—this to Chenn, who looked so sad that I lost my breath again. In the moment of quiet that followed I saw it, as clear as if it were really happening before me: Chenn and Yigranzi sitting in Yigranzi's room of coloured cloth and shells. Chenn drinking from the cup with the crab on its side. Talking; both of them talking, but Chenn more. Tracing her old cuts with her fingers. Telling.

"How dare you," I whispered to the Chenn and Yigranzi who were in front of me. I pushed past one, then the other; I ran over the walkway and into the shadows of the walls. I did not truly know why I was running, which only made me hurry more.

Chenn came to my room that night. She knocked on my door as she usually did—four short raps followed by a scrabbling of fingers that sounded like tickling, or an animal digging. I did not answer. I lay on my bed, sunk in a loneliness that felt warm.

"Nola," she called. "Nola—I'm going to the receiving chamber now, but I'll be back at dawn. I want to talk to you. Please?"

I did not answer.

She left—I heard her footsteps in the hall, soft and quick. I thought: *Going somewhere else, like always*. I stared up into the dark air, and at the even darker patches that I knew were the ceiling beams. I almost hoped she wouldn't come back, so that I would be able to hold onto my anger or my hurt or whatever it was that made me feel suffocated and protected at the same time. *Almost hoped*—because when the silence stretched on and the sky in my open window paled to grey and she still did not come, the loneliness in me turned cold.

If I had let her in, when she knocked. If I had gone to find her. If, if—but no. I did not find her. He did.

CHAPTER FIVE

I had just managed to fall asleep when the screaming began. I was so accustomed to this sound that at first I only burrowed deeper into the bed, pulling the blanket up over my ears to shut it out. This did not work because several girls were screaming now, all at slightly different pitches. I felt the shuddering of the floor and thought, *So many people running—must be something very nasty.* But I did not move until Bardrem called my name from the corridor in a breaking, broken voice.

"What is it?" I was aware of the cold as I stared at him, air like wind, the last of winter, burrowing beneath my skin.

"Chenn," he said—and I pushed him out of the way, flew on feet I could not feel to the door where everyone had gathered.

"She is not here," the Lady said to me as all the girls fell back, letting me through. "We will find her and Yigranzi will tend to her." These words made me hope, for the space of time it took for me to step into the room—but then I saw.

I had seen blood before. I had imagined, before this, that I had seen a great deal of blood. This, though: dark pools, livid sprays on walls and even ceiling, every surface patterned wet. *Too much for one person—perhaps some animals'?* I thought dizzily, but when I looked at the dripping mess of Chenn's bed I knew this was not true.

I left, while the others stood and gawked. Ran again, as Bardrem and Yigranzi called out behind me. Bardrem had finally been getting taller this past winter, but even his newly lengthened legs could not keep pace with mine. I ran around corners and down the rickety flight of stairs by the kitchen and out into the daylight that had turned to gold.

It was the gold that made me stop, at the walkway. The hue of my vision—the one with Chenn sitting on the throne—and Chenn *was* sitting, but with her back against the tree.

"Chenn?" Just a whisper, so I was not surprised when Chenn did not look up. I walked. The wood was cold and smooth against my bare feet. The light was thick; I peered through it, saw only clean, graceful lines—the slope of Chenn's shoulders and her crossed legs and the fall of her long, dark hair. Her head was bent forward, a little. Sleeping, I thought, because I had made myself forget the room behind me in the glow of what was in front. I heard Yigranzi call my name again but did not pause. There was only Chenn.

I knelt beside her. "Chenn," I said. "Chenn, Chenn," and reached for her shoulder. The cloth of her sleeping shift was soft and white. Her skin was shining, damp, and I thought of dew. I gave a gentle shake, and another, and Chenn's head lolled slowly, slowly.

At first I saw only her eyes, which were open wide. They were light green with black centres. Green without gold. Normal eyes—and this was so shocking that I looked away from them, and down.

The wound was as it had been in my vision: the lips of a lycus blossom, curled outward. This was no Otherseeing, though, not a thing glimpsed swiftly, which would fade to nothing as I blinked. I stared at the pale, glistening hole of Chenn's throat. There was a sudden sound in my ears, like the wings of hundreds of birds all trying to fly at once. When it passed I heard my own blood, pulsing *alive, alive* within me.

"He washed her," Bardrem said. He was crouching on Chenn's other side, clutching her hand in both of his. "He cut her and let her bleed dry and then he washed her."

I could hardly see him through the haze of gold; I could hardly hear him through the clamour of my heartbeat.

Yigranzi's shadow fell across Chenn's lap and up over her face. I looked at Yigranzi's fingers, which were swollen and gnarled and grasping the rounded top of her walking stick. "The mirror," Yigranzi said. Only now did I notice it, lying on the ground near Bardrem's knees. It was shining as I had never seen it shine before, copper fire on the dull, black earth. Its wrapping cloth was spread smooth and flat beneath.

"We must look," Yigranzi said.

I tried to find words. I felt my voice stir in my throat; felt how whole my throat was, closed and filled with breath—so unlike Chenn's. "But," I began, "she is dead—she can't ask us to Othersee, so—"

"Sometimes," Yigranzi said, "fresh blood is enough. Blood and flesh."

"But her Pattern is done—there is nothing to see."

"Except how it was set. If we are quick enough, we might catch a trace. But we must be quick, and Bardrem must speak the words."

"We'll look together?" Yigranzi finally turned her eyes to me. "We shouldn't," I said, "you told me that two seers looking at a single Pattern at the same time could hurt—could be confusing and strange. . . ."

Yigranzi leaned down and picked the mirror up in her twisted hand.

She's becoming a tree, I thought; a stray, fleeting idea that I remembered only later.

"You've always wanted to know the hidden things, Nola-girl. So come here by me now, and learn."

I expect darkness. There is light, instead: a stark silver-white that is everywhere and nowhere, curved and flat. I am within it but also above—for there are shapes, and they are far beneath me. I am Nola, I think, to keep the light from burning me to smoke. I am Nola, and for now I am a bird. I hover, though there is no wind, no breath—only a crushing stillness.

All of a sudden I am lower, or maybe the shapes below have risen toward me. One is Chenn. I cannot see her face, since the other figure is bending over her, but I see her hair, spread out around her like a spill of ink upon the white. She is naked, and I can barely make out her skin. Chenn, I think, it's me; I'll listen to you this time; show me who he is. . . .

His head is golden-brown. The rest of him is blurred, strangely shaped, but he looks short and round. I thrust closer, through the air that seeks to crush me.

Someone is holding onto me; hands around my wings. Yigranzi, let go: I'm nearly there. I cry out silently and the brown-gold head lifts. Feathers, not hair, and a hooked beak trailing crimson, and Chenn's throat crimson too—only it is not Chenn any more. The eyes that stare above the bloody wound are mine.

I try to scream and I try to fly but he has me; he reaches down with talons and up with beak, and his hunger turns the sky to gold. I stop imagining I can or even want to struggle.

Yes, I think—blinded, weightless, ready—but then the hands around me tighten and pull, and Yigranzi calls my name so loudly that the gold shudders.

"Nola!"—again and again, as shards fall: sky, beak, skin and blood, until nothing remains but me.

I woke in my bed. It was dark except for the flickering of the single, squat candle that sat in a bronze dish atop the washstand. This weak light bruised my eyes, my temples; the aching I always felt after a vision, only more powerful. I rolled my head on the pillow and swallowed over a surge of nausea.

Yigranzi was sitting beside my bed. Her chin was bent to her breast, and for a moment she looked like Chenn—but for a moment only, for when I gasped out her name she lifted her head and smiled at me. "My girl, my girl," she said, like a lullaby, "you're back again."

"How long?" My voice echoed in my head and down my arms. I could almost see it throbbing out from beneath my fingernails; a bright, branching pattern in the darkness.

"Two days and nights," Yigranzi said. "I thought you were lost; thought the Otherworld had kept you."

"I saw—" I began. She leaned over and put her fingers on my lips.

"Not yet," she said. "Not if it will hurt"—but I told her anyway, in a long string of words like one of Bardrem's, with no room for breath. When I was done she rose and shuffled to the washstand to get me a mug of water.

"I did not see Chenn at all," she said as I drank (and choked a bit; so thirsty). She looked up at my window, pursing her lips in the way that meant she wished to say more but knew she shouldn't.

"What, then?" I asked, though I already knew.

"You." Her eyes were on me again, their black trembling with candle flame. "You in a desert of white sand, sinking up to your waist and then your neck. I could feel him there"—she was whispering now, her face so close to mine that her words brushed against my cheek—"but I could not see him. He was beneath you; he was everywhere, but I could not see him."

"So I am in danger," I said, "the same as Chenn."

Yigranzi held my hands as if they were shards of glass—so lightly, when in my vision she had gripped me, saved me. I waited for her to say, "That is one

Path, yes, but not the only one" or "Perhaps, but say 'might be' instead of 'am.'"

I waited, but she said nothing more.

It rained for months after Chenn's murder: a steady, relentless downpour that washed away the fuzz of new grass and turned the courtyard to quagmire. Or so I assumed—for I never tried to go there. Yigranzi had Bardrem bring the Otherseeing tools inside and saw the few men and girls who came to her in the Lady's public chamber. Yigranzi did not ask me to help her, in part because there were hardly any customers, but mostly, I think, because she could tell how afraid I still was. This fear kept me away from the mirror and the coins I could have made; kept me curled on my bed for hours at a time, listening to the rain that would not stop.

Bardrem tried to help. He wrote me nonsense rhymes, dragged me to the kitchen and juggled turnips, spun himself until his eyes crossed, trying to make me laugh. He put bread and cheese in my hands and glared down at me with his hands on his hips until I ate. When all his attempts at levity failed he came to my room and sat at the end of my bed. Sometimes he spoke, but usually he just watched me drift in and out of sleep. One afternoon he came in and stood beside the bed. I waited for him to sit down, but he did not. I glanced at him, then sat up myself (my limbs so heavy, trapped by mud).

"What is it?" I said thickly. I hardly seemed to speak any more.

He bit his lip. There was a strand of hair stuck in the corner of his mouth but he did not notice it. "The girls are talking; they heard it from the Lady. . . ."

"*What*?" I said. My annoyance felt sharp, like blood returned to a numb limb.

"Seers at the other brothels are being killed. Three so far, that the Lady's heard of. Some of the regular girls, too—a few of them."

I thought, *I suppose I'll never leave my room at all, now.* I said, "And no one's seen him?"

He shook his head. "Guesses, only: a suspicious man who was short and fat; another who was tall and thin . . ." He took a noisy breath, clenched his hands. "I hope he comes back here, Nola," he said, so quickly and smoothly that I could tell he'd heard the words before, in his head. "I hope he comes back—I'll know him as soon as I see him, and I'll kill him—I *will*, I'll kill him before he can hurt you."

"And how will you do that?" I said, as dryly as I could, trying to keep the tremor in my belly and legs from touching my voice.

He lifted the fold of shirt that fell over his belt. A small leather scabbard hung there, with a worn, wooden hilt sticking out of it. "It's not big," he said, "but that means I can always carry it. And it's the sharpest one in the kitchen."

"A kitchen knife," I said, making the tremor into a laugh. "That will be perfect, if he happens to be a potato, or a medium-sized haunch of beef." I bit my own lip, to stop these words I did not even mean, and I looked away from his open mouth and his round, stricken eyes. I lay down again, this time with my back to him, and covered my face with my arm so that I would not have to see him or hear the rain. When I rolled over, after minutes or maybe hours, he was gone.

The rain stopped a few days later, and I woke wrapped in silence. I listened to it for a moment, then stood up and pushed the shutters open. Sunlight washed over my face, and a smell of earth and drying stone. I thought, *Enough of this room*. I splashed water on my hands and cheeks, slipped on a brown dress that was very nearly too small for me, and went to find Bardrem.

It was midday, between the noon and evening meals, and he was in the tiny closet that was his bedchamber. It was next to the kitchen, and stank of everything that had ever been cooked there—most recently, apparently, cabbage. He stared at me with his hands behind his head and said nothing.

"Let's go somewhere." My voice sounded too bright, and my smile felt taut, but it did not matter: I was full of restlessness and remorse. "Somewhere outside."

His eyebrows arched. "Outside."

"I know—I don't usually like going anywhere—but please, Bardrem. It rained for so long and now it's a beautiful day, and if there's trouble that'll be fine, because you can bring your knife. I'd like that; it'll make me feel safe."

He sat up, angling his head so that it would not knock against the slanted ceiling. "Oh, very well," he said gruffly. "But only if I get to choose where."

"Yes," I said, too excited by his forgiveness to point out that he always chose, on the rare occasions when we left the brothel.

I did not like going out into the city. Most of the girls did; sometimes they argued over which of them would get to have a free day, when the fair came. (Once two of them returned from the fair with torn clothes and bloody scratches on their cheeks and arms: they had fought each other for a length of satin ribbon. The Lady took away the ribbon, and their wages for the month.) I had no desire to see such things. Until Chenn arrived, I had given little thought to the world beyond the courtyard.

It was a bright world Bardrem led me into, that day. I stood outside the brothel's door and blinked at the sunlight, and at the stone and wood of houses and shops, all of them washed by rain. "Come on," said Bardrem, who was already picking his way through the churned mud of the street. "Let's go before someone sees us and claims there's work to do."

I followed him. At first I kept my eyes on the road, which was rutted with wheel tracks and footprints and scattered with deep, murky puddles. But Bardrem soon guided me from this path to another, which was cobbled, and I looked up as I walked. I did not recognize the houses here. They had two storeys and intricately carved shutters painted in colours so bright that I blinked again. There was more colour, too: tapestries and rugs hanging from high-up windows, drying in the sun. *At least I won't see my mother here*, I thought, and remembered our table and our old, dirty rushes and the walls that had leaned in to squeeze my breath away.

Bardrem walked very fast. "Where are we going?" I called once, and he only waved at me over his shoulder. The street began to climb, and I gasped with exertion, bent over a knot in my side, but I was determined to keep up. I focused again on my feet (my shoes were sodden and stained; the Lady would be angry) and saw everything else peripherally: a black dog curled in a doorway; a line of people holding empty baskets, waiting outside a barred gate; two little girls rolling a ball between them. I wheezed up a flight of twisting stairs and ducked beneath a low archway—and then I straightened and stopped, because Bardrem had.

"Here," he said. "Look."

I thought, *But there's nothing to look at*. After all the streets, all the houses and courtyards, we were standing at the foot of a wall. Its stones were reddish-gold and threaded with ivy. I was about to say something puzzled to him when he took my hand and placed it against a stone and said, "Look *up*."

The wall stretched on and on, higher than any wall I'd ever seen. Its top seemed to hang against the sky. There were notches in it, there, and fluttering from these notches were banners of silver and green, stitched with patterns I could not make out.

I looked back at Bardrem. "The castle," I said, and he nodded and smiled the smile he used when his mind was on words, not on what was before him.

"The castle," he said, and laid his hand beside mine. "Just the north wall, but

I can still feel it all—can't you? The towers and the great halls and the people. The music and the feasting."

A bird called and I looked for it, found it wheeling in the blue above the battlements. It was very far away, and I could not see its features, but it cried out again and I thought, *Eagle*, and caught my breath.

"There's also truth in there," I said. "About Chenn."

Bardrem narrowed his eyes at me.

"About what happened to her before she came to us," I continued, "and maybe even what happened to her after."

"Maybe," Bardrem said. "Maybe we should try to get in, try to ask someone."

I shook my head. "Look at it—just at this part. We'll never get in there. Perhaps we shouldn't even want to."

But I did. I felt the stone beneath my palm; I almost heard it, humming with danger and promise.

"Let's go back," I said, already turning away. "Now. People will be missing us."

"Nola." Bardrem spoke quietly; he sounded older than fifteen, suddenly. "It's all right to want something you think you can't have. It's all right to say so, too."

"No," I said, to something, to everything, and pushed past him on the steep, sunny path.

It might seem as if the next part of my tale is something I created—or something real, but stitched onto the story in a place other than where it truly belongs. But it is true, and happened precisely in this way and at this time: The evening of the day of my walk with Bardrem, one of the girls came to my room. "Yigranzi wants you," she said. "In the courtyard."

I went. It was dusk; the spindly upper branches of the tree were burnished, the leaves bronze and gold over their spring green. The tree shadow was long, dancing a little on the ground in a wind I did not feel. There was a man standing with Yigranzi by the tree. He was tall, dressed in browns and blacks that made him hard to see until I was in front of him.

I try to remember now what it was I saw, that first time. Or rather—I remember precisely what I saw and try to convince myself to see more, all these years later. But I cannot. He was a tall man, dressed in a brown tunic and black cloak; a man with such a beautiful, sad face that I'm sure I stood and stared like a mouse before an owl.

"This is Master Orlo," Yigranzi said. "He is an Otherseer from the castle, and he is here because of Chenn."

He smiled at me, gently, sadly, and bent his head in the dying light—and that was all. That was all I saw.

CHAPTER SIX

The stubble on Orlo's chin and cheeks glinted red, though the hair on his head was the colour of honey.

"Nola," he said. His voice was quiet and grave. "Yigranzi tells me that you were Chenn's friend. I am sorry you have lost her."

His eyes were not quiet. They were the blue-black of Chenn's, only the colour seemed to ripple, and their centres were a gold so bright that I looked away.

"Thank you," I said, gazing at his mouth. His upper lip was thin and his lower one full, and the teeth behind them were even and white.

"I sent for you as soon as Orlo came to me," Yigranzi said, "so that we could hear his tale together." There was nothing strange about her words, but I heard hesitancy beneath them, giving them slow, blunt edges. "I offered to receive him in the Lady's chamber but he refused."

"Because I would rather stand by a seer's tree than sit on an overstuffed chair," he said, and I smiled. The chairs in the Lady's chamber were all hard and lumpy.

"This tree must not be nearly so grand as the one at the castle." Yigranzi was not smiling, so her words did not sound admiring.

Orlo did smile. "There are several at the castle, all very grand, but this one . . ." He put his hand on the bark, flat, though his fingertips arched a bit. "This is a fine tree. So . . . delicately leafed."

"Hmph," said Yigranzi. She sat down slowly on the stone and twisted her head toward him. "Enough about trees, now. Tell us about Chenn."

Orlo hesitated for a moment, his eyes cast down. He scuffed a foot, just as Bardrem often did. He said, "It is difficult . . ." and looked up at me. "It is a difficult tale to tell, because there are parts of it that cause me shame. But you must hear it."

"Yes," Yigranzi said, "we must."

He nodded at her. There was no smile about him now. "I had just begun instructing child seers when Chenn was brought to the castle. This was nine years ago, and she was very young—four or five, I think."

And how old are you? I thought, then flushed, as if I had spoken aloud. He looked young, except for the lines around his eyes and in his forehead—though these could have been from Otherseeing, not age. *Chenn,* I reminded myself, and tried to imagine the child, and the tall, windy castle.

"She was the daughter of a wealthy family, pampered and strong-willed, but as her schooling progressed she grew in skill and character. There was always a gleam in her eye, though, no matter how weighty her visions or how difficult her lessons. Her fellow students adored her. As did one of her teachers, a seer named Master Prandel." He frowned, squinted up at the leaves, which were just a dark green now, untouched by sun. "Here is my first shame—for I should have acted. I saw his desire, and she was just twelve, and I should have spoken to him, at least, or gone to Master Teldaru with what I knew . . . but I did not. I imagined that Prandel's infatuation would pass, or I hoped that someone else would confront him, or some such cowardly thing." Orlo shook his head, dragged a hand roughly through his hair, which stood on end afterward.

"I'm not sure when he acted on his desire. All I know is that she changed. She stopped laughing, grew quiet and pale and afraid of her own visions. And then, this past winter, she disappeared."

He was staring at the bottom of the tree. *Maybe Yigranzi's already told him that that was where we found her,* I thought, and the pain I saw on his face and in the slump of his shoulders made my own stir and sharpen.

"Prandel was not distraught, as the rest of us were—he was furious. Which made me furious. I faced him, though too late. He is a small, plump, weak man, and I admit that I did him some harm. Before I left him I took a lock of her hair, which he had hung next to his bed on a yellow ribbon. I had another student speak the Otherseeing words and I used Chenn's hair to find her Pattern."

"Really?" Yigranzi's voice made me start, because its edges were no longer blunt. "You saw her using only a lock of her hair? That's a thing that takes a great and practiced grasp of the Othersight."

Orlo gave a slight shrug. "My gift has always been considerable, and my training was rigorous. Though the visions I saw that night were weak, of course, as they always are without the person in front of you. Weak, but enough. I saw faint images of naked limbs and small, dark rooms; girls and men . . ." He glanced at me, cleared his throat. "Enough to show me that her Path would lead her to a place like this one. But although the visions I saw were unpleasant, there was no danger in them. No"—another vehement shake of his head—"no danger, or I would have begun my search then. But I did not, and this is my other shame. I, of all people, should know that the Othersight is not always a complete view—just a glimpse, there and gone in a blink. But I chose not to think of this. I thought: Chenn is safely away from here, where she might have come to great harm. Prandel has been punished and is a changed man. Only I was wrong about this, too." He gave a short, breathless laugh. "Because Prandel disappeared a few months after Chenn did. And he found her. Somehow he found her."

"Small and plump?" It was the first time I had spoken to him, and I was pleased with my voice, which was firm and older-sounding. "I think that's what he looked like—the man in my vision."

"Your vision?" His night-dark eyes shimmered and this time I could not look away. "You have seen him? How?"

Yigranzi opened her mouth and I said, quickly, "Yigranzi and I used the mirror when Chenn's body was still here. Right here." I gestured at the place where Orlo was standing and he flinched, stared at the tree's roots as if she were there again, her throat gaping. Then he stared at me.

"You looked into the Otherworld when she was dead."

"Yes. Yigranzi and I. And I saw a man who was short and fat—or just round, somehow. But it was hard to tell, since . . ."

When I stopped speaking, neither Orlo nor Yigranzi noticed. They were gazing at each other; gold at pearl, far beyond me.

"A dangerous thing," he said at last, "for one so young."

"I'm thirteen," I said, but they did not look at me. I thought, *I'll swing from the tree, I'll stand on my hands and sing Bardrem's longest poem*—but I watched them instead, in silence.

"Yes," Yigranzi said. "But it was necessary. Chenn was only just gone; it was necessary." She rose, leaning on her stick. I saw Orlo eye her hump, which seemed to be lurching in its own direction. I wanted to say something that would make him stop, but I did not.

"And what of the other girls who are dying?" Yigranzi was out of breath, just from standing up. "Why did this Prandel not stop with Chenn, if it was she he wanted?"

Orlo took a breath of his own, which was deep and smooth. "I believe that he only *started* with Chenn. That hunting her and killing her only made his hunger keener. So now"—slow words, and a slow smile—"I am hunting him."

"I will come back." This was the last thing Orlo said to me before he left, and it circled in my head like a melody whose beauty fades with persistence, but will not go away.

"He will come back," I said to Bardrem, many days after that first meeting. Then, hastening to explain my eagerness, "To tell us if he's found Prandel."

"I hope he doesn't find him," Bardrem said. "I want to kill him, remember?"

I looked at the thin, gangle-limbed boy in front of me and thought of the man with the hunter's smile and I said, "Yes, Bardrem," as if he were three years old. To Yigranzi I said, "Orlo will find him, I know he will," and, "It's been two weeks: he'll be back soon to say Prandel is dead."

Yigranzi peered at me after I'd spoken, so intently that I wished I had said nothing. It was dark in her room, but I might as well have been standing before her in full sun. "Take care," she said, too quietly. "You are old enough to feel the force of the wave but too young to see the water."

"Riddles!" I cried. "Why do you give me riddles when I want something simple and simple things when I want mysteries?" I did not understand what this meant, even though I felt the truth of it, and I ran from her as tears hardened in my throat.

She and I must have spoken to each other again—I am sure of this, but have no memories with which to prove it. There must have been a few more lessons, a few more customers, a few more coins passed from her hand to mine. I long to remember, and I cling to the imagined certainties and the must-have-beens with a doggedness that would make her smile her gap-toothed smile. "Nola-girl," (what would she have called the woman I've become?) "you can't keep the tide on the sand; let it go. . . ."

But there it is: I remember running from her room, and the next thing I remember is running to it, a week or so later, drawn by a sound I had never heard before. It was not screaming, not shouting; not any noise ever made by one of the girls (even the few I'd heard birthing their babies, or ridding themselves of them). It was a choking, gurgling whine. I can hear it even now, though I still cannot describe it.

I threw open Yigranzi's door and took two quick steps into her room. I looked first at her bed, blinking in sudden darkness (although it was bright midday outside, her shutters were closed). When my vision cleared I saw that she was not there but on the floor, twisted in a way that was all wrong, as if she were broken. Her back and face were both turned to me. Her bare heels drummed against a space of wood between two rugs, and it sounded like my heart.

I yelled over my shoulder, but people were already coming, drawn, as ever, by dread and excitement. They did not enter the room, though, or even cluster at the door as they usually did. They gathered in knots along the corridor and would not come closer, even when I screamed at them to help me.

Only Bardrem came, long moments later, when I was hoarse and gasping with tears. I was kneeling beside her, trying to roll her over or straighten her, but mostly gazing at her own closed eyes. She must have known me, for the high, terrible whining had stopped, though the gurgling continued.

"Here," I heard Bardrem say, "I'll hold her under her arms and you take her legs—just there—good—now *lift*."

She was too twisted, and her hump was too big; we had to settle her on her side. I covered her with a blanket, which the beating of her feet soon dislodged.

"Yigranzi," I said, "what is it, what happened?"

She clung to me with trembling, digging fingers, as if these things would give me my answer. She choked and coughed, and spittle ran from the corner of her mouth—but no words.

"Help her," I said to the Lady, when she finally came. "Send for a seer from another brothel—an old one, because she might know healing, like Yigranzi does."

The Lady looked away from Yigranzi's straining, stranger's face, at me. She did not look back at the bed again. "No," she said, lifting a hand to curl a strand of lank hair behind her ear. Her rings winked colours and metal. "Her Pattern is ending and there is nothing we can do to stop it."

Bardrem reached over and put his hand on my arm. He must have seen my anger, or felt the wave of words I was about to speak. "Nola," he said, "it's true. Look at her."

I did not. I glared at the Lady, who seemed impossibly tall just then. She towered above me, her head nearly touching the bundles of herbs that hung from the beam.

"In any case, child," she said, "the end of her Path means the widening of yours. You will take her place as Otherseer and we will all benefit. For now," she continued, turning so that the velvet dragged into a tangle around her feet, "you may stay with her. Come to me when she is dead."

I stayed. For three days I ate only because Bardrem told me to, and slept only for moments, sitting forward with my head beside Yigranzi's on the pillow. Everything blurred: rug hues, volcano rock, a clay crab that somehow scuttled from mug to floor and up my bare leg. I did not flinch. I watched daylight and darkness on Yigranzi's sunken, twitching cheeks, and on the eyelids that fluttered but still did not open.

"Look," Bardrem said once, "the mirror—what's it doing here?" It was on the table among the combs and pots of oils; it was bright, polished, wrong.

"I don't know," I said. "It shouldn't be here"—only in the tree, or in the Lady's receiving chamber, but how could this matter now?

I dripped water from a cloth onto Yigranzi's lips, which trembled and cracked; the water useless, soaking the bed beneath her head, but I imagined she would drink it, anyway. I touched her face, her shoulder. I had never touched anyone so much before, but I had to show Yigranzi that I was there. I did not speak, though, to show her this—not until the dawn of the third day, when I bent and whispered, "I need you; don't go."

Later that third day the room was flooded with sun. "You must sleep," Bardrem said. "You must eat. It's hot in here, and it smells—come with me now." I only hunched closer to Yigranzi. I heard him leave, and then I heard nothing but her breathing. It was just as loud as it had been before, but there were more spaces in it, so it seemed quieter. I put my hand on her hair, which was the last remnant of before: thick and crinkly, filling my palm. *Still here*, I thought with every one of her halting, slower breaths. *Still here*.

I was nodding asleep when Yigranzi thrashed once, violently. Her fingers raked my arm and I started awake. I leaned forward again, ready to comfort, to reach for water or a groping, beseeching hand. Then I saw her face, and froze.

Her eyes were open.

I lurched to my feet. My stool tipped over and my ankles caught and I fell. I sat on the floor as she sat up in the bed, effortlessly, her legs swinging over the side.

Her eyes were brown.

She was trying to speak; her lips and throat convulsed and she made a sound like *oh oh oh*, low and urgent.

Brown, I thought. *Regular brown, with regular black centres—like Chenn's, at the end. Like Chenn's . . .*

Yigranzi stood. For a moment her back seemed straight; she was entirely different, some new woman formed from the bones of the old. She lifted a hand that did not waver and stretched it toward me. I scrambled back, raising my own arm as if she meant to strike me—but she did not. She only reached, her brown eyes wide and clear. "*Oh*," she said again, and fell.

I crawled across the floor, clumsily, catching fingertips and toes in gaps in the rugs. I touched her shoulder and one warm, limp hand and said her name, over and over, to make up for all the words I should have spoken, on this day and others. I waited for the eyes to blink but they did not; waited for them to close on their own but they did not. I touched them gently with the pads of my thumbs, held them shut until they stayed that way.

I closed my own eyes and pressed my hands to my ears and rocked myself, alone.

CHAPTER SEVEN

I must breathe. I must lift my head from these pages and wriggle my stiff fingers and roll my shoulders until the knot between them loosens. The words that I thought would take time to choose and set down in order are coming so swiftly, crowding my head and the paper and making me forget everything else.

It is Sildio, now, who makes sure that I eat. He raps on my door a few hours past dawn and again at noon and once more at dusk. If I'm too absorbed in my writing to answer, and if he must leave the post he's appointed for himself outside my door, he sets the food on a tray in the hallway. (It must be the hallway. If he left it on the floor of my room, one of the animals who shares this space with me would eat it before I could.) And if the food is still there when he returns he knocks again, much less politely.

But sometimes it's so difficult to remember to look up beyond the page beneath my nose. I must remember. Because the tiny strip of sky can be so lovely. Like now, for example: it is dawn, and the clouds are several shades of pink.

Dawn now—and dawn in my story, too. (How neatly done! Bardrem would approve of this, though not of my desire to draw attention to it.)

Dawn, and courtyard, and one last, lonely girl.

Her name and her face are long gone but I still remember the vision I had of her. It was simple, lovely, uncoloured by copper. She had brought me a handful of barley, "Because the mirror is probably too grand a way to see my Pattern."

It was there as soon as the barley had settled on the ground: a hillside so green that it seemed made of paint, not grass, and the girl walking up it. The slope was steep but she was moving easily, gracefully, tipping her face to the sun. She stopped just a few paces from the peak and raised her arms above her head and suddenly there were butterflies around her, their wings silver and blue and green and yellow, blurred with light and flying.

That was all. I told her, expecting impatience or even anger—some other girls would have cried, "Try again! Tell me what can be seen from the hilltop or I won't pay you!"—but she smiled.

"My grandmother's village was always full of butterflies in the early fall—my mother told me this. I have been thinking of going there, and now I am sure." She unclasped a silver chain from around her neck. A single ruby hung from it.

"No," I said as she was handing it to me, "this is far too precious. . . ."

She nodded. "It was to me, too, for a long time. Now I don't need it any more. Take it—and thank you, Nola. Yours is about the only city face I'll miss."

I collected the barley, after she had left me, and set it in a pile by the mirror. The mirror in its cloth, the grain, the goblet in which wax and water swam; the tattered tree and its worn-smooth carvings. All mine, now that Yigranzi was gone. In the two weeks since her death many people had come to me—many more than I'd ever seen come before.

The Lady had noted this, of course. One afternoon when she came to take her share of my payment she said, "For years Yigranzi's island skin and accent made her a curiosity here, and this was good—but then she grew old, and that hump . . ." She twitched, as if she were warding off a fly. "I am happy she is gone. And you have turned out better than I expected, when you came to me with your filthy nails and your hair crawling with bugs. We will do well for each other, you and I."

I should have been proud, or at least excited. But as I sat among the Otherseeing things that were mine alone, all I felt was a hollowness beneath my bones.

Perhaps it was because I was immersed in this feeling that I did not see him come. I was fastening the pendant around my neck when I heard a footfall on the wood. By the time I lifted my head, he was in front of me.

"Nola," he said. Dawn was giving way to morning; the light was more white than gold, and I squinted to see him clearly.

"Orlo," I said, as calmly as if I had been expecting him. I laid my hands on my thighs; the sweat that already slicked my palms belied the steadiness of my voice.

"I came to see you and Yigranzi—both of you, to tell you that I tracked Prandel to a brothel by the western gate, and that I missed him only by moments. But I've just heard . . . the Lady told me that Yigranzi . . ."

His eyes are wild, I thought, *too black, half in the Otherworld, or someplace just as far away from this one*. He rubbed a hand roughly over his stubble, which was thicker and redder than it had been the last time.

"She was old," I said—words that had angered me when spoken by others.

He said, "Yes. But I am still sorry to hear she is gone, and so soon after Chenn."

I clasped my hands now, because they had begun to shake. "Thank you. I—I miss them very much."

He crouched next to the stone so that his head was level with mine. "And what will you do now?"

I looked into the restless dark of his eyes. "I will stay here." These words rang as false as the ones about Yigranzi. "I will be the brothel seer. The Lady has asked me, and I've already had many customers."

He smiled at me and raised a honey-coloured brow. "You do not sound certain. Is there another choice you would make?"

"No." The word was too high, too quick, and it seemed to echo in the space between us. Images came to me, as suddenly as if I had summoned them in the mirror: a girl surrounded by butterflies; my hand lying against the stone of the castle wall; Chenn's face, distant with secrets. "No," I said again, blinking these images away so that all I saw was the courtyard. "This is where I should be."

"I understand." Orlo hesitated, cocking his head to one side as if he were listening to a voice I could not hear. "But think, Nola," he continued, his eyes back on mine, "think of your own safety. Prandel is hunting girls like you more and more frequently now; it would be best if you—"

"Nola?" Bardrem's new, steady voice had arrived with the summer. It was deep, and sometimes I still did not recognize it right away—like now, when I was slow with recent Otherseeing, and Orlo's gaze.

"Nola," Bardrem said again as he walked from wood to grass (the beautiful, soft green grass that would live only until midsummer, when the heat would turn it brittle and brown). "Who is this?"

Orlo and I stood up. Orlo was taller than Bardrem, but not by much, which took me aback, somehow.

"This is Master Orlo," I said, "the man I told you about—the one who's looking for Prandel, who killed Chenn."

"Ah," said Bardrem. "The man from the castle."

Orlo inclined his head. "Indeed. And you are?"

"Bardrem," he said before I could answer for him. "Cook and poet."

I glanced at Orlo's brows with expectant dread and was rewarded when one of them arched. "I do not believe we have such a job at the castle. The ways of the lower city continue to amaze me."

"Perhaps you mean 'amuse'?"

"Bardrem!" I hissed.

He held up a hand. "No, Nola—wait—I have a real question for *Master* Orlo. Why would an important castle seer come down to the lower city to look for a girl?"

"A murderer," Orlo said, as if between gritted teeth. "I seek a murderer who was also, once, an important castle seer."

"Yes," I said hastily, "of course—I *told* you this, Bardrem—"

"Oh, you told me—so I must believe it?"

"Bardrem, stop! He's from the *castle*!"

"When have you ever cared so much about the castle?"

"When have you ever cared so little?"

"What—"

Orlo stepped away from us and we fell abruptly silent. "This is obviously not the time for a quiet, reasonable conversation," he said with a small smile that took any sting from his words. "I will return soon. Soon," he repeated, looking at me.

I nodded, watched him walk back into the brothel. Then I whirled to face Bardrem.

"I can't believe it," I said, my voice high and thin with anger. "You finally get a chance to talk about the castle with somebody *from* the castle, and—"

"I don't like him." He spoke quietly, which made me snap my mouth shut in surprise. "He doesn't look right. He doesn't talk right. He doesn't *fit*."

"Maybe because he's a castle seer standing in a lowtown brothel. But that's not even the thing, is it? You're jealous, Bardrem." I tossed my head as if there were hair to billow out behind me, and stamped my foot. "You're jealous because he's where you want to be, and he's a man, and—"

"And you admire him—don't forget that—you look at him like the Lady looks at silk—and yes I'm jealous, yes yes *yes*—how else could you expect me to feel?"

He had been coming closer to me as he talked, and I had retreated until the tree was at my back and there was nowhere else to go. "Bardrem," I said, holding my hand up—and it was against his chest, he was so close. I felt his heart beneath my palm and his breath on my cheeks, and just as I was thinking that his breath smelled of carrots he kissed me.

It was clumsy—a tangle of hair (his, of course) and tongues and knocking teeth—but I did not pull away. It was the taste that held me—his taste, which was carrots and also porridge, but which was other things, too, that I could not name; warm, wet, dark things that made him someone new.

I did not pull away; he did. He stared at me for a moment, his mouth open and glistening, and then he turned and ran.

I did not follow him until much later. For most of that day I sat at the foot of the tree, shifting sometimes on the roots that made parts of me completely numb. My body's lethargy felt strange, for my mind was spinning, a blur of vivid, tireless wings: *He'll come back—which he?—but she never will—which she?—and I am here, here because I am here and that is where I must be. . . .*

The Lady loomed over me at one point. "You aren't ill, are you?" I heard her say, though the noise in my own head was louder than her words. "Some of the girls told me you looked ill. . . . There was another girl murdered, you know, by the western wall; another seer, this one was . . . You'll get no customers today, so you might just as well come inside. . . . There—do you hear that? Thunder. Now come inside; you'll be no good to me soaked and feverish."

I closed my eyes. When I opened them again I was alone, and the courtyard was sunk in an Otherworldly light: dark purples and yellows that matched the thunderclouds massed above. A flash of lightning turned everything white and black and I started as if I'd just woken up. The rain began—fat, warm drops that drove me to my feet at last.

I headed for the kitchen, where Rudicol was plucking a chicken, cursing as each feather came free. "Where is he?" he shouted when he saw me in the doorway. "Where is that accursed boy—this is *his* task—tell me, girl, for you always know." I shook my head and backed into the corridor as he flung a handful of down at me (I saw it settle on the floor directly in front of him, gentle as snow). As he yelled more words I could not hear, thanks to another clap of thunder, I ducked beneath Bardrem's low door. His tiny room was empty.

Lightning showed me the way up the stairs. On the second floor the air seemed heavier and darker, and the thunder louder, rattling shutters and even stone. I trailed my hand along the wall, expecting to feel puffs of mortar dust. There was no light here—no candles burning, nor oil lamps; no glimmers from beneath doors that proved there were people behind them, too. My own door was just as dark as all the others, but I opened it with relief.

I stood with my back against it. "Bardrem?" I called. I could see nothing, and thought, more irritably than fearfully, *Now I'll have to go all the way back downstairs to find a candle, and I'll probably have to talk to the Lady about the newest murder, even though she cares only for lost money, not for dead girls.* . . . I took a step forward and felt my foot hit something. It was light, and I had to get on my knees and grope a bit before I found it: a piece of paper folded into a shape with many facets, like a gem. *Bardrem*, I thought, placing the paper in the front pocket of my dress. I stood back up. I would really need a candle now, to read the words he had written me. I wondered whether they would be about the kiss, or whether they would be meaningless, foolish: *cabbage tendril toad tomorrow* . . .

Thunder tore the room apart—or so it seemed, for I stumbled forward as if the floor had pitched, and the shutters above me flew open with their own, lesser crash. A few heartbeats later, lightning filled the chamber and seared everything into my eyes: the washstand, Yigranzi's goblet, the rumpled rug, the man rising from my bed.

If I managed to scream, the sound was lost in fresh thunder, and his hand was over my mouth before I could draw another breath. "Nola," said Orlo in the shuddering quiet, his lips warm against my cheek, and his chin rough. "Hush. Hush; I have you now."

CHAPTER EIGHT

"Shh, Nola. I won't hurt you—but Prandel will, if he finds you. You must come with me now, before he does. There's a place, a safe place; it's not far."

I heard only him. The thunder was retreating now, grumbles instead of roars; his voice was the nearest thing, closer than my own breath.

"I must go to Bardrem first," I stammered, "I must tell him—"

"No one can see us. No one can know that you are going, or try to stop you. Secrecy will be your only protection."

I thought, with a twisting in my belly, *I'll come back, Bardrem—I will, after Orlo has killed Prandel and the danger has passed.* I nodded at Orlo, over and over again. Even in the dark I could see his eyes stirring, awake—a deeper darkness, like cloud against starless sky.

"The door," I whispered, "locked from the inside tonight, so no girls get out and no one else gets in." My words made no sense to my own ears, but Orlo nodded, still smiling. He held something up, something that glinted in the thin light from the window. It was the front door key—heavy, notched, silver—that usually itself lay locked in the Lady's oak desk. "How . . .?" I said, but Orlo only shrugged. His teeth glinted too, so even and white.

We walked, me in front. I felt his hand in the small of my back, its pressure light but warm. Down the hall to the stairs, turn—and there was another girl coming up, shielding candle flame with her hand.

"Nola?"

I thought, wildly, *Just when they start addressing me with respect instead of fear, I leave.* Orlo's hand was gone from my back.

"I'm . . ." I cleared my throat. "I'm going to get a candle. And some water for my room."

"But you don't have your pitcher," the girl said, squinting at my empty hands.

"No," I said, "no—I . . . I need a new one; my old one's cracked. Rudicol will have an extra."

"Are you all right?" The girl was frowning, and I grinned back at her, far too broadly.

"Yes. Fine. Perfectly fine. Just . . . thirsty. Excuse me. . . ." I walked past the girl, feeling my breath catch in my throat and stay there. I waited for a screech and a scuffle, for more lights and running feet and the arrival of the Lady. For a moment there was silence behind me, then soft footsteps.

"Go on," he mouthed at me, his lips serious but his eyes shining, as if he were a boy with a secret.

The front door was close, but the Lady's was closer. It was open a bit; a branch of light shivered on the hallway floor. I pressed my back against the wall across from it and edged forward. I thought I would slip past, but when I drew level with the Lady's door I paused, looked. The Lady was sitting very straight, in her high-backed chair of wood inlaid with something that looked like gold but (Bardrem insisted) was not. The desk in front of her was covered with papers and books, one of them held open with an inkpot. There was a quill in her hand but she was not writing; she was staring and still.

Orlo nudged my foot with his and I moved, imagining the Lady's eyes shifting and her voice calling out, sharp and thin. As before, there was only silence. *She will hear the door*, I thought as Orlo passed me and set the key to the lock. *It always squeaks, always, always. . . .*

It did not squeak. Orlo stood with his hand on it, gesturing at me with his head: *out, now; out*. I squeezed past him, my bare arm brushing his, and suddenly there was rain on my skin. I stretched into it—summer rain, warm and gentle as fingertips. The door closed behind me with a muffled thud.

"Run!" Orlo cried.

He was past me, vanishing into an alley across the street. I followed, my feet sticking, sucked down by mud. "Who's there?" The Lady's voice at last. I did not turn, but I could picture her anyway, tall in the doorway, a candelabra sputtering in her hand, making her shadow leap. "I see you: stop! Come back!" I scrabbled at my cloak's hood as I ran, and pulled it over my head just as I reached the alley. I plunged into its darkness, gasping, waiting for the Lady's hands to find me. Orlo's did, instead; he put one around my wrist and one, briefly, to my cheek.

"Good," he said, and drew me forward. "She will not follow us here."

He led me a very long way, through a maze of alleys and over low walls, and onto wider streets paved with cobbles that made me slip. "I thought you said it was close," I said after he steadied me. I was bending over, my hands on my thighs, but also looking up at him.

"Of course I said it was close." He smiled, tugged my lopsided hood straight over my head. "You wouldn't have come with me if I'd told you you'd have to walk half the night, would you?"

I rolled my eyes at him. "*Now* are we close?"

"No," he said. "So walk, Mistress Seer, and ask no more questions."

The rain had turned to mist and the sky to silver when he finally halted. "Here," he said, and I looked where he was pointing.

"Here," I repeated, the word a slow release of breath. In front of me was a fence made of iron, curved into graceful shapes at the top. Behind the fence was a garden of dark, hanging leaves and flowers bent by rain. I could not make out their colours but guessed that they would be brilliant in sun.

Orlo pulled open the gate and bowed to me, deeply, with a wild flourish of arms that nearly unbalanced him. I laughed. The sound seemed very loud, in this place of tall walls and taller houses, at this hour just after dawn, but I did not care. I walked into the garden, onto a path of glinting pebbles (glass, I saw later: little pieces of blue, green and dark red glass, their edges rounded smooth). This house, too, was tall—three storeys—and not attached to any other houses. Its great stone blocks were a light, sandy colour. There were carvings around the arched windows, of animals whose names I had heard in Bardrem's poems: stags, peacocks, lions. The windows had no shutters, for they were made of glass, and bound with iron bars that looked like the garden fence. I reached through the bars and touched the glass, which was green-tinted and thick and scattered inside with tiny, frozen bubbles.

"Nola," Orlo said. The word had a smile in it. I smiled back at him and followed him through the enormous wooden door.

"This was my great-aunt's house," he said as he walked around the entrance hall, adjusting the oil lamps that hung from walls and sit on tables.

"Oh," I said, as light bloomed. Mirrors and portraits in gilded frames; my own eyes and others' (an old woman's, a young woman's, a boy's) gazing back at me. Carpets on the floor and tapestries on the walls, among the frames. A ceiling so high I almost could not see it, and a staircase that spread out and up like a fan.

"I'll show you these rooms later, after you've slept." I nodded, too distracted to tell him that there was no way I'd sleep at all, not soon. "Up here"—the stairs creaking, maybe, somewhere beneath the carpet—and up again—"I'll put you on the third floor, next to the room you'll study in."

I stopped, my feet on different steps. He did not notice until he was about ten steps above me, when he turned and looked down at me with his eyebrows raised.

"I'm to study here?"

"Yes. What did you think I'd brought you here for?"

I swallowed. My throat was dry and my heart hammering; sickness, if I hadn't been so happy. "I . . . I didn't think about it. You just said it was somewhere safe, where Prandel wouldn't find me—I never thought of lessons. . . ."

He looked very serious, suddenly. The darkness of his eyes seemed to still. "Of course you never thought of it: there was no time. I surprised you in your room during a storm and told you to come with me, and you did." He was coming down to me, step by slow step. "And I am so glad you did. Glad that you trusted me enough to leave your home, and so unexpectedly." He was directly above me. He eased my wet hood back (I had forgotten it) and I thought that it must be heavy, that my whole cloak must be dragging and sodden, but I could not feel it.

"So let me tell you now, a little too late: you are here to be safe, and here to be taught. I saw it as soon as I met you, Nola: your power is great. You glow with it, with its promise. You could not have stayed in that place and let it wither. I could not have allowed you to."

I wondered if I would fall backward, dizzy with the empty space behind me and him in front, close enough to touch. He put his hand on my arm as if he knew, as if he had heard my thought. "I will teach you here, when I'm not needed at the castle. And someday, if your instruction goes well and I feel the time is right, you may come with me."

"To the castle." My voice was hoarse and quiet.

"To the castle." Another smile, as gentle and strong as the hand on my arm. "But let's begin with some sleep, shall we? Up here just a little further . . . that door there, you see? The one with the cut glass knob. My great-aunt was so proud of it; got it from some sort of gypsy peddler who told her she'd live to over a hundred, which she did. She always wanted me to use the knob for

Otherseeing, since—she claimed—the gypsy obviously had. Look at this! So bright you won't need a light—though you wouldn't anyway, as you'll soon be sleeping."

Again I thought, *No, I won't*, and again I did not say it, because wonder had risen in my throat like tears. The room was huge, full of windows and pieces of furniture fit for the castle itself: cushioned chairs, long couches, two wardrobes inlaid with (I was certain) real gold, in patterns of leaves and flowers. The floorboards were dark and polished beneath the carpet, which was the colour of wine. But it was the bed that drew my gaze most insistently: a wooden headboard carved like the wardrobe, and fat mattresses (at least two), and a tumble of pillows with bright, tasselled covers.

"Do you like it?"

I made a sound that was half laugh, half gasp. "It will suffice," I said, and he did laugh, his golden head thrown back, his eyes briefly closed.

"Good," he said when he was looking at me once more. "I had hoped . . . I am happy that it will suffice. Are you hungry?"

"No." I was thirsty, though, and glanced around until I saw a water jug on a stand by the door—a jug so tall and slender and delicately decorated that it hardly seemed to resemble the one that had sat in my room at the brothel. But everything here was like that. I recognized and could name each thing, but it was as if they belonged to the Otherworld, to a place both brighter and blurrier than any I had seen before.

"Good," Orlo said. "I will have a fine breakfast prepared for you when you wake." He gestured at the wardrobes. "Make sure to look in those, too; you should find something dry to wear. And now"—at the door, his hand on the blue glass of the knob—"I must take myself to my own bed for a few hours before I return to the castle."

"So you won't be here when I get up?" I asked, twisting my damp cloak in my hands.

"Likely not," he said. "Even when I'm not teaching, the king and Teldaru often request my presence. I must not be too long away from them during the day. But at nightfall I will be yours, Nola." He smiled one more slow smile, with lips and restless eyes.

I stared at the door, when he was gone, as if a shadow of him still lingered. Then I turned to the wardrobe closest to me and tugged its double doors open. "Oh," I said, hardly noticing that I had spoken aloud. I reached for silk and velvet, for scarlet and green and gold stitched with silver. There were so many dresses—gowns, really—one for every day of the month, perhaps (if every day featured a ball or a visiting dignitary or a wedding). I did not wonder if they would fit me; would only have wondered if they had not.

The second wardrobe contained sleeping shifts: long ivory ones, short white ones trimmed with lace, which should have reminded me of the brothel and the girls—maybe even Larally, for whom I had seen snakes of blood—but did not, because they were so clean and soft. I chose a long one with two tiny pearl buttons at the collar and each of the wrists. Took my wet, dark, ragged clothes off and laid them carefully on the back of a chair. The cream-coloured cloth slipped over me, hung from my shoulders and arms as if it were not there. I wanted to feel it, so I turned, quickly, and it wrapped around my legs. I turned faster, faster, until I was spinning, and then the world lurched and thrust me face-first onto the bed.

This morning, I thought as my breath warmed the coverlet, *I was in the courtyard. The courtyard! I cast barley for one of the Lady's girls and saw butterflies. I kissed Bardrem.*

I sat up slowly and stared at my old clothes. Stood and went back to them (my toes sinking into the carpet) and put my hand into the pocket of my dress. The paper there was no longer the shape it had been when I had first picked it up; it was flattened, bumpy with folds. I opened it back on the bed, smoothing it on my lap. There were four words, one at every corner of the paper. I read them once in the wrong order and again so that they made sense:

You are beautiful help!

I realized I was crying only when the neat curves of Bardrem's letters began to wobble. And as soon as I realized I was crying, I realized I was crying hard, in wrenching gulps that hurt my chest. I peered from the note to the room, whose wood and cloth and tall, brightening windows were smudged now, but somehow even lovelier than before. *But I'm not sad!* I thought. *I'm the happiest I've ever been*—and I was crying harder still, curled on my side, clutching coverlet and paper in a moist ball.

When my tears were done, full morning was shining through the window glass. I pushed the coverlet down and pulled it up again, over my body, all the way to my chin. *I'll just lie here for a moment*, I thought, *and then I'll go down to breakfast; he will have made it for me by now. Perhaps I'll see him before he returns to the castle....*

I slept, and my dreams were black and gold.

CHAPTER NINE

Bardrem once said that poets should write of passion without any. Something to do with great works requiring care and rigour.

This thing I am writing is neither poem nor great work, and I am not sure where I am. Sometimes I am Nola, *here*, choosing words for old pain and writing them with a steadiness that is almost pleasure. Sometimes a few of these words dig their claws into me and pull, and I am lost among them, and no pain is old.

I have written nothing at all for three days. The last section was so easy, at first, which surprised me; I had been dreading it, certain there would be no words at all. But they came, so smoothly that I barely paused to eat or stretch—until I began to write of opening the wardrobe. I started to shake, then. Then. Not when I was describing Orlo's eyes, or Bardrem's note, though the shaking did worsen. But it was the wardrobe that began it. The gowns, and my thirteen-year-old hands reaching for them.

It is strange, this unexpected passion. Beautiful and frightening—and also, when I am feeling impatient with myself, a little silly.

But enough. I am back now, after three days of sleeping and comforting the princess (who cries so much now, especially at night). I am ready again, because I am unready. A mysterious contradiction: for all my youth, I have become Yigranzi!

The words for this latest beginning:

I woke to a tugging on my sleeve.

I saw no one I expected, as I struggled up from sleep; not Orlo, or the Lady, or Bardrem. (He would have followed us, of course, and climbed over the fence. I would have to tell him to go back. He would try to kiss me again and I would have to turn my face away—perhaps.)

None of these people were by my bed, but the tugging continued. I rolled toward my arm, which was dangling over the edge, and peered down.

I think I would have jumped and scrambled to the other side of the bed, if I had been more awake. As it was I just lay and stared. A bird stared back at me. A very large bird with amber eyes, blue head feathers, a scarlet body, a green and yellow tail that swept along the floor behind it. Its beak was hooked and black and looked very sharp, though it held my sleeve quite gently, between the two pearl buttons.

"Greetings," I said after we had been gazing at each other long enough that I felt alert. "I have seen you before."

I had not known this until I spoke. I narrowed my eyes, trying to remember, and it cocked its head carefully, twisting my sleeve only a little. "I haven't *really* seen you, of course, so it must have been a vision. I can't recall. . . ." But, suddenly, I could. Grown-up Bardrem screaming rage and sorrow at grown-up me; a glorious, bright bird rising into the sky behind him. Yigranzi's mirror in my lap for the first time.

"You," I whispered to the bird, "and Bardrem and me. I had a long, thick braid. . . ." My Path, my Pattern; this house, and the tall, tall someday-stones.

The bird made a clucking noise and gave another tug. I smiled. "Very well—I'll get up. But you'll have to let go of me."

It clucked again and opened its beak.

I chose the plainest dress in the wardrobe: a dark green one with darker green stitching around the neck and hem and copper-coloured ribbon laces up the bodice. It fell to my ankles. A woman's dress, not a girl's.

The bird cooed at me when I turned back to it, and I laughed. "Ah—you like it? So do I." I twirled once and the soft, light cloth rose in a bell-shape around me. "Very well, then," I said when the dress lay once more against my bare legs, "show me this house."

The door was open a bit. I remembered Orlo closing it behind him and gave my own low whistle. "I don't know how you did this," I said, opening the door wider, "but I commend you."

The bird preceded me into the corridor, its silver talons clicking on the wood, then silenced by carpet. It paused at the door next to mine, which had a regular metal knob. "The teaching room?" I said, recalling what Orlo had mentioned on the stairs. The bird bobbed its head. This door was also open, just a little, and I put my hand to the knob, but I did not push. *No*, I thought, *he should be the one to show me what's inside.*

Despite its slender grace, the bird waddled to the head of the stairs. I waited for it to fly to the bottom but it did not; it hopped instead, from stair to stair, sometimes raising its wings for balance.

There was a mirror at the bottom. I had not really looked at any of the mirrors, earlier; now I looked into this one. I saw myself—my whole self, from head to feet. I had only ever seen my face reflected back at me, and that only in thick, dented pieces of metal. This was glass, and it was smooth. I touched it—fingers meeting fingers—and my image was so clear that I did not recognize myself. A girl with short, reddish hair and skin made golden by the courtyard sun. Freckles across my long, straight nose, which somehow did not look quite as long as it had in the brothel mirrors. My eyes were very green—or perhaps the dress was making them appear that way. I leaned closer, staring at my own stare. There was a narrow rim around the outside of my eyes, between whites and centres. It was dark grey or light black, just a shadow now, but someday more. I remembered seeing Yigranzi's eyes for the first time and shivering. I remembered Chenn's. Othersight, Otherworld; people marked by power. I smiled at myself: at my eyes, my freckles, my breasts (small but noticeable beneath the cloth), my waist, which looked narrow because the hips below it were widening. "You are beautiful," Bardrem had written—and I thought, *Yes*, with a certainty so strong and sudden that it was not even pride.

The bird burbled and I turned away from the mirror. I followed it into another corridor, lined with portraits and dark with closed doors. The bird was the only brightness, bobbing in front of me with its tail feathers splayed and dragging like a gown of impossible colours.

We turned a few more corners and came to a hallway with narrow windows and no portraits. At the end of it was an enormous oaken door with a brass ring in it instead of a knob. "What—you can't open this one?" I asked the bird, which blinked at me but stayed silent. I pushed on the wood and the door opened.

My mother's scarred table and dirty rushes and guttering, smoky fire;

Rudicol's stone hearth and cluttered countertops and the narrow pathways between them. These were the kitchens I'd known. This one was like the rest of the house: it had details familiar to me, but so grand that they looked Otherworldly. There were two hearths so big that I could have walked into them and spun around with my arms out and not touched their stone walls. A counter of some dark, burnished wood ran down the centre of the room. Pots and skillets and large-bowled stirring spoons hung from hooks above it. The walls were lined with shelves that held smaller bowls and plates—plain brown ones and lovely, blue-and-gold painted ones that must have been used only for special meals.

It was a very neat room. Everything was clean, hanging or standing in place; even the wood for the hearths was stacked in perfect, matching piles against the wall next to me. I thought of Rudicol, who always shouted about cleanliness and order but never produced them. I thought of Bardrem, of what he would do if he were standing beside me (his eyes would widen beneath the loose fall of his hair, and he would gape, then seize me and dance me up and down the wide spaces around the counter). These thoughts made my chest ache. I turned to face the three windows, as if the sight of flowers and trees and sky would distract me. And it did—for I saw that the light was the deepening bronze of late afternoon, and I realized that I was ravenous.

Orlo had left my meal at the end of the counter closest to the hall door. There was a wooden stool there, and I sat down on it, already reaching. Brown bread and honey and clotted cheese; apples and one orange and dark, glossy, wrinkled fruit I'd never seen before (dates, I later learned); salt fish and chestnuts, roasted and peeled. I ate as I had on my first morning at the brothel (though that meal had been thin porridge and a slice of stale bread, toasted over the fire to make it more palatable—not that it had mattered to me, eight years old and partly starving).

I was licking orange juice off my fingers when I remembered the bird. It was beside me, gazing reproachfully—I was sure of it—at my face. "Oh," I said, around my fingers. "Would you like some?"

It stretched up on its silver-scaled legs and plucked a date from the bowl. It transferred the fruit from beak to claw and nibbled at it, looking at me again as if to say, This *is how you should eat, here.*

I rose and groaned at the fullness of my belly. "Yes," I said to the bird, though I did not turn to it, "you're right: it's my own fault. Perhaps a walk will help."

There was another door, set between two of the windows; a low, wide one made of unvarnished, pale wood, which had probably been used for deliveries and as a servant entrance. I gripped the knob, jiggled it, leaned against the wood, but the door did not open. I looked through the window—between the iron bars— and out at the garden. Its blossoms were as vibrant in sunlight as I'd thought they would be: pinks and indigos, white with darker whorls inside and out. The trees were very tall, their trunks so broad that I would not be able to touch my hands together, if I put my arms around them. The grass around the glass-pebbled path was thick; I thought of how cool it would feel against my calves and rattled the knob again, as if I had merely done it wrong, the last time.

"Very well," I said when it was clear that the door was, indeed, locked. "Let's go back to the front hall."

The front door was locked too, as was a side one to which the bird led me. I sat on the lowest step of the entrance hall staircase and leaned my head against its banister. The bird cocked its head at me and I sighed. "If I can't go outside I'll wait here for him. It's getting dark; surely he won't be long."

I did not feel myself fall asleep. When I started awake the air around me was black, except for a wavering light that blinded me for a moment. I rubbed my eyes and blinked the lamp into focus. The lamp, and the hand that held it.

"Mistress Weary Seer," said Orlo, "you do not need to sleep on the stairs when there is a perfectly good bed available."

I stood up quickly. My feet tangled in the folds of my dress and Orlo gripped my arm so that I would not fall. "I'm sorry," I said, hoping my flush would be invisible in the weak light, "I'm very clumsy. The Lady was always scolding me for it."

Orlo's smile gleamed. "It is a good thing, then, that grace is not a requirement for Otherseeing. Though we'll make sure that you won't be tripping over your own clothing by the time you arrive at the castle."

By the time, I thought, as warmth spread through my stomach. *Not "if."*

"I'm glad you slept a bit," he said as we went up the stairs. "You'll have to learn to rest during the day, since your lessons will almost always be at night." He turned to me; I hoped he would not notice how awkwardly I was holding my dress, trying to keep it above my ankles as I climbed. "Did you enjoy the food I left for you?"

"Oh yes—I ate far too much, and too fast, and then I thought I'd take a walk, but all the doors were locked."

We were at the top of the stairs, now. Orlo raised the lamp so that its glow lit both our faces. He was all hollows, in the shadow-light: his cheeks, his eyes, his mouth. "You must have wondered why," he said.

"Yes," I replied, though all I really remembered feeling was a mild sort of annoyance.

"Prandel is a clever man. I fear that he knows I am hunting him. I fear *he* will follow *me*, someday. What if he were to follow me here?"

I said, "Yes—that would be terrible—but if the doors were locked from the outside, surely that would be enough? If he couldn't get into the house . . .?"

"And what if he got into the garden and waited there? You would go out, during the day when I wasn't here; you would go into the garden and he would be waiting for you. . . ." Orlo was so close to me that I could feel his breath. It smelled of something strong and sweet—mead, perhaps, or wine. I should have wanted to turn away, for the smell reminded me of the few men who had tried to kiss me and paw at me, in the hallways I had known before. Drunken, brothel men. Instead I imagined leaning up and in, catching Orlo's breath between my own lips. This time the flush swept from my face to my ears and down my chest, and I did not care if he saw it.

"I will keep you safe, Nola," he said, very quietly. "If you wish to walk in the garden we will do it together—but when I am not here, you will be inside. You will *stay* inside. And only I will be able to get to you."

"Yes." An answer, though he had not asked me a question. My voice was hoarse.

"Good." He stepped back. "Now, then. Did you go into the lesson room, on your journeys today?"

"No. I saw that the door was open, but I . . . I wanted to wait for you."

He frowned. We had reached the door in question, which was firmly shut. "Strange," he said, "I did not leave it open. I never do." He gazed at his own hand on the knob and shrugged. "No matter. My great-aunt used to say that this was a house of mysteries, and she was always right about such things."

The bird, I thought as he pushed the door open. I glanced behind me and saw only hallway.

"Come," Orlo said, and I followed him into the room.

In the entrance hall he had lit lamps; here he walked about lighting candles, which bristled from two enormous candelabra. I expected to see a riot of furniture and decorations—but this room was different from the others. It was larger than mine but seemed enormous, as it was nearly empty. The candelabras stood in each of the far corners. In the centre was something that I took at first to be the bowl of a fountain. It was round and shallow, set on a low stone plinth. I stepped toward it and the candlelight glinted, reflected—for the bowl itself was not stone, but metal. I drew closer yet, as Orlo watched me, and then I was above it, looking down into a pool of gold. Golden ripples, golden waves, facets and sky that opened up and drew me in and under.

"You will see many things, in this mirror," Orlo said, from across the gold.

"This is a mirror?" I felt slow and dizzy at the same time. "It's so big, and it's made of real gold—isn't it?—and I've never . . ." I swallowed, thinking of Yigranzi's mirror, small and copper, warm from her knobbly-knuckled fingers. "I've never seen anything like it."

"I know. You cannot imagine, Nola, how grateful I am that I will be the one to show you—that you will come into your true power here. Here." He swept his arm out and I followed it with my eyes, looking over my shoulder when it pointed that way.

There was a cage by the door. It, too, was gold, and its bars stretched nearly to the ceiling, where they were fused together in a shape as intricate as spider's web. Inside the cage was what seemed to be a real tree trunk, its leafless branches short and widely spaced. The bird was perched on the highest branch. Its feathers looked like silk, in the candlelight, and its eyes like real amber, hard and translucent.

"That is Uja," Orlo said as he walked from the mirror to the cage. "Isn't she a lovely creature?"

"Yes," I said. "Yes—I saw—" I meant to tell him that I had met her already— that she had woken me and led me to the kitchen—but as the words formed, Uja spread her wings wide and gave a piercing squawk.

"Uja!" Orlo said sharply. "Quiet—you must not frighten our guest."

She lowered her wings slowly. Her head was cocked; she was looking at me steadily, unblinkingly.

"You saw?" Orlo said, turning to me.

"I meant . . . I meant I *heard*. I heard something from my bedroom, and it sounded like a bird, but I thought I must have dreamed it." I did not understand my lie, but Uja appeared to: she straightened her head and cooed, just as she had before, when we had been alone.

"She's no dream, no—though she's no ordinary bird, either. I use her to bring on the Othersight, and to show me someone's Pattern with her talon-tracks and sometimes her beak." He put a forefinger between her bars, reaching up toward one of her silver claws. She sidled along the branch, just far enough that he could not touch her, and he scowled. "When she's not half in the Otherworld, however, she can be downright unpleasant. Perhaps she may be convinced to be friendlier with you."

"Perhaps," I said. This time my reticence did not feel like a lie; it felt like a game, or a strange, harmless, shared secret.

I looked away from Uja, at the wall on the other side of the door. (I think it was then that it struck me, belatedly, that there were no windows at all in this room.) The only piece of furniture was here: a sideboard with wooden drawers at the bottom and glass doors at the top. I saw shelves behind the doors, holding things I recognized: goblets and bowls, lidded glass containers full of different kinds of grain and different-coloured sticks of wax. I smiled at their familiarity—and then I glanced at the highest part of the sideboard and saw the knives.

There were six of them, hanging in brackets above the shelves. They were arranged from smallest to largest. The largest was about as big as the one Bardrem had used to slice heads of cabbage and lettuce, but its blade was different: curved like one of Uja's talons, and notched at either end. The smallest blade had so many notches that they looked like tiny teeth.

"What are those for?" I asked, even though part of me did not want to know.

Orlo clucked his tongue, and Uja, on her perch, made a sound very much like a dog's growl. "Dear girl," he said, "you've had no lessons yet and already you seek to know the deepest truths?" He was beside me, his arm nearly touching mine. I thought that I could feel heat rising from his skin and wanted to put my own cool fingers on him—wanted it so suddenly and strongly that I had to press my nails against my palms, instead.

"Not yet," he said, serious again. I had protested when Yigranzi had said these words to me, but I only nodded at him. His eyes, which always seemed to move, made me still. "But," he went on, stepping back, smiling, "there is much that I *can* teach you now. Shall we begin?"

CHAPTER TEN

In the beginning, the lessons unfolded as they had at the brothel: with much talking and no doing. I hardly noticed, during those early weeks at the house, and I cared even less. For Orlo came to me at nightfall, or sometimes a few hours later, and he talked and talked as darkness held us close together, alone in the world. He spoke mostly of the history of Otherseeing, which should have grown dull. It did not. I watched him stride around the mirror (we never sat) or back and forth before one of the great garden trees, and every gesture, every quirk of lips or brows, made his words live. I remember him acting out the Betrayal of Seer Aldinior—all the parts, from the each of the foreign emissaries to the queen's lady-in-waiting, who was actually a rebellious student seer in disguise. I remember laughing until I wept, and then—when the story turned tragic—weeping again so that the mirror's metal and Uja's feathers blurred.

He told me to read about these things in the books he kept in the library (another huge room, all wood and leather), after he discovered—to his surprise—that I could read. But beautiful and mysterious as these books were, with their gilt pages and ancient paper smells, his words were better.

I talked too, because he encouraged me to. He was mostly very patient with my castle questions, and asked me many questions of his own, which it seemed no one else ever had.

These lesson-talks are patchwork, now; I remember the bits, in their colours and textures, but they no longer exist individually. One long, breathless conversation that lasted all summer.

"How many Otherseeing students are there at the castle?"

"Only four, since Chenn left."

"How old are they?"

"Ten, twelve, fourteen and eighteen. And before you ask, I will answer: two are boys and two are girls."

"And how many teachers?"

"Two, and myself."

"And Master Teldaru—does he teach, too?"

"He sometimes visits the classes, to observe. Now and then he speaks."

"How old is he?"

"You should be able to answer that yourself, Nola. If he was five when he was taken to the castle, and he served King Lorandel for fourteen years, and if he has so far served King Haldrin for sixteen, then he is . . .?"

". . . thirty-five? But that seems too young; he is so—"

"Yes, yes—his legend has lent him years beyond the ones he actually possesses, and he is said to be wise even beyond these. . . ."

"You sound impatient. Do you like him?"

"I like him very well—but if you do not stop asking questions about him, I shall have trouble liking *you*."

"You're jealous!"

"Perhaps a little. He and I are close in age—and no, I will not tell you how old I am!—and I have known him since we were both young. It is hard, sometimes, to be so close to greatness and to share none of it. But that is enough. You will meet him soon and have all the answers you desire. Until then you are mine."

"And what of the king?"

"We were speaking of the properties of wine. What *of* the king?"

"He must be of an age with Teldaru—and you. Do you know him well? He and Teldaru must be like brothers, and—"

"Indeed, yes—they grew up side-by-side, and Teldaru is the elder by several years, and the king trusts him with his life—and they are both staggeringly handsome, though I am even *more* handsome, which makes them both sick with envy. Will this suffice, Mistress Overcurious Seer?"

This was the day that he first brought his dog Borl to the house. I remember that Borl burst from the bushes right after Orlo said, "Mistress Overcurious Seer." He dropped a rabbit at Orlo's feet and stood waiting, his lean flanks heaving and his tongue lolling from mottled, brown-and-pink gums. I drew back from him; I had never liked dogs.

The rabbit was small and brown and twitching. Orlo chuckled and said, "He pretends to be gentle, bringing them to me alive." To the dog he said, "Well *done!*" Borl whined and rolled his long head on the grass.

Orlo crouched and picked the rabbit up. He twisted its neck in his hands and there was a cracking sound. I had seen Rudicol and Bardrem do this many times and had not flinched, but for some reason this time was different. I sucked in my breath, as the creature's neck broke.

Orlo looked up at me. "Ah, Nola—so soft-hearted. You'll be glad of Borl's prowess when you're eating rabbit stew. Though we'll need a cook. I can manage soup and bread, but stew . . ." He rose, gazing thoughtfully at the shadows of the trees. "A cook," he said again.

He brought Laedon with him the next day. The talking part ended, then, and the doing began.

At first I was excited.

"There's someone you should meet, Nola," Orlo said. "Someone who will cook you real meals and help us with our lessons."

I uncurled myself from my favourite library chair. For a month I had sat in the one that looked like a throne, because even though its grandness made me feel a bit silly, there was no one else to see me. Recently, though, I had been using one that was low and round and fashioned from what seemed to be thick reeds—a strange thing that I thought must have been made in another country. But it had a deep, soft cushion, and I dozed in it as much as I read.

"Oh?" I closed the book I was holding—a slender tome on the Otherseeing uses of sparrow bones during the reign of the Boy King. *Someone else here,* I thought, and this thought was followed by a flurry of others: *It will not be us alone, any more, and I am sorry for this . . . I am not sorry—I'm lonely when he's not here . . . a cook and a helper; by Pattern and Path, he's brought me Bardrem. . . .*

The kitchen smelled of simmering wine and meat and rich, dark broth. The table was covered with knives and platters stacked with vegetables and bones. It looked like a kitchen, and smelled like one; I thought, *Bardrem*, one last, breathless time—even as Orlo called, "Laedon?"

A very old man shuffled out of the shadows at the far end of the room. *Maybe* an old man: he was swathed in so many layers of cloth—coloured rags, really—that his body was shapeless. There was a tight leather cap on his head; wisps of yellow-white hair had escaped from it and were clinging to the stubbled hollows that were his cheeks. His eyes were white-filmed blue, and they wandered and rolled.

"Laedon can hear us," Orlo said. "Can't you, Laedon? But he's been mute for years, and blind for even longer."

"But he can still cook?" I said. Laedon's head jerked in what might have been a nod, and I drew back, just as I did from the dog—who, I saw, was lying in front of the fire, gnawing on what looked to be a small skull.

Orlo walked over to the iron pot that was hanging above the flames. "Oh, he can cook. Come and see for yourself."

I followed him, and the old man's eyes swivelled to follow me, or the sound of me. Orlo held up a wooden spoon and I sipped from it. "Delicious," I said loudly (because it was; it was the most delicious thing I had ever tasted).

"He is blind and mute, remember," Orlo said, "not deaf. You do not need to raise your voice."

"All right." I glanced at Laedon. I wondered how he could bear the heat of fire, clothing, heavy midsummer air.

"He used to work in the castle kitchens—didn't you, Lae?"

A twitch of the lips, this time. I saw two blackened teeth.

"He befriended me when I was new to the place, and missing home. His kitchen always reminded me of my tavern's, though the two were really nothing alike. Perhaps you understand this, Nola?"

I nodded. Orlo waved me over to my customary stool; I sat, and he put a bowl of stew in front of me. Even though I was ravenous I ate slowly, placing the spoon carefully in my mouth so that none of the liquid dripped. Some moments in this house were for teasing and jests; others felt like practice.

"When Laedon lost his sight and then his voice," Orlo said as I sipped and nibbled, "the castle kitchens grew too much for him. He worked in the seers' kitchen, then. A smaller place, but his handiwork was much appreciated by the students. Recently even this job has seemed too difficult for him. How perfect, that I could bring him here."

"So no one will miss him?" I asked—for Orlo had told me that this house was a secret from the castle folk, just as I was.

Orlo smiled a sad, gentle smile. "Likely not. I am the only one who's paid him any mind, these last few years."

I looked at Laedon—stared, now that I was sure his swivelling eyes were sightless. "You said he would help us with our lessons. How?"

Orlo stirred the stew, then knocked the spoon against the pot's edge. "I will explain this to you when—"

"Explain it now," I said. "Or better yet: show me."

The broth wine, I thought; *it has made me even freer with my words than usual.* I kept my eyes steady on Orlo's. He did not seem angry—though he had never been angry at me, and I did not know how it would look. He was silent for a long time. The only sounds were flame pops and the crunching of the skull between Borl's jaws.

"Now," he said at last. "You are certain?"

I pushed my stool back and stood up. My hair slid out from behind my ears. (Now that it was growing, it was as wayward as Bardrem's.) "Yes. I've been here for a long time, and all I've done is read and talk to you. Which has been good," I continued hastily as his eyes narrowed, "wonderful, in fact—but I'm ready. I want to *do* something."

There was another moment of motionless quiet before he smiled slowly. Something in my chest pulled tight. "You remind me of myself," he said. "How can I deny you?" He placed the spoon across the top of the pot and pointed at the table. "Choose something—an Otherseeing tool."

I said, "But the mirror, or the wax—"

"You said now, Mistress Hasty Seer, and now it will be. Choose."

Bones on a plate, dried herbs in a bowl, wine in a squat earthen pitcher.

"Remember," Orlo said, "that some will bring on stronger visions than others."

"Yes. Things that were alive, and recently, will be strongest. . . ."

"Things that have bled." His voice was low.

I wanted to look at him but did not; reached instead for the plate.

"So it is strength you desire," he said, more lightly. "An excellent choice. Laedon—come here to us."

The old man's feet scuffed on the floor as he walked to Orlo's side. He was shorter than Orlo, and looked quite round (I thought this must be the bulk of his clothing, since his cheeks were so gaunt).

"You will Othersee for him," Orlo said.

"But . . . but he is mute. He cannot speak the words of invitation."

Orlo cocked his head to one side, just as Uja did when she was listening to me. "Remember Chenn," he said.

"Chenn? I do, but—"

"Chenn dead beneath the tree, where you and Yigranzi found her. What did you do there?"

"I . . . We both had visions. Of her."

"And did she speak any words of invitation?"

"No—of course not."

"How did Yigranzi explain this to you?"

The golden light; the deep, curling wound. "She said only that there were things I did not yet know—mysteries. I never asked her, afterward. I was too . . . It was Chenn. I didn't want to know."

"How unlike you," Orlo said with a smile that passed over his lips like a shadow. "Let me explain, since she did not. When blood has just been spilled, even if a person is dead, it is possible to Othersee with someone else speaking the words. The Otherworld is close, as long as there is blood, or something else that is from a body. As Laedon will show you."

I swallowed. "But he is not dead, and he is not . . . not . . ."

Laedon was holding a small knife. It shone, clean and sharp; he could not have used it for vegetables or meat. His cloud-eyes rolled up toward the ceiling. He closed his hand around the knife's blade and held it there.

"Cast the bones, Nola."

I watched my fingers grasp and tighten on the plate. The bones were small and jagged and wet. *The big ones are in the soup*, I thought, with a part of my mind that was clear and separate. I held them and imagined that they were pulsing against my own vein-lined skin. I held them and remembered.

"My mother," I said. I had already told him about this memory, but it seemed like more than that, suddenly. "She spoke words, and she bled, and I was watching her blood on the tabletop, and that's when I had my first vision. I used no Otherseeing tools." I licked my lips, which felt cracked. "Is blood enough, then?"

Orlo let out a long, slow breath that I could hear. "It is. Good girl; it is. But what do you think happens when an Otherseer uses both? What do think would happen if you looked at the shapes made by Laedon's blood *and* by the bones?"

"I . . . it would be very powerful." I did not need to see his nod; I knew I was right. *Maybe I should wait*, I thought. *Maybe this would be too much, or too soon.* But I thought of him saying, "So it is strength you desire," and knew that he, too, was right.

I opened my fingers and scattered the bones away from me. I heard them skitter along the wood. I heard Orlo say, "Look at Laedon," and I did. Laedon pulled the knife sharply, down and away from his body, and he shook his hand, and I saw blood spray—fat droplets hanging, then falling over the bones.

"Tell him, Nola. Tell him what will come."

The kitchen flows away from me. All that remains is fire: two pale, blue fires, which I know are Laedon's eyes. They are far away, so I push my Otherself forward—and I move, just as I did in my vision of Chenn. This time I am not a bird; I am something low and small, perhaps a snake, or a vole. I slither, scurry through a darkness that parts like water. As I do, the eyes multiply—two to four to six—and begin to spin. I twist so that I can catch them, and what is in them—because there are images there, limned in blue flame. A boy with a harp in the crook of his arm, singing soundless words; a skull pillowed on layers of coloured cloth; a field of tall russet grass. I am dizzy but strain to hold the other eyes too, and do. An eagle on a wall, its beak stained red; a naked woman asleep on her belly, one hand holding a lock of her own dark hair, as if she is a child (though she is plainly not). And in the last eyes, a wolf. My Otherself shrinks back, and I turn, seeking the boy or the lovely, empty field—but these eyes blur past me, and I know, anyway, that it is the wolf I must watch. It is a tawny brown. Its teeth gleam—a grin of sharpened knives—and yet its eyes are dull and flat. I ease closer, for the eyes are the most important, somehow, and maybe just one more turn, one more stretch will show them to me. I reach with fingers or claws I cannot see. The beast lunges. For a moment my eyes are filled with flames, and then the flames give way to a heaving blackness that presses on my nose and mouth and crushes my screams to silence.

I was kneeling on the floor. I was making a low, rough noise—but no, the noise was not mine: it was Borl's. He was standing by my head, too close. I did make a sound—a strangled one—and Borl snarled and snapped his jaws so that I felt wind and smelled a waft of meat.

"Borl!" Orlo's legs; his hand descending, grasping the brindled fur at the dog's neck. The fur looked green, and Orlo's skin looked orange, and slender black shapes darted over everything like a cluster of startled fish.

Borl whined and padded away, his long, thin tail tucked between his back legs. Orlo raised me up as if I were a child and set me on my stool. He put a mug in my hands and helped me tip it against my lips. The wine was harsh and sour and I choked a bit, dribbling it, before I really swallowed.

"Do not speak until you are ready. If—"

"There were six things," I rasped. "Six pairs of eyes with different . . . things." Words hardly ever matched visions, but this was worse than usual. I clenched my fists.

"Laedon," Orlo said, as if he was reminding me.

I blinked at the old man, who was standing where he had been before. His eyes were closed; the little black shapes squiggled across their lids.

I told Orlo, the words halting, then smoother. When I was done, everything was the right colour again, though my dizziness remained.

"And how was this time different?" he asked.

"I felt like I could move—like I was inside the vision, not just seeing it. That happened with Chenn, too—when I was like a bird above her, and Prandel."

"You saw Prandel?" Orlo's voice was sharp, and I flinched.

"I . . . yes. Not clearly, though: he was far below me. I tried to drop closer to him, just like I tried to get closer to the wolf, to see . . . but I couldn't. Or I did, with Chenn, but Yigranzi stopped me. I can't remember."

Orlo smiled, though it looked strained. "What else? What else was different this time?"

"There was more. I saw six things—six parts of his Pattern—and I think I could have chosen which one to look at, if I'd been more sure of myself." I wanted Orlo to look like himself again, so I added, "Why did these different things happen?"

It worked. He straightened, narrowed his eyes as he always did before he instructed. "Because visions grow more complex, the older you get. And yes, you must sometimes choose, from within the Otherworld, which one to follow. There is art to this choosing, and to the telling of it afterwards. For you should never tell the person all that you have seen. You must be clear and firm, and speak as if you saw but one Path."

He paused, leaned across the table toward me. Our fingertips were almost touching. "You will see and feel more strongly once your monthly bleeding begins. The vision you have just had gives me hope. The time must be close now—at last."

"Blood power," I said slowly. "My own."

"Yes," he said, and smiled in a way that sent heat and cold chasing through my belly. "There is so much more to learn, Nola. What we—what you will be able to do, when the time comes."

"Yes." Only a breath of a word, but it filled me.

Something moved beside me, and I turned. Laedon had lifted his arm; his hand was pointing at the ceiling. Blood was still easing from the wound on his palm, wending its way down pale, wrinkled flesh and beneath cloth that clung, sticky and damp. "Laedon," Orlo snapped, "that's enough—press the wound now, so the blood will stop"—but the old man stood still, staring at me with his blind blue eyes.

CHAPTER ELEVEN

My head aches today. Too many words already, and too many still to come; all of them as oppressive as they are exciting. (And how can they be exciting—even the ones that I fear?)

I did not think that I would remember so much. Part of me is impatient: *Just get to them, Nola! Get to the words that matter most!* But it seems to me that they wouldn't matter quite so much without all the others.

And then I think: *You're delaying, dripping water into an ocean that will never be full. You're afraid, Nola-girl—because beyond these pages there is something you have to* do.

All right—enough. One more sliver of lycus fruit from the platter Sildio left for me and then I'll go back to filling up the sea.

Bloodseeing was like a fever. It began as a shivering under my skin and stayed that way for a few weeks, while I wondered whether I was really feeling anything. I knew I was when Orlo spoke the words of invitation and Laedon drew out his knife (sometimes he only pricked his finger, and I tried to ignore my disappointment). I knew I was when the Pattern's spinning pictures spun me too, and when I blinked myself back afterward, to strange colours, dizziness, and terrible thirst. But when I was not Bloodseeing, my desire for it was quiet and sly. It rested in my own blood like fever does, waiting for weakness.

I stayed away from Laedon when Orlo and I were not using him. I told myself that I did not want to intrude any further, but really it was just that he unsettled me. I had seen visions of his boyhood and youth—"When people age it is sometimes easier to see the Pattern that lies behind them," Orlo told me—and strange, sometimes inscrutable ones that were obviously of time-to-come, but none of this truly unsettled me. Much smaller things did: his sallow, grizzled skin and his fingernails, which were yellow and so sharp that he could have used them instead of his knife. And that leather cap! He never took it off (or not that I saw), and the thought of what the hair and scalp beneath it might look like made me shudder.

He was never in the kitchen when I ate. I had no idea where he went, but was always relieved when I entered and found only food, always freshly prepared, arranged neatly on plates and in bowls.

In fact, I do remember looking up from my meal one night and seeing him. I glanced up and saw him by the door that led to the garden. He was staring at me. One of his hands was on the knob.

"It's locked, you know." I don't know why I spoke to him. Perhaps to prove to him that I wasn't afraid—though of course I was. Uja wasn't fooled; she plucked at my skirt and made the low, calming noise that made me feel as if I were her chick. That was one way I could tell that Orlo would not be arriving soon—when Uja let herself out of her cage and came downstairs with me.

Laedon's hand tightened on the knob. I thought that he must be scratching himself with his own fingernails. "You can't get out," I said, thinking, *He* must *already know this—or maybe he's as much of a fool as he looks.* He did not move. I pushed the food around on my plate for a few minutes, but my hunger was gone, and soon I stood and left, hoping he would not hear my haste.

And there were a few times, when Orlo and I were conducting our lessons without Laedon, that I saw him watching us. "Watching," with his wobbly blind eyes, standing at the kitchen window while we were walking in the garden, or at an upper window, his hands pressed against the glass. I never mentioned these sightings to Orlo.

When Laedon was with us, though, in our lesson room, he did not unsettle me. Then he was ours.

I was in the library, the day my Bloodseeing-fever turned from shivering to heat. It was a rainy day in late summer. I was restless, listening to the rain on the windows, imagining how it would feel on my face and bare feet. I was not sure why I'd come to the library, since I had no desire to read. I sat in my favourite chair, which felt lumpy; I paced, whirling when I got to the room's corners, to make my skirt billow.

I saw the book in a still moment, between paces. I craned up at the top shelf. I was certain I'd never seen this book before, for it was bound in bright red leather with golden claw-clasps, and I would have noticed it. I pulled the stepladder over to its shelf and climbed. The ladder was not quite tall enough and I had to clamber up onto one of the shelves, leaning back and up at the same time, scrabbling for the book. I nearly fell when I pulled it free, because it was very heavy, and I could only grip it with one hand. I did not fall, but it did; it landed on the floor with a dull thud, its covers splayed. Some of the gold-edged pages were creased, and I smoothed at them frantically, then closed the covers as if this pressure would do the rest. I carried it over to the chair that looked like a throne and opened the book again, over my knees.

The script was very old-fashioned, with curling lines and rows of dots that made it difficult to read. I squinted and concentrated, and after a few moments I began to understand.

. . . a treatise on the use of blood for the Seeing of the Pattern; which use the King has forbidden, deeming it a peril and a threat to the goodness of his land and laws. We, the Otherseers of Sarsenay, do protest the King's decree. Bloodseeing will give strength to our friends and weaken our enemies. Bloodseeing is Pattern and Path revealed, but also transformed. Who among us can deny the necessity of transformation? Who, though cleaving to writ and form and fear, can say with honesty that he does not desire transformation? . . .

I read more—much more, even though I did not understand a good deal of it. There were diagrams drawn in many colours that had faded; I saw blues and reds that must once have been vivid but were shadows now. The diagrams were of arms, torsos, ribbons that could have been veins.

Take care to make your enemies' cuts in places that cannot be seen when he is clothed. Such care, along with a Bloodsight order of silence, will keep your actions hidden from those who might seek to stop you. When making cuts upon friends, however, such care is not required. There are many, indeed, who in the days before the King's writ bore their scars with pride, knowing themselves to be true instruments of Pattern and Path.

I stopped reading, here. There was a tingling, almost-sick feeling in my belly, because I was remembering Chenn, and the scars she had tried to hide beneath her sleeves. The scars she would not explain to me. But now that I had these words, these pictures, I was close to knowing. I sat with my hands folded on the book, and by the time I heard Orlo's footsteps in the corridor, I was ready.

"I need to know something."

He raised an eyebrow. "No 'Good evening, Orlo'? No 'I have a question; may I ask it'?" He looked and sounded tired. He was always either weary or restless; there was nothing in between.

"Good evening, Orlo," I said, to make him smile. He did, a little. "I have a question; may I ask it?"

He sat down in the round chair, groaning as he did. "You may. But only if it has a simple answer, and only if you will bring me some wine after."

I ran my fingertips along the edges of the book. "I found this book today." I watched his eyes shift to my lap. They did not widen, which meant I had to try harder to surprise him. "I'm sure it wasn't here before. Was it?"

He was smiling now, the lines around his eyes more amusement than weariness. "If you're sure, why must you ask?"

"What can you do with Bloodseeing? What can you really *do*?"

I no longer wanted to surprise him, but his sudden stillness was gratifying. He stared at me and I stared back.

"I've shown you," he said at last, slowly, "how blood may open a person to Otherseeing, even without his spoken consent."

I shook my head. "But there's more. This book says there is, but I don't . . . it's written in old language, and it's hard to understand. It says you can transform things, if the blood is from two . . ." I cleared my throat. I felt a flush easing up along my cheekbones; I had had so much time to prepare what I would say, and now that he was here I could only stammer.

"There *is* more. It is better to show than to tell, however, and—"

"And you're going to wait until sometime else to show me." My indignation made my words smooth.

"Yes," he said. "Precisely. I believe you know me, just a little." He paused and frowned at me, as if he was trying to understand something. "What else did this book tell you?"

He was trying to distract me, and I wanted to resist—but I did think of another question. "Whatever this special transforming Bloodseeing is, it's forbidden. It was whenever this book was written, and it must be now, for Yigranzi never taught me about it and you haven't either."

"Yet," he said, and the tingling in my belly spread, outward and down. "But you're right, Nola—this use of Seeing is not permitted, not taught. And now," he continued, holding up a hand, "you will demand to know why, and I will make you even more frustrated than you already are when I say, 'No, Mistress Headlong Seer, this too must wait.'"

He stood and walked over to me. Bent a little to cover my hands with his. His palms were warm and very slightly damp. His thumbs traced circles on my knuckles. Maybe I was not breathing. "Your curiosity does you credit. Your questions deserve answers, which I will give. Perhaps"—he slipped his hands away from mine, drawing the book out of my grasp as he did so—"it is time that I allowed you another glimpse of what is to come. Time I gave you more."

I nodded. All I could see was the darkness of his eyes, lifting and falling like water.

"Come," he said, and I rose and followed him.

Laedon was standing by the mirror. He was not usually waiting for us (Orlo would fetch him), and so I was surprised, and hesitated just inside the door. Orlo put his hand on my shoulder, turned me away from Laedon so that I was gazing at the cabinet.

"Choose one," he said. I knew that he did not mean a stick of wax or a kind of grain. I stared at him as he drew a leather cord out from the neck of his shirt. There was a ring of keys on the cord: four of them, all small and slender. I had never noticed these before—and now I noticed the hollow of his throat too, and the smooth ridges of his collarbone, and the skin below it. I swallowed, or tried to.

"You will do no choosing while you are looking at me." He smiled. The restlessness was about him again; waves I could sense, even without seeing them in the tensed muscles of his forearms and the tapping of his right foot. I smiled back at him—probably too pink already to flush any more deeply—and looked at the knives.

They were all beautiful, and at various times I had imagined each of them in my hand, without imagining what I would do with them once they were there. But now that it was time—*For what?* a small, fading voice asked me—I pointed and said, "That one."

Orlo opened the glass doors. He took the middle knife down and held it out to me. My fingers closed around its hilt, which was wrapped in leather—thicker, darker bands than the one around Orlo's neck. It was cool, but I had only been holding it for a moment before it felt as warm as my skin. The blade was the simplest of the five: curved, but not as much as the large one. A sliver of moon.

"Tell me," Orlo said, stepping back toward the mirror, "what you have learned about Bloodseeing so far."

I twisted my hand, watching the candlelight play along the steel. "I've learned that the blood of the person to be seen is enough; that the seer requires no other tools."

"What else?"

"That the words of invitation do not need to be spoken by the person to be seen, if that person is bleeding, or if they have just bled."

"And who *has* spoken the words of invitation, when Laedon has cut himself?"

I glanced at Orlo. "You, of course."

"Yes." He was tracing circles on the mirror, just as he had on my knuckles. "But I do not have to. A seer does not need another speaker at all. Not if . . .?"

I looked from him to Laedon to the knife in my hand. "If . . . if I—the seer . . ." My throat was dry, closing in on itself. It was late; I was probably hungry and definitely thirsty, but this did not matter. "If I cut him."

Orlo did not nod or smile, and yet I took a step backward, as if a sudden wind had pushed at me. He said nothing, which meant I had to say more. I straightened my shoulders. "So this is what I will do. I will . . . cut him, and I will ask his Pattern to show itself to me."

"And will you use tools?"

I knew immediately that I would. I felt taller, stronger, as if I had grown older just since coming up from the library; there was no need for restraint or reluctance.

"I will." Not wax on water, though, nor bones, nor mirror. "Uja," I said.

For a moment I thought he would refuse; he had refused until now, saying that Uja was another thing I was not quite ready for. But this time he nodded once, almost sharply, and said, "Know that it will be like nothing you have seen so far." I nodded too, because he seemed to be waiting. "Very well. Go to Laedon, then, and choose where you will cut."

I heard Orlo behind me as I walked to stand with the old man. The cabinet doors opened again; a glass lid came off a jar with a ringing sound; grain sifted.

I heard these things and I heard my own breathing. Only Laedon was silent. He stood like a statue, gazing over my head, pretending I was not there. I looked at his face quickly, then only at the cloth bulk of his body. I would have to touch the cloth; I would have to touch his skin.

"You will not need to make a deep cut," Orlo said, "and you should not, this first time."

I swallowed. The fingers of my left hand closed around the material that lay against Laedon's right arm. It was more ragged, and trailed more ends of thread, than the layers above it. It was a light, washed-out blue—like his eyes—with darker patches that must have been cooking stains. I eased the cloth up, gingerly at first—but I had to be faster and firmer, so I pressed my fingers into his skin and thrust until the material was up above his elbow. It stayed there, even when I took my hand away. It was easy because I was not looking at his face. I took his wrist and turned it and his whole arm turned, and it was just a thing; just something I was examining. Despite this detachment, I did think, *Please the Pattern, I will not have to look anywhere else for a place to cut. . . .* I did not. I saw the place, and looked back at Orlo. He was waiting, one hand in a glass jar that was resting on his hip. I nodded at him and he scooped, pulled his hand out. He crouched and drizzled the grain on the floor in front of him. "Uja likes rye best," he said. He turned himself around until he had covered a large, circular space with grain.

Only now did I look at Uja. She was on her upper branch, her wings and beak tucked in against her body. I could not see whether her eyes were open.

"Come here." Orlo was speaking to me but it was Laedon who obeyed him. He shuffled past me, to the edge of the rye circle. I followed. When I was beside him he shifted a bit, so that he was almost facing me.

Orlo used another of the keys at his neck to unlock Uja's cage. (Is it strange that I never wanted to tell him she could get out on her own? Some premonition about my own Path that kept me quiet?) She hopped from branch to branch and sidled out the open door. Waddle-walked around the circle and stopped precisely where she had begun. Straightened her head, at last, and looked at me.

She does not know me, I thought wildly—but after a moment she blinked and I realized that she did. She was readying herself, half in her own Otherworld.

They were all waiting for me.

Laedon's arm was as heavy as a fallen tree branch. It was not that he resisted me; he simply did not help. I lifted it, angled it until I saw the hollow of his elbow, and the green vein that bulged there (so fat, while the rest of his arm was sinew and bone). I raised my right hand. The knife trembled until I set its blade against him. I gazed at it there. I was trembling too, somewhere very deep; maybe this should not be now, not yet. . . . My eyes flickered up and found his. He was staring at me as he had that once in the kitchen, as he had done through windows and probably from other places I had not even noticed—and suddenly I was angry. The anger was formless and cold, and I felt nothing else. I tilted the knife and pushed its tip into Laedon's flesh. One push, and I drew the knife back and let it fall, for I did not need it any more.

The blood welled. It looked like one drop, blooming, blooming; then it burst into a thinning, snaking line. This one line became many, which branched around forearm and fingers and dripped, one by one by one and soon all together, onto the grain.

I gazed from blood to bird. "Show me." I did not know how I managed to speak—or even why I had, since I realized it was not necessary—but the words were clear and felt right. "Show me what will come, for him."

Uja began to walk. Not her customary waddle, punctuated by ungainly flapping, but a graceful dance, dainty, lifted feet and wings opened, poised, tucked softly back again. She lowered her neck, every few paces, and plucked up a bit of rye. And there it was, so quickly: a path made by talons, tail and beak. A pattern edged in blood.

The vision came on gradually. I was expecting shock and speed and glaring colours, but for many long moments there seemed to be nothing at all. My eyes leapt from Uja's marks to Laedon's with anticipation that soon became impatience. *Where? When? Why not already?* Nothing was heightened or more vivid; in fact, the corners of the room were paling, quite gently. Nothing to see.

Nothing, creeping up walls and across the floor. A whiteness that is more than lack of colour; a whiteness that is no sight, no sound, no touch. It seeps over my feet and up my legs, and I remember my mother, devoured by black mist. I am disappearing, and this is not even really about me; where is Laedon? Where is the boy I have seen in so many other visions; where are the wolves, the eagles? Frost crystals reach for one another in my lungs, and join, and I try to lift my hands to clutch at my chest. My hands are there—I feel them—but they do not move. I am mired in the whiteness and there is no Path, no Pattern—nothing ahead or behind. Yigranzi, I think, because she rescued me before, when I was lost in Chenn's Otherworld. Yigranzi pulled me out and away—but she is not here, and there is no here. The white is filling up my nostrils, clotting my throat. I will die, and I will never see the castle. One last attempt at movement, but my bones are white now, bare and fused to nothing. I scream silence and they shatter.

I was choking. I was pressed to the floor, facedown. There was so much pain that I almost, almost wished the nothingness back. So much noise, as well: Uja crooning, rye grains skittering, the cabinet doors opening or closing—all too close, swollen as the inside of my head was swollen. The one thing I had none of was sight.

Orlo picked me up. I felt the muscles of his arms and chest, and when he said my name I felt it too, like a drumbeat that was inside, not outside, me. He smelled like wine and salt. He carried me and I thought I would vomit from the up and down, up and down, but I did not. He laid me on my bed, which was horribly soft—fleshy, sinking. I thrashed once, twice, and he held my wrists. I felt his breath on my face.

"I'm blind," I said, in a whisper or a shout—I couldn't tell.

"Not for long. Here—drink this"—cool clay, water a new kind of agony, tracing down—"and then sleep." His hands and breath were gone. The bed creaked as he stood. "You did well, Nola."

Well? I thought. Well? I saw nothing—truly, nothing—and now every one of my bones is broken and I am as blind as Laedon—but as long as I did well (and you would know, of course), then fine, I will simply go to sleep. . . .

I did, somehow. And when I woke the next morning, my own bleeding had begun.

CHAPTER TWELVE

The brothel girls talked about it all the time. "Ohhh, it's so awful; at the start I get headaches that make me vomit." And: "Don't bother looking for Mahelli. She's in bed, and she'll be there two more days—but at least the bleeding draught worked; she was afraid it hadn't." Or: "I wrap myself in hot cloths but it doesn't help the pain." I envied them their shared complaints even as I feared understanding them. I never expected my bleeding to begin as it did— so quietly that I did not notice.

There were other things distracting me, of course. My pounding head, my aching muscles, the sunlight that made my returned vision ripple with tears. I lay in bed and wriggled my toes, flexed my fingers and my arms. I gazed around the room, hungry for images, even though my blindness had only been brief. Everything looked paler than usual, but there were no squiggly black lines, and the colours were right. *Maybe I slept through the worst of it*, I thought. After all, it was full day, and Orlo had brought me to Laedon just after dusk.

I was ravenous. There was a tray beside my bed; I saw this when I sat up, slowly and awkwardly, like a creaky old woman. Lemon water, rolls with raisins baked in, and pickled fish. The fish was the most delicious thing I thought I had ever tasted; when it was gone I lifted the plate and licked the vinegar off.

The food steadied me. When I had finished all of it, I sat and looked out at leaves and sky. The windows were open, and a warm breeze stirred my hair and the sleeves of my dress. A bit of outside, creeping through the iron bars.

Laedon, I thought. Now, with no hunger and very little discomfort to distract me, I remembered. It was like probing a bruise: round the edge and in, seeing where it might hurt. It should have hurt; I knew this, in daylight. Yigranzi never would have allowed me to draw blood for Otherseeing. She would have told me about Bloodseeing only to warn me against it. And yet, when I remembered how the knife had felt in my hand, and how Laedon's blood had blossomed, I smiled. (It did not occur to me to check on him.)

When I finally stood up, I was briefly, sharply dizzy. I leaned on the bed until the feeling passed. Just as I was going to straighten again I saw a mark on the bed sheet. A dark smudge—brown, or dark, dark red. I wondered if I had had some of Laedon's blood on me, and checked my hands, my feet. The smudge was in a strange place, though: right where I had been sitting. I twisted, grasped the bottom of my dress. The cloth was blue; the blood on it looked black.

I sat down again, hard.

Orlo was in a terrible mood that night. Maybe that's why I didn't say anything right away, even though I knew how important the news would be to him. I remember feeling a sense of weight, while I waited for him to arrive: embarrassment (which I hadn't expected), and longing for Yigranzi. At some point after I'd folded several kitchen cloths and wadded them into my underclothes, I even thought of my mother. Perhaps she would have been moved by my new status; there might have been a bond. . . . This thought was quickly succeeded by a more rational one: she would likely have complained about all the extra washing and commanded me not to get myself with child until her own were out of swaddling clothes.

In any case, I wanted a woman's presence. I went and sat by Uja, who did not come out of her cage. She stood motionless on the floor and blinked at me. "My bleeding has started." *Blink, blink.* "It's strange, isn't it? That this happened right after I used a new kind of Bloodseeing?" *Blink.* "I miss Yigranzi. And I wish you could talk." Uja made a low, tongue-rolling noise and I laughed a bit.

I did not see Laedon that day, and though I was mostly relieved, I also felt even lonelier. So maybe I would have blurted it out to Orlo the moment I saw him, despite my embarrassment. Maybe I would have, if he hadn't swept in with all the force and fury of a thunderstorm.

"What are you doing in here? I've just spent five minutes looking for you."

I was standing in the art room: an enormous chamber on the lower level that was filled with sculpture and paintings. (Standing, because I was afraid that my new, clean dress would also get stained, if I sat.) My hand was on a statue of a girl about my age, clad in a shift so thin she might have been wearing nothing. I liked to touch the folds of cloth; marble ripples that looked as if they would crumple like silk in my fist.

"I'm sorry—I—"

"No excuses; we've wasted enough time already. Upstairs."

I had never seen him so angry before. He was very pale, but there were two streaks of scarlet along his cheekbones. His forehead shone with sweat.

I turned back, just before I stepped out the door. "Is it Prandel?" *Perhaps if I get him to talk*, I thought, *he'll calm down.*

He stared at me as if I had spoken in another language. "Pran . . .?" Incomprehension. No understanding at all.

"Prandel," I repeated. "Has he slipped away from you again?"

One more empty-eyed moment, and then Orlo raised his brows and let out his breath with a *whuff* of air. He sounded like Borl. "*Prandel*—of course . . . No. I lost his trail weeks ago."

"Oh." My voice was low with disappointment. "You didn't tell me. You haven't mentioned him in so long, but I thought that you were still looking."

"I *am* still looking." Words squeezed between his teeth. "Upstairs, Nola. *Now.*"

Despite the fact that I had no excruciating bleeding pains, I felt weak; I dragged myself up the staircase and into the lesson room. I needed Orlo to see my difficulty. I thought that he might ask me about it—that his concern for me would overcome his anger—but he only snapped, "What is *wrong* with you tonight, girl?" and strode past me in the corridor.

I leaned against the mirror. Answered his questions in one or two words. He bit at these questions, snarled them at me while Borl gazed at me with half-lidded eyes from the floor by Uja's cage. There were so many questions. I was sagging, gripping the mirror's edge; my legs felt like the fruit jellies Rudicol had made for special occasions.

Still, several hours had gone by when Orlo finally slammed his fist down on the gold and shouted, "Nola!" I stared at him as the word, and the metal, thrummed to silence. The cloths in my underthings had shifted and I could feel wetness between my pressed-together thighs. "If this is the best you can do," Orlo said slowly, "you will never be ready for the castle."

"There won't *be* a castle, for me. You'll never find Prandel. And I think you like me here; I'm your pet—only I don't get to leave with you, as Borl does." My voice was very high, and shaking. I remembered the girls saying that their bleeding made their anger and sadness more intense than usual. This idea comforted me for a moment, until I saw Orlo's glower and his black, furious eyes and thought, *And what is your excuse?*

"How dare you?" They were nearly whispers, but his words struck me like blows—one, two, three, all in the belly. "After all I've done for you."

My mother had said this. My mother, who had done nothing good for me until she sold me. And although Orlo had, in fact, given me much, much more than she had, my old anger was enough to give me strength.

"My bleeding started today."

He gaped; another thing that should have been amusing but wasn't. I stood taller.

"You . . ." He took a step toward me. Another. His eyes were briefly still. The scarlet on his cheeks seeped downward and I thought how beautiful he looked, aflame, quiet. Only he was not quiet for long.

"When today?" Yet another step. He was close now, but I did not move.

"This morning. Or maybe during the night, but I only noticed in the morning."

"And why did you not tell me immediately?"

I drew my shoulders back and tipped my head to look into his face. "Because you were in a foul temper the moment you walked in."

"A foul . . .?" He took one more step and there was nowhere for me to go but back. My spine and shoulders were pressed against the door. "You know how long I have been waiting for this news." His hands were on my shoulders, fingers digging. "You know—you ignorant, *idiot* girl." He was shouting again, and shaking me. My head cracked against the wood and my ears began to ring and I could no longer hear his words—just a roar that enveloped me and fell as spittle on my skin.

He let me go, suddenly. I slid down the door to the ground, where I sat like a boneless thing. I closed my eyes. When I opened them again, a few minutes later, Orlo was sitting next to me. Borl's head was in his lap; he was stroking the dog between the ears, in large, slow circles.

"I'm sorry." He hadn't even glanced at me, and yet he seemed to know I had opened my eyes. "Nola . . ." His hand slipped from Borl to me and lay upturned on my left thigh. It was both so strong and so helpless that I put my own hand within it. His fingers curled to cover mine. I felt a rush of relief and desire. I wanted to touch the underside of his arm, and reach over to put my lips against his throat.

"Walk with me," he said.

It was hotter outside than in, despite the darkness. The glass pebbles of the garden path were warm; I could feel them, even through my slippers.

The lycus blossoms were finally done blooming. They lay thick on the grass, and when Orlo led me off the path I tried to step on as many as I could. They changed colour when you touched them—bruising from white to purple—and released a gentle, sweet scent that could almost make you think they were still alive.

"I do not enjoy keeping you here," he said. We were standing under a tree with cascading, enclosing branches; alone together in the world, yet again. I said nothing. Watched the moonlight speckle his hair like moving jewels.

"If I did not fear for your safety I would have taken you to the castle weeks ago—for you are ready."

I shook my head, partly because there was a dull, throbbing ache settling into the back of it, where it had hit the door. "But you're not afraid for the other students who are already there. If they're safe, why wouldn't I be?" As I spoke, I thought, *I should have asked this before; maybe the bump has made me cleverer.*

Orlo was silent for a long time. I imagined he was gazing at me, but there was not enough moonlight for me to be sure. "There is another thing," he said at last. "Another reason why I need to keep you a secret, for now."

This time the silence went on long enough for my cleverer mind to grasp at a possibility. "The Bloodseeing," I said. "You aren't allowed to teach it to your other students. You need me to be separate so that you can teach it to me."

His teeth glinted as he smiled. "Yes—good, Nola. You're far more special than the others; that is precisely why you must stay here."

"But what does this mean?" The panic that was rising in me made my voice rise, too. "How long will it be before you teach me the rest? When will you take me back with you? Because you promised to—you promised! But it's been months since you took me from the brothel and I haven't been outside this house *once*, and if I have to stay here alone for much longer I'll go mad."

"You won't," Orlo said. "You have more strength than any other student I've ever had—and that is why I chose you. I will need someone strong, when the time comes to reveal my work."

"If I'm so strong," I said quickly, "let me prove it—let me use my power to help you. I could hunt Prandel with you. We could find him together, and now that my bleeding has started I could *really* help. We could hurt him even more than you could by yourself. But let me go out—let me leave here with you to do this. It will be enough. I won't need the castle yet. Just a walk in the streets . . ." I had not realized how badly I wanted this, until now. I was breathless, stinging with tears.

Two steps brought Orlo even closer to me. He raised his hands and sank them into my hair and eased my face up so that I could not look away from him. "Soon," he said. His thumbs were moving, stroking the arcs of my brows. "Patience, my sweet, stubborn girl. So much will come to both of us, in time."

He bent down. His lips brushed my forehead, back and forth, back and forth, lightly, trailing goosebumps and fire. "But"—warm, damp words, muffled against my skin—"there is more I *can* teach you now. This is what I have been waiting for, and it's why I was angry. My own kind of impatience, and I should not have let it hurt you."

My body forgot its exhaustion. It leaned into his fingers and his lips with a weight I had never felt before. "Show me," I whispered.

He drew back, and I cursed myself for having spoken. His hands slipped along my cheekbones and down to his sides. "Not now," we both said together, and he threw his head back and laughed. "Mistress Saucy Seer," he said, smiling still, "respect is one thing I have obviously *not* taught you. No doubt it's too late." He took a deep breath, and when he spoke again his voice was serious. "I am as eager to begin this next lesson as you are. But you are tired—no! Do not protest! You are tired. And you will need all of your strength for what I will be showing you."

He took my shoulders and turned me around so that I was facing the way we had come. "Go on, now. To bed with you."

We walked back together, over the blossoms and the pebbles. A cool wind had risen, and I lifted my face to it. I was free, for just a moment—unbound by walls of stone or iron, humming with a need that hurt only enough to remind me that I lived, and that I was glad of this. Then my gaze fell upon the house. There was a light burning in my room, and a shape in one of its windows. A shadow, but I knew him, saw his features as clearly as if he had been standing in sun.

I halted. Orlo took a few steps past me and stopped, looking over his shoulder at me. "Nola?"

"My window," I said slowly. "There's . . ." But even as I spoke and Orlo turned, Laedon's shadow melted away. Orlo arched an eyebrow at me and I shrugged. "I am tired," I said, and tried to smile. "It was nothing."

CHAPTER THIRTEEN

"Transformation."

I blinked at Orlo, and the candlelight seemed to swim around him. I had been in bed most of the day, resting but not really sleeping. And when he had arrived—not too late, tonight; just after sundown—he had had me drink a flagon of wine with him. So the light was swimming, now—everything was, gently, around the edges.

"What does it mean, Nola? Transformation."

I swallowed. The wine—sweet, amber like Uja's eyes—had made me thirsty. "Change," I said.

"Yes. And where have you seen this word, recently?"

"In the book—the red one with gold pages."

"Yes. You wanted to know what it meant; what it had to do with Bloodseeing."

My turn for "Yes," as the tingling began again in my belly.

He walked to the cabinet and set the key to the lock. "Choose," he said, "and I will show you."

I picked the smallest one, this time. Its tiny teeth would likely be useful only for sawing, but it had a beautiful tip, which would work nicely. (I could already see the vein, green when it was beneath skin, red when it opened above.)

"Your bleeding has begun," Orlo said. He was smiling at me. "Your new power awaits you. When you cut Laedon now, you will do more than see his Pattern. You will control it."

I was smiling too. He came to me, touched my lips with his fingers, held flat.

"I will tell you what to do, this first time. When you have had more practice you will be able to guide yourself—but for now you must listen to me. Now, and when the vision takes you."

His fingers slid down my chin and away. "I will," I said. "Tell me what I must do."

His smile widened. "What is your favourite cake?"

I laughed. "Apple," I said, remembering Bardrem peeling and slicing while Rudicol shouted about spilled batter and not enough rum in it.

"Very good. Apple it will be. Imagine it, when you are in the Otherworld. Imagine it as clearly as you can."

"All right. But what—"

The door opened. Laedon shuffled in, his hand trailing along the wall. I started, but I was not afraid, as I had been last night when I saw him in my window. I felt no fear, no anger; just a deep, waiting quiet. The knife was cool in my hand. My skin was cool, though the wine had warmed me, within.

Orlo put an arm around Laedon. "He'll feel this one, if you do it right. Not as pain, exactly, but he'll feel it. You're used to it, though, aren't you, Lae?" A little shake of the old man's shoulders. Laedon's eyes did their rolling dance.

"Now, then. No tools, Nola: the vision would be too strong. Just his blood. And I will stay very close, to help you remember what we talked about." He winked at me. I did not smile back. I was already walking toward them.

It was not so easy, this time. Maybe I had the angle wrong; it was a smaller knife, after all, and I had not had time to get used to it. I pushed its tip against Laedon's skin—exactly the same place as before, because I knew it. The skin puckered inward but did not break. I pushed again, and again. Anger surged through me. I pulled the blade back, then jabbed down. His arm jumped. I had not found the same place, after all, but that did not matter: blood spattered and flowed.

"Show me," I said, and gasped, because it felt as if there was a knife in me too, slicing from my thighs to my belly and up, up until it rested behind my eyes. I doubled over. At first all I heard was my own whimpering, but as I breathed I heard something else: Uja, whistling high, sweet notes that seemed to turn the agony into aching.

I straightened. I saw Laedon's blood, dripping onto a piece of white cloth (Orlo must have put it there). I saw Laedon, staring at me from behind a crimson gauze that wrapped him. Everything I looked at was crimson, except for his eyes, which were diamond-clear, all colours. I stared at his blood again—a single spray and the rest droplets—until it spun and blurred and the world around me vanished in red.

A silver road cuts through the red. I move toward it as I have moved in other visions, expecting to feel myself a bird or a vole—but I am myself. My own feet are beneath me, bare, sunk into the soft, warm stuff of the path. The Path, I think, and see that it stretches on and on, over red hills and along the bottoms of red canyons, and that it ends in Laedon's clear, bright eyes.

I walk slowly, because I feel heavy and strange. The Path ripples, and I dig my toes in, between steps. When I glance to either side I see other roads—so many, too many; which is the one I should follow? They are silver snakes, writhing, making me even dizzier. They all wind up to Laedon's eyes. I stop, sway.

"Choose, Nola." Orlo's voice is so close that it is nearly inside my own head, but he is nowhere I can see. "Choose one and make it the only one."

I do. It looks like all the others, but when I hold it in my gaze it stops its wriggling. I think, Walk, now—but my feet (so solid and near) will not move. I whimper again.

"Nola. Stay still—it is all right." I take a great gulp of crimson air. "Concentrate. Imagine tomorrow. Imagine tomorrow, and the thing you described to me earlier."

Tomorrow, I think. Imagine . . . The sun rising into blue sky, not red. Sunlight on the dark green leaves that brush against the kitchen windows. The kitchen—the cake. Apple slices laid in a circle; batter poured. A round, brown cake on a windowsill. I see it, but only for a moment; it is too silly, a thing from my world steaming in the Other. I laugh and the cake vanishes, as do the leaves and the light and the window glass. I laugh at my bare toes, and at the road that squirms away from me like a snake. I look along the road and see the diamond-flash of Laedon's eyes and my laughter turns to pain.

When I opened my eyes I was in bed, in my room; I guessed this from the wobbly shadows, then squeezed my eyes shut again. I was spinning. My insides throbbed, and I remembered red, pulsing hillsides, red sky. I hardly felt myself moving, but I was—I was across the room, retching into the bowl that was supposed to hold only fresh water. When I was done I sat on the floor. I could tell that there was wetness seeping between my legs, but the ache in me was so huge that I didn't think I would ever move again.

I must have dozed; when Uja pecked at my fingers I started and flailed my arms. She sang the four notes of her "calm yourself, little chick" song, over and over, until I said, "Thank you, Uja—I'm fine now." Though I was not. I could hardly see her; she was a shadow like the other things in the room, her glorious colours smudged to black.

She picked up the edge of my dress in one of her talons. She tugged. "Oh, Uja," I said. My voice burned my throat, which was bitter with sickness. "I can't go anywhere with you. I can't get up."

She tugged and tugged. She gave a piercing whistle, right into my ear. She scratched her beak along my palm. "Stop, you horrible creature! Stop! Leave me alone!" But I was up. I was standing, my arms out, balancing on the ground like a marketplace tumbler atop a tall, wavering pole.

Uja did not let go of my dress. She was holding it in her beak, now. "I should change," I said. "There's blood on this dress. . . ." She pulled. I shuffled after her. Pull, shuffle, pull, shuffle, all the way out the door and down the hallway.

She allowed me to rest on the stairs. I sat, breathed, edged myself down, sat still again. She burbled and popped her tongue, as if she was not sure whether to praise or scold me. By the time we reached the bottom my vision was a bit clearer; her red feathers looked pink. I stood with my forehead against the enormous mirror until my ragged breathing smoothed. I pulled back and caught my own eyes, and I made a sound like one of Borl's puzzled whines. My eyes were dark. It was not just the remnants of Othersight: they were dark blue, nearly black. They were Chenn's.

I hardly noticed myself walking, this time. Uja led me slowly, though she nipped my fingertips whenever I stood still. I thought, *She did it too—of course she did—Chenn used the Bloodsight and he taught her to—of course, of course.*

I lifted my head, when we got to the kitchen door. Uja scratched at it with her claws. "Why do you never open this one?" I said, and opened it myself.

I smelled it first: a sweetness of fruit, butter, sugar. I had never smelled this particular sweetness here, and for a moment I expected to see Bardrem, elbow-deep in flour, and Rudicol sucking in his thin cheeks, preparing to shout. I saw Laedon instead, standing by a window. Its two panes had been unlatched and opened (though they could not open far, because of the iron bars). I stared at his eyes, which seemed to be staring at me, and then I looked down at the cake that was sitting on the sill beside him. It was perfect: brown, round, so hot that the air around it shimmered.

"Orlo told you to do this," I said, loudly, because I did not believe it. I did not believe that Orlo had told him; I also did not believe that I had. I walked to the window with Uja clicking along behind me. Laedon's gaze stayed on me as I drew closer, but I ignored him. I looked at the cake. I touched its apple-pitted top and drew my fingers swiftly back before they scalded. A few moments later I reached again. This time I dug my fingers in, heedless of the heat. I gouged out a piece that left a shallow, unsightly hole, and I put it in my mouth. It burned along my tongue and all the way down my throat, but before this burning numbed me, I tasted it. It was delicious.

"Othercake," I said, and I laughed until I cried.

I woke at dawn and

You would think that there couldn't possibly be any more blood. But there was—so much more, in fact, that all these memories seem washed in crimson, just as that vision of Laedon was. If this were not my own story, I would roll my eyes and grumble something about exaggeration.

So—the *next* blood.

I was desperately impatient that day, waiting for Orlo. I had been unsure about talking to him when my bleeding began, but now I paced and paced, afire with the need to tell him about a cake. Of course, since I wanted this so badly, he did not come. Not that evening, nor that night. I woke at dawn and padded through the house with a candle, thinking he might have returned very late and decided not to wake me, but I found only Uja, perched on the highest branch of her cage with her head beneath her wing. I sat and waited for her to wake up. When she showed no signs of doing this on her own, I rattled the bars and called her name and gave some piercing whistles of my own. "See?" I said when she finally shook her head erect (all its feathers puffing, then subsiding). "It's unpleasant, being woken up like that. If I could get in there with you and pull on your feathers, I'd do that, too." She blinked at me, her head cocked, and I groaned. "I'm sorry. But Orlo didn't come and I couldn't sleep. Please come out?"

She did not move.

"Ah," I said. "You *won't* come out—which means Orlo's on his way? Why haven't you ever shown him that you can leave your cage on your own? Why do you not *like* him?"

I talked and talked, while she regarded me calmly. I talked about Orlo, and eventually about Chenn. My words about her were even quicker than the rest. "He taught her too. He was showing her about Bloodseeing—that's why she didn't want to tell me about the cuts on her arms—it was a forbidden art, and she was afraid to mention it to me, just as she was afraid to mention Prandel."

The day passed. My meals appeared in the kitchen, as usual, but I did not see Laedon. "Where does he *go*?" I said to Uja when I returned to the lesson room in the late afternoon. "Is there a secret room here somewhere? Or maybe when he closes his eyes he becomes invisible." I giggled—a silly sound, and it went on too long. I felt half-mad with waiting.

I paced and sat. I changed the cloths in my underthings more often than I needed to and washed them in a bucket in the kitchen. I stared out the second-storey windows, because although the streets beyond the house were hardly visible (the trees were tall, and the house was at the top of a hill), I might be able to see him—just a glimpse of him, opening the gate, coming up the path to me.

He did not come at sunset, nor in the hours after. "If he never came back again," I whispered to Uja, "if something happened to him, we'd all die in here." This thought had not occurred to me in daylight; now, in darkness, it made my head hum with fear.

I fell asleep, somehow. I had been pressing my forehead against the library window, staring at the moon, which hung fat and white among branch shadows. I was aching with solitude, and, with the stubborn contrariness of the young, I was making it worse—forcing myself through memory after memory of Bardrem, Yigranzi, Chenn, the Lady, the spindly courtyard tree. I was consumed, certain I would never know peace of any sort, ever again—and then I was asleep.

And *then*, with a start that drove me to my feet and backward, I was awake again.

A sound had woken me. I had not heard it, with my sleeping ears, but I had felt it, and I felt it still, as I stood shaking by the door: a violent, echoing crash. "Orlo?" A thread of a voice that he would only have heard if he had been beside me, which he obviously was not. I eased the library door open and peered into the hallway. The lamps I had lit earlier shone on emptiness. I waited for a moment—for more noise; for him, approaching, explaining—and then I crept out into the corridor.

By the time I reached the entrance hall I had convinced myself that I had heard nothing. *A dream*, I thought. *Maybe the beets I ate for supper are to blame. . . .* I was relieved enough that this thought of beets made me hungry. I walked to the kitchen, scuffing my slippers loudly on the floor so that I would be able to imagine I was not alone. I raised my hand to turn the knob—but the door was already open a crack. I pushed on it, just a little, and as I did I heard another sound.

Words, muffled but furious, unintelligible, snapped off with teeth and sucked-in breath.

And another sound: a rhythmic, dull pounding.

My heart began to pound too, but I pushed at the door a bit, and a bit more, until I could see.

Orlo was sitting on my stool. He was wearing a dark, striped shirt—only he wasn't; he was wearing no shirt at all. His shoulders, chest, back and arms glistened with blood. There was a bucket on the floor beside him, and a cloth on the table, but he was not using them. He was hunched over, his head bent; he was slamming his fists against the table, one after the other. Borl was stretched out at his feet. In the brief silences between words and fists I heard the dog whimpering—a high, thin, unbroken question.

I whimpered too—I must have, for Borl sprang to his feet and ran at me, barking, spraying spit. Orlo did not look up. Borl lunged and bit the hand I had lifted to stave him off and I cried out, but still Orlo did not look up. "Orlo!"—I kicked, caught Borl in the ribs and sent him skittering back—"*Orlo!*"

He lurched to his feet. His shoulders were rounded and he had to crane to see me, and even then he did not truly seem to be seeing me, for his black eyes leapt and rolled like Laedon's. "What?" he cried. "Who is Orlo? By Pattern and Path, who is Orlo, and who are you?"

Borl was beside him again, panting, gazing up into his face with one ear cocked toward me. "Orlo," I said, and my voice trembled. "That's you: Orlo. And I'm Nola—I'm *Nola*; why don't you know . . .?"

He groped behind him for the stool and sat down. "Oh," he said. "Yes. Me . . ." He shook his head, ran a bloodied hand over his hair. "Yes. And—" He blinked at me. "You. Ah."

I took a step toward him. "What's happened? What's wrong with you—why are you bleeding?"

"I . . ." He was running his hands over his skin now, smearing. "Sometimes they fight me."

"What?"

"When I try to take them—they . . ." His head snapped up. His eyes were focused, seeing me at last, but I felt no relief at this.

"Let me help you." I walked to him. "Let me clean it off." *Be busy, sound firm; maybe he won't notice your fear. . . .*

I dipped the cloth in the bucket. The water was so cold that I felt I had awoken a second time, just as abruptly as the first. I wrung the cloth out. When

I set it on his back he flinched—muscles bunching, so beautiful, so close. I wiped, dipped, wrung, over and over, and yet I found no wound on him—just smooth, firm flesh.

"Where are you hurt?" I asked as I dabbed at the hollow below his shoulder blade.

He frowned. "Hurt? No, no—it's not mine. Not my blood."

He sat up, stretched so that his back arched, and I saw his chest clearly (as I had not when he had been standing). Despite the blood, I saw the scars: corded, puckered, some white-healed, others purple, still others fresh and red. They crisscrossed each other from his nipples to the clenched ridges of his belly. I hesitated only for a moment; continued rinsing and washing, as if I was perfectly calm, not shuddering all the way to the soles of my feet.

"So whose blood is it?"

He stared at me. I could tell that he was no longer confused. He could have answered me, but he did not—just stared, with a small, tight smile. I could have waited for him to answer. I should have. But I was so alarmed by his silence that I said, in a rush, "Is it Prandel's?"

His smile disappeared and his eyes narrowed. "Prandel?"

"Oh, Orlo—please don't tell me you forget him too, *again*?" I was relieved that I sounded angry, not afraid (though I was afraid; was cold with it). "Prandel! Prandel, who killed Chenn—why don't you *remember* him?"

Another smile. This one was slow and broad and familiar, but it made me even colder. Water dripped from the cloth that hung from my fingers, and these drips made light pink tears of his blood.

"Yes," he said. He reached for me, cupped my chin in both his hands. His thumbs rested, warm and gentle, on my lower lip. "Yes, that's it. It's happened, at last: I've killed Prandel."

CHAPTER FOURTEEN

Sildio came to me a few hours after sundown, last night. He must have knocked, but I didn't hear him; I was bent over my paper, of course.

"Mistress," he said, and I started. "I'm sorry—I don't usually like to disturb you—but I heard you and had to check. . . . Were you laughing, just now, or crying?"

I lifted my hands to my cheeks, which were dry. "I don't know," I said. My voice sounded very rough; when had I last spoken, had a drink?

"I worry, Mistress. You hardly sleep, and sometimes you don't eat for an entire day."

I stared down at my ink-stained fingers and cleared my throat. "I know. But I need to finish writing. If I don't write as much as I can every day, it'll be years before I'm done. And in any case, was it not you who wanted me to do this in the first place?"

He smiled. (He has a sweet, lopsided smile. I never used to understand why Grasni flushed every time she mentioned him; now I do.)

"It was." He walked over to me. "But I didn't say you should starve. Now hold out your hands." I did, and he slipped an apple into my right, a piece of bread into my left.

"Sildio," I said, "you'll make me plump."

We both laughed. Such a simple exchange, and such a simple sound, but they made me feel dizzy.

I must begin again, now, before I gape at sleeping bird, dog and baby all day.

The kitchen. Orlo's clean, wet skin. His hand around my wrist, clamped like iron. And his voice, low and breathless, stirring the hair by my ear: "Nola. Let me show you one more thing."

"But," I said, "Prandel! *Prandel*—that's wonderful! Where did you find him? Did you speak to him before you killed him?"

My words were ragged, some of them only half-said, for Orlo was pulling me, so hard and fast that I had to jog to keep up. He did not reply. He did not look at me, either; maybe this was why I kept talking. This, and my need to fill my own ears with words, so that I would not have to think. "You can take me outside with you now. Just for a walk, like I asked for before. Just—" A particularly violent tug on my wrist, and I stumbled forward, gasped. "Orlo, you're *hurting* me!"

He rounded on me so abruptly that I ran into him. I did not recognize his eyes. "Take me out. Take me to the place where you killed him. I want to see." I steadied myself with breath. "I need to see him."

Orlo grasped my jaw and squeezed until I flinched. "Why?" he said, his voice light and mild. "Don't you believe me?"

I did not know how to answer, but did not need to. He pulled me again and I lurched after him, into the entrance hall.

Laedon was there, one foot on the bottom step.

"Laedon!" Orlo cried. "Lae! On your way to the lesson room, were you? I'm glad we found you here. Come. Come *here*, old man." Laedon took his foot from the step. He walked to us. When he was close, he swivelled his eyes to me, and he kept them there, even when Orlo spoke.

"Mistress Bloodthirsty Seer." He was glittering: his eyes, his hair, his teeth, his naked skin. I saw suddenly that he did have an injury—a jagged, almost circular one that looked like a bite mark, below his collarbone. It was trickling blood. "Cut him," Orlo said. "Now."

"But," I said, "I have nothing—there is no knife—"

"Oh?" He bent, groped for his ankle. When he straightened he was holding a dagger. Its hilt glinted with tiny jewels. Its blade was short and very thin. When I did not reach for it he gripped my hand, pressed the knife's hilt against my palm until my fingers closed. "Come, Nola," he murmured. "Do this. This one thing. Do it and I will take you to the castle. I will take you to Teldaru and tell him that you will be as mighty as he is. King Haldrin will place you at his right hand. Only do this one more thing, dearest girl."

I believed him. I must have, for why else would I have clutched the knife and stepped up to Laedon? I lifted his arm and twisted it round. He was trembling, which made me pause; he had never trembled before. I looked into his face and saw fear, and for the first time I wished he could speak to me.

"Nola."

I thought of the castle's soaring stone and Bardrem's words—all of them written for the king, in hope. I thought of Teldaru, a boy facing a lord across a wine-soaked tavern table.

"*Nola.*"

I believed Orlo, even though I didn't. My own hope made me set the tiny dagger against Laedon's flesh. I cut.

It is the same scarlet landscape as before, and the same pain. I wriggle my toes and look at all the snake-roads and am just about to choose one when I hear Orlo.

"You see the paths? Many of them?"

"Yes," I say, inside or aloud. The pain is blurring my sight and my mind, but still I think, He is not where I am; he cannot see what I do.

"Pull them toward you." His voice sounds slower and deeper than usual. "Pull them into yourself."

"How?" I want to say, but I am already obeying him.

I try a slender one first: lift my hands and think, Come here to me. The silver lashes at its far end, but it comes, jerking over the red ground. Soon it is a coil at my feet—so much smaller than the road it was, and slippery when I touch it. Slippery and moist; not just silver any more, but colours of earth, stone, water and leaf. I think, What now?—but again I know, somehow, my Othermind strong and certain. I raise the thing in both hands. It writhes and I nearly drop it; I squeeze and it is wet, suddenly: dark, flowing along my skin and then beneath.

"Do you have it?" Orlo hisses. "Is it in you?"

It is. It courses through me, leaving a trail of wind and flame. I am larger, making room; my eyes are keener, lighting on the roads and hills and seeing below them, to a latticework of bones. I am ravenous. The roads pulse and I grab at them.

"Slowly," Orlo says. But I am too hungry: I pull them in, in squirming ribbons and knots, and moan as they become my own veins.

The red is receding. I notice this when there are only three paths left, because I have trouble distinguishing them from the ground. They are pale; the ground is pale. Sand. It does not matter that I can hardly see the paths; I smell them (rotting meat and fruit), and they are weaker than the others. I grasp them, absorb them, stretch my longer muscles and my thicker, wider skin. I am still hungry.

"You have done it." *Orlo sounds further away than he did before. I feel myself smile; I am alone.* "Don't linger where you are, Nola. You must leave the Otherworld before you lose yourself in it. Come back now, and see what you have done."

I lift my hands and hold them up to the white-gold sky. I am alight; flame, in this desert. This desert . . . I sweep my gaze around its emptiness.

I have been here before.

"Nola!"

I turn toward his voice. He is there, in the front hallway—but he is also here, across a space of sand. How? I think, *but then remember the bite mark, the thin trickle of his blood. I must be very powerful to be seeing him too, so effortlessly. He does not know,* I think. *And he will not feel me, if I do not try to transform anything. And I won't, even though I'm still hungry. I'll just look. . . .*

I begin to walk across the sand. I am awkward because of my swollen body, but I do not care; I feel like a gathering wave.

He is crouched, his head bent. There is a shadow before him on the ground—not his, for the sun is directly above us. I have been here before. I have seen this before. I was above him then, a bird, dropping closer, closer, trying to see his face. Chenn's hair was a spill of ink on the sand.

I stop. No—that was Prandel. I was in the sky; he was below her, short and plump. But above? I think now. How could I have been able to tell that, from there? I saw a man—that is all. A man crouched over Chenn, who turned into me.

"Nola—what is it? Where are you?"

Other-Orlo says nothing. I walk toward him again. With each step the shadow beneath him grows. It seeps over the ground, curving into shapes of arms, legs, lolling heads.

"Come back! Now, Nola!"

Other-Orlo is smiling. He is not looking at me. He is crouched on the edge of a dark, still lake of sprawled bodies and tangled hair. The small, jewelled dagger is in his hand.

"You will listen to me! You will come back to me—"

I see Chenn's cold, bloodless face among all the others. Her eyes—one blue-black and gold, one brown—stare. Her throat is open to bone. I look away from her, wildly, and Yigranzi is there. Another limp, lifeless body—but no—she is lurching to her feet, her hands held out, gasping a word I still do not understand. Yigranzi stumbles over the bodies—so many of them, more with every step—and she is nearly there, nearly touching me with her shaking, knobby-knuckled hands.

Other-Orlo rises. He thrusts the dagger into Yigranzi's belly, wrenches it around and around again, until she falls. He kneels beside her. She is bleeding. He sets his mouth to her wound and opens his lips

"Nola—"

—and I was screaming, thrashing in his hands in the entry hall. I twisted, seeking Laedon in the lightning-shot dimness of my after-vision. He was not there—not standing, nor sitting on the steps. I twisted one more time and saw him on the floor. He was a dark, broken shape; his eyes were open and still.

"You killed him too!" I shrieked, clawing at Orlo's arms.

He clenched his hands around my wrists. He was baring his teeth in something like a smile. "No," he said as I sagged in his grip. "No, dearest girl: you did."

CHAPTER FIFTEEN

I could not move. I did not even think to, or want to.

"I hardly even needed to tell you what to do," Orlo was saying. He was still clutching me, even though I was no longer struggling. I was staring at Laedon's body. I was thinking that I could have run away from Orlo and all the other bodies, deep and forever into the Otherworld.

"You took him, Nola—all of him. Every one of his paths; his entire Pattern. I knew you would understand. I didn't want to tell you: I wanted you to find out for yourself how sweet this power is." He leaned in toward me. My head was level with the bite mark on his chest. I could have moved just a little and opened it up again.

"This is the highest known form of Bloodseeing. The hardest. And you have done it—you have . . ."

He frowned slowly, and I wanted to whimper. I did not.

"You said 'You killed him too.' What did you mean?"

He does not know, I thought, *and he cannot.*

"I . . ." My voice tasted rotten, the way Laedon's last, dying paths had smelled. I swallowed a cough which would have brought sickness up and out of me. "I was thinking of Prandel."

It was a ridiculous thing to say. Orlo's eyes narrowed.

"I hardly knew what I was saying. Oh, Orlo"—*look at him, Nola, and press his hands a bit*—"it was so wonderful and so horrible at the same time. How do *you* stand it?"

His frown lingered around his eyes but his mouth smiled. "Dear, sweet Nola—you will understand even more, soon. You will understand that taking a life in this way is pure. It is joy."

My normal vision was returning. His face was sharpening, brightening, and I could not bear it. I lowered my head. "I . . . I feel sick. I need to lie down."

"Of course you do! You must rest; you must sleep for a month, if that is what you need. Come."

He lifted me as he had before. Before, when being held against him had made me ache with longing. Now I looped my arms lightly around his neck and gazed away from him. Laedon was sprawled just as the others had been. The only blood on him was drying on the inside of his arm, where I had cut him. The knife was lying beside him. His leather cap had fallen off. I recognized the fringe of yellow-white hair, but other than that he was bald, which surprised me in a distant, useless way. I kept him in my eyes for as long as I could, but Orlo walked swiftly up the stairs and soon all I saw were doors and darkness.

"There, now."

No, I thought as he hovered above me. *Don't touch me. Go.*

He bent and brushed his lips across my forehead. Stroked my hair smooth over the pillow. "Sleep well," he said, and rose, and smiled at me, and went.

I lay stiff and sleepless and could not think. I *needed* to think. I needed to get up, break the glass of the cabinet, take one of the knives—though even all five would not be enough—and find him. Hunt him, as he said he would hunt Prandel, who had never existed. I needed to carve Chenn's pain into him; I needed to hear him make Yigranzi's garbled, urgent noises. I lay in bed and thought only about how I should be thinking, until dawn light began to spread across the ceiling.

When the room was golden-bright I felt a tugging on my sleeve. I rolled over and looked into Uja's amber eyes. I did not speak to her, because I knew that a word would loose all the tears that were pressing on my throat. She gave a piercing whistle, which made me start up onto my elbow. She gabbled at me—a stream of sounds I had never heard before. They shocked my tears away.

"Uja?"

She chattered and clacked her beak and bobbed her head up and down so quickly that her colours blurred. She seized my sleeve and wrenched it violently and it ripped. I stared at the dangling lace, then at her. She waddled to the door, which was open. The door she had opened.

I sat up. The inside of my head flashed white. When I could see again I said, "Uja?"—plaintively, since I wasn't sure, but wanted to be. She burbled and disappeared into the corridor.

He's not here, I thought as I set my feet on the floor. *She wouldn't have come out of her cage if he were here.*

I hobbled to the wardrobe (my muscles all hurt terribly) and opened it. If my old brothel dress had still been there I would have put it on, but of course it wasn't. I chose the most opulent gown I could, instead: a thing of pink shell buttons and gathered silk and a train that dragged on the ground behind me. If I could not be invisible, I would be a lady. I fumbled with buttons and sash and slipped on a pair of white shoes embroidered in a pattern of purple vines. I turned away from the wardrobe and back again; I took a crumpled piece of paper out from where it had been lying, amongst the shoes. "Beautiful," I read, and "Help!" I folded Bardrem's note and bent to put it into one of my slippers. Then I turned and left the room.

Uja was perched on the top step. When she saw me she spread her wings and flapped them. I walked slowly to the staircase and down, expecting her to keep pace with me as she usually did (hip-hopping from stair to stair), but she did not. I looked behind me and saw her poised, her wings still outstretched—and then she was flying, gliding past me like a blossom caught in wind. She was so beautiful that I forgot where I was, for a moment. She sketched a wide circle that became a spiral and landed by the front door. She cocked her head up at me and whistled a question ("What are you *waiting* for?") and I continued down the stairs to her.

Only when I was at the door did I begin to think clearly, or indeed at all. Uja stood up on her talon-tips and inserted her beak into the lock. She wiggled her head and I heard a click.

"Uja," I said when she was looking at me once more. I was trembling with anger. "Why didn't you do this for me months ago? You knew. You *knew*, but you didn't help me."

Blink, blink.

"You could have . . ."

Blink.

My anger was gone but I was still trembling—because there probably had been a reason that she hadn't helped me before, and because the door was unlocked. I pulled it open and stepped onto the path. *I* blinked, now, in the early morning sunlight; it had been months since I had been outside in anything but darkness. The air was warm but tinged with autumn, and I took great gulps of it. I walked along the glass-pebbled path, and each step was firmer than the last. The black iron fence was before me, and Uja was beside me, and the gate, too, was unlocked and waiting.

"Come with me?"

She rolled her delicate bird shoulders and cooed and stepped back, gracefully, just as she had within the circle of grain.

"Uja," I said, one more time. Not a question, any more; just a word. I reached out and laid my hand on her head. I had never touched her before. Her feathers were as smooth as the silk of my dress, though they prickled when I drew my hand back over them. I ran my finger along her beak—which was cool—and she nibbled it. "Thank you," I whispered, and then I was thrusting my way clumsily out the gate and she was singing me a high, sweet, vanishing farewell.

I knew where I was going. Maybe I had actually managed to think, as I lay motionless in bed, or maybe it was just that there was only one place to go and my embroidered shoes realized this as soon as they touched the cobblestones. I had no idea how to get back to the brothel—and anyway, that was not where I needed to be. Later, perhaps, after I had done what must be done.

I tried not to be distracted; tried to look only at the castle and the way in front of me. But there were people in the streets—so many of them, shouting laughing, some singing from open windows. Most of them paused to look at me—a wild-eyed girl, lost on her way home from a royal ball?—and I avoided their eyes, kept my feet moving. It was almost too much: the noise, the smells of cooking and midden heaps, the smirking urchins who darted at my skirts, imagining coins. I kept walking. I strode through alleys and along broad avenues and narrow pathways, and if I needed to double back and find new ways I hardly noticed. I was breathing open air and I had words to speak and I was very, very close.

The road that led up to the castle gate was wide. Only here did I slow. I felt a first sickly lurch of fear, looking at the five guards and their spears and shields, which glinted like Otherseeing mirrors in the sun. I watched them speak to a man on a wagon covered in scarlet cloth (they turned him away), and to a group of women and girls holding armfuls of scrolls (who were gestured inside). I hesitated. I stared at my shoes. I picked up the slippery folds of my dress and walked over to them.

"Yes?" The man's voice was rough but not unfriendly. He was not smiling, and his helmet hid his eyes.

"I must speak to King Haldrin," I said, too loudly.

"Indeed," another guard said. He sounded bored.

"Yes." I breathed in deeply, silently. "One of his seers is a murderer."

The other three guards had gathered around me. All five stared at me, then at each other.

"And who are you, to know this?" asked the first one.

"I was his captive. He taught me and promised to bring me here, but he was lying. He held me prisoner for months."

"And how did you escape?" The second guard, no longer bored, grinning.

"A bird," I said, and, quickly, over the swell of their laughter, "It doesn't matter. I must tell the king. He must be warned."

"Awfully pretty dress, for a prisoner," one of the ones behind me remarked, and they laughed again.

"Look at me!" I cried, and they fell silent. "Look at my eyes! What do you see?" They did look, as I gazed at each of them in turn. They looked and were still silent. "I have the Othersight. My eyes are dark with it already and will only grow darker, until they are black like his."

"Like whose?" the first guard asked. "What is this man's name?"

"Orlo."

I waited for them to gasp, but instead they shifted and chuckled. "There is no Orlo here," the first guard said.

"There is. He teaches. He serves the king and Teldaru. He grew up with them. *Let me in.*"

"She's mad," someone beside me said, and someone else grumbled in agreement. A third spat over his shoulder.

"I'm not," I said quietly.

The first took off his helmet. His hair was short and grizzled and the skin beside his pale green eyes was crinkly with lines.

"Jareth," another said, "don't go all soft now, like always. She's a mad child or a criminal—doesn't matter which."

Jareth looked at me, and I at him. "Maybe," he said slowly, and a chorus of groans rose. "But she has the Othersight. Someone inside might know how to help her, at least."

"Another wounded birdling for Father Jareth," a guard said in a high trill of a voice.

Jareth scowled. "Enough, Marlsin. You'll do an extra two hours' watch tonight." He took hold of my arm, just above the elbow. "I'll take the girl in and you'll none of you give me more trouble. Back to your places, now."

I heard them move away; heard Marlsin mutter something. Then Jareth drew me under the great arch of the gate.

We crossed a dusty courtyard. I smelled horses and baking bread but did not turn my head to seek out the stables or the kitchens. I looked where Jareth took me, up a flight of steps so long that my legs ached when we were only halfway. People spoke to him on the stairs, and when he led me inside the keep at the top, but I did not look at them, either.

The keep was dim. We paused for a moment. "King Haldrin?" he asked someone—another guard, for while I did not look up at his face, I saw his sword and shield. The other man said, "His reading room—where else?" and Jareth guided me on, down a hallway lit by lanterns. I expected a series of halls, more steps; a place that was enormous and grand. The door we came to was quite plain, as the others in the hall were: wood and bronze, without insignias or ornament. For a moment I thought he had brought me to a prison cell, and I pulled my arm back, trying to wrest it from his grip—but then he rapped, and a man's voice called, "Enter."

The room was bright. I blinked, and the wash of sun hardened into a series of arched windows that looked onto sky and green. Bookshelves lined the walls. The books upon them were not neatly arranged, but scattered, leaning against each other, or lying on their backs or fronts, or even open. Some of the shelves bristled with scrolls. I looked from them to the tapestries on the walls between the shelves, to the worn carpet on the floor and the large, scarred table upon it. To the man sitting at the table, twisting around on his chair to look at me.

Orlo was right; he is young, I thought, as if Orlo might have lied about this too. King Haldrin's hair was brown and curly enough that I could barely see the golden circlet that lay upon it. His eyes were blue. They narrowed as he gazed at me, but not really in a frown. He was clean-shaven, as Orlo was.

"Jareth," the king said. His voice was warm, and I felt a surge of hope. "How did you find me?"

Jareth cleared his throat. "You are always here, my lord. When you are not in the Great Hall, that is. And Larno told me, too."

The king sighed. He was smiling. "And I try so hard to be elusive." He rose, stepped closer to us. "Who is this?"

"A girl, my lord, who claims . . . well, she claims something that sounds a little mad, really."

The king stepped even closer. He was gazing into my face, into my eyes. "She has the Othersight," he said.

"Yes." Jareth sounded relieved. "She does. And she says—"

"Perhaps she should tell me herself."

My throat was dry. As I was walking here I imagined a great hall that would echo with my words; a hall full of people, and the king on his throne above me. I had been ready for this—not for a room of books and one smiling, waiting man.

"There . . ." I bit my lip, wiped my palms on my dress. "There is a seer here at the castle who kills people. He uses the Othersight—Bloodseeing—it's forbidden, and he uses it to murder them."

"So you see," Jareth said, "I thought to bring her to you, because you could decide whether to take her to Mistress Ket for help"—he gestured at the windows, and at what lay beyond them—"since she does healing. The girl may be mad, but—"

"Jareth." The king's voice was quiet. "Leave us, please." After the door had closed, he leaned back against the table. "How do you know this?"

"He held me captive at a house in the city—he took me from a brothel and told me he'd teach me, told me he lived here at the castle and that he knew you well, ever since you were boys."

"What is his name?"

"Orlo," I said, with the last of my breath.

The king did frown, now. "Orlo?"

I nodded.

"I knew an Orlo once, when I was very young, but he died."

"No," I said, "no—he's a seer, and he lives *here*; he told me so." I swallowed tears. "He told me."

There was a door set in the far wall, between two windows. A door leading out to the leafy courtyard, where the seers' pool was, where the school was. It opened, as my words faded. I did not turn to it, at first, but clung to the king's gaze as if I would convince him silently, since my speaking could not. But then I heard a growl, and knew it, and I did turn, slowly.

Borl was in the doorway. He was growling at me, his ears back against his skull.

"Borl!" King Haldrin said sharply. "Quiet, now!"

No, I thought—because there was a man behind the dog, blocking out the sun.

"That's him," I said, too hoarsely. "*That's him*"—lifting my hand, pointing at Orlo, who was looking at the king with his honey-coloured brows raised.

King Haldrin's frown was puzzled, as was his voice. "Teldaru," he said, "what is this?"

BOOK
TWO

CHAPTER SIXTEEN

They put me in another prison. More walls and locks—and him. Even now, years later and surrounded only by branches and sky and doors I can open, I can hardly catch my breath, remembering.

I thought I would write and write, once I'd set down that first "Teldaru?" Because that was it—the one word I'd been writing *to*, all this time so far—and surely everything after it would be like the loosing of a deep, held breath. But it did not happen that way. I slept, or did not sleep, but lay looking at the midsummer sky, with its heavy grey storm clouds.

Yesterday morning, in a fit of restlessness, I put the princess on my hip and walked out my door. Sildio sprang from his stool. I don't think I've ever seen him so surprised. I told him to close his mouth and added that I was going out. We went through the keep, the princess and I, and down into to the central courtyard, where a troop of players and artisans from the north had set up their tents. I watched the child's sightless eyes roll as they followed all the sounds: the fire-weavers' hissing patterns and the actors' strange, swirling words. These things distracted me too, so that now and then I thought, *I have not worried about my writing in minutes!* with a start of surprise and relief. When we returned to the room I was exhausted and achy (my body hasn't been the same, since I was ill last spring), but still restless.

This morning I woke to rain pouring in through my partly-open shutters.

Time is passing. I am making this Pattern by *not* making it, and it is knitting around me, and I do not want it to be this way. So I am ready, again, to write the Path behind and then to walk the one ahead.

I remembered, in my newest cell—a tiny room with no windows and a door made of oak that shuddered when it closed. There was nothing to do here except remember.

I remembered how Teldaru had frowned at Haldrin and said, "I don't know what you mean. Who *is* this girl?" And then, when the king explained, how Teldaru said, "She must be mad."

"She doesn't look mad." The king searched my face, which had gone as numb as the rest of me.

"Hal." Teldaru looked regretful. (*Teldaru*, I thought, over and over, the word a heartbeat under my own.) He was absolutely clean-shaven. No tiny red-gold hairs to catch the sun or scratch along my forehead. "You've seen it before: people unable to bear the weight of their own power. People who desire the Otherworld but cannot stand its glow."

I laughed. It was more of a cackle, and it would not help me—except that Haldrin, still gazing at me, said, "Yes, I've seen such people. But she's different. She . . ." *He will do it*, I thought as he looked at me. *He will understand. He wants to.*

"What is your name?" he asked me.

I turned to Teldaru. "Why don't *you* tell him?" I said, then laughed again at his regretfully shaking head and his regretfully uncomprehending eyes.

"He knows," I said to the king. "I didn't know his, but he always knew mine. I am Nola. I am also Mistress Hasty Seer and Mistress Overcurious Seer and . . ." A broken breath, nearly a sob—and no, I *must not* cry.

"Nola," said the king.

I heard things, from my cell. Muffled footsteps and voices; laughter and shouting.

It's the opposite of the house, I thought as I stared up at the ceiling plaster. *There I had space and it was full of things, but empty of people. Empty rooms and an empty garden beyond them. Here I have nothing but a pallet and a chair and a lantern, but the world is right on the other side of my door. I can hear it. I can smell it, onions and bread and meat—Laedon's kitchen—or was Laedon also a lie?*

"Nola," the king said again. "Teldaru will take care of you."

"No." I sounded quite reasonable now, which was strange, since there was a knot of screaming in my chest.

"Yes." Teldaru took a step toward me. Borl barked, once. "You are an Otherseer. You are unwell. I will find somewhere quiet and private and I will tend to you."

"Is there anyone we can tell?" Haldrin said. "Any family in the city?"

I saw: it was so simple, the way out. "Yes," I said quickly, "Bardrem—he lives at the brothel where I—"

"Good." Teldaru nodded briskly. "We will find him and tell him where you are." He smiled at me—concerned, reassuring.

"No you won't," I said, even more quickly, so that Haldrin would hear at least some of my words, "you'll *say* you've looked for him and then you'll say you couldn't find him, or maybe that you found him and he didn't care, and everyone will believe you because—"

"You see?" Teldaru's voice was louder than mine. He lifted both hands, shrugged, quirked his brows again, at the king. "She is raving. But she is lucky that her madness led her here, for there would be nothing but misery for her in the city. She is lucky, too, that she is young. Young and strong."

I could not look away from him. (*Teldaru Teldaru Teldaru* said my pulse.)

"Come with me now . . . Nola." He said my name like a question, as if he might have got it wrong. "We will begin by finding you a more appropriate dress. And some food."

"I'm not hungry," I said. "And why don't you like my dress? You gave it to me."

I thought, *I could reach up and unhook the lantern and smash it against the wall.* I imagined flames catching on the bedclothes and mattress and on my clothes as well, beginning with the hem of my plain brown skirt. They would have to open my door then. They would pull me out, coughing and blistering—or, even better, Borl would pull me out with his jaws clenched around my flesh or my belt, and Teldaru would say, "Well done, Borl" and pick me up and carry me to another locked room where I would have no light at all.

How long had it been? A day, two? The door had opened several times (keys jingling, bolts sliding)—on him, of course, bringing trays of food that smelled wonderful but tasted like dust. He did not speak to me. He stared at me as I picked at my food (I'd rather not have eaten at all, but after a few days I needed to), and took the corner bucket out to dump its contents somewhere. I blushed, the first few times he did this, but after awhile it was just another thing he did, silently and swiftly.

The first time he spoke, Haldrin was with him. I did not know what time it was, of course, but I was sleeping, and woke to the rattle and slide of the lock and bolt. When I saw the king I struggled to sit up, holding bedclothes around my shoulders, even though I was dressed.

"Nola." The king sat on the chair, pulled close. His tunic was very fine: a deep red stitched with golden thread and studded, at its hem, with tiny circles of copper. The lantern light plucked at him, and his shine made me blink. "How are you?"

"She is—" Teldaru began, but Haldrin stopped him with a glance and a, "She will tell me herself."

Teldaru's scowl was enough; I took a deep breath and said, "I am much better." Sweetly, lightly, as if there were no darkness, no bucket in the corner, no Teldaru standing against the closed door.

The king smiled. "I am glad to hear it."

"Yes," I said. It was difficult to think quickly and speak slowly. "And because I feel so much better, I am wondering when I will be permitted to go outside."

Haldrin looked over his shoulder at Teldaru again. "She has not been out?"

Teldaru shook his head. "She is not ready. The reason she has improved at all is that she's been inside, protected from upheaval and excitement."

"I'm fine now." My voice was climbing. "I am. I would like to go out, please. My king."

"She really should not." Teldaru was still speaking evenly. That regretful expression—but his black eyes were on me, and I felt them like weight, like cold. "She is right: she has improved. And when I am certain that she is strong enough, she will leave this room. But not before then." He lowered his voice, murmured, "And Hal, you cannot want to risk her standing in the courtyard screaming about . . . well. You cannot want this."

No, I thought as Haldrin turned back to me. *Please.*

"Also," Teldaru continued, "I have selfish reasons for wishing her truly well. I believe she is a strong Otherseer, and I will have much to teach her, when she is ready. And isn't this what you want, Nola?" He smiled; the wolf with jewelled teeth. "Isn't this really what you've always wanted?"

I sat. I was squeezing the sheets so tightly that I could not feel my fingers.

"Very well." The king rose. The chair scraped along the flagstones. "But only a little longer, Daru, yes? We don't want to weaken her in a different way by keeping her from sunlight, and from other people."

They left together. The bolt slammed home.

Teldaru returned alone not long after.

I pressed my back against the wall and wrapped my arms around my pulled-up legs. I prepared to watch him watch me from across the room as he usually did—but he took three long strides and was there with me, kneeling on the edge of my pallet.

"I couldn't do this before," he said, softly. "Couldn't come near you, speak to you. I knew that if I did, I would kill you." He took a strand of my hair, rubbed it between his fingers. Hooked it gently behind my ear. "And I did want to kill you, Nola. Especially when I first saw you in Haldrin's study and realized what you had done. But I commanded myself to wait. To be calm. Because you will serve me even better, now, than you would have before."

"I will not," I said, my voice low and steady.

He seemed not to have heard me. "How did you do it? How did you get out of the house?"

I smiled at him; showed him my teeth and my narrowed, gleaming eyes. I said nothing.

He shrugged. "It does not matter. You are mine."

"I am not," I said, and he threw his head back and shouted a laugh.

"Oh, Nola! Mistress Defiant Seer. It will be such a pleasure to break you."

He leaned forward. There was nowhere for me to go; I twisted my upper body, ground my cheek against the wall. He grasped my chin and pulled it slowly around. I was facing him and he was closer, the dark water of his eyes moving, moving. Closer yet—and his mouth was on mine, warm and sweet. I felt a brush of teeth and tongue against my own closed lips. I thought of Bardrem kissing me beneath the courtyard tree. *Carrots*, I thought desperately, *and porridge; he tasted like that. He*, Bardrem, *so thin and bony*—but it was just a memory, weak and slippery and gone.

"Nola." Teldaru's lips slid along mine, and down to the hollow of my throat. He must have been able to feel my blood throbbing there, beneath, giving me away as my rigid arms and neck did not. "Dearest girl." I felt his teeth and his breath and they tickled and I *had* to squirm, had to moan a little, as if I were some other girl without will. I felt him smile. He drew back slowly, traced my mouth with his thumbs. My mouth was wet and my skin was hot—probably glowing with heat, though my insides were so cold.

He rose and looked down at me. He was not smiling any more. "It begins tomorrow," he said, and turned away.

CHAPTER SEVENTEEN

He brought a mirror and a knife. So much gold: the mirror and its filigree rim; the knife's hilt; the sleeves and hem of his tunic. His hair.

"So will I be playing Laedon, and you me?" I spoke lightly (I'd been practising) and held out my arm, turned so that its pale, smooth inside was toward him. My veins branched, green and swollen-looking; I could almost feel them, aching as my chest was.

He was silent for a long time—so long that my arm began to tremble. I lowered it. *Idiot girl,* I thought. *Idiot,* idiot; *be quiet now, and wait like he does.*

"I have stories to tell you." His voice was gentle. My flesh rose in goosebumps, as if he had touched me. "Like our lessons at the house—only these will be far more diverting for both of us." He ran his finger over the filigree and gazed at me. I said nothing, this time, though I wanted to. "I won't listen!" I wanted to cry, and I swore to myself that this was true, that I would somehow have the strength to deafen myself to his words. "Just do whatever you intend to do!"—another shout that never left my throat. "Just hurt me and be done with it. . . ."

"The first story is about girls." He grinned. I wondered, wildly, if I would be able to use the even, glinting surfaces of his teeth to Othersee. "All stories are, I suppose. But these girls . . . Sisters. A princess and a seer." He turned the knife over and it made a quiet clinking sound against the mirror. "Zemiya and Neluja. Strange, savage names, no? Like your Yigranzi's. Dark-skinned island girls, like your Yigranzi." Another smile, this one slower. "I left just a little of her; did you like that? Just enough for lingering and pain. But those others, now. Those sisters from Belakao."

Zemiya was bold and Neluja was shy; you could see this right away.

Teldaru was fourteen and Haldrin was nine and they had been waiting all morning for the Belakaoan delegation to arrive. Which it finally did, around noon. The Belakaoans must have planned it for this time because they wanted the sun to be at its brightest, to catch all the colours. Haldrin was far too obvious about his excitement, as always—jumping from foot to foot, leaning halfway over the tower wall, waving at the procession as if he knew them all. When his nurse scolded him he pouted, but a few minutes later he was leaning out into the air again, babbling back at Teldaru. "Daru, look at that—the big man must be the king, but he's wearing a sleeping shift! And those fans—they're so shiny—are they made of shells? Their clothes are so green—and I've never *seen* that kind of green before; it's more like yellow, but not exactly. Their skin is even darker than I thought it would be. Daru, Daru—look at those drums! How have they carried them so far? Why didn't they sink the boats? I'm so glad they're not our enemies any more!"

Teldaru noticed the sisters then, even before the delegation arrived in the Great Hall. He did not know they were sisters, nor did he know their names, as he stood at the tower's top, but forever after he remembered: Neluja was tall and slim and staring straight ahead of her. The cloth over her hair was dark orange, tied in a knot at the back of her neck. Zemiya, beside her, looked as if she was dancing. She was shorter than her sister, but was more like a woman: high, full, firm breasts, high, full, firm buttocks; her legs all curves over muscle. There was a wind, so it was easy to see these details: the cloth of her long, shapeless dress kept blowing and clinging. Her hair was tied with jewelled ribbons into what seemed like hundreds of little knots. She was looking everywhere—even up, at the Sarsenayans who were waiting. Her teeth gleamed, far too white, surrounded by her skin that was far too brown.

There was much talking, in the Great Hall. The Belakaoan king (*moabu*, as they called him) spoke Sarsenayan with an accent that sounded like poured honey, which made the familiar words difficult to understand. Teldaru hardly listened, anyway (first official visit . . . years of hostility followed by years of friendship . . . trade, trade, trade . . .)—until the *moabu* introduced the girls.

"*Moabe* Zemiya," he said, and the knot-haired one stepped forward, smiling her too-white smile. "My youngest child. And *ispa* Neluja, my second youngest." The tall one also stepped forward, but she did not smile. "My son is at home. He is sixteen, old enough to play at ruling for awhile." The big man turned his eyes to Teldaru and Haldrin, who were standing together, as they always did, at the foot of King Lorandel's throne. "And these," the *moabu* said, "must be the sons of the king of Sarsenay."

King Lorandel shook his head. "No, brother king. Not both—just this one—Haldrin. He is my only child. I lost two others to fever, years ago, before the death of my queen. No, this"—gesturing at Teldaru, who was glad he was standing beside Haldrin, so short and slight even with his riot of white-gold curls—"is Teldaru. He is an Otherseer—a student—and a great favourite of his teacher, and of my son."

Teldaru's teacher, old man Werwick, glowered. He was mean-spirited, and probably hated Teldaru nearly as much as he hated Belakaoans.

"Otherseer," said the *moabu*, and frowned into his bushy black beard.

"Visions," Werwick snapped. "Of future time, or past time."

The *moabu* smiled and set one enormous hand on his daughter Neluja's shoulder (he had to reach up to do this). "Ah! *Ispu*. And she is *ispa*. Visions, yes."

"Well, then!" Lorandel said as Werwick, beside him, turned an unhealthy shade of red. "Two royal children and two seers! They must go off together and share these things—perhaps to the seers' courtyard. Haldrin, Teldaru: show the girls the way."

The seers' courtyard: so lovely, with its trees, its pool, its snaking pathways.

"Are these your biggest trees?" Zemiya, her hands on her hips (cloth pulling taut over curves).

"Yes," said Haldrin. He was staring up at her—such a child, so innocent and protected—he had never seen any of the horrors Teldaru had, in the lower city.

"Hmph." Zemiya was walking now. Neluja was behind them all, her face raised to the sky. "And this," Zemiya went on, pointing to the pool, "is it your only water?"

"We have wells too," Haldrin said, "and fountains, and there's a river just outside the city, and—"

Zemiya laughed. The first of her many laughs—low and throaty and scornful.

"You speak Sarsenayan very well," Teldaru said, as Haldrin scuffed at the path with his toe.

"Of course. Our father has us learn the languages of all the countries we'll conquer."

"Zemiya." Neluja sounded tired.

"Really?" Teldaru said. "And how will you conquer them? With sharpened shells and fierce warrior fish?"

The whites of her eyes were like her teeth: *unnaturally* white, as if some artist had made them out of polished marble. The centres of her eyes were dark brown and black. Her lashes were very thick, and she batted them at him. "Come to Belakao," she said with cloying sweetness, "and I will command our minstrel fish to sing for you."

He tried to smile back at her, casually, but the smile felt more like a grimace. He was angry—had been angry since he saw her dancing up to the castle gate as if she had always known Sarsenay. A spoiled Belakaoan girl—what had she ever known but island savagery? "There are fish here," he said, gesturing to the pool. He was speaking to Neluja now. "You can only see them at night."

"Then perhaps I will come tonight to see them," Zemiya said. When she looked down—with false coyness, as she was doing now—her eyelashes were invisible against her skin.

He waited for her until long after the moon had set. He waited and felt like a fool—for the longer he sat by the pool, the more it might seem that he wanted her to come. At last he stood, disgusted with himself and furious at her—for she had never intended to come; had only wanted him to—

"*Ispu* Teldaru."

She was next to him and he had not heard her. Her feet were bare, and her arms too, even though the air was cool and she must be accustomed to hot nights. Her dress was long and dark, but so thin and tight that when she turned to face him he could see her puckered nipples and the hollow of her navel.

"Don't call me that." His voice was too loud, but it did not matter; no one ever came here so late.

"Why not? It's what you are, no? You see time"—she was so close; he smelled the fragrance of a flower he did not know—"you see the currents that drive the great tide, just like Neluja. . . ."

"Currents," he scoffed. "Great tide—you must mean the Pattern."

"Words," she said, leaning even closer. Her breasts were brushing the front of his tunic. Her breath was sweet, or maybe it was her skin—whatever it was, he wanted to take a gulp of pure air that was not there.

But then it was. She stepped away from him. "So where are these fish?" A normal tone, without mystery—though the lilt of her words made him feel dizzy.

"There. Wait; you'll see them."

They were tiny, hard to see at first—but once you'd glimpsed one you saw all the rest, darting, glowing faintly green. When Teldaru had been brought to the castle as a boy, he had sat here for hours, entranced (and he had always fallen asleep at his lessons, afterward).

"Those? *Those* are your wondrous night fish?" She looked at him. The whites of her eyes were greenish, too. He imagined her flashing teeth in the mouth of a much larger fish—something sleek and ugly. "In my country we have crabs that are red under the moon and come up onto the beach in thousands for one night in the storm season. We have—I don't know how you say it—things with long arms and bodies that change colour every time you blink. But," she said, glancing back at the pool, "I suppose your tiny fish are fine. For this sad place, anyway."

"You . . . you can't . . ." he sputtered, clenching his fists, and she laughed. Again that laugh, rich and mocking—and her dark flesh, her woman's hips and breasts that would be dark too, maybe even the nipples, and her strange, dizzying smell—

Her body was soft and hard at the same time. He ran his hands down her back until they were at her hips and then he pulled her up against him. She yielded. She was the one who opened her mouth on his. It was her tongue that forced his lips open. He tasted her and wanted not to; he thrust her dress up until he felt only the muscled smoothness of her thighs, and no Sarsenayan girl had felt like this—none of the many who had yielded to him before, in the lower city or in the beds of the castle. She made a low, growling noise that he felt in his own mouth and through his chest. He pushed her dress higher and one of his hands found her breast, and he did not *want* to, but he had to taste it too—had to move his head away and down—

Pain. Her fingers raking his cheek; her teeth tearing at his neck. He shouted and stumbled backward. For a moment she was before him, standing tall, taking up all his vision—some terrible night beast, glinting and dark. Then she spun and ran.

※

"She ran from me. She knew, even then, that she should fear me."

"I don't believe you," I said. "I don't believe anything you tell me."

Teldaru pouted, though his eyes were grinning. "You don't? Truly? Well, this pains me terribly—for is it not important and comforting to be believed?"

He seemed to be expecting an answer. I stayed silent.

"As a seer, Nola, would you not say that others' belief in your words is vital?" Still silent. I thought I was managing to keep the confusion from my face.

"You will understand," he said—for he saw it, of course. My confusion, and probably also my fear. "Soon. When you are transformed, and after I have told you more stories."

He set mirror and knife on the floor and rose. There was a length of rope in his hand. Perhaps he had had it in the pouch at his belt, or perhaps it had been under the mirror—but it was the first I had seen of it, and its appearance seemed like some kind of enchantment.

When he sat beside me on the pallet I saw that it was, in fact, two lengths of rope, one longer than the other. "Do not struggle," he said, "and do not scream. No one will come."

He bound my ankles. I did not move while he knelt by me, doing this, but when he lifted the shorter rope to my hands I lunged at him, snapping my teeth. He drew swiftly back and I laughed, giddy, terrified, trying not to care. "I would like Zemiya," I said, and then he slapped me so hard that I could not say anything else.

He knotted the rope around my wrists very tightly, but I did not wince. He bound them behind my back, which hurt my shoulders and neck terribly, right away. I stared at him, when he was done. A trussed animal awaiting the knife— which he lifted, along with the mirror, and brought back to me.

"Now then, Nola," he said, and sliced my dress from neck to waist.

My shoulders, my belly, the tender place beneath my breasts. He touched them lightly, tracing lines and circles with the knife's point, his eyes and hand steady. When he finally cut, he did it so gently that I thought there should be no pain, somehow—but it was vast and red. I screamed, because the pain made me forget my defiance, but no one came. "The girl is mad," he had probably said to whoever might have passed by the door. "All my efforts with her will be in vain if we are interrupted. Do not come near, no matter what you hear from within."

I stopped screaming and panted, instead. I gazed down at my blood, which looked darker than any shade of red, in the dimness. Snakes and ribbons; paths on my skin. I wondered briefly whether he would see my Paths in the same way as I had seen Laedon's. Whether they would look like roads, or like things

I'd never seen. Then I wondered nothing, for he was bending over the mirror, angling it so that I was in its gold, and his black eyes were fixed and Other.

I had never watched him Othersee. In all our lessons, all those months, I had never seen him do this. I watched him now. He was so still, every angle and hollow of him breathing lamplight. He was beautiful. Far away, seeing me as I had never even seen myself—and my heart pounded with more than pain, more than fear.

The first sensations are flutterings, deep beneath the wounds. Tiny creatures beating their wings, making my stomach lift and fall. That's him, I think, and my pulse sends tingling waves to the ends of my fingers and toes and the roots of my hair. Very quickly the fluttering becomes a scraping, which eases its way along my bones and my veins. I moan a long, low note that does not change, and the vibration helps a little. He is pulling. Though his body does not move, he is drawing something within me, slow and hard. I fall to my side on the pallet. I fold into myself and arch out again, rubbing my cheek on the rough blanket. He is knotting, snipping, burning ends until they crumble like spent wicks. My vision is clouding. He blurs in the light and the gold swims up and around him. I clench my eyes shut and see nothing but orange-tinted darkness, but it does not matter: he is everywhere, inside and out. All the pain is one. Take me, I think, and it does, in a surge of deeper darkness.

When I opened my eyes I knew that it was much later, though I didn't know how I was so certain of this. The lamp's flame was flickering lower. I was numb, but also shuddering. I watched my legs buck and thrash on the blanket. My toes dug and curled. I felt nothing; I was here but gone.

Teldaru was slumped against the wall by the door. The chair was lying on its side between us. He was looking at me, almost without blinking.

"What . . ." My voice and my eyes—all I had from before. I had no idea how I found them. "What did you do? What did you change?"

He did not answer for so long that I thought, *He is paralyzed . . . he is dying . . .* But then a corner of his mouth lifted, and an eyebrow. "Mistress . . . Hasty," he said. His voice was even rougher than mine, and as thin as smoke. "You'll see. When I'm done."

"Done?" I whispered, and I closed my eyes again so that I would not have to see his smile.

CHAPTER EIGHTEEN

I felt no different. After the numbness had passed, there was fire—fever under my skin; I wondered why it did not blister—but a few days after that I was myself again. Everything was as it had been: Teldaru brought me my food and dealt with the bucket, and he did not speak to me, and I did not speak to him. All I could think when I looked at him was, *What have you done to me?*—but I never said this. I waited to wake one morning and discover that I was lame, or that my hair had all fallen out, or (and this seemed the likeliest, the longer I thought of it) that I was blind, but every morning I was just the same as ever. I almost convinced myself that I had imagined his "When I'm done." Perhaps I had been dreaming; perhaps he was finished, and whatever he had tried to do to me had failed. I almost convinced myself. But when he appeared one day with the mirror, the ropes and the knife, I was not surprised.

"How do you feel?" he said, quite solicitously (after all the previous days of silence).

I glared at him.

"I need to know," he went on, "because how you feel now may affect what I—"

"I feel fine. And how are you?"

I saw him frown, just for a moment, before his smile returned. "I am glad you are well. This means we are ready to continue." He stretched his legs out in front of him and moved his feet back and forth, back and forth, lazily. "We will begin, as before, with a story."

"About Zemiya?" I asked brightly, sitting up very tall with my hands clasped in my lap.

If I had hoped to annoy him again, it did not seem to work. "Yes," he said smoothly. "And about Ranior and Mambura."

I was so surprised that I spoke before I remembered that I should not show any true interest. "What?"

"Yes—Ranior, who united the quarrelsome tribes of Sarsenay, three hundred years ago, and raised this great keep above a cluster of huts—and Mambura, the island savage who slew him before himself being slain—"

"Everyone knows about this"—so many statues and paintings, books and poems, and the great midsummer procession.

"Well, then. A story about Ranior and Mambura—and Zemiya too, and Neluja, and their green islands and blue ocean. I went there with Haldrin's family, you see. When I was eighteen."

Teldaru was seasick. Haldrin was too, but only for the first day; Teldaru was rushing to the ship's side up until the last morning of the journey. He hated the water—the pure, clear water that was as green as it was blue, in patches that stretched like ribbons around the ship. He had hated the water off Sarsenay, as well, which had been rough and grey—but this was worse. So calm, so beautiful, and yet still he retched until his ribs ached, while Haldrin made maddening, comforting noises beside him.

He felt much thinner when he alit on Belakaoan soil. He held himself very tall, though, amidst the drums and dancers, with their gem-encrusted hair and clothes. He thrust his shoulders back, because they were quite broad now, just as his chest was. And Zemiya noticed. She stood on a ledge that jutted from one of the painted, patterned black rock spurs that seemed to act as houses, here, and she looked him up and down with a slow and hungry smile. He looked back at her—such smooth, dark curves; and he could almost smell her—and smiled himself, triumphantly.

She had apparently forgotten to fear him. Perhaps her desire was too great for caution. He woke on the first night to her hands on him. Her hands and then her lips, warm and wet on his belly, trailing down as her fingers did. He was awake; this was glaringly obvious, though he kept very still. She lifted her head and he saw the white flashes of her teeth and eyes.

"You are more handsome than you were," she said in that throaty, accented voice that made his people's words into a new language. He lifted himself onto his elbows, about to say something commanding, even harsh, but she rose and gazed down at him. Her lips were still wet. He was wet—bathed in sweat that made his pale skin shine.

"Now it is time for me to show you *my* water," she said, "and *my* fish"—and she disappeared beneath the jagged arch of door.

He commanded himself to stay where he was.

He rose and followed her.

He rushed along the tall, crooked hallway, past the room where Haldrin would be sleeping, down the twisting steps that led out into the night. She was a shadow among the black rock spires, but he never lost sight of her. The jewelled ribbons in her hair caught the moonlight. They winked down a slope that was covered in creepers and onto the black-rock beach. She climbed swiftly over the rock with her bare feet; he had to pick his way, feeling for pits and bumps. His slowness annoyed him—but better to be slow than to sprawl at those bare feet of hers like a clumsy child.

"There," she said when he was finally standing beside her, on a rock that made him a head shorter than she was. "Look."

Dark water. The Sarsenayan ship lifting and falling, the only familiar thing in emptiness. Flickers of fire in the distance that he could not measure with his eye or his mind. He said nothing, determined to betray no interest.

"Your awe makes you silent," she said. He could hear the insolent grin in her voice. "I understand."

He snorted. "What is there to say about so much water?"

"And what of its shining"—long, iridescent streamers, he saw, fluttering pink and green; tentacles, scales?—"and the flames?"

"What *of* the flames?"

"How thoughtful of you to ask. The flames are new islands—fire mountains . . . volcanoes, rising up from the sea. Belakao is always being born." He felt her fingers tracing his eyebrow and then his cheekbone and then his jaw. "That is why we are so strong. Our land is always young."

"Ha!" he said, leaning his head away from her hand. "But what of the wisdom of maturity? My land is ancient and wise and made of stone and wood, so you can *see* what it is you're ruling. This," he went on, waving an arm at the darkness, "is nothing."

He looked up at her, waiting for a blow or a bite or at least some shrieking. He was dizzy with need.

She did not speak. She stared at him. Waves sloshed over the rock, and the volcanoes across the water sent tremors up through his feet, and the iridescent streamers flickered. He waited—but it was not Zemiya who spoke next.

"Zemiya-*moabene*." Neluja said something else in her own language, but Teldaru hardly heard it; he was gaping at the bird beside her. A creature that stood as tall as her waist, with glossy feathers whose colours he could not see well, in the moon-dark. It gazed back at him, its head cocked. Its beak glinted like a blade.

"I will guess," Zemiya said to him (having apparently ignored her sister's words), "that your birds in Sarsenay are small and brown."

He would have reached for her, as he had four years before, if it had not been for Neluja. Instead he hissed, "We could crush your island bones, if we wanted to. If the king didn't need your gems and cloth and horrible fruit—if your father offered the same insults to him that you offer me, we would drive you and all your people into the sea; you would drown in your own hateful water."

He was panting. The bird made a rough, low sound and Zemiya smiled at it and then at him, her eyes narrowed to slits.

"Yes? How interesting. Because I believe we Belakaoans know some other truth." She looked away from him, at the shifting, flame-spotted distance. She was biting her full, dark lower lip.

"And what other truth is that?" he asked.

"Your people believe in words of future time. In the pictures you see for them."

"Visions," he said. "Prophecies—yes."

"Well, we have a . . . prophecy here. A vision seen by an *ispa* long ago. It was of your country and mine."

"Zemiya," Neluja said, slowly and clearly, "what are you doing?"

Again her sister paid her no heed. "The greatest Belakaoan *moabe* of all history was Mambura, Flamebird of the Islands. Yours was Ranior. The . . . War Hound. They fought. They died together, in your country." The sound of these words in her mouth made Teldaru dig his fingers into his palms. "The prophecy was: the cold stone country will only conquer the islands when bird and dog rise again. Only," she said, speaking faster, "if another, new, great leader brings them together in battle will your Sarsenay prevail." She smiled once more, while the real bird trilled a long, sweet note. "So you see: this will never happen."

"No," he said. "It could. If your seer saw it, it could."

"I do not think so," said Neluja quietly. Her hand was cupped over the bird's head. She was looking at Zemiya. He wished there were light, so that he could see what was passing between their eyes.

"Maybe *ispu* Teldaru is right," Zemiya said. "Maybe his small friend Haldrin will be the next great leader, and maybe he will wave his small magic hand and bring back these dead."

"Maybe *I* will." Teldaru spoke in a rush, and he stood taller—as tall as he could, on the rock that still made him shorter than her. "Maybe I will be the great leader."

She tipped her head back and laughed. He saw her closed eyes and the line of her throat, her arched back and her breasts, pressing against thin, taut cloth. The bird clacked its dagger beak as if it, too, were laughing.

"Mambura and Ranior and Teldaru," he said as she wiped at her eyes with the backs of her hands. The names were right together; they filled him with such certainty and strength that he felt as if he were partly in the Otherworld, surrounded by what would be. "You won't be laughing then."

***

"She was lying," I said. "She made it up just so she could mock you."

"No." His eyes seemed more golden than black, as if they had changed to match the knife that waited upon the mirror. "Listen."

***

"No," Zemiya said, "I will no doubt be weeping, begging you for mercy while your Dog bares his teeth at our Flamebird and my people flee and scream. Yes, I'm sure that is how it will happen, Great Teldaru."

"*Zemiya.*" He had never heard Neluja speak with such force. "Do not play with words of *isparra*. Do not—" And then her own words were Belakaoan, thick and rich and angry.

The sisters argued, Zemiya gesturing, Neluja glaring down at her, twisting her hands in the loose fabric of her dress. Teldaru was gazing at her hands, thinking how long her fingers were, when the bird leaned forward and bit him.

He had been bitten by dogs before, and by cats, and by a chicken that Laedon had told him to kill. He had also been cut by knives, in Laedon's kitchen and in the lower city, when he had been a poor boy serving rich, drunk men. The bird's beak cut him like those knives had, except even more smoothly. The flesh of his forearm parted. He watched his blood well and flow. He blinked and then he felt the pain, and he lunged at the bird with a strangled cry.

"No!" Zemiya was between him and the creature. She held his shoulders, and her arms were dark, rounded muscle. "Uja has marked you for *isparra* and now my sister must look." She was gazing past him at Neluja, her eyes bright with excitement or maybe triumph.

"Look?" he shouted. "What do you mean?"—because he did not yet know about Bloodseeing. Because this was the first time.

"I must look at you as *ispa*." Neluja was where Zemiya had been, though she did not touch him. He thought, *Run!* but did not.

"You mean you will Othersee?" he said. "You can't!" Relief, as warm as the blood. "You can't do that unless I tell you to."

She lifted his arm. Put her finger in his blood and drew it over the skin above his elbow, which was still clean. She made spirals and waves with fingertip dots between. "I can," she said, and raised her eyes to his.

Werwick had looked at Teldaru's Pattern when the boy had first been brought to the castle; Othersighted children were always examined like this when they arrived. But Teldaru had asked him to, and had felt nothing—only watched in fascination as the old man's eyes turned an even darker black and bulged, along with a vein in his forehead. Afterward Werwick had drunk an entire pitcher of water and said, in a quavering voice, "I see greatness. The child must stay."

But now, staring into the black-and-pearl of Neluja's Otherworldly eyes, he felt a tremor in his gut—a swell like anger or desire that moved without his control. He bit his lip until he tasted blood—blood everywhere, in his mouth and on his skin and dripping onto the black stone beneath them. The bird Uja was moving its wings in a gentle, sweeping way that made him want to glance at it, but he could not. Neluja was all.

She cried out. Took two steps back and stumbled to her knees on the rock.

"Neluja?" Zemiya said. "*Ispana* Neluja . . ." She bent over her sister, frowning, stroking her forehead. Teldaru sat down heavily. He felt breathless and sick and did not understand—and then Neluja spoke in a torrent of words he also did not understand, while the bird clacked and cackled.

"What?" he said roughly. "*What*?"—high and loud, above the other noise.

Three pairs of eyes on him. A quiet of waves and his own ragged breathing.

He stood slowly and looked at them. He was finally taller, finally strong, and they shrank from him just as Werwick had, all those years ago.

"It's true, isn't it?" he said. "Mambura and Ranior and Teldaru."

Zemiya swallowed. "I don't believe it," she said.

He laughed.

"I don't believe it, either." I knew there would be pain, soon, and I wanted to provoke him, wanted to keep him talking. He rose, ropes and mirror and knife in his hands.

"But you will," he said, smiling. "You will, when you help me remake the Patterns of Mambura and Ranior."

I gaped but made no sound.

"Ah," he said, shaking his head, "I have leapt ahead again, when there is much to do first. To do now." He was in front of me, looping, tying, tightening. He undid the laces of my bodice and stepped back to look at me.

"You are mad," I whispered.

He bent and kissed both my breasts—and then he raised the knife.

CHAPTER NINETEEN

I kept bleeding, after that second time. I slipped in and out of consciousness, aware sometimes that the pain was just as burning and numbing as it had been the first time; aware that Teldaru was sitting where he had been before, sprawled, staring at me. Aware of little else. I was heavy, which was new. I could hardly move at all, even after Teldaru had gone and the numbness had mostly passed. I lay and half-slept and was too deeply weary to wonder what was wrong.

I woke fully when he started to shake me. A day later, maybe, when he came with my food? "Nola!" Shouting and shaking, and then he rolled me over and gave a ragged, fearful cry.

There was much coming and going, after that. Teldaru, and someone with cool, slender hands and a blonde braid that swung beside my head. They put cloths on me—on my forehead and below my breasts, where he had cut me. Poultices, too, which were so hot that I yelled. Bandages wrapped so tightly around my ribs that I thought I would suffocate. They tipped my head up and I drank warm, bitter concoctions that tasted like the mud beneath the courtyard tree would have tasted—and I squeezed my eyes shut and saw Bardrem's feet in the mud, and Yigranzi's lumpy fingers polishing her mirror, and snow falling on Chenn's head—so cold on my feverish skin and on my tongue.

And then one day I woke and everything was clear again.

"So." Teldaru was sitting beside me. I could see his crossed legs and his hands clasped over his knee. I felt much better and could have turned my head to look at his face, but I did not. "I just had an extremely awkward exchange with the king. He heard about all the commotion, somehow, and came to ask about it—tried to come in to see you, in fact. I convinced him that you were finally resting peacefully and should be left alone." A pause. My belly grumbled loudly, as if it had no idea that the rest of me was upset. "I also told him that you had broken one of your food bowls, which I had foolishly left you alone with. That you sliced yourself open and nearly bled to death."

"I wish I had." I did turn, then, and gazed up at him. His face was almost as still as if he were Otherseeing. "You should be more careful with crockery," I said, and he smiled.

"You'll be relieved to hear that I won't require a blade, this last time."

"Last time?" I said.

"It seems," he continued, as if he had not heard me, "that your monthly bleeding has begun."

I glanced down at myself. I was under a sheet, and it lay on skin that felt mostly bare—except for strips of cloth around my ribs and between my thighs. "Yes," he said, "I've taken care of you. Arranged things so that you'll be clean and comfortable."

I rolled away from him, pulling my knees up to my chest.

"I know you feel weak and tired, Nola. But we must finish, now. We are so close." I heard the mirror's gold clink against the flagstones as he lifted it. "Look at me, dearest. I need your eyes."

For a long, long moment I stayed as I was. I imagined his hands on me, turning me over, and my naked flesh was hot again, beneath the sheet.

"Nola."

I rolled over.

"Good girl." He laid his palm on my forehead, drew his fingers through my hair. "One more story, first. Just one more." He sat back in his chair. The mirror glinted at me. I saw, only now, that there were shapes in its filigreed rim: leaves and branches and tiny, plump birds.

"I am still eighteen, in this story. Still on Belakao. Does this please you? This time I am in a cavern—a grotto. Imagine: a place between land and sea. A deep, savage, dangerous place."

Neluja stood on the tallest of the black rock spurs that rose from the water. All the other people, Teldaru among them, stood or sat on lower outcroppings. Teldaru stared at the water below—the sea, easing in the daylit entrance of the grotto.

A shaft of sunlight fell upon Neluja. There were openings above, and faces clustered around them. Belakaoans inside and out, waiting.

"You must come to the choosing," the girls' father had told Teldaru. "It is our most sacred time, and it is *isparra*, which is something you know. The others cannot see it, however." Teldaru had glanced at his king's arched brows and at Haldrin's crestfallen frown, and he had nodded at the *moabe*, firmly, trying not to smile.

Now that he was here, though, and the sea was coming in ("the highest tide of the year," the *moabe* had said), and the Belakaoans had fallen silent and were gazing at Neluja and her bird, he felt a quiver of dread in his belly. Zemiya was solemn and still, at her place between her father and brother, and this, too, worried Teldaru. She had refused to tell him what this "choosing" was, other than to say what her father had. Neluja had added, "It is the time of greatest blood-power. The only such time, for the power is hungry, and must be ruled on all other days."

"But what does that *mean*?" he had demanded. They had both blinked at him, silent. Even the bird had blinked at him as if it knew but would not say. He wanted to wring its neck.

Some of the islanders in the grotto looked terrified. Some looked at him with their wide, white-rimmed eyes, and he looked back at them defiantly. *I am Sarsenayan*, he thought. *Whatever this blood-power is, it cannot unman me.* But the water was rising. It was nearly at his feet. It made sucking, seeking noises against the rock and he tried to edge backward, only there were people there, forcing him to stay where he was.

He focused on Neluja because now all the others were. She cried out a long, harsh word and turned to the bird. Laid her hand on the creature's glossy blue head and closed her eyes.

Nothing happened. Nothing except the swelling of the water and someone's rasping, ragged breathing behind him. Nothing—until the bird Uja gave a piercing cry and spread its wings.

It flew. Up to the grotto's roof, where faces gaped at it from safety; down, in a looping, graceful glide. The light from sun and water turned it into a falling spark. Even in the shadows, it glowed. It circled, and some people craned to watch, while others ducked. Teldaru watched—Uja, and Zemiya, who was smiling a little now, and shining in her own way, in cloth of yellow and blue.

Uja passed so close to him that he could have reached up and touched its wing. It gazed at him—deep, steady amber that made him shiver. Then it angled away from him and hovered above a knot of people on the rock to his right. Four of them shrank back; the fifth, a girl no older than ten, lifted her arms and closed her eyes as if she waited, and accepted. Uja landed on the rock, wings beating more and more slowly, until they folded. The girl whispered something, and the men and women behind her huddled even father back, against the pitted rock wall.

Uja walked past the girl. Three stately paces took it to the wall, and the people there. Their eyes widened even more. Someone behind Teldaru sobbed. The bird cocked its head and plucked at a woman's dress. The woman—not old, not young—said three breathless, broken words, and Uja ran its beak along her arm, very gently. Woman and bird made their way over the rock to where Neluja stood. She spoke quietly to the woman, then raised her hands into the sunlight. Her voice rang from the stone. Other voices began to murmur, surging like the waves, and Teldaru wrapped his arms around himself as if this would steady him. The water was washing over his feet now.

The bird touched the woman's arm again, drawing its beak up and down, up and down. The woman turned to look over her shoulder at someone, though Teldaru imagined she would have trouble seeing through her tears. Up and down—and there was blood dripping onto the stone. Neluja said something else and the woman turned back to face her.

The water was at Teldaru's ankles. No one else seemed concerned; they all watched Neluja, their murmuring dread replaced with a silent, strained eagerness. *Surely we won't all die*, he thought, his toes wriggling and gripping. He wished Haldrin were beside him, so that his fear would make Teldaru's into scornful strength.

Neluja lifted the woman's arm and looped her fingers around her wrist. The bird moved to the edge of the rock and lowered its head to its puffed-up chest feathers. Blood fell, almost invisible against black skin. The two women stood gazing at each other as the waves pounded and sprayed. Teldaru shifted. Something must happen soon or he would throw himself at the wall and climb (a fruitless effort, given the angle of the wall, but it would not matter—he simply had to *move*).

The woman's head snapped back. Neluja's black eyes flooded with whorls of pearl. *Isparra*, Teldaru thought, because he could not imagine calling it "Otherseeing." The woman fell to her knees, choking, gripping her own throat. Neluja did not touch her. *And yet she's killing her*, Teldaru thought. His heart hammered at his ribs.

The woman was on her side, her body lashing. Her head hit the rock with a sound that was dull and sharp at the same time. She bumped down the rock slope, flailing. Foam flew from her lips. She came to a stop directly above the water and lay with her gaze fixed on the roof. Liquid too thick and dark for tears oozed from the corners of her eyes. She gurgled and frothed and was silent. The blood-tears kept seeping, over her cheekbones and into the fuzz of her hair.

Neluja picked her way down to the body. She stood looking at it; raised her face and arms and called out a stream of words that sounded both triumphant and sorrowful. She crouched, touched the woman's forehead, cheeks and chin. She held her palms over the eyes and said one more word. Then she pushed.

The body rolled into the waves with a splash that was nearly inaudible. The water took it—tossed, pulled, thrust it against the rock and then away, to the mouth of the grotto. For a few moments the tide breathed it in and out, but soon it was out, only, lost to the open green sea.

Teldaru found Neluja later, at the feast. She spoke first, raising her voice above the drumming and clapping. "You will ask me why, again," she said.

He smiled at her. "I don't care about the why, any more. No—just tell me how."

"She didn't," I said. "She wouldn't."

Teldaru tapped his fingernail against the mirror. "No," he said, "she didn't. But it was enough. I'd witnessed the power of Bloodseeing, and when I returned here I pursued knowledge of it, in books and from other seers."

"Werwick?"

Teldaru grinned. "He nearly fell over when I asked him. Sputtered and spat and turned purple. Which told me all I truly wanted to know—though I did *need* more. The rest I found out from brothel seers who were less concerned with the forbidden-ness of it all. And they gave me other ideas, too, without realizing it. Ideas I put to use once I understood Bloodseeing."

I pressed my hands against my belly. It had been cramping since he began his story, but now the pain had intensified. I remembered the brothel girls I had known; remembered how they had complained about their own cramps and headaches and other monthly troubles. "You started using the Bloodseeing on the girls there," I said. "You killed them. Like Chenn . . ."

He nodded. "I never told her about my nighttime trips into the lower city.

And how fortunate that I did not—for that was where she ran, thinking she was escaping me." He bent so that his face was close to mine. I wanted to shy away from his eyes and I wanted to be lost in them—again, as always. "All those girls, Nola. Their flesh, so solid, yet as thin as paper beneath my knife. Their blood, which I can almost smell. Sometimes I say, 'Come,' and hold out my hand. All of them are poor, and used to fat men, toothless men who scuttle off without paying. But I hold out my hand, with its black glove and bag of coins, and they look from the bag to my face and smile. It is the smiles that excite me most, next to their blood-strength. So full of power, and yet their lips and teeth and sometimes the wet tips of their tongues are all ignorance."

I felt sick. I could not look away from him.

"But how much more profound it is with you," he said. He stroked the curve of my hip, his hand light and warm on the sheet. "Because you know. Because you have already shared my power, and will someday understand it as I do. You are mine in a way none of those others ever were, and now there is only you."

This time he bound my hands in front of me, and not as tightly as before. He did not bind my ankles. Again he sat in the chair, not touching me at all with his body—but again I felt his Otherself inside me like a blade. When I woke up, he was lying on the floor by my bed, his eyes closed and his body limp. I wriggled free of the rope and sat up. This happened very slowly, and I watched him, feeling each breath of mine, each blink, as if it marked a year. I eased my feet to the floor. There were so many different kinds of pain—in my belly, my head, my bones; real pain and Other, which felt just as real—that I could not think. I asked myself no questions, like, "Where will you go, once you open the door?" or "You are naked and bleeding: how will you explain any of this?" The only words in my head were "King Haldrin," and they forced me up, forced me to stand and take enough shaky, tiny steps to get me to the door.

"Nola."

My hand was on the latch. I was trembling so violently that it rattled when I lifted it.

"Nola."

He was up; I felt him behind me. His feet scraped along the flagstones. He was limping, weaker even than I was. I tugged the door open with what little strength I had, and sunlight beat against my eyes and skin. I gulped fresh air and stepped out beyond the doorframe, trying to see, trying to find the muscles that would help me run—but the sun was too bright, and he was right behind me now, his hands at my shoulder and hip, pulling. I was back in the room, and the door was smothering the sunlight, and he was pressing me against the wood, leaning so heavily into me that I could hardly breathe. He lowered his lips and my own lips opened (my shame, my horror—but I must tell all of it); my lips parted and let him in.

"You will not tell," he said. His mouth barely moved against mine. He tasted, smelled, of earth and wine. I bit his lower lip, hard, and he staggered backward. He lifted his hand to his face. I could not see if he was bleeding.

"You will not tell," he said again, his voice muffled by fingers, "because you cannot. The curse is cast."

"I do not care," I said, defiant and bitter. Because I did not understand—not yet.

CHAPTER TWENTY

When Teldaru finally returned to my room, he brought a girl.

She was beautiful. I stared at her green eyes and full, pink lips, and at the dimples that appeared in her cheeks when she looked at him. Her hair hung down her back in a thick blonde braid. My own hair had not been washed since I arrived. The girl stood with her clasped hands resting on the light purple cloth of her dress. I wanted to pull the sheet up over myself, from dirty shift to dirty hair, but I did not.

"Nola, this is Selera."

I said nothing. Selera smiled a false, sweet smile.

"She helped me tend you, when you were so sick."

I remembered the braid, the cool hands; I said, "I know." Then I, too, smiled. "So you know about him, do you?"

Selera glanced at Teldaru. "Know what? That he is the greatest Otherseer who has ever lived? That he is the greatest teacher?"

"Hmm," I said, "yes, of course, all that." I thought about adding, *But are you also aware that he intends to raise Ranior from the dead using Bloodseeing? Ranior and Flamebird Mambura, too, who will fight and probably die again and somehow confirm that Teldaru is, as you've already said, the greatest man who's ever existed?* I said none of this, though; I would wait, speak the words when they would surprise the most.

"And what has he told you of me?" I said, lightly.

Selera's blonde brows drew together and her smooth, white forehead wrinkled. "He has told me of your madness, and of his efforts to cure you."

I laughed. There was a strained giddiness to the sound, which was so appropriate that I laughed harder. "Well done, Master Seer," I gasped at last, gesturing from Teldaru to Selera. "She's perfect."

Teldaru nodded. "She is." Selera's dimples wriggled. "And she is going to help us again, now. She is going to show us whether you have truly been . . . healed."

"Healed," I said. "Is that what you call it?"

Teldaru glanced at Selera apologetically, as if my madness embarrassed him. "You will Othersee for her," he went on, turning back to me. "You will look on her Pattern and tell us what you see."

Selera gasped. "But master . . ." she said. Her hands fluttered at her narrow, silver-belted waist. "This is . . . this would be . . ."

"Forbidden?" He smiled at her. "Of course. You have always been taught that Otherseers should never ask to be seen themselves. You have been taught that this detracts from the Otherseer's power and reputation." He touched Selera's arm with his fingertips and she flushed (prettily, not awkwardly). "But now I ask you to let go what you have learned and serve me in a different way. Will you do this for me, Selera?"

She nodded, her green eyes round, her lips parted on a silent "o."

Then he turned to me. "You will look on Selera's Pattern," he said again, and I felt a rush of excitement I could not quell, despite the confusion and dread that lay beneath it. For what if *this* was the curse? What if he had stripped me of my Othersight, and we were all about to discover it?

I let them see none of these things. I shrugged, said, "Very well. What will I use?"

Teldaru set my metal water bowl down beside the bed. He drew a vial out from his pouch. "Ink on water," he said.

Enough, I told myself; *don't be so nervous; don't be so eager*—but my head hummed and my hands shook a bit, as I reached to reposition the bowl. The water sloshed and settled.

Selera knelt on the other side of the bowl. Teldaru passed her the vial and she tugged the stopper out. "So, mad girl," she said softly, "tell me where my Path will take me." She poured.

Dark spirals and circles, thick, thinning. The Otherworld rising around me in trembling clear waves shot through with crimson.

A wolf, an eagle, a knife, a severed hand; all of these suspended, frozen, until they are swept away in a flood of dark, boiling water. A flood, but soon the water vanishes into baked, cracked earth. Nothing left behind but bones: ribcages and hips and pointing fingers, and one clean, polished skull. A place with no paths, no roads: only the cracks that gape beneath the white sun.

I was on my back. The ceiling wavered and solidified as I blinked. Its surface rippled with the black lines I always saw, after the light of the Otherworld passed. I held my breath for a moment; held the wild, aching, fearful joy of vision.

"She is finished." Selera's voice, far away.

"Yes." Teldaru's, much closer. I breathed out. "Yes—and she will tell us what she saw, now."

He held a cup to my mouth and I took a great, clumsy gulp—wine, bitter, hardly watered at all. I coughed, saw Selera snigger, behind one of her shapely hands.

"Oh, I'll tell you," I said. I thought, *Teldaru's failed: there is no curse. I had this vision—and how I'll enjoy making those awful, pretty dimples disappear when I describe it to her.*

"I saw flowers," I said.

The words echoed in my ears. I wanted to laugh in disbelief, but there was something in my throat—a hollow; a strange, hot lump—I hardly knew what I felt, but it was there.

"I saw three children with golden hair. Two of them had green eyes. The third one's eyes were black."

Selera was gazing at Teldaru, her lips still parted, her own green eyes glowing.

No, I tried to say; *that is not what I saw.* "They were laughing," I said. *No, no, no:* but these words, too, were silent. I heaved myself to my feet, ignoring a surge of dizziness. I stumbled to Teldaru and seized his tunic—two handfuls, right below his shoulders.

"Yes, Nola?" he said mildly, covering my hands with his. "Is there something else?"

What have you done to me? I whirled, faced Selera. *Look at me—surely you see? I will scream; I will throw myself on the floor and scream until King Haldrin comes and I can tell him.*

I did not move, and I made no sound.

"Well?" Selera demanded, frowning. "Is there?"

I said, "No." This false word rose effortlessly over all the true ones.

"She may be mad," Selera said to Teldaru, "but I think I like her visions." She looked back at me. "You will Othersee for me tomorrow."

No. Never again.

"Of course," I said, and bowed my head.

"The most difficult part was first." Teldaru was pacing. He looked at me every time he spun to walk the other way, but he was not seeing me: he was lost in the memory of my Paths, and what he had done to them. "I suffered more exhaustion the second and third times, but it was the first that truly shook me. I had to find so many separate strands—vision and speech, volition and will; all the ones that ran toward your time-to-come. It was excruciating, but I expected this; I've tried such things before, on others. I made mistakes before, but not this time: I knew this even before I brought Selera to you."

Selera was gone. He and I were alone, as we always had been. I was curled on my bed, crying. I did not care that he would see me cry. I hardly noticed it myself, except that now and then I made deep, wrenching noises that shook my whole body.

"*You will see true visions but all the words you speak about them will be false*—I had to find all the roads that would make this possible, Nola! Imagine that! Find all the ones that would threaten this, too, and pinch them out. Burn them black."

He took a long drink from the wine ewer. Wiped the wetness from his mouth with one savage sweep of his arm. "After that it was easier. *You will not be able to refuse a request to Othersee. If the words of command are spoken, you must answer*—nothing terribly difficult about that, once I had altered those first Paths. *You will tell no one of what I have done, or what we will do together* and, *You will never leave me*—these ones were the easiest of all. Though by the time I was finished I hardly had the strength to move. I nearly did not catch you when you ran, you know."

He was seeing me, now. He smiled, knelt by my bed. Drew circles on my cheeks with my tears and his fingertips. "But now you understand: it would not have mattered, if you had escaped me. For if you had tried to tell anyone about me, about what I have been doing—if you had tried to tell the truth, you would have failed."

He lay down beside me. I thrust at him with hands and feet but he did not move, except to draw me against him with his muscle-roped arms.

"I'll break it," I said. *The curse*, I wanted to add, but could not. *I'll break the curse.* He was so close that my own breath was warm on my face.

He chuckled. "Break what, dearest? More crockery? Your arm?" He paused. He rubbed my back, which had stiffened; long, slow strokes, up and down. When he spoke again his voice was serious. "You won't, you know. Not unless you find another seer powerful enough to alter all the Paths I did. Powerful enough to remake them. And how will that happen, if you cannot ask them to?"

"I'll kill you, then."

He wrapped his hand in my hair and pulled until I was looking up at him. His eyes shifted like the black, boiling water of my vision. "If you do, your Paths will stay as they are now. Only I can restore them. No, Nola: if you kill me, you'll forever lose the chance to free yourself."

"You're lying."

"And yet you will not harm me, in case I am not." He ran his hand from my shoulder to my thigh; his thumb kneaded, there.

"I'll kill *myself.*"

He smiled. "You won't. Feel your breath, your skin—you're young, my dear—you won't. But hold your rage close. It makes you beautiful and it makes you strong. And you will need strength, for what we are to do together."

"I'll do nothing." My voice broke on the last word.

"You will—yes, because I will tell you to. And because, if you are very, very good and do as I say, I shall remake your Paths myself."

I wanted to believe him, and he must have seen this on my face. He smiled. "I promise, Nola. If you help me and forgive me, I will undo what I have done. But you must be good." He drew me to him again. I shuddered and gasped the last of my tears, and I listened to his heart, and then, somehow, I slept.

He was still there when I woke. He was sitting on the bed now, with one hand on my hip and the other on a dress. I remembered everything, as I stared at its clean, flat, blue folds and its silk ribbons. I remembered in a rush and thought, *No—that cannot have happened; it cannot be true.*

"Are you hungry?"

I did not look at him. I was terribly hungry—cramping with it—but I said nothing.

"Put the dress on, Nola. We're going outside."

Outside, I thought—and everything else fell away.

He stood and walked to the door. I waited for him to turn his back but he did not, and even this did not matter. I tugged the filthy linen shift up over my head.

"You'll have a new room, of course," he said. "And a bath. Right away." His eyes leapt and lingered and I bent to hide my flush (for apparently it did matter, after all). I picked the dress up and it slipped over my hands like water. I pulled it over my head and let it fall, and I thought of that first dress—the one I had taken from the wardrobe at the house. *So that wasn't really your great-aunt's house*, I would have said, if I could. If the words had not been about his hidden life, and thus unspeakable. *And I already know that Uja isn't really your bird.*

He smiled broadly, as if he had managed to hear what was in my head. "Let me pin your hair up; it's terribly dirty, but this should help."

Outside, I reminded myself as I walked to him. *You're about to go outside; stay calm.* He drew a collection of pins and combs from his pouch. I expected him to fumble with them (as Bardrem had once, when he tried to help Chenn with her hair), but he did not: he inserted them quickly and firmly. When he was done he teased two strands out to fall at the sides of my face. He cupped my cheeks in his hands.

"Good enough," he said. "Now come."

I expected it to be day: dazzling, blinding, like the last time I'd been so close to outside. But the light was soft and indigo, and I only squinted a little bit as I stepped out beyond the doorway. There was a warm wind blowing, and I turned my face into it. It smelled like rain.

"This way."

I hardly heard him. I felt as if I were floating, so light that I noticed nothing but the touch and colour of the air. I suppose I followed him. Trees, a dusk-darkened pool, the stones of the keep—they all flowed past me, or I past them. People, too, their faces gentle and featureless. A sweet, soft, drunken blur, until Teldaru grasped my wrist and squeezed it, hard.

The first face I saw clearly was the king's. He was smiling, though his eyes were worried, as he looked at me (at my gaunt, sallow face and my too-thin body, on which the blue dress hung loose). I smiled back at him. Then I looked around at the hall: a large, dim room lined with tapestries and filled with long tables. No one was sitting on the benches, though there were servants moving about, gathering up plates. I stared at the food on the plates; I could not, in fact, look away.

"Nola. Nola—sit—eat, please. . . ."

I sat. There was a bowl in front of me. A piece of bread in it, and some bean stew that was no longer hot enough to steam, but that warmed my tongue and throat. Haldrin and Teldaru did not speak while I ate. I thought fleetingly of the Lady, and her horror of noisy, voracious eating. I imagined her seeing me now, hunched over a bowl, shovelling food into my mouth in front of the King of Sarsenay and Great Seer Teldaru.

When I was done I straightened on the bench. I was full, and every bit of me, inside and out, wanted me to be happy. But I could not be; I remembered this, truly understood it, even as Teldaru said, "You see, Hal: she has evidently regained her appetite, along with her senses."

The king leaned forward. He was sitting on a dais, upon a wooden throne that was inlaid with whorls of pearl and strips of gold. "Is this true?" he asked me. "Are you feeling well, now?"

Teldaru has cursed me. He is the mad one. He will use his forbidden power to destroy the peace of this land. He is not your friend.

"Yes," I said, "I am."

CHAPTER TWENTY-ONE

I spent three days alone, in the room they gave me. It had coloured glass bottles on its shelves, and little carved wooden boxes. Two horses made of fabric so worn the straw stuffing was coming out. They never quite stood up on their own.

"You'll be interested to know that this was Chenn's room," Teldaru said from the doorway, that first time. I think he expected me to be afraid, or at least unsettled. I might have been, if it had been night. But the sunlight was shining past the open shutters and onto the blue and red glass bottles, and the horses seemed to be smiling lopsided smiles. I smiled too, and said, "Good."

So for three days I was by myself in this room. I threw the door and shutters wide, even at night, when the air was early-winter sharp. There was always a man outside—a succession of men, in fact; Teldaru must have had them on a schedule. They wore no armour, but their thick necks and bulging shoulders would have revealed them as soldiers, even if the short swords at their sides had not. They began by standing, tensing whenever I appeared. I would glare at them, then turn to look out at the seers' courtyard. I only ever looked—at the other small, stone rooms that clung, like mine, to the red wall; at the drifts of fallen leaves and the bare branches above them; at the sky. Especially at the young people who would gather at their own doors and out under the trees. Two boys, two girls: it seemed that Teldaru had told me the truth of this, anyway, when he had still been Orlo. They stood, singly or in a group, and stared at me—Selera most often, though thankfully she did not come too close. She made a show of whispering to the others, and her rolling eyes and scornful smile were obvious enough—but I was not sure what I saw in the faces of her companions. I showed all of them—guards and youths—an expression of defiant helplessness. *See*, my eyes and straight, stiff body said, *I am not afraid, but I am also frozen here. I could not move quickly, even if I truly wanted to.*

The guards seemed to believe this, for they all began to relax. They leaned and watched me with hooded, careless eyes, and I thought, *Yes, you think this. Think that I will just stand here forever.*

Because I meant to run.

At first I was too tired to think about this with any precision. I simply knew I would reason it out when I could. But before I could, Teldaru came for me.

He had not appeared at all, those first three days. A silent, stooped woman had come instead, with my food, and to take me (escorted by whichever guard was nearby) to the dark, dank outbuilding I was now permitted to use, rather than a bucket in the corner. I had tried not to think at all about Teldaru, and I really only failed at night, when every scraping branch or pacing guard became him, coming to me again in darkness.

He came at noon. I had just eaten and was sitting on the chair by the desk. (There was nothing inside it: no papers, no quills or ink. Nothing that could help me, now that my own voice could not.) I saw him when he walked out of the naked trees, along the path of tiny white stones. He was wearing a deep red cloak that he twitched at, every few strides, to keep it from tangling in his legs. Borl loped beside him, his tongue lolling. Teldaru nodded to the guard, and then his eyes found me. He did not smile, and my insides clenched. I knew what his smiles meant; his smooth, expressionless face could mean anything.

"Good," he said when he was in my room. "You're dressed and you've eaten. We can go."

"Where?" I did not want to speak to him, of course, but I needed to know this.

"To the history lesson room. It's time you met the others."

I followed him outside, my belly sour with nervousness. Borl rose and planted his legs wide and snarled, showing his pink-and-black mottled gums. I snapped my own teeth at him. "Enough," Teldaru said brusquely, maybe to both of us. He walked, and I hurried to walk beside him. (Borl loped behind, still growling deep in his throat.) We stopped at a building that was nestled in the crook of the courtyard wall. This building had two floors and a much larger door. A great tree stooped in front of it, its branches touching the upper casements. There was a corridor inside, and a flight of smooth, uneven stairs, and a dimness that made me hesitate.

"Up," Teldaru said, and wrapped his fingers around my arm, just above the elbow. He pushed me before him on the stairs, which were unnervingly slanted, worn down and inward by generations of student-seer feet. When we reached the top he put his hand against the small of my back, just as he had when we had crept out of the brothel. He kept his hand there as he rapped at a new door, this one painted green. It opened. Heads and eyes turned to us.

"Master Teldaru!" The teacher was a short, round woman with white hair that had been pulled into an unruly knot. Behind her were a high table, shelves of books, an open window filled with a tangle of bare tree branches. All four students were sitting around the table. There were books open in front of each of them: slender ones with large, colourful pictures for the two boys and thicker ones with only text for the older girls. Sheets of paper too, and quills and ink. My palms began to sweat; I pressed them against my dress.

"We were not expecting you today! But welcome, of course; we were just reciting the twelve laws of the Paleric Age. . . ." Her black eyes leapt from Teldaru to me and back again. I could tell that she did not want to stare, as all the students were, but that she also could not resist.

"Ah," Teldaru said, "the Paleric Age. Excellent." I could hear his smile. His warmest, most relaxed tone; everyone else smiled too, though all of them except Selera lowered their eyes to their books or hands. "You must forgive my interruption, but I have brought someone to meet you. You may have seen her in the courtyard." I thought he had probably watched them there, as they watched me, and whispered. *And now I am one of them*, I thought, with another thrum of eagerness and dread.

"Her name is Nola. Her Otherseeing power is so strong that it made her sick, for a time, but now she is well again. She will be studying history with you."

A pause. The younger boy wriggled on his chair. Selera twisted a long, blonde coil of hair around her forefinger.

"Only history?" the teacher said.

"Yes." He was stroking my back. I wanted to whirl and cry, "What? Now that I'm finally here you won't even let me take lessons with the others?" Instead I flushed slowly, as his fingers circled.

"As I have said already, she is powerful. In fact, she could probably teach several of your classes." He chuckled low in his throat, and it sounded like one of Borl's growls. "So I will be taking charge of her Otherseeing instruction."

Selera stopped playing with her hair. Her emerald eyes widened. And I felt triumph, flooding over everything else. I smiled a tiny smile at her.

"I will leave her with you now. If you could just step outside with me for a moment, Mistress Ket?"

"Certainly. Children, write down laws eight and twelve without consulting the texts."

She was gone. They both were.

I walked to the table. There was an extra stool pushed beneath it; I pulled it out, sat down between Selera and the littlest boy.

"What are your names?" I said as I reached for paper and quill. My voice was steady; my heartbeat was not. Perhaps my hand would be unsteady too, and I would blot the ink, smudge it so that no one would be able to read my words.

"I believe Mistress Ket told us to write." Selera glared at each of the other students. The two boys avoided her eyes; the girl looked back at her with an expression of profound disinterest.

"She did," I said, and dipped the quill in Selera's ink pot.

I had imagined what I would write, when the opportunity arose. The words had been very clear, these past few days:

I am Teldaru's captive. He uses Otherseeing for evil purposes and has cursed me so that I cannot tell anyone. Please give this information to the king. Please help me.

I did not expect anyone to believe me, but I did think they might fetch King Haldrin. I would write much more for him, of course, but now I needed to set down only enough to bring him to me.

I placed the quill's tip against the paper, aware of everyone's eyes on me. My hand moved and letters scratched forth, dark and wet.

Teldaru Teldaru Teldaru Teldaru

Selera giggled.

Teldaru Tel

"Well. It seems that Master Teldaru's special student wishes to learn more than visions from him."

I set the quill down. Folded the paper in half, and in half again. *Of course,*

I thought, flooded now with a numbness that was too familiar. *Of course he would think of this; he would make sure to take everything away from me* . . . There was a warm pulse, in the numbness: the memory of another Path I had not even known about until it was gone. I lowered my head for a moment, so that my freshly washed hair hid my face.

"*Anyhow*," said the other girl, who was sitting beside Selera. This girl was covered in freckles (even her arms) and had greyish eyes and lank brown hair. She was shapeless, too—fourteen but somehow old as well, all rounded edges but no curves. "My name is Grasni." She nodded at me as if we had just conducted a satisfying bit of business. I nodded back at her.

"Grasni is tedious and annoying," Selera said. "You and she should be fast friends."

"I believe Mistress Ket told us to write?" Grasni said in a high, querulous imitation of Selera. Selera herself scowled and the little boy to my left cringed back on his stool, but Mistress Ket came back in then, and we all bent over our papers.

The eighth law of the Paleric Age, I wrote, as familiar numbness gave way to familiar pain.

I ran that night.

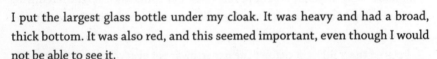

I put the largest glass bottle under my cloak. It was heavy and had a broad, thick bottom. It was also red, and this seemed important, even though I would not be able to see it.

"Help me . . . Sir Guard? Help . . ." I made my voice thin and weak and leaned on the doorframe, both hands beneath my cloak, as if I were clutching my belly.

It was very dark, beyond my door. The branches were black and there were stars among them, but no moon. My breath was white; the brightest thing I saw.

"What is it?" He was dark too, though as he neared I made out the silver glint of his eyes. He had a beard, contrary to the custom begun by Teldaru. This almost made me regret what I intended to do.

"I'm ill . . ." I retched—a wracked sound that produced no vomit but was nonetheless convincing. "I need . . ." I leaned over, heaved again.

"Very well," he said hastily, "I'll take you."

I stumbled after him to where he had been sitting. He picked up his lantern (which glowed only weakly) and led me to the latrine. I thought, as I lurched inside and slammed the knot-holed door, that it did not stink as much at night.

I straightened up against the wall and waited. The bottle was in my hand, which was already raised. I counted my own heartbeats; twenty of them, before the guard rapped on the wood.

"Come on, then," he called. "Come out."

Fifteen more heartbeats.

"Girl . . . Nola. Come out now or I'll come in."

Five more, and the door creaked open. I was relieved that he did not pound it open, because I was behind it, and needed him to be tentative in order to carry out my plan. I was relieved, but sorry again, in a clear, sudden, silly way—and then he was in, head and neck, and I was bringing the bottle down on him with all my strength.

He fell onto his stomach with a grunt that sounded puzzled. He tried to twist onto his side when I stepped over him; I slammed my foot against his forehead and he fell back again. I ran out the door and into the shadows of the trees. I ran as if I had done it before, here: skimming over roots and crackly grass, toward the keep that flickered with red-orange light. I heard only my own footsteps—no one shouting; no one following.

At the double doors to the keep I halted. I leaned against the stone, panting in long, vanishing plumes. *Think*. Think: *this part will be harder. . . .*

I pulled the doors open and saw a stretch of torchlit corridor. No guards; no one at all. I stepped inside and pulled the doors shut behind me. Walked quickly, but not too quickly. I remembered this place a little; I knew I would see a staircase, at the end of the hall, and yet another set of doors, and another guard. I did. I stood and watched him. *Think, Nola, think. . . .*

I burst into the brighter light of the entrance hall. He saw me almost immediately and stiffened, though he did not draw his sword. "You must come!" I cried. "The guard in the seers' courtyard—someone has attacked him!"

He stared at me for a moment, then rushed off the way I had come. I scrabbled at the double doors until they creaked open and flung myself down the long staircase outside. It seemed very dark here, after the keep, and I was moving swiftly; I slipped several times and flailed my arms gracelessly to keep my balance. There were knots of people at the bottom but I flew past them, and past the guards who were standing by a wagon at the main gate. My feet pounded the cobblestones that sloped away from the castle. I made for an alley that branched off the main street. It was narrow and dank and there was no light at all, so I slowed, dragging my shoulder along a rough wooden wall. The alley twisted downward.

Yes, I thought as I followed it, *take me away from him; take me to a street I know—the one with the brothel, so that I can find Bardrem. We'll leave the city together and he'll write a poem about it someday, when we're old. . . .*

Light flickered ahead of me. I quickened my pace, blinking, clenching my hands to try to keep them warm. A pony clopped by where the alley met the street. I edged forward and peered out after it. The castle was there, very close, looming against the sky. I stared at the shapes of its gatehouse towers and walls, thinking, *No—that's impossible—I ran down, away. . . .*

This time I took the main road, and I walked. Down again—I was sure of it, because when I glanced over my shoulder I could see just the black shadows of the gatehouse banners. I breathed and wrapped my arms around myself and kept walking. A woman carrying a yoke and two buckets was coming up toward me, and I stepped to the side to let her pass. When she had, and I went back into the middle of the street, the castle was directly ahead of me.

I stopped. Everything swam in my vision, as if I were beginning to Othersee. I staggered where I stood, and turned around to look behind me. I saw the castle again: a mirror castle and a real one, or maybe neither? Men were approaching from both. Guards—four of them, led by the bearded one I had hit. As he drew closer I saw that his left eye was swollen shut. I spun and spun and there was no path away from them. Even if there had been I would have been too dizzy to follow it.

"Nola," the bearded one said softly as the others fell in behind him. He closed his big hands around my upper arms so tightly that I cried out. His mouth was nearly touching my ear. "He warned us you'd be tricky."

"No." I whimpered and wrenched myself around in his grasp, but it did not matter—not only because he had me so firmly, but also because the castle was there, where it should not have been. It was everywhere.

"Back we go, mad girl," he said. "Master Teldaru's waiting."

He did not come until dawn.

I heard him, after hours and hours of silence. It was almost a relief to hear him: his footsteps, his voice murmuring to whichever man was outside my door. I sat on the edge of the bed, holding one of the cloth horses in my lap. I thought of Chenn.

Borl came in with him, this time. Teldaru was holding a lantern; its light glanced off his belt buckle and Borl's bared teeth, and something that was between his teeth—something metal. They both stood just inside the door and stared at me.

"Well, Nola," Teldaru said at last. My muscles ached from gripping the horse, but I held it even closer. "You still do not appreciate all I have done for you, it seems. You still seek to defy me, even though I have offered to lift the curse if you obey." He stepped toward me, and I flinched. "And you evidently had little faith in the curse itself. *You will never leave me*—I bent your Paths to make this true. Perhaps now you understand? You can try to run, but your feet will always lead you back to me."

I remembered the alley and the street, and the castle that had waited at the end of both. Sickness bubbled up into my throat.

"And yet," he continued, "even though you have been disobedient, I have brought you something. Something you might have been missing."

This something was small and pale, and he was holding it between his fingers. He dropped it onto the bed beside me and I reached for it, even though I did not want to. Paper. Just a square of it, wrinkled where it was folded—but it was not folded now.

"Do you remember it? You should: it was in your dress—that lovely pink dress you were wearing when you first arrived here. Remember?"

You are beautiful help!

I nodded.

He whistled and Borl came toward me, too. He opened his jaws and the metal thing he was carrying fell.

"And this, dearest—do you remember it?" I looked. I knew but did not know; I waited because I could not move. "Go on," he said. "Pick it up."

It was Bardrem's knife—the small one, the one with which he had sworn to kill Chenn's murderer. The one I had scoffed at because I had been thinking of Orlo's black, restless eyes and broad shoulders. I picked it up and turned it over and over, and I saw dark streaks on the steel.

"He defied me too, your Bardrem." Teldaru shook his head, smiled. "He yelled 'Orlo!' and ran at me, but too late."

My breath shuddered in my chest. "You killed him," I said. The blood on the blade smudged under my fingertips.

"No. Why would I be so foolish? No: he is alive now. But if *you* are foolish enough to try to escape me again, he dies. He dies, Nola. Do you understand?"

I did not nod or speak, but he leaned down to me and said, "Good," as he plucked the knife from my hands. "And now we are done with foolishness."

He traced the line of my cheekbone, smoothed his thumb along my forehead. Bent even closer and whispered, "Goodnight," against my hair, as Borl growled from the doorway.

He left the door open when he went. I stared after him, at nothing—until someone else appeared on the threshold, maybe minutes later, maybe an hour.

"May I come in?"

I blinked, heard myself say, "Yes."

The girl Grasni came to stand in front of me. She plucked at her voluminous brown dress with one freckled hand. "I heard," she began, and cleared her throat. "We all heard the commotion last night, with you and the guards. No one will tell us what it was about, and I'm not here to ask you—just to say that I'm sorry. You must be feeling unhappy here, lonely—I know what that's like, so I thought I'd come and give you these."

She put something down on the bed where Teldaru had dropped Bardrem's note. I reached out again and felt cool metal against my fingers. "They're for your hair," she said in a rush, as I picked up two of the dainty bronze butterfly pins and turned them over in my palm. "Now that I think about it, I'm not sure why I imagined they'd help you be less lonely. But my brother gave them to me, and he was the one I missed when I came here. They always slide right out of *my* hair—yours is so much nicer than mine, and I saw that it was falling in your eyes, yesterday in the classroom, so I thought that you should try them." She drew a deep, gusty breath and let it go again.

I looked up at her. "Thank you," I said, quietly enough that I hoped she would not hear the wobbling of my voice. "Help me with them?"

She gathered one thick strand of my hair up and away from my forehead, gave it a deft twist, and thrust one of the pins in. She did this three more times, then stepped back and cocked her head at me. "Well," she said, "you look just lovely. Selera will be jealous."

She smiled at me—and despite the note, the knife, and the road that would never lead me away, I smiled back at her.

CHAPTER TWENTY-TWO

Sometimes I stare at the papers in front of me and am still surprised. I should be accustomed to it by now: to my hand holding the quill, making shapes that match the ones in my head. Words, thousands of them, and none of them lies. Every "Teldaru" intentional.

It interests me that my desire to speak true words is far less strong than my desire to write them. I never really tried writing anything except lessons, after that first attempt, whereas the words flowed from my mouth every time someone asked them to. I've grown terribly weary of listening to myself.

And now? My fire is tall and bright and I've just eaten and I'm not tired and animals and baby are all asleep—so what's next?

There's this, I suppose, which seems ridiculous and frightening at the same time:

I got used to it.

I got used to it—to almost every aspect of my imprisonment. Partly because Teldaru (to my great surprise) was distant, almost aloof, and so I actually began to enjoy myself—and also because you can accustom yourself to anything, if you feel you have no choice.

Years passed. Teldaru kept me by him in public but almost never came to me alone, and I was too relieved to question this. "Do not think I have forgotten you," he said to me once. We were walking around the seers' pool; I could feel the other students' eyes on us, as they always were, wide or narrowed, curious or furious or admiring. This had been very easy to get used to. "Do not think that I have forgotten what we will do together. It is just that there are things I must try alone, first. Plans that must be made with clarity and care."

"And you can't be clear or careful with me around?" I was probably about seventeen by then. I had despaired of ever having Selera's lush curves, but I had grown my hair as long as hers, and it was thick and red-gold and made her jealous.

"No, Mistress Alluring Seer, I cannot." He smiled and bent his head close to mine.

Grasni would be turning to Selera now, saying something like, "I'm sure he's positioned himself that way so that he can see *past* her to you. Yes, I'm sure of it, Lera: his fingers just twitched! He's sending you a secret message!"

"It will be your time soon," he said to me. "Not yet—but soon."

I grew accustomed to hearing this and not believing it. Years had gone by, after all. Maybe whatever foul experiments he was conducting were failing; maybe he had realized how impossible his plans were and was simply too embarrassed to admit this to me.

I was comfortable. People envied me. Fear and revulsion and rage were memories. Grasni was my friend. Even Chenn's bottles and toys and Bardrem's note were things I looked at, but did not think about. I saw King Haldrin less, but when he did visit the school he always paid particular attention to me. The King of Sarsenay, asking after me! And his kingdom continued peaceful, I heard—peaceful and prosperous. Maybe Teldaru *had* forgotten. Surely he had.

I somehow got used to my curse-twisted Otherseeing, as well—probably because Teldaru hardly ever had me use it. I had been afraid that he would force me to come with him to Othersee at court, but he did not, in those first years. He had me teach the young ones (and there were more of them, as time went on), and sometimes he brought a scullery maid or guard to me, and the exhilaration of Otherseeing for them lessened the sting of false words that came after. And they were innocuous words, really, or so I insisted to myself. Words of triumph when I had seen defeat; of sadness when I had seen joy. Not big things, I thought, when I thought about it at all. Nothing that would change the world's Pattern.

But then Grasni came to me, on a night in spring, and asked me to Othersee for her.

Selera had been doing this for years. It was a game she played without even understanding the rules—only that it was enjoyable, as it had been that very first time, when I had been the mad girl who had spoken to her of laughing blond children with black eyes. She never told me that she was coming; she simply appeared at my door. If someone else was with me (which rarely happened) she would send them off with an imperious word or two and a wave of her pretty hand.

She would not tell me to Othersee right away. No: first she had to talk about Teldaru.

"He kissed me yesterday. In the kitchen. He unbound my hair and wrapped it around his hands and smelled it."

"Lovely, Selera."

"He pressed me back into the grass, last night. He unlaced my bodice and ran his lips over my breasts."

"Did he find them to his taste?"

"Finally—oh, *finally*, Nola! He woke me with the gentlest kisses, and he was in me—he was moving, so slowly—"

"Yes, yes, fine; I need no more details."

That last time I was very quick to lose my patience, but on other occasions it took longer. This was part of the game: she would prattle about how, *precisely*, he had loved her—on which chair, up against which tree—and she would wait for me to snap at her. Which I always did, despite the resolve I felt when she first swept in the door. I told myself that I snapped because she was simply intolerable, but there were other layers there, beneath my angry words. Once I threw one of the bottles at her, which made her laugh and laugh. When she had gone I cried and cut my fingertips on the blue shards as I gathered them into a pile on the floor.

After she had provoked me to frustration or anger she would lean back in the chair (she always took the chair) and ease open the lid of my desk, where all my sticks of wax and jars of grain were. She would smile sweetly while I stared at her, both of us motionless, knowing what was next.

"Now then, Nola. Othersee for me. Tell me what will come."

She had no idea why I never refused her. Maybe she thought her power was so great that I could not. Maybe she did not think about it at all. What mattered most was that she got what she wanted.

This I did not get used to. Every time I reached for the jars or the wax my insides clenched. My hands sometimes trembled, and she never failed to comment on this.

"It gratifies me to see how overcome you are by the prospect of Otherseeing for me."

"Overcome by that old pork we had for dinner, more like."

My only consolation was that, though the words I spoke to her were always lovely and golden, the visions I saw were always dark. Both Yigranzi and Teldaru had told me to speak only of the strongest image, if there were many differing ones and I was unsure which was truest. But there were no differing images in Selera's Otherworld—and how could I have chosen which of them was strongest? The skull, the fire, the flood; the eyes that wept blood?

There wasn't one baby or music box or swan among them, and yet these were the pictures I gave her, with my cursed voice—and as I did I smiled, inside, thinking of the truth of things. I did, though I shudder to remember this now.

⁕⁂

When Grasni arrived, that night in spring, Selera was just leaving.

"She's doing very well tonight," Selera said, waving her hand at me. "I'm sure she'd tell you something spectacular, if you were brave enough to ask for it."

I snorted. Grasni would never come to me for Otherseeing. She thought that seers should never ask for the Othersight to be turned on themselves; it was what our teachers had always said, citing the importance of purity of vision and maintenance of power. Selera enjoyed thinking she was breaking the rules in this respect. The fact that Teldaru knew about it—that he had, in fact, encouraged her to do it—surely sweetened the transgression all the more.

Grasni believed in keeping seer and seen separate. And she claimed, too, to have no desire to know where her Path would take her. I had seen her reprimand younger students, when we stumbled upon them crouched over pot lids or globs of wax stolen from the classroom or our desks. "I know what you're intending to do," she said in her gentle, scolding voice as they shrank from us. "And you mustn't. All you need to know about your Path is that you will tell other people about theirs. You give; you do not take. You are too important for that. Yes?"

Selera took; Selera told me to help her do it. Grasni would never do the same. Only that night, she did.

Before she did, she said, "Why do you keep letting her *in*?" Selera was gone, leaving behind a swath of her scent, which her father sent her in tiny bottles from some far-off country that had no rain, or some such thing. The perfume smelled like too many cut flowers, all of them just about to rot. I thought this in general, but especially after I had been Otherseeing, when all my senses were too acute.

"She amuses me," I said thickly.

Tonight's visions had been disturbing, as usual: a severed hand with emeralds for nails; a wolf shaking a cat in its jaws. "An apple tree," I had said. "A woman dancing by a river."

I waited for Grasni to respond with one of her dry, withering comments, but she did not. She sat down, stood up, walked over to the bed and back to the window. She stared out at the moonlit leaves—all of them unfurling, at last, after a long, bitter winter—then turned and strode back to the bed. I watched her, struck yet again by how badly her clothes fit her. She was a plump young woman—we were about nineteen, at this point—but her dresses were far too large, and entirely shapeless. (Selera had once told her to stop stealing curtains from the castle.) Looking at Grasni always made me feel better about myself, though I had the grace to feel guilty about this.

"Grasni. Stop pacing.She whirled; her dress billowed and subsided, slowly. "I'm sorry. I just ... I ..."

I had never seen her struggle for words before. "Grasni—*what*?"

She raised a freckle-splotched arm and held it over her eyes. "Othersee for me."

I laughed, but she didn't.

"Nola." Her arm was still up, hiding everything but her mouth. "Do not make this more difficult."

"I ... all right. Is ..."—now *I* was struggling, casting about for explanations even as a hard, cold weight settled in my stomach—"is it to do with your brother?" He had joined a band of rebels in northern Lorselland, whose rulers were preventing their people from using or even speaking of the Othersight.

Grasni told me about such things, which I'd have had no idea about otherwise—political things; matters of injustice, violence and scandal that existed far beyond our walls.

"No. It's . . ." Her arm came down. Her eyes were bright, but not with laughter; with that hunger, instead, which made people helpless and greedy. "It's someone else—a guard. Sildio."

"A man." My voice was harder than it should have been, but the cold in me was spreading. I had no trouble using my cursed eyes and words on Selera and others I did not know enough to care about—but on Grasni? "You wish me to search Pattern and Path because of a man."

"I know I've given you no warning—never talked about him with you—but I was too ashamed; I care about *big* things; I'm a stronger, cleverer person than this—only I'm not, Nola." She drew a deep breath and cleared her throat and rolled her eyes toward the ceiling. "Please don't look at me like that. I already feel as if I've grown a tail; don't make me grow fangs too. Because then I'd drool, and—"

"Think on this," I said. "Think of the rule you'd be breaking—the one you always remind the children of. 'You are too important for that'—remember—"

"And when have you ever worried about rules?"

"This isn't about me! It's about you: what *you* care about! And anyway, you've always mocked the girls who come to ask you about love."

She smiled a smile I'd never seen before—thin and careful. "Well, then, I suppose it's up to you to do the mocking, from now on."

"Please, Grasni"—one more entreaty, even though I knew it would do no good.

She drew a mirror out from somewhere in her voluminous dress. It was small (would fit in a palm) and copper and she had brought it with her from her home when she had come to the castle, at ten. It was the first thing she had ever Otherseen with, when her brother (who had no Othersight but wanted it, desperately) had asked her to. She passed it to me, and I took it. Ran my thumbs over its dents and felt a stirring of anticipation, despite all the dread.

"Tell me, Nola," Grasni said. "Tell me where my Path will take me."

Grasni's images were so bright, after Selera's. *Here* were the lycus blossoms and the waterfall; the smiling woman and the baby's dimpled fingers. There were shadows, but only at the edges.

When the brightness faded I lifted my eyes from the little mirror. Grasni was leaning against the wall. She was pale; her freckles—which were dark red and brown—looked livid. Other spots danced over her skin: the leavings of my Othersight, which I knew would fade, along with my dizziness. I wanted to smile at her—I tried to, but could not.

You will be happy. "I saw a sea of shadow. A purple thunderhead shot through with lightning."

Her shoulders sagged.

You'll cut your hair: it will be short and curly and it will suit you, just as your joy will. "An empty cradle." *Oh, please,* I thought—*an empty cradle? She'll never believe that; she'll think I'm being melodramatic to tease her*—but she was turning her face away. *No—those aren't the right words; they* aren't.

How could the truth be so loud inside my head and silent on my tongue? Where were the pathways he twisted and snipped? I had to find them; I reached inward and strained to see, to feel, but there was nothing but a seeping white pain behind my eyes. This happened every time I tried, and it is why I had stopped—until now. This was important; she was my friend.

"A sea of shadow." Grasni was smiling again. This smile I recognized; it was her wry, "ah, well" one. "I think I already know where it is. Do you promise to visit me there?"

"Oh, Grasni," I said, and, "I'm sorry," though she would not understand what I really meant.

And then, in a rush that swept the pain from my head, I knew what I must do.

"Now it's my turn."

She frowned.

I rose, walked to her, thrust the mirror into her hands. "Take this. Look at my Pattern, now that I've looked at yours. We've never done anything without each other, after all—not since that morning you came to me with the butterfly pins." My excitement was like wind snatching the words from my mouth. Why had I not thought of this before? Why—had I been so lazy, so complacent simply because I lived at the castle (not in a brothel; not alone in a house), and because I had a friend, and because the king knew my name? Because I, too, had simply been reluctant to break an Otherseeing rule?

No, I told myself, clenching my trembling hands as if this would still my thoughts, as well; *it is just that the time has not been right. Grasni was the one to show me this Path, and she did it tonight. This is the way, and I am glad of it.*

"I'll tell you what I told the children," Grasni said. "You give; you do not take. Don't try to just because I have."

"No—it's not just because of that. Truly: I want you to look. I need you to. Please, Grasni." Those words again, breathless now.

She gazed at me for a long time. I heard a bird singing, in our quiet. There would be baby birds soon; bits of eggshell scattered in the new grass, and sometimes the babies themselves, fallen from their nests before their wings had had time to grow.

"It's not a man, is it?" she said at last. "Because at least one of us should have loftier concerns."

She wanted me to laugh. "Maybe," I said instead. "I don't know."

She nodded. Gave me one more long look from her brown-grey eyes, then sat down on the chair with the mirror in her left hand.

"Tell me." The words felt terribly strange on my tongue. They even sounded strange. I'd heard them so many times before—but now, suddenly, they were new. "Speak of what will come, for me."

She bent her head. I saw the reflection of her eye—just one; the mirror was that small, and so battered that the image was warped and blurry. I edged away. I was dizzier than I had been; I felt behind me for the bed and sat down hard. Only Teldaru had done this for me (to me) before, and I could not tell Grasni. I couldn't tell her anything important—but maybe she would see, now. Maybe I wouldn't need my voice, or a quill and ink and paper. I wrapped my fingers in the rough twine mane of one of the toy horses and waited for her to look up.

When she did her eyes were black. I had not expected this to surprise me, for this was what happened when seers were caught in a vision. But this was Grasni, and she was seeing the Otherworld—*mine*—and I sucked in my breath noisily and pushed myself back still farther on the bed. She stared at me, as the leaves hissed in wind and the night bird sang and my heart thumped its hope above every other sound. She was motionless until the black gave way again to brown, and then she blinked at me. Her mouth opened and her legs jerked and the mirror fell with a clang.

"Grasni?" My voice cracked.

She wet her lips with her tongue. I thought I should get her a drink from the pitcher of water by the bed, but I could not move. "It was like rock," she said in a ragged whisper. "Rock with branches sticking up—burned ones, all black and bare. I didn't know where I was. It wasn't your time-to-come and it wasn't your past. It was . . . now?" She stood but did not straighten; her shoulders stayed rounded, as if she were an old woman.

I was up too, lurching toward her. The old woman and the drunk woman; we made a fine pair. "But did you see anyone?" I asked. "Anyone at all? Did you understand that—" But my words tangled in my throat, too close to unspeakable truth, and I could say nothing more. I reached out, and when my hands were almost touching hers she stumbled backward.

"*What's wrong with you?*" she cried. Just before she whirled and ran from me, I saw her tears.

Nothing will be the same, I thought—and I was right.

CHAPTER TWENTY-THREE

Grasni came back to my room a week later. It was a wet spring night, this time, and she stood in the open door.

"You're soaking," I said, as casually as I could. I had missed her terribly but could not let her hear this. "Your hair's sticking to your neck. And there's rain on the floor—come *in*, Grasni. Sit with me."

She had managed not to look at me at all in our history classes, and in the ones on Otherseeing tools that we taught the "babies" (as we called them), and she did not look at me now. "I haven't been able to sleep," she said in a hoarse voice that sounded nothing like hers. "I'm afraid I'll dream of . . . that place. But I see it anyway, even when I'm awake. It's behind my eyelids."

"That happens sometimes with strong visions: you know that. It takes a few days, but—"

"I told Mistress Ket." She looked at me then. Her eyes were bright. *More tears?* I wondered, and my own eyes blurred, washed red with rage and fear. *Teldaru*, I thought, very clearly, *I'll kill you for this.*

"I had to, Nola. I'm so sorry. I thought it would ease my mind a little— weaken the image because I'd shared it. But it hasn't."

"Please come in," I said, though I don't think I truly wanted her to. What could I have said? *What you saw is Teldaru's doing* would have become, "Rain is good for flowers," or some such thing.

"No." She was already turning. A gust of wind made the flames in my hearth gutter and spattered rain all the way to my bare feet.

"You've been my friend for five years," I said. I had practised these words, in my solitude. "I am still the same person, no matter what you have seen." I drew a trembling breath. "And who else will help me do battle with Selera? You're the only one who knows how."

Grasni almost smiled—or so I told myself. She seemed to hesitate, between the rain and the firelight. But then she shook her head and bit her lip; said, "No—I'm sorry, Nola; I can't," and fled from me. Again.

It only occurred to me much later that night to wonder what Mistress Ket had said, or what she would do. I didn't have long to wonder, because Teldaru came to me the next day.

"Walk with me," he said. He was standing where Grasni had stood the night before, but now the sun was shining. Everything (his hair, the leaves and sky behind him) was very bright. I blinked at him and did not move.

"Get up, Nola, or I will fetch Selera and ask her to walk with us."

"May your Path end in torment," I said pleasantly, "and soon." I rose, stretched, bent to put on my slippers.

"You'll need sturdier shoes than those," he said. "We have a long way to go."

Teldaru was wearing one of his finest tunics: deep blue, embroidered with whorls of silver and gold thread. His cloak was mostly gold, and seemed to pulse in the sunlight. Borl walked at his right side. He was the Great Teldaru, and everyone who saw him in the city recognized him. I watched them gape and murmur to each other. A group of girls by a well let out a series of squeals. Teldaru paused and turned to them and they clustered together, gasping now, clutching each other's hands. He produced a slender lycus branch from beneath his cloak and held it out to the girl in the centre, who was short and plump and had lank brown hair and sweat-sheened skin. "Mistress," he said, in a sonorous voice. He smiled as she took the branch and held its white and pink blossoms to her face. His perfect, "my world is you alone" smile.

The girls began to whisper as soon as we walked away. I looked over my shoulder and found their eyes on me, and again my insides crawled with pride and shame.

"So you always carry flowers," I said. "Just in case."

"Yes," he said, already smiling at someone else.

A little boy ran up to give *him* a flower, when we were walking along the wide road of the wealthy east-town merchants. Teldaru wound it around his cloak pin. There were many children in the poor lower town, with its narrow streets and mud and the smell of rot and waste that I remembered so well. He gave them coins—every one of them, even when more came running from alleys and houses, whooping and holding out their dirty hands.

"And me, O revered Master Teldaru?" I said, cupping my own palm. The children were behind us now. He did not respond; he was walking faster, toward the faded awnings of the lowtown market. When he reached the stalls (with me behind him, trying not to pant) he slowed again, and put a hand on my arm.

"Look, Nola." I did. "What do you see?"

The ragged cloth of the awnings; lengths of bleached, weathered wood covered in salt fish or fruit—pale lycus, picked too soon, and other scarlet ones I did not recognize. Women with dresses as worn as the awnings, and faces pinched beneath headscarves that were not faded, but bright greens and oranges. Like Yigranzi's.

He saw where I was looking. "Belakaoan cloth," he said. "Yes. And Belakaoan fruit. I have ensured that even the poorest of our citizens will be able to obtain at least some of the items that are so prized among wealthier Sarsenayans."

The giggling girls by the well had been wearing jewels in their hair, I remembered. And strips of bright material tied around their waists.

"Belakao," he said, as if to himself. I was suddenly cold. *He has forgotten nothing,* I thought. *He has been busy for years, plotting, and I have no idea what's been going on outside the school.*

"So this is what you wished to show me?" I said. "Some scarves and fruit? And how beloved you are to girls and poor children?"

He gazed at me. I was as tall as he was, but this look of his always made me feel smaller—a girl again, craning up at him. "In part. I thought it would help you, after all this time, to see that I have been hard at work, drawing Belakao close. For it must be close, before we break it." He shook his head, smiled a slow smile. "But there is more. There is something to be *done.*"

He led me swiftly away from the market. Whenever I lagged too far behind, Borl growled and snapped at my heels. I was so intent on avoiding his jaws that I hardly noticed where we were. Only when Teldaru halted abruptly—and I stepped aside to keep from walking into him—did I raise my head.

We were at the city gate. The eastern one, with the great carved doors and the round towers with conical tops and the green banners that were prettier than the silver ones that flew above the southern gate. I had walked between these doors once a year, since my arrival at the castle, on Ranior's Pathday. The entire city seemed to empty out on that day in late summer. I had never joined the procession as a child; the Lady had not allowed anyone to leave the brothel, since business used to increase dramatically during the festival.

The guards atop the towers saluted Teldaru, and we walked together onto the road that stretched like a ribbon or a snake—like a vision from the Otherworld, except that it was not. It was a real path, made of cobbles, crowded with wagons and people. But we walked among these people, all of them staring, whispering as the others had, and very soon there were fewer of them, and the way unfolded before us, among trees and over hills, beneath the empty sky.

"You see now where we are going."

"Yes."

I had never really noticed the details of this road and the land around it. All the other times I had come this way I had been giddy, surrounded not by walls but by people I knew: Grasni, who would insist on holding onto my skirt so that we would not be separated, and the younger students behind us, wide-eyed and gripping each other's hands. Teldaru had stayed close to us, but I had not cared: there was too much singing and laughter, too much sun.

Now there was quiet. Our footsteps, and the clicking of Borl's nails on the stone, and the wind stirring leaves and the tall, slender grasses that lined the road. Once or twice something moved in the grass and Borl plunged after it, but Teldaru whistled for him and he came, whining and slavering, and resumed his place behind me. The light was a pressure now, thrusting at my face, and then—as the sun moved, above—at my shoulders and my back. I was so tiny, here.

"Tell me."

The first words in several hours; I started. "What?" My voice seemed too loud, even as it vanished.

"Tell me where we're going."

I swallowed. Thirst and dread; I wondered if there would be room for words. "Ranior's Tomb," I said, and just as I did I saw the turning—the place where a path of beaten dirt began. It curved away from the road, into a copse of trees. Beyond the trees was a meadow, which I did remember. I also remembered watching the line of celebrants surge up and up, toward the rocky hill that reared like a ragged tooth from the meadow. The high place where the War Hound had finally died, at the hand of the Flamebird of the islands. The place where Mambura too had died—his throat torn out by Ranior's own dogs. The place where Ranior's bones rested; where, once a year, his descendants came to give thanks for the Pattern he had made, and for the Pattern that had made him.

The climb was difficult, and knots of people settled at the base of the hill to watch the others wend their slow way among the rocks and the bent, squat trees. There were many paths up to the single stone at the summit—many ways moulded by centuries of feet and hands, by people who had struggled to feel, in some small way, as Ranior must have felt. Grasni and I had reached the top last year; it had been our first time, and we had spun each other around as the wind tore at our hair and skirts and voices. The world below had been both vast and tiny: the crowd, the road, the farmers' fields, the city itself, with its wall and its castle. Even the castle was dwarfed, from here. Just some spears of red stone surrounded by sky.

With Grasni, pressed about by others, I had been able to gaze upon Ranior's monument with simple awe. I could forget, as I looked at the carved lines and spirals that showed the hero's Path, that Teldaru was behind me. I could forget the stories he had told me as I lay on my narrow, filthy pallet and waited for him to use his mirror and his knife. *Mambura and Ranior and Teldaru*—these words were echoes, snatched away by wind. Now, though, I stood where the path began to climb and he was the only one beside me and every one of his mad words rang in my ears, as if he had spoken them days, not years, ago.

I started up the hill. I had taken about twenty steps when he called, "Mistress Intrepid Seer. Where are you going?"

I turned. A stream of pebbles skittered down the slope; Borl barked and lunged at them. "To the top," I called back. "Where you will do whatever it is you mean to do."

He was shading his eyes with his hand but I could still see them. Black waves; they would have lapped up around my feet if I had let myself look at them for too long. "No, dearest Nola," he said, "we're going in and under. Beneath. *That* is where I will do what I mean to do."

He led me around the base of the hill to a low stone door. The stone was the same colour as the hillside's dirt and spreading plants, and even when he brushed at the ivy that concealed the latch I had trouble seeing its whole shape. He drew a bunch of keys from beneath his tunic and up over his head and I thought suddenly of Uja and her cage. Uja, who had belonged to an island Otherseer; Uja, who did not need keys.

"You must lead now."

I looked from him to the open door. Stepped toward it and crouched to look inside. "We'll need a light," I said. I smelled darkness and earth.

"No," he said. "This is a place where seers become like their unsighted fellows. Where they stumble down pathways, seeking a bright centre that will make sense of the rest. No, Nola—here you have only your eyes."

I crawled forward before I could feel fear. I heard Teldaru behind me; I heard Borl whine and scuffle. The door shut the outside away. I groped and felt an edge that was a stair, and another below it. I reached above me and found only space, and stood.

"I hear your own Paths are black," Teldaru said. His breath was warm on my neck.

Mistress Ket, I thought. *Grasni*. "I had to know," I said—just a murmur, but it wrapped around us both. "I had to try."

"Of course you did." I could hear his smile. "I'm a little disappointed, in fact, that it took you so long to ask someone to help you try. But I told myself that you were happy, and that this was good for both of us."

"I wasn't happy." Louder, so that my real voice would drown out the one in my head: *He's right, he's right.*

"I was relieved when Mistress Ket came to tell me what you'd asked Grasni to do. When she told me what Grasni had seen. Because now you are ready to return to me."

His hands were on my neck, beneath my hair. I remembered how I used to stand and tremble, when he touched me like this years ago. I twisted around and found him in the darkness: his cheekbones with my fingertips, his lips with my lips. He started backward and I drew my hands over his chest and down his sides and held him still. His mouth was open a bit; I ran my tongue around and in and forced it wide. My head was filled with words—chattering, noisy ones that were more insistent than the throbbing of my skin. *You have no idea I'm grown now I'm not fourteen any more I'm not yours I'll show you I'm not afraid. . . .*

I pulled away. His breath left him in a rush that was almost a whistle. Before he could speak or grope for me again I turned and began to pick my way down the stairs. I moved slowly from step to step, words still spinning. *Idiot; he knows the way and you don't; he could reach out anywhere and have you.*

At first my breathing and footsteps were so loud that I heard nothing else. I imagined him three steps behind me, smiling, listening. Ten stairs, eleven, twelve, and then floor; I shuffled forward, drawing my hand along the wall. It was stone, pocked with holes or carvings, and so cool that I longed to pause and lay my forehead against it. I followed the wall—its bends and sharp corners—my free hand waving in front of me, lest there be a dead end. Which, very soon, there was.

I turned and retraced my steps. More bends and corners, and another wall before me, as well as the ones beside. I leaned against this one, my fingers feeling for a door or a crack, a space I could climb through, but there was only rock.

"Teldaru." I expected my voice to echo, but it was flat. I set my back to the dead-end wall and called, more loudly, "Teldaru! I'm lost—I'm sure this will please you. I need your help, which will please you even more."

I tried to be very quiet. I listened for his footsteps or Borl's wet panting. Silence pressed on my ears. "Teldaru!" I shouted as loudly as I could, yet still my voice was swallowed before it could truly sound.

Maybe he is angry at me for having Grasni Othersee . . . maybe he doesn't need me at all any more and this is where I'll die.

"No," I said, to the darkness and to myself, and straightened.

"The Pattern is ocean," Yigranzi had said to me once, "too big to see entire, its currents too numerous to feel all at once. So we watch our own shores—the tides and waves we *can* see—and we hope they show us more." I—only eight or nine—had frowned my incomprehension and Yigranzi had clicked her tongue against her teeth. "But how will this ocean talk help you, Sarsenayan land-girl? Let me try this: the Pattern is all the roads, all the paths that lie across the world. You see only the one your own feet are on; you feel its little familiar stones and you know that it will lead you to walk some of the others that you do not know."

The small, I thought, in the night-dark beneath Ranior's Hill. *The small within the large. Something I can feel.*

I put my hands back on the wall. Traced bumps and zigzags and spirals: the frenzied, inscrutable shapes of the Pattern. So many shapes; I could feel nothing but confusion, beneath my fingertips. I took several paces and my hands slipped from the raised carvings into the hollows among them. These hollows were smooth and long—so long they had no end I could feel. They ran around the carvings and off into the black, and as I traced one and then another, the space around me shifted. Perhaps it lightened, too; I blinked and saw the wriggling, wobbling images that usually appeared after I had Otherseen.

The Otherworld, I thought, wondering and certain; *it's here.*

The hollow lines led me. I walked more and more quickly because I knew that no more walls would rise before me. Paths in stone, and the one beneath my feet; I was swift and sure, bathed in a light that only my Othereyes could see. I did not think about where the path would end. I was here, rounding corners, taking stairs two at a time, stepping over tumbled rocks and pools of dark, still water. I breathed deeply, and even the dank air seemed Otherlit as it filled me.

And then there was a door.

I stopped before it, my hands still on the lines that had brought me here. The lines that ended here. The door was very tall, unlike the one in the hillside. It was unmarked stone, with a metal ring in its centre. I put both hands on the ring, which was scratchy, ridged with rust. I pulled, expecting it to open just a little—but it swung wide and I stumbled backward.

Four steps rose beyond the door. I went up them slowly, suddenly aware, again, of the noises my feet and breathing made. At the top there was more darkness; the Otherworldly glow had faded, inside and out, and I stood motionless, my arms outstretched.

"Teldaru!" His name echoed; I was listening to its throbbing, thinking of Yigranzi's waves, when light blazed around me. I dug the palms of my hands against my eyes, rubbing at tears. A very long time seemed to pass before my vision was clear.

Teldaru was sitting on the edge of an enormous stone sarcophagus. Two lanterns burned beside him, and two torches behind him, in wall brackets. The sarcophagus was painted in patterns of scarlet, white and gold, as were the walls that stretched up and up, into a dome that was all gold. I caught glimpses of figures in the paint—Ranior with his hounds behind him, and his army, and his enemies. I did not look at these. I looked at Teldaru, who was leaning forward, his legs swinging like a boy's.

"Come here." He sounded like a boy, too; happy, eager. I took two steps over red flagstones. Two steps; I saw a knife in his hand. Bardrem's knife, so small and simple. I stood still.

"Come *here*, Mistress Reluctant Seer."

Two more steps; I saw Borl, lying on his side beneath Teldaru's dangling feet. I waited for him to leap up and snap at me, but he did not.

"Look at you." Teldaru was smiling. I had forgotten how bright he was, in firelight. "How have I kept myself away from you, all these years? But this is what I needed to do. I needed to be sure that we were both ready."

I touched him, I thought as I took another step. *I kissed him, and he was surprised—but now he is above me, watching, and the knife* . . .

I glanced again at Borl. I was close now; surely he would growl, at least. I saw his sides rising and falling—only I didn't: it was something else moving, easing outward, darker and larger than he was.

"What have you done?" I said as Borl's blood seeped toward my feet. His eyes were half-open and his tongue was lolling, nearly touching the blood. His neck was soaked black, except for the lips of the wound that ran across it. These were a livid, wet pink.

"I have killed him," Teldaru said in a low, warm voice—a voice for secrets and plans. "As you can see. I have killed him, and now you will bring him back again."

CHAPTER TWENTY-FOUR

Borl's blood was nearly at my feet and I could not move them. "I can't bring him back," I said. "It's impossible."

Teldaru frowned. "Nola. When have I ever told you to do something impossible?"

"And forbidden," I said, my voice rising. "Even looking into the Otherworld of an animal is forbidden, just—"

"Just as Otherseeing for a seer is forbidden? Just as using Bloodseeing is forbidden?" He pushed himself off the edge of the sarcophagus and landed lightly on the floor. "Your 'forbidden' is not the same as 'impossible.' Do not let your fear make you careless in your thinking."

"I'm not afraid." And I was not. I did not believe him, and I was not afraid.

He crouched by Borl, balancing away from the blood. He put his hand on the dog's head and rubbed it so vigorously that it flopped against the stone. "I suppose it would be unreasonable of me to hope that *you* were already bleeding?"

"I'm not," I said. I was relieved, for a fleeting, deluded moment—and then I looked at the knife.

He shrugged. "A pity. I hate to hurt you."

"Liar."

He smiled up at me. "Listen, now. This is how it will go."

I am alone in thick grey fog. It is in my eyes and nose and between my fingers. I turn myself around and around, or I think I do, since the view does not change.

"I can't," I cry. My mouth is full of mud, porridge, sweet rotten fruit, but he hears me somehow.

"You can." His voice is so clear; I should be able to see him. "His Paths are fresh. Look for them."

"But I don't know what to look for—"

A wisp of orange like flame that flutters by me and vanishes.

A flash of yellow.

Red that rises and froths around my knees.

"Colours or shapes, Nola—you'll see them—weave them together."

"I don't know how."

"You will."

If it were somewhere I recognized, like the desert of Chenn's death, the desert I made of Laedon when I undid his Paths—but this place is strange and suffocating, and it throbs with the throbbing of my cut skin, drips with the dripping of my blood, and I cannot concentrate.

Another yellow flicker, this one brighter. I reach with my aching hands and catch the end of it. It is rough, pocked like a tongue. I grip it, even though I do not want to. Let go, I think; turn away and close your eyes (all of them, real and Other)—because what is he going to do? Kill you too?

But I grasp the colour, and as I do I feel what Teldaru told me I would: a tremor in my veins; a new pulse so strong that I lurch, on the hard, splintered ground. Something flows from me to the yellow, and it is not a flicker, any more—it is a ribbon, slender but solid.

I stoop and run my hand over the red foam. It is real, just as the ribbon is; it gathers in my palm and hardens to the pulse that is mine and more than mine. Other colours, other shapes; I reach for each of them and somehow do not drop the rest. My arms move fast and faster and so do my feet, as if I am dancing. I gather in the vein ribbons and the bone roots and spin and they arc away from me, though I still hold them.

"Nola—good; very good, my love—you are doing it."

Doing what? I think. I don't understand—but my Otherself does. I dance through the pain that blooms in my hands, feet, legs and then all the way into my chest. The ground is no longer hard; it yields beneath me, and the fog lifts, and I see dark earth and a horizon, close and curved. I run toward it. If I run far and swiftly enough I might plummet off an edge.

"No!" he shouts, and he is beside me, matching my stride, reaching for me with huge, crooked hands. I scream at him and at the soft, bright web that I am still weaving, even as I try to escape it. He cannot be in this Otherworld with me. Another impossibility—and yet I suddenly remember when I nearly lost myself in my vision of Chenn. The eagle with the golden head and crimson beak; its wings filling the sky

until Yigranzi pulled my Otherself free. We were together, I think now, as Teldaru
runs beside me. Yigranzi was with me in that vision and he is with me in this one
. . . I whirl, or try to, but the pain is too great and he is too close. He wraps his hands
around me and we fall.

I was so cold I could not even shiver.

"And now . . . you see." His voice was thin and halting and close. I opened
my eyes. Tried to, thought I had, but saw nothing. Not even grey fog or dancing
black shapes. I was completely blind.

"You see . . . the last thing about blood. Two Otherseers together. Both
bleeding. Same vision."

"Impossible," I wanted to say, one more time, just to make him angry, but my
voice did not work either. My sense of touch, at least, seemed to be returning; I
had begun to feel the stone beneath me. It was so hard that I nearly forgot the
cold.

"You see . . . another thing," he rasped. I wondered, with a jolt of annoyance
that made me feel abruptly alert, why my hearing was the only sense that
seemed truly intact. "Why I need you. So much. Remaking is . . . not like
unmaking. Gives no strength. Steals it, instead. Took me too long to realize.
Now I am certain . . . I need your help. When the time comes."

I tried to remember how I had felt after I had killed Laedon—whether I had
felt strong. I could not. Though I did remember staring down at his twisted body.
His bald head and his eyes weeping blood. I wondered suddenly where Teldaru
was bleeding now; where he had cut himself, to enter my vision. Probably just a
prick on a finger. Something tiny. (He had cut me on the underside of my right
arm, which was throbbing—from the wound itself and from the tightness of
the cloth he had already managed to bind around it.)

The air seemed to be lightening. *I hope it isn't,* I thought. *I hope I really am*
blind and can never do his bidding again. Only I did not believe this, for as the
world did brighten a bit, there was more relief in me than disappointment.

He was silent for a long time. I dozed; he might have, too. I started awake
when he spoke, closer than before, in his own smooth, light voice.

"Many things must change. You and Grasni and Selera can no longer be
students. You will take your place at my side and I will send the other two away.
Find them posts in other royal households. Selera will like that, though she will
stamp her feet and cry when I tell her she must go."

Another silence. I was definitely beginning to see again: stones and muddy colours that hurt my eyes, just as the quiet hurt my ears and the floor hurt my back. Everything too heavy, with too many edges.

"Up now, my sweet."

His hands were on me, easing, propping, smoothing at my clothes and hair. I managed to wrench an arm away from him and he laughed, said, "Good girl!"

I was sitting against the sarcophagus. *Ranior's bones*, I thought, and felt no awe or even interest.

"Look, *Mistress* Nola. See what you've done for me." When I did not move he took my chin in his hand and angled my head down, to what was beside me.

Borl was lying as he had been before. His head was resting near my left hand. He seemed indistinct, outlined in blurry purple, and I strained to make him clearer, even though I did not want to.

"Still can't see well enough?" Teldaru said. He leaned across my lap and took my hand, stroked the back of it with a fingertip that was more like a needle. "Feel, then."

Coarse fur with bumpy ribs beneath. Warm fur, warm flesh—but he had only been dead a short time; surely he could still be warm. . . .

His side rose and fell beneath my hand. Once—an imagining, an impossibility—but no, twice, and again. I felt Borl breathe. I heard him too, making wet, wheezing sounds. Had he been making these before, or had the pressure of my hand prompted them? It did not matter. He was breathing.

Teldaru whistled. The same few notes he always used to bring Borl back to his side, or simply to attention; they echoed in the domed chamber and behind my eyes. My vision was much clearer: I saw the clean, pink edges of the dog's wound meet as he lifted his head, very slowly.

"Good boy," Teldaru said, and reached out his hand. Borl ignored it. He whimpered. He held his head shakily up. His eyes were brown beneath a gauze of white—rolling, unblinking above the moist red of his tongue. His eyes rolling, wide and blind as Laedon's.

"Borl!" Teldaru spoke more sharply, and his fingers stiffened into claw shapes. Borl could have shifted his head to the side just a little and touched him. He did not. He lowered his muzzle, instead, down into my upturned hand. He licked my palm in long, rough strokes that did not change, even when Teldaru gave a ragged shout and lurched to his feet. I laughed; when he struck me across the face with the back of his hand I kept laughing. Borl raised his head again and snarled, baring his teeth. By now my laughter was thin and breathless. It ached against my ribs. Teldaru kicked Borl in the side, over and over, and even though the dog whined and thrashed on the floor, he never stopped growling.

Teldaru spun and grasped the lantern. He strode to the stairs that led down to the doorway, where he turned to look back at me. He opened his mouth as if he would say something, but he did not. He gazed at me a moment longer and then he left me alone in the dark.

Only it was not quite dark, and I was not quite alone. Borl wheezed beside me, the whites of his eyes shining in the torchlight that guttered, now, as the flames burned low. I wheezed a little too. Neither of us moved very much. Borl's paws twitched and I bent my legs up and flat, up and flat. It was all I could do for quite awhile.

Perhaps I should have been frightened, but I was not. I had been earlier, lost in the maze of dead-end corridors, but now I was quite calm, and not because I was numb with shock. I knew, despite horror and revulsion, that I was safe.

Many, many hours must have passed. I imagined the sun setting above the hill, Ranior's monument a long arm of shadow on the ground. I imagined stars and wind. I slept.

When I woke I could move again, and the torches had gone out. Borl's head was in my lap. He was no longer wheezing; just panting lightly, as if he were hot. I stretched my arms up and jiggled my legs until he lifted his head.

"Come on, now," I said. My voice hurt my throat, but mostly because I was desperately thirsty. He whined questioningly. "Up you get. And me too."

I managed this before he did. My legs buckled and I leaned against the sarcophagus, gripping its top edge so hard that my fingernails bent. When I felt steady I let go and stood with my arms out, like a child balancing upright for the first time. "Up, boy," I said to Borl. His legs scrabbled and his claws clicked wildly on the stone and he blew his breath out in great, heaving gasps, but he could not rise. "Fine." I bent carefully and scratched his ears. "You stay there until you're stronger." He laid his head back down but his rolling eyes followed the sounds I made.

Once I was upright my own strength returned quickly. I set my hands and feet to the carved bumps in the sarcophagus' side and pulled myself up, slowly and steadily. I twisted onto the lid, on my belly like a snake. I sat up and swung around so that I could peer down again.

"Easy, Borl," I said as he whimpered and scratched again at the floor. "Rest a little more. All we have to do now is wait."

Teldaru came in very quietly. Perhaps he intended to surprise me, or to watch me sleep—but I was awake and sitting atop the sarcophagus with my legs dangling. He put the lantern down by the stairs and walked over to me. There was a bag in his hand. He looked at me—only at me; not even once at Borl.

I took the bag when he held it up to me. It was heavy, full of lumpy, bumpy things: a waterskin, I saw when I opened the cloth, and an apple, a rounded end of bread, a block of yellow cheese. I ate and drank everything, but not greedily. "I have better manners than I did the last time you watched me eat," I said, between bites. "Good castle manners. Must be much less interesting for you."

He said nothing. Just stood below me, watching me with still, black eyes.

When I was done I dabbed at my mouth with the hem of my skirt. We looked at each other for a very long time. "You didn't expect that," I said at last, gesturing at Borl. "You expected me to succeed, but you had no idea what would happen after. It *surprised* you."

Another silence. I had no trouble meeting his gaze. I was strong and sure, and I knew that this feeling would not last, and the knowledge only made it all the sweeter. "Isn't there anything you want to tell me? Like why he's blind?"

Teldaru frowned but I knew he would speak; he could never resist an opportunity to instruct. "It is a result of remaking. Those who are remade are always blind. Also, sometimes they can only move a bit, and sometimes not at all—this depends on how long they were dead."

"How do you know this?"

"I have done just the tiniest bit of studying, in my time."

"Studying? That is hardly proof. In fact, you have hardly ever *proven* anything to me—I wonder if you really—"

As I was saying those last three words he drew the knife from his belt and plunged its blade into Borl's side. I leapt from the sarcophagus as he went on stabbing: belly, throat, belly, while I hammered at him with my fists and wrapped my arms around his jerking shoulders. Borl made no sound. A few moments later, Teldaru sagged back into my arms, pressing them against his chest so that I could not move them.

"So," he said, and poked Borl with the toe of his shoe. The dog was oozing black liquid that did not quite look like blood. His breath whistled. He lifted his head and blinked at me with his new, blind eyes; a moment later he sat up, shook himself, and growled. "The creature cannot die again, for good, unless you do," Teldaru said. "Shall I prove *this* part to you, now?"

I shook my head. All my bravado had been swept away by a sickness that made my limbs judder. When he let me go I crumpled to my knees.

"No?" he said from above me. "Well, then. Let us go home."

He walked to the door and I rose and took a few wobbly paces after him, then stopped and turned. Borl was panting, his black-streaked tongue lolling. "Come," I said, and he whimpered. I went to him and knelt and put my hands on his flanks. They were trembling. "Come, Borl," I murmured. "Get up. Walk. We'll go together." He licked my hand. His breath was hot and smelled of rotting meat. "Up, now. Up you get." He trembled and trembled.

"Move aside, Nola." Teldaru bent down next to me. He lifted Borl and cradled him. The dog was silent. His sightless eyes did not leave my face.

Teldaru walked down the stairs and out through the door. I picked up the lantern and followed. "Close it," he said, and I pulled the great stone slab shut behind us.

This time I did not need to touch the walls. I glanced at the shadowed grooves that had led me here, but not for long; it was easier to concentrate on Teldaru's back, and anyway, he was walking swiftly. There was no Otherworldly glow in my eyes or against my skin; just the lantern light. We passed through corridors and beneath low doors with painted lintels; we climbed stairs so close together that Teldaru took them four at once. It seemed to take no time at all to reach the final doorway—the squat, low one that opened onto dusk. I knelt beneath it and coughed, choking on fresh air. There was a gentle wind; it flowed around me from the hill and meadow, wrapped me in green, growing, flowering. I could almost see it.

We paused only a few times on the road back to the city, so that Teldaru could set Borl down and shake the stiffness from his arms and shoulders. He did not speak to me or even look at me. I hardly noticed. I watched the last of the sun as it turned the grasses to gold and the far-off castle stones to fire. I watched the leaves darken. I watched my own shadow on the ground and thought that it was taller than I'd ever be, and I saw it get fainter and fainter yet, in the darkness that grew around the small light of the lantern.

The sky was blue-black and speckled with stars when we reached the eastern gate. Teldaru stopped for the last time, here. Borl barked once and Teldaru put him down, and this time the dog stood firmly on his feet. He turned to me and wagged his tail. I held my hand to his damp muzzle and said, "Well *done*, Borl," and he barked again, as if he was answering me.

Teldaru waved at the tower guards and we walked into Sarsenay City. It had been so long since I had seen these streets at night, and they seemed magical—even the smelly, muddy ones—and despite all that had happened at Ranior's Tomb, I looked on the darkened stone and flickering torches with something that felt like joy. I thought of the brothel and of Bardrem, and this caused me no pain. *There is such beauty in the world, to balance out all the horror*, I thought, and then: *I must be drunk*—and I smiled at nothing and everything.

Borl and I both had a bit of trouble with the castle steps. Teldaru let us rest. He stared up at the keep with an intensity that should have unsettled me but did not. I wondered, when I was walking again, whether Borl would stay with me when we reached my room—but we did not go there. Teldaru led us into the keep and stopped, turned to block our way when we reached King Haldrin's study door. He knocked on it.

"Yes?" The king's voice. My joy fluttered in my chest and vanished.

Teldaru opened the door. I saw a blaze of light and faces—ones I didn't recognize, except for Haldrin's. He was not smiling.

"Teldaru," he said in a tight voice I had not heard from him before. "I was looking for you—I wanted you here for this, but I could not find you. Come to me later; in an hour, say, and—"

"My king." The words rang. Five men—for I had managed to count them, by now—stared at the Great Teldaru. "I am sorry I was not here when you sought me and I am sorry to disturb you now, but something terribly important has happened. Nola has had a vision and you must hear of it."

The king's eyes shifted to me. I looked at my feet, but it did not matter; I could still feel his eyes. "And what was this vision?" he said. A mild question, but I thought I heard uneasiness, beneath.

"Haldrin," Teldaru said slowly, "it is as I have been telling you; it is what I have seen myself in the Pattern of this land. In your Pattern. The fact that Nola, too, has been shown—"

"Daru," said the king, "just say it."

Teldaru waited one long, quiet moment more. Then he took a deep breath. "For yourself and for your country," he said, "you will marry Princess Zemiya of Belakao."

CHAPTER TWENTY-FIVE

I've been having a dream—the same one for years and years. I am standing by my mother's old, scarred table, but not in the house, nor even in a room. My surroundings change: sometimes desert, sometimes lush riverbank, other times a plain of waist-high grass. The table is always there, though, as are the paths: giant, red, wet-looking ones that hover above the ground and flow around me. These paths bring me people. They bob along, just specks at first, then shapes with some definition, and finally themselves: men and women, children, all of them familiar to me. Larally has been among them—the first person I ever Othersaw for; the first person I wounded. Grasni is there, floating, looking down at me. Selera, lazily plaiting her blonde hair. There are so many others whose names I have forgotten, but this does not matter. I know I have wronged each of them. They return to me, on their river-paths of blood, and I try to turn away from them, but the only other place I can look is down at the table. Potato slices there, and a bag of coins, and a row of severed fingertips that I know are my mother's, and probably the other children's, too: my siblings', whose names I have also forgotten. The red rises, and arms reach out to wind around me, and I wake gasping and sobbing to be forgiven, and saved.

I had the dream again last night. It was not enough, this time, to thrash my twisted sheets away and take a few paces around my room. This morning I poked the almost-dead fire into a fitful glow; I cracked the thin layer of ice on my basin (quietly, so as not to wake the princess) and drank enough water to numb my throat—and I still had not shaken off the dream's weight. So I went to the door and stepped through it. It was so early that Sildio was not on his stool. I walked by it and out into the dawn, and down to the main courtyard.

It was such a strange, headlong feeling: my feet bearing me over the patches of snow and the crinkly grass between. My lungs filling with sharp, cold air that was all around me, not just gusting in my window. Full winter is coming; I smelled it, felt it beneath my feet and on my skin.

It was the dream that sent me outside. It was winter. It was the press of all the words I've written, these past many months. And it was my stillness. For all these months I've been in my room. I've been still. This morning I needed to *move*.

The tower guard opened the gate for me. I wrapped my cloak more tightly around me, for it is always windy at the top of the road that leads down into the city. I did not know where I would go, but I suppose I expected to walk a ways. As it was, I took a few steps and then I turned back. Because I wanted to look at the castle from the outside, for once, and also because I heard the fountain.

This fountain is built into the castle wall. Its bowl (a half-bowl, really) is very large, with a lovely scalloped edge, but no one sits on it to gossip or cup their palms for a drink. This is the king's fountain. The stone hands that channel the water are his hands: protector's hands, worn smooth and white by centuries. I turned expecting to see only these things—the stone, the water—but there were others too. Lengths of cloth and ribbon, I saw as I stepped closer. Scraps of colour fluttering from the wall beside the fountain, held by nails that had been driven into the spaces between the red stones. I have seen such offerings before, around the fountains and sometimes the trees of the lower city. They are for mourning, for people beloved and lost. I had never seen them by this fountain. It was only when I was very close that I realized why they were here. For whom.

Layibe. A name, sewn into one of the broad pieces of cloth. The thread was silver, and caught the light that was spreading behind me. Red and purple ribbons, blue and gold cloth, and this name in ink, in thread.

Layibe. Haldrin's little, lost daughter. The princess who was sleeping in a cradle in my room, guarded by a bird and a dog. The girl whose face also appears in that nightmare of mine, because I have wounded her, too.

I hardly remember going back into the castle. I only began to breathe again when I was at my desk, clutching my quill as if I would protect myself with it. Or harm myself—I don't know—it seems like the same thing, sometimes.

And so I am still sitting here, gazing from my paper to the bright blue-white of the sky and sometimes down to the child who is sleeping in the cradle at my feet. My need to go forward—to write and then to ready myself for whatever comes after that—is so strong that I am frozen.

Move, Nola. Back to the king's study—to all those eyes on you.

To Haldrin, breaking a long, long silence: "What have you seen, Nola? Why must I marry Princess Zemiya?"

* * *

You mustn't. I've seen nothing. It's Teldaru's plan and I don't understand it yet but I know that it will hurt many people.

I could not say this but, as I swallowed and blinked away all the faces except Haldrin's, I knew that I could try to say something else that might be almost true. I had had no vision of Belakao or Zemiya; there were no true images that the curse could twist. I would only have to take care, choose words that would be vague.

"It is not certain," I began. One man leaned forward and another leaned back. I felt their scrutiny, their waiting, and drew myself taller.

"Not certain?" Haldrin said. There was a tiny crease between his brows, just above the bridge of his nose.

"Of course it is certain," Teldaru said from behind me. He sounded amused and perhaps a little impatient. "The Pattern is a maze of possibilities, but only the Belakaoans themselves believe that there is no—"

"That is nonsense," I snapped over my shoulder. "You always teach that there are often many images; that an Otherseer must choose among all the—"

"Enough." Haldrin did not shout, but his voice rang in my ears anyway. "This is not the time for a debate about the characteristics of Otherseeing. Nola—speak to *me*."

I wish I could, I thought with a surge of despair and need that made me dizzy. "I am sorry, my king," I said. I bowed my head, then lifted it again, and brushed a strand of hair away from my eyes. *There was no vision, but there is so much I must tell you. . . .* "One of the images was a volcano in the sea, it's true, but another was a northern mountain range, and yet another—"

"Nola," the king said, and I stopped speaking, my mouth open a bit. "Lift your arm again, as you did a moment ago."

I did, and the sleeve of my blouse fell away from it. All the men stared at my arm. Haldrin looked only briefly before he raised his eyes to mine.

"You are bleeding."

"Yes," I said, flushing, dizzy again—so close to truth. "I was." The bandage around my arm felt hot, as did the trail of blood that had escaped it, hours ago, and dried. The cloth was dark and damp, growing brittle against my skin. *Teldaru cut me. He forced me to use the Bloodsight.* "Teldaru took me into the city and I stumbled and cut myself." The lies came so smoothly, though there was a place in my throat that ached when I told them.

"Yes—an old rusty brothel sign that had fallen and was lying in the street." Teldaru stepped up beside me. He was shaking his head. "I had no desire to take her back to that neighbourhood, of course, but we were looking for a kind of plant I have only ever found in the lowtown markets."

A brothel sign. I felt my flush drain away to pallor. A brothel, and Bardrem; a threat that Teldaru knew would still frighten me, after all these years. I would not be able to bear his triumph, so I kept my gaze on the king.

"Sit," Haldrin said to me as he rose himself. He walked to the only empty chair and pulled it away from the table. "Rest here a little—unless you would like to go directly to your room?"

"She will stay," Teldaru said. "These matters concern her, since she has seen what I have."

Borl walked over to me, then, only a little unsteadily; he was already used to being blind. He laid his head in my lap. The king frowned again—at the gesture, and probably too at the blood that had dried and matted on the dog's already dark fur.

"And what of Belakao, Master Teldaru?" said one of the other men, and Haldrin turned away from the dog and me and returned to his own seat.

"Lord Derris," Teldaru said, "I thank you for reminding us of our purpose, here. I will tell you of my vision while Nola thinks on hers."

I had seen Lord Derris before; he was the king's cousin, and attended all the feasts and processions that I did. I had never heard him speak. He had a breathy rasp of a voice—from an arrow taken in the throat. I thought I saw the white-pink tip of a scar, below his beard. His eyes were blue, like Haldrin's, but hard.

Teldaru walked over to the window. The sky was very dark, though I could not see any stars from here. "A volcano spilled its fire into the sea." Even I went still, listening to him. "The water boiled and foamed and rose in waves that threatened to sweep toward land. Except that the land, too, rose. Trees and vines coiled down to the shore and out upon the ocean's skin. Rocks tumbled and sank into a wall that wound its way beneath, toward the volcano. In this union of land and sea, the fire sank to smoke and the waves subsided and all the world was filled with stone and growing things."

"A powerful vision," the king said after a moment. It felt as if the room remembered to breathe, when he spoke. "But how do you know that it does not indicate that I am simply to forge a closer alliance with the new *moabu*?"

"No." Teldaru's hands were clenched around the windowsill; he was gazing out at the night. I thought, as I had before, *He is beautiful.* The thought was too quick, too fluid to stop. "It was a *union*, Haldrin. A joining of land and sea, stone and fire. It was you and Zemiya."

"She is not young."

"Forgive me, my king, but nor are you. But it will still be a fruitful union: I am sure of this."

"Sarsenayans might not accept a Belakaoan queen."

"Sarsenayans will be relieved to *have* a queen, and heirs to your throne. They do not understand why you have waited so long."

King Haldrin picked up a quill. I noticed only now that the table was strewn with maps, some of their corners held down with books. He twirled the quill so that its curved end brushed a map—up and along the black arches of a mountain range, I saw.

"And why would Belakao give up one of its princesses?" Lord Derris said. The other three murmured in agreement.

Teldaru turned back to face the room. "She had no children with her first husband. She is a burden. She has no power except that to be gained by another marriage. And"—he walked to the table, nudged a book aside, traced a fingertip along what looked like the undulations of a shoreline—"as we already know, her brother the new *moabu* wants more from us than his father did."

"His father was a reasonable man," said someone I did not know.

"Ah," Teldaru said, "but this Bantayo is not. He is not content with the treaties that bind our countries. He has made this clear from the moment his father died."

"And now," said yet another man, "he tells us that Lorselland is offering more."

"But they will not offer him *this*." Teldaru smiled. "Such a bond—it will go beyond any treaty imaginable. He would be a fool to refuse."

"And what of me?" The king's voice was mild, but the frown still wrinkled that place above his nose. "Tell me, Teldaru, since you are so certain: how should *I* feel about this?"

Teldaru's smile changed a little, softened, as if they were both younger, and alone. It made me prickle with cold or warmth; I was not sure which. "The Pattern is clear, Hal," he said quietly. "It will be a Path of power and joy, for you and for your people."

No! No: it will be twisted and terrible because he is making it, my king. . . . I pushed my chair back, still sitting, my arms braced on the edge of the table. Borl whined and settled back on his haunches.

"What are you doing?" My words hung among them, heavy as rain about to fall. Teldaru's eyes narrowed. I thought of Bardrem and spoke again anyway, in a rush of desperation—around the truth, as close to it as I could get. "Why do you speak of such things? And why," I continued, glancing at each of the other men, "do you believe them? Because he is the Great Master Otherseer? Because he is Teldaru—only that?"

"You are unwell," Teldaru said swiftly, starting toward me. "Your wound—perhaps there is a fever starting."

"Or perhaps it is the return of my madness? That madness that possessed me when I arrived here six years ago; I'm sure you all remember, for he made much of it." The truth so close, and Haldrin's keen, kind eyes on me once more, but this would be all, for Teldaru was wrapping his hand around my good arm and pulling, and I was up.

"Come, now; I will walk you back to your room and fetch Mistress Ket, and then"—to the king—"I will return and we will discuss how to put our proposal to *Moabu* Bantayo."

Haldrin put the quill down with a sharp, snapping sound. He was no longer looking at me, though the others were, with distaste and discomfort and maybe a bit of awe. "I am glad that you have decided for me," he said to Teldaru, "for there is not much time. We have only just learned—and it is why we met, tonight: he is on his way here."

Teldaru's fingers dug even more deeply into my skin and I flinched. His face hardly changed but I felt his surprise, and something else too, which trembled after the first pressure was gone. "Here," he said steadily. "To Sarsenay."

"To Lorselland as well," said Lord Derris. "He is a new king assessing his allies. We must impress him."

"We will." Teldaru turned his black eyes to me and I looked into them, defiant and lost. "Won't we, Nola?"

CHAPTER TWENTY-SIX

Moabu Bantayo went to Lorselland first. It took him two months to arrive in Sarsenay, and by the time he did the capital city was a riot of banners and garlands and washed, shining stone. It had been nearly thirty years since a Belakaoan dignitary had visited. And this was the new king.

"The *mo-a-bu*," Selera said with her lips pursed, as if she were tasting something sour.

"Now say *ispa*," suggested Grasni.

We were sitting in one of the classrooms on the second floor of the school building. The room was shaded by the tree, which trailed its leaf-thick branches in the window, but the air was still smotheringly hot. Grasni and I were running with sweat; our dresses clung to us in dark, damp patches. Selera's dress was dry. Her face and hair were dry. She was fanning herself languidly with a rolled-up scroll.

"Or just say *moabu* again," Grasni said. "I could tell how much you enjoyed it."

Selera scowled, and I laughed. Grasni did not look at me, but I did not mind: she was sitting near me, hadn't risen to leave as soon as our students had. She was close.

"It's an ugly language," Selera declared. "And they're ugly people. But there are so many of them living among us now; I suppose I should be accustomed to them."

"As you're accustomed to their jewels," I said. "And their cloth."

Grasni smiled a little. Selera raised her hand to her braid, which was wound with green ribbon studded with gems: amber, crimson and blue ones, polished but uncut, born in Belakaoan fire.

"I like their things, yes," she said, rising, "but that doesn't mean I have to like them." She looked down at me with a little smile of her own. "And anyway," she went on, "certain *other* people enjoy my ribbons too. Certain other people enjoy drawing them out of my hair one at a time."

"How lovely for other people," I said, as dryly as I could. I was thinking: *Don't leave.* I wanted her to, of course, but then I would be alone with Grasni, and then *she* would leave, with some awkward word or glance, and—

"Girls." Mistress Ket was in the open doorway, leaning heavily on her stick. She hardly ever came up the staircase, these days; we all gaped at her. "There has been word—*Moabu* Bantayo is close. A day away, perhaps, no more."

Selera gasped. "So the feast may be tomorrow!" She glanced at me. "I must find some particularly fine jewels for my hair." As she passed Mistress Ket she bent and kissed the tangled, white hair at the top of her head.

Grasni stood. "As must I!" she said with fervour so false that I snorted.

"Shall I help?" I said. "You never have been any good at choosing colours that match."

"No." She spoke quickly. Blinked at me, ran the back of her hand across her sweat-sheened forehead. "Thank you, Nola, but no." And then she was gone, as I had known she would be, and I did not have the courage to follow her.

In any case, there was someone else I needed to find.

Mistress Ket leaned heavily on my arm as we went down the stairs. When we reached the bottom she kept her hand where it was, squeezing a bit.

"It's difficult for you," she said. Her eyes were dark, dark grey—fading from the black they'd been when she was younger. For some the Othersight grew gentle; for some it disappeared. A very few, Yigranzi had told me once, were consumed by it and never saw with their own eyes again.

I thought, with a wave of relief, *Now we'll talk about it—about what Grasni saw when she looked at my Pattern.* . . .

"For all three of you."

I said, "What?" I sounded like a child.

Mistress Ket peered up at me. I wondered suddenly what it would feel like to lose the Othersight, to be blind to the Otherworld. No teachers had ever talked to us about this.

"You and Grasni and Selera are in a difficult place. You are no longer girls, yet you are not quite women, because we have kept you here too long—yes"—a tighter squeeze of my arm—"we have. Master Teldaru knows it too. You've just been so useful—such fine students, and good with the little ones, too. But now

we've decided to give you postings, when this excitement with Belakao is over."
She smiled. Her two front teeth were a peculiar shade of purple-brown; we had
mocked them, years ago, but not any more. "You will all be happier. Perhaps you
will even find love, as I have not, as so many Otherseers do not. You are sweet
girls."

"Mistress Ket . . ." I put my hand over hers. "What about Grasni? She told
you something a few months ago." It was agonizingly close to the truth; I would
not be able to say much else before the curse took the words away. "She did
something for me, though we knew she should not, and—"

"No, Nola." She was frowning now, clutching my arm even more tightly. "No.
Master Teldaru has commanded me to speak of this to no one, not even to you.
There are mysteries, and only he can understand them, and the rest of us must
keep silence."

"Of course," I said, breathing around a suffocating weight that could have
been laughter or tears. "That's very true. And Master Teldaru . . . where do you
think he is, now?" A clumsy way to ask, but she smiled again, probably relieved
that I was no longer speaking of mysteries.

"He is in his rooms. It was he who sent me to you with the news—and soon
he will be joining the king. There will be many preparations to make."

"Yes," I said, with pretend eagerness. "I will go to him—see if I can be of
help."

One more smile, and a pat. "Nola," Mistress Ket said, "you're a good girl."

His rooms were in the keep. I knew precisely where—we all did—though
I had never been there; never in six years, for he had always come to me. I
wondered, as Borl and I walked through the trees, whether anyone other than
the king had seen Teldaru's rooms. Even Selera had not; I had asked her about
this once and she had spluttered something about the sensual possibilities of
the outdoors, and the ecstasy of waking in her own bed to his hands on her.

I had listened to the younger students whispering about what Master
Teldaru's rooms might look like. Statues of marble and gold (for he was known
to enjoy sculpture). Strange musical instruments from far-off lands (for he
had an ear for music). Golden cushions, golden washbasin and ewer, and an
enormous golden mirror. *No*, I thought when I heard this, *you will find that last
item in a house in the city—that, and a bird whose colours would amaze you.*

When we turned the corner that would bring us to his door, Borl began
to whine. "Yes," I said, "I know—you used to live here with him—it must be
terrible to remember that." He sat down in the middle of the corridor and

turned his blind white eyes up to me. I scratched his ears and bent to run my hand under his muzzle. "I wish you would come with me—but very well. Wait here." He lay down with his flank pressed against the wall. I stepped past him and rapped on the door.

As it turned out, there was no gold in the rooms through which Teldaru led me. Three rooms: one with a plain wooden table and two chairs, another with a narrow bed and washstand, and a third (which I glimpsed through a half-open door) with a floor tiled in brown and white, and a low, square tub built into the floor. A private bathing room—and I imagined him there, washing blood from his body as candlelight flickered over his hair, his skin, his midnight eyes.

"Teldaru." I spoke suddenly, to force the image away. He motioned me to one of the chairs. I sat, wishing that Borl were at my feet. I glanced out the window and saw the courtyard trees and the ribbon of path and, quite clearly, the window and door of my own small room.

"Do you have some sort of magnifying lens?" I asked lightly. "So that you can see straight in to my bed?"

"A fine idea," Teldaru said. I had not expected him to reply; I shifted on my chair and hoped he would not notice my flush.

"Oh, Nola." His eyes on me; just the hint of a smile. "What I could show you, in that narrow bed of yours."

"So why don't you?" I said, too quickly to stop myself. "Why haven't you, when you claim to have wanted me for so long? Or do you only want young girls? Though," I finished in a sickening rush, "that would not explain Selera."

His chair creaked as he leaned back. I stared out the window, seeing nothing.

"Really remarkable things," he said at last, slowly, "take time."

"Ah"—looking back at him—"so you may yet honour me with your attentions. How reassuring." *Enough*, I thought. *Nola—enough.*

"What did you really come here to ask me, Mistress?"

I laughed breathlessly. "It doesn't matter. All I can do is talk around what I want to say."

"As you tried to do in Haldrin's study, in front of all those people. Tell me," he said, leaning forward now, "how did it feel to make a fool of yourself in front of all those people? In front of the King of Sarsenay?"

I leaned forward too. "Belakao," I said. The curse stirred in my belly with just this one word. "*Moabu* Bantayo. Zemiya. Tell me exactly what you mean to do."

He chuckled. "Do you truly believe you deserve this information, after all the betrayals you've attempted? Truly, Nola? It is as if you do not *want* me to lift the curse."

I flinched, and spoke again before he could. "It wouldn't make any difference, telling me. I can't tell anyone else, and I won't try, because no, I did not enjoy humiliating myself in front of the king, and yes, I do want you to help me, someday. And surely," I added in a low voice, "surely you long to tell *someone* of your plans."

He was no longer smiling. "My plans," he said at last, "continue to grow and change. There are so many Paths, and the Pattern is vaster than I have ever seen it, and all I know for certain is that we must draw the Belakaoans close, as I said to you before. We must draw them close before we break them."

I squirmed in my chair, because I knew that every word I intended to speak would feel like a stone in my throat. "You hate Zemiya and Neluja," I said. "But why do you hate Haldrin too?"

Teldaru snorted. "I do not hate him. I feel nothing for him—I never did, even when we were boys. 'How handsome the prince is—and he'll be even handsomer when he's king.' People feared me and fawned over him—but even then I thought of him as little as a horse does the fly that sits on its flank."

I wanted to say, *Indeed? So why do you seek to usurp him and lay waste to his land?* "If that is so," I said instead, "why do you make these plans?"

I thought he might smile, but he did not—he rose and gazed out the window. I watched his jaw work, as if he were tasting his words before speaking them. "Hal is a small man—a king only by accident of birth. He does not deserve Sarsenay."

"And you, who were born in a tavern, do?"

He turned his head slowly. I straightened, beneath his gaze. "It is a tale often told, in the lower city," I said quietly. "The little boy, son of no one, who became the Great Master Teldaru."

"I know the tale," he said, also quietly. "I know, too, that little boys who are sons of no one never become kings. Our world would have to change, for this to be the case. And that is what I, the great Master Teldaru of lowtown tales, will do—what *we* will do, my Nola. Together we will change the world."

"It will be difficult," I said, "if you won't tell me how."

Teldaru threw his head back into the sunlight and laughed.

Bantayo, *moabu* of Belakao, arrived at midday. The moment the cry sounded, atop the highest tower, the walls of city and castle filled with people. I stood beside Teldaru on that highest tower. The king and his cousin were with us. I saw Selera and Grasni on the wall below; Selera scowled at me and Grasni gave me a quick wave and an almost-smile.

There were no clouds at all, and, even so high up, no wind. I wiped sweat from my eyes and squinted at the road, which rippled with heat and distance. I saw glints on the furthest part of the road; flashes of light that, after hours had passed (and I had ducked inside for shade and water), became spear tips and polished drumskins and the jewelled clothing of many people. *Zemiya already*, I thought, remembering Teldaru's tale of the *moabe*'s years-ago arrival here, but it was soon obvious that there were no women at all, this time. Only men— thirty or so of them, wearing flowing garments that were every bright colour imaginable. Their drumbeats shuddered through the air.

"How did they manage to get the drums here?" Haldrin said. "First on the boats and then overland?"

Teldaru said, "You asked the same question nearly thirty years ago," and the king said, "Did I?" and smiled. His curls were dark with sweat, flattened against his neck and forehead, but he looked quite calm, as the sun beat down and the Belakaoans drew nearer. It was Teldaru who paced restlessly to the battlements and back to the others again, humming urgently and tunelessly under his breath.

"Daru, stop," Haldrin said. "I'm afraid you'll fall over."

Teldaru glared at him and continued pacing.

"Master Teldaru," said Lord Derris in his odd, half-voice. "Please." Teldaru stopped.

Moabu Bantayo was a small man. I looked down at the broad-shouldered drummers and the tall, gleaming spear-carriers, and then I looked at the man who walked among them all, and I could not believe that this was he—the new *moabu* who had already been so harsh and demanding. A few hours later, in the Great Hall, I saw that, although he was short and slight, he was also sleek. The muscles in his arms stood out as he gestured, and he moved with the grace of a hunting cat. His beard was short and pointed at the tip. The cloth of his robe was covered in tiny gems and shells that flashed every time he moved. And he moved a great deal. He stood before the dais where King Haldrin was sitting and he turned and turned again, looking at the room while everyone else looked at him.

"Welcome, *Moabu* Bantayo," the king said in a loud, firm voice that made me blink. I was sitting at the long table that had been placed closest to the dais. I could see all their eyes, from here: Haldrin's, Teldaru's and Bantayo's. Blue, black and brown. I was not sure whose I should watch most closely.

"King Haldrin," said Bantayo.

I remembered how Teldaru had described this *moabu*'s father's voice—"poured honey"—and thought that this was not true of Bantayo's. Just two words, but I heard metal in them, and my heart began to pound.

"I trust you have had a pleasant journey," said King Haldrin. He was not smiling. His hands lay loosely on the arms of his throne.

"Pleasant enough," *Moabu* Bantayo said. "Lorselland was a most delightful place. Their roads are better than yours."

The king's brows rose, just a little. "Indeed?" he said, and then he did smile. "But their wine, I happen to know, is worse." He gestured and a serving boy scuttled forward, clutching a pitcher. "*Moabu*, we have much to discuss—but first you and your men must sit and rest and drink *our* wine."

More servers arrived, bearing another long table that they placed on the dais in front of the throne. They brought other chairs, too, and Teldaru sat, as did Lord Derris. Bantayo watched this activity, his men standing in a circle behind him (their drums and spears had been left elsewhere). They did not look hot—maybe because this Sarsenayan heat was nothing to them, after their black rock and sand and their own ocean sun. I thought of Yigranzi; I wished, with pain that felt new, that I could run to her room and sit down and say, "Tell me about drums and *moabus* and polished shells, because now I've seen all of these things."

The music began as Bantayo took his seat between the king and Lord Derris. The harp and flute sounded too sweet to fill the quiet—but soon there was murmuring as well, at the high table and at the ones around mine. The Belakaoans were led to places among the Sarsenayans. One of the island men sat next to me, and I watched his dark fingers plucking at chicken and bread. I wondered what I would say to him, if he spoke to me, but he only ate and sipped from his goblet and stared at the high table.

Bantayo, seated, was a full head shorter than both Haldrin and Teldaru. He should have looked like a mere youth, between them, but he did not. Because of the beard, yes—but also because of the smooth, purposeful movements of his hands as he ate and the tilt of his head as he listened to the other men, or spoke himself. I had never seen such power contained, controlled—and it frightened me, excited me, especially when I looked at Teldaru.

This will be harder than he imagines, I thought. *This man will not be led.* I also thought, *Whatever happens, it must be soon; no one will be able to bear waiting.*

But everyone did wait, for days and days. King Haldrin and *Moabu* Bantayo met in the study. They ate together (privately, and at yet more feasts, which Selera attended adorned in Belakaoan jewels) and walked together and rode around the city in a closed carriage. The Belakaoan soldiers showed Sarsenayan soldiers how to throw spears into straw-stuffed targets in the main courtyard, amid wagers and much laughter and shouting. Sarsenayan soldiers showed the Belakaoan soldiers how to hold swords—more laughter but no wagers, since the Belakaoans refused to do any actual fighting. I walked about, alone or with some younger students, and I watched, listened and counted the hours until sundown, when Teldaru would come to tell me what had happened that day.

"Bantayo has now taken issue with our ale, our vegetables, our women and our sunsets. The Lorsellanders have offered Belakao three times more lumber than we currently give them. He is unimpressed with each of our offers; he is losing patience."

"And what of *the* offer?" I asked on one of these nights.

Teldaru shrugged and said nothing.

He came to me on the morning of the sixth day. It was early, but already the heat was settling onto skin and cloth and the bowed tops of the trees. I was splashing tepid water on my face; he touched my back and I whirled.

"Nola." He seemed very still. "It is happening. Now. I was with them all night and past dawn, and Haldrin asked about Zemiya—about all Bantayo's family, and her too. He has tried to ask before, but Bantayo did not answer. Until today."

I tried to picture it, as he told me the rest.

"Neluja is a strong ispa, *a credit to our blood."*

"And your other sister? Zemiya?"

"A proud woman, though she has no reason to be."

"But she too is of your blood—royal blood—surely she is revered as the rest of you are?"

"She shows me little honour."

"But the people—"

"They love her. It is difficult for me to do the same."

"I will ask the others here to leave us now, moabu. *You and I must talk alone."*

Teldaru was holding my shoulders—the bare skin beneath my sleeping shift. "It is as I have seen. This is the Pattern that will shape my triumph. Our triumph." He smiled and dug his fingers in. "And it has been so *simple*! Will it always be so simple?"

Please, I thought as I crossed the courtyard with him, *let him be wrong. Let this Path twist all of us away from him. Let him be wrong.*

We stood outside Haldrin's study with Derris and the other lords. No one spoke. The only voices came from behind the closed door: a rising and falling, words blurred, impossible to understand. Then, after a time, silence.

The people in the corridor stood straighter as the door opened. King Haldrin stepped out, and *Moabu* Bantayo behind him. Now, so close, I saw that Bantayo was even shorter than I had thought he was, and that his eyes (which lit on me briefly) were very beautiful—several shades of brown shot through with green—and very cold.

Both men were smiling.

"You, my trusted advisers, shall know first." There were purplish shadows under Haldrin's eyes, and a smattering of golden-brown stubble on his cheeks and chin, and his tunic was rumpled. He was like a boy who had just risen from a too-short rest—hungrily, wildly awake.

"The *moabu* and I have reached an agreement that will unite our lands forever."

I saw Teldaru's hands clench and thought, *He was right.*

"*Moabe* Zemiya of Belakao will be queen of Sarsenay."

No, I thought as the others moved to clasp Haldrin's hands and bow to Bantayo. Teldaru did not step forward with them. He was still beside me; I felt his gaze and turned toward it because I knew I must, eventually.

"So simple, love," he said. "You see?"

"No," I whispered, over and over, so that I would not have to hear the voice within me that said "yes."

CHAPTER TWENTY-SEVEN

"Tollic!" Grasni cried. "Dren! Stop immediately before you fall in!"

We were outside—all of us, nine younger students and Selera and Grasni and I and even Mistress Ket, who was sitting on a bench beneath the shadiest tree. It had been too hot indoors; the students had been sodden and querulous and impossible to teach. So we had all come out to the courtyard, where there was the hint of a hint of a breeze, and Tollic and Dren had discovered enough energy with which to wrestle each other.

We were not doing much to stop them. Grasni was laughing as she shouted, and some of the other children were cheering. Tollic and Dren were now the oldest boys among the group—eleven and ten—and they were clumsy and graceful, a delight to watch. Selera was the only one protesting; she was waving her arms, trying to stand between the wrestlers and her own small, excited charges.

Dren, who was shorter than Tollic but also broader, lunged at the other boy, and with a scrabbling, desperate flurry of limbs they both fell into the pool.

Everyone was silent, very suddenly. The pool was sacred; it had been in this place before the castle had, and Sarsenay's very first Otherseer had used it for her visions. Also, it was full of those tiny fish that glowed green in darkness. You might dabble a hand in it, on a hot day like this, but nothing more.

Grasni and I knelt and reached for the boys. They were thrashing, stirring the clear water to murkiness. It was not deep, but they were panicking, choking, slipping away before we could get a grip on them.

"Nola!" Selera's voice was shrill.

"Selera," I said loudly, "I'm busy—just wait—"

"Nola," said a new voice, and I froze. "Move aside, now." Teldaru leaned out over the pool and hoisted Tollic and Dren up. He deposited them onto the yellow-brown grass, where they hunched, sputtering and coughing, and not looking at any of us.

I sat back on my heels. Teldaru was standing, brushing dirt from his knees. He was smiling. *He should be angry*, I thought, and, *What now . . .?*

"I tried to make them stop." Selera was beside him. I wondered yet again how she managed to be simpering and solemn at the same time. "They are incorrigible, all of them." She glared from Grasni to me, as if we had leapt into the pool ourselves, against her express orders.

"They are," Teldaru agreed.

"I tried—" Selera began, and he held up a hand.

"Yes, Selera, I'm sure you did. And I'm appreciative of your efforts, as always."

Her simper wobbled into something less confident. One of her students (a little girl no more than seven) giggled, and Mistress Ket thumped her stick against the ground and cried, "Quiet while Master Teldaru is speaking!" Master Teldaru himself continued to smile.

"I have come to give you good tidings," he said.

Selera brightened again. "About the wedding?" The students murmured, and another few giggled.

"No," he said. "About you—about my three lovely, grown girls."

Grasni glanced at me. I shrugged a bit, not caring if he saw. My belly was crawling with dread.

"Stand with me, Mistress Ket." She rose slowly; Selera rushed over to her, helped her shuffle across the grass to Teldaru.

"Selera, Grasni and Nola, you are not students any more. You have known this—we all have—for months and months, but it is time to make the knowledge real. It is time for you to take your places as Mistresses of Otherseeing."

Selera gave a gasp that sounded very loud.

"Nola," he said. That benevolent smile, those calm black eyes; I swallowed dryness and a taste of bile. "You will stay here." Hardly a shock—so why did my heart give a great, lurching thump? "Mistress Ket and I need you, for, as you well know, there has not been a full complement of teachers at the castle since Master Parvo and Mistress Mandola left." They had run away together, Selera told us. "Even if she did look a little like a toad," she had said, "and he was old, it's terribly romantic, don't you think?" *Terribly lucky*, is what I had thought; *they're free.*

"Grasni," he went on, and looked down at her. She was sitting quite straight among her dress' riotous folds. "You will go to Narlenel. It is a fine city, and its lord and lady are fine rulers."

"And it is near my own town," she said. "Thank you, Master Teldaru."

He nodded, let his eyes slip from her to Selera. "Selera."

"Master?" she said brightly. She looked very beautiful just then: soft green dress, gold at her ears and throat, Belakaoan gems and ribbons in her hair. She glowed with certainty.

"You will go to Meriden—another city of vital importance to Sarsenay. It is second only to our own in wealth and influence."

"But . . ." A dimming of the glow. She twisted her hands in her dress. "Master, I thought . . . I thought you would keep me here?"

Her voice cracked on the last word. I looked away from her, pitying her even as I exulted.

"No, my dear," he said, "Nola is the only one to stay. And you will be grateful when you see your new home. They have silks there that will—"

"I don't *want* silks!" she cried. One of the students whimpered. "I want to stay! I need to be here, Master—you know that."

Grasni's mouth was hanging open. The whimpering student began to sob. Teldaru frowned—in consternation, not anger—and stepped toward Selera, but before he reached her she lifted her skirts and whirled and ran.

"Do not worry about her," he said as we watched her go. She stumbled once, where the grass met the path, but she did not fall (and I was surprised to find that I did not want her to). "It is difficult to embrace change right away. She will soon be happy. Especially," he added, smiling again, "when I tell her about the celebration we will have."

A feast, as it turned out. I watched the tables being set up in the seers' courtyard a few days later, even as the lower courtyard was filling with tents and performers' stages. Zemiya would be arriving in a matter of weeks; the king had called upon Sarsenayan artists to gather at the castle for a celebratory competition. Singers, poets, sculptors, painters, dancers: they flooded onto the castle grounds and into the inns of Sarsenay City, all of them hoping to win fame at the royal wedding. We could hear their clamour from here. Distant music, clapping and laughter and some shouting. Singing. A hum, beneath everything else, of bodies alive and together.

"I'd rather be down there tonight," said Grasni. I started and turned to her. She was gazing at the tables and the benches, and at the lanterns that had been hung in the branches of the trees. I had gone looking for her earlier, rehearsing what I would say to her and trying to anticipate what she might say to me. I had not found her—but now here she was beside me, and I almost did not want to speak and risk the moment's end.

"Ah," I said (because I had to speak, of course), "but only here, tonight, will you see Selera disguised as a serving girl as she attempts to avoid the Path her true love has set before her."

They were hollow words, echoes of ones that might once have made us laugh.

"It will be hard to leave," Grasni said. "For Selera and for me."

Just as I was noting, with some relief, that she had no tears in her eyes this time, I realized that I did. "Grasni," I said, "I don't know what I'll do without you."

"You'll teach," she said, "and you'll find a friend who knows not to wear purple with red, and who *won't* know . . ."

"What my Otherself looks like?" I said when her voice faltered and faded. "Someone who won't be disgusted and afraid, as you are?" I did not know if my own voice was trembling because of sadness or anger—for I felt the latter, all of a sudden, thrusting heat outward from my belly.

"No," she said, turning to me, her face twisted, "oh, Nola, you *know* how sorry I am—"

She did not flee from me again, as I half-expected her to. I fled from her. I dodged among the trees and the tables and the people laying them with silver plates and goblets, and I dashed into my room and slammed the door. I cried for a long time, with my face pressed against one of the toy horses. I had not cried like this in many years. I felt like a child, gulping and sobbing, consumed by something I could not name. Except that I was not a child, and I could have named it—all the layers of it. I could have dried my eyes and washed my face and gone back out into the courtyard to talk to my friend, who was leaving.

Instead I stayed where I was. I waited, after my tears had stopped—just as I had waited for Chenn, so many years ago, when I had slammed another door and hoped she would come to me anyway. The light in my room turned from gold to bronze to blue-black. I did not touch the lamp on my desk. No: I would sit in darkness, while the courtyard danced with flame and silver. I would be miserable and alone until someone came to fetch me: one of my students, perhaps, or Grasni, or all of them together.

The knock finally came hours after night had fallen. I waited for a long, silent moment before I called, "Come in."

Selera shone, with all that light behind her and all the dimness in front. She was silhouetted in points of fire: her curves both gentle and sharpened, her hair a glittering mass of gold. I had never seen it down before—not like this, in rippling waves that had no pins or combs or ribbons in them.

"Go away." I still sounded like that child, sullen and hurt.

She stepped into the room.

"Selera. Please. I want to be alone." My voice wobbled and leapt.

She took another step, and another. "What do *you* have to cry about?"

She was right in front of me, and I could see her better: her wide eyes and the tears on her cheeks. "I'm the one, Nola. I . . ." She sat down beside me on the bed and I did not think to tell her to get up again.

"You what?" I said. There was something different about her—the unbound hair and something else. As she turned her head to face me I knew what it was: she was not wearing any scent.

"Take my place," she said. "Go to Meriden."

I laughed. "And you will stay here and be Mistress Teldaru, is that it? And what would *Master* Teldaru say to this?"

"I've already asked him." She was speaking so softly I could hardly hear her. "He said no. But I thought if I asked you, and if you agreed . . ."

I snorted, rubbed my hands over my eyes and under my nose. "And what else did he say?"

"That he will let me stay until the Princess Zemiya arrives, if I wish."

"And do you wish?"

She leaned over so that her forehead was almost touching mine. "Of course I *wish*—do not ask me questions you already know the answers to—do not *mock* me." Her spittle fell on my face but I did not wipe it away. "You . . . you. You and he." She sagged backward as if I had been holding her and had let her go. "What is there between you? You can tell me, now that it doesn't matter any more."

"What do you mean?" Because I wanted to know, suddenly, with a desire that made my flesh throb.

She laughed, this time. "You and he, Nola! Looking at each other all the time and pretending not to! Together all the time, even when you're not! Ever since that first day, in that tiny smelly horrible room, when you were so filthy and mad—I tried not to see it then but I did, and I still do, and I don't understand—he loves *me*—*what is there between you*?"

I heard singing, in the silence—two of our girls, whose voices rose above all the other courtyard noise like smoke. Weaving a pattern too lovely and vivid to endure.

"He will have to tell you," I said at last. "I cannot."

She stood up. It was strange that she was just herself, with no perfume to waft every time she moved, and no jewellery to rearrange. I thought with a stab of envy that she was even more beautiful than she had been by the pool, just before Teldaru had told us what would happen.

"I hope he ruins you," she said.

I laughed as I had cried, earlier: wildly, desperately, aware of nothing but the pressure in my head and chest. When I finally opened my streaming eyes, Selera was gone.

I slept, for a time. When I woke the night was deep and moonless. It was not quiet, though; I could hear the thrumming from the main courtyard. I could feel it—all those people, awake.

My own courtyard was empty. The tables were gone; the lanterns were still hanging in the trees, but no longer lit. *Maybe they looked like stars*, I thought as I walked beneath them. I imagined flames shattering the glass and streaking through the leaves. A smell of burning wood and cooked fruit; the water hissing and bubbling; the air brighter than day. *Am I dreaming?* I felt the pebbles of the path grind against my bare feet, so I had to be awake—but no—even dreams could be this clear. Even visions could.

There were extra guards at the doors to the keep. For safety, Teldaru had told me, because of all the outside people here. Lord Derris had not wanted them here at all. He had asked the king what the princess would make of all the noise and the crowds, when she arrived.

"I have met her, remember," Haldrin had replied. "I do not think she will mind." He had smiled.

I stood on the staircase above the main courtyard. Here were the lantern stars, the torch stars, flickering below me so brightly that I could not see the ones above. Shadows moved among them. The people of Sarsenay, dancing, eating, fighting, singing, all within the red stone arms of the castle. I felt a slow, sweet bloom of joy, looking down. I almost did not want to go down myself and see the torches that were not stars—but I did, stair by stair, until I was among them.

It was hot—no breeze, and so many bodies, so much fire. I tied my hair back as I walked but the sweat still gathered at my temples and slipped down my cheeks and neck. I saw a man wearing only a strip of cloth around his hips, squatting before a block of stone. I saw a woman in the stone: brows and eyes and the curves of nose and chin. An unfinished woman. The man looked at me, a chisel and mallet in his hands, waiting.

There was a stage hung with coloured sheets. Three girls—my age, perhaps—were dancing on it. They were wearing loose, light shifts that slid as they moved; I glimpsed thighs and breasts, skin that gleamed with moisture and muscle. I was staring at them when arms come around me from behind.

"Lovely lady." A man's voice, rough and slurred; a man's hands clutching my dress into bunches, drawing it up my legs. "Come with me. . . ."

I wrenched myself around, caught a glimpse of him (bald, shiny head, grizzled cheeks) and ran. I heard him grunt another word, and I heard his feet pounding after me as I darted among the fires and wagons and people. Very soon I had left him behind, but I hardly slowed. I did not stop until a woman reared up before me and we sent each other sprawling.

"My apologies!" she said as she helped me to my feet. "We poets are always getting underfoot."

"Poets?"

"Yes," she said, and gestured. "I'll show you."

She led me beneath some low awnings, where people were standing, talking, or sitting, reading, scribbling on scrolls or gazing at them as the sculptor had gazed at his stone. "The king will be judging our poems very soon," the woman said. "No one can sleep—it's wonderful—we're all half-mad, just as poets should be."

You annoy me, I thought—my first clear thought since waking. I let my feet drag, ready to turn back.

"Oh!" the woman said, and gripped my arm. "Listen . . ."

Someone was speaking in a loud, sonorous voice—so sonorous that it had to be a jest. As my guide and I pushed our way through a knot of onlookers the voice rose to a tremulous, breathy height. People laughed; the woman laughed too, and squeezed my arm. "Listen to him!" she hissed. "He's marvellous!" We were at the front of the crowd, now. I saw him.

He was taller and not quite so thin and his hair was very short, but I knew him right away. The shape of his eyes; the quirk of his mouth as he rolled the word "ravaging" around on his tongue. He waited for the laughter to subside and opened his mouth to say some other word that belonged to the silly verse he was reciting. Then he saw me—and the word that came instead was "Nola?"

I walked to him. I reached for the one thing that was new: the long, white scar that ran above his eyebrows. I touched it with my fingertips, which trembled. "Bardrem," I said.

CHAPTER TWENTY-EIGHT

He smelled of bread and wood smoke and onions, just as he had when he was a boy. But there was something else—sweat; something rich and different. I discovered all this because we held each other tightly for a moment, before he thrust me away.

He pushed through the crowd and I followed. He did not look back at me but he knew I was there, for as soon as he had ducked into a tent he rounded on me.

"Go away," he said.

The tent was very small. Its sides pressed against us both every time someone passed outside.

"Go away," he said again, in his deep, harsh, man's voice. "You had no trouble doing this before—why hesitate now?"

"No, Bardrem." I could already feel the ache of the curse in my throat. "I didn't. I won't."

"You won't." He gestured wildly and smacked the cloth and someone on the other side of it called, "Mind your arm, Master Bardremzo, or take the lady somewhere else!" Bardrem ignored this. He was so close, staring down at me with such raw, fierce anger—and even though I knew I should feel only dread, I was breathless with joy at the sight of him.

"Tell me, then. Explain yourself. Make your excuses, six years too late."

Orlo was Teldaru. He lured me away. He said he would kill you if I ever tried to escape. I have never stopped thinking of you. "I was apprenticed. To Teldaru. Someone from the palace came, and he took me with him right away; I had no time to find you."

Bardrem smiled a wide, false, crooked smile. "Ah, so *that* was all! Well. Did you think"—his voice dropping, suddenly; the smile gone—"to write, perhaps?

To tell me you were fine and happy and living at the castle instead of *dead*, as I thought you were?"

Teldaru's cursed me; I have no words that are true, any more. None to speak, none to write. "I couldn't."

"What—no paper, here? No ink?" He laughed as he had just smiled, and I flinched back against the cloth as if his bitterness had actually touched my skin. "I never thought that you would be like that. A person who forgets her friends as soon as she finds something better."

"I didn't," I said, but he waved my words away.

"But we were young—how could I have thought I knew you?"

"You did." I reached for him and gripped his wrists until my fingers went white. "You did, Bardrem. It . . . it is impossible for me to tell . . ." I was crying, each sob a word I could not say. He stared at me with a confusion that looked familiar, and he was so much the same and so different that I cried harder, dry and wracked, hardly any tears. I thought I had finished with those earlier that night.

"Do you know what was the worst?" he said when I had quieted. I was still holding his wrists, loosely now. "I thought you were dead—and I thought that this would be easier to bear than if you had gone away without telling me."

"I would have thought the same thing," I said in a low, rough voice that some far-off part of me found rather alluring.

"But do you know what convinced me that you *were* still alive?"

I shook my head.

"That Orlo man appeared one night, years ago. He asked if I knew where you were, and when I said no he attacked me. With my own knife." He lifted his hand to the scar above his eyes. "I don't know why this made me think you still lived, but it did."

"It must have been a terrible cut," I said, remembering Teldaru with Bardrem's knife and Borl with Bardrem's note, coming slowly toward me in the darkness of my room. "Though," I added, "you must be just a little proud of the scar."

He gazed at me for a moment and then he smiled a real smile—slow and slight but there—and in the rush of relief that filled me I had my first clear thought of that evening.

Orlo. Teldaru. Bardrem.

"You mustn't stay here," I said, the relief sinking, spreading into heaviness as he frowned. "You can't be near the castle."

"Oh? And why not?"

I let go of his wrists; he would soon have twisted them free, in any case. *Teldaru will see you and you will recognize him and he will hurt you.* . . . "I can't," I said brokenly. "I can't—"

"Can't tell, can't say—how very convenient for you, Nola, to make pronouncements that don't require explanation!"

"You must not enter this competition," I said, my voice as shrill now as it had been husky before.

"So you're a person like that, as well!" Again I felt a strange, keen thrill, because his breath was hot on my face; because he was here. "Someone so mad with selfish weakness that she can't bear anyone else to succeed! You're living the life you've dreamed of and yet I'm not allowed to try to do the same—is that it?"

"No"—a soft, ebbing word that neither of us truly heard.

"I'll stay at the castle, Nola, but I won't stay here now; I won't stay with you." He pushed past me. Wrenched the cloth door open and ran—or so I guessed, for I did not watch him go. I stared at the door, and I was still and empty and cold. I heard some murmuring and incredulous laughter from the other side of the wall; two men, maybe more, probably wondering what "Master Bardremzo" had got himself into.

When I finally ducked back out into the night, I seemed to be moving very slowly. I found my way back to the place where I had first seen him, but there was an old woman speaking there, and he was not among the crowd watching her. I wandered among fires and stages and embracing people, sleeping people, people who reached for me and then recoiled (something in my face?). I dragged myself up the stairs to the keep and looked back down into the courtyard for a long, long time, as the sky paled above me.

Bardrem, I thought, and even his name like this, silent, was a gift. *Bardrem— where will this new Path take us?*

I hardly ate or slept, in the week or weeks that followed that night. Every young man I saw became Bardrem, at first glance, and my heart would stop, then pound again when I realized it was actually a soldier or a gardener, someone who did not resemble him at all. Mistress Ket asked me what was wrong; even Grasni did. Selera had not spoken to me since she left me laughing in my room.

I have no idea what I told them. All I remember is that I was close to some sort of collapse—and then Zemiya arrived.

"Mistress Nola." One of the boys—Dren—was standing in my doorway. The sky behind him was purple-black; his own black curls looked even darker than usual, and his face was a sickly white. I blinked at him from the bed. I was sitting at the very edge of it, as if I might rise at any moment. I had probably been sitting this way for hours.

"Yes, Dren?" I said, thinking, *I must go back down into the courtyard; it's been two days since I was last there; this time I'll find him. . . .*

"Mistress, the Princess is coming. I mean"—he shifted, cleared his throat— "she's nearly here. Mistress Ket says go to Master Teldaru and King Haldrin in the Great Hall, please."

Suddenly my head was clear again—too clear—and I realized that I was wearing an old, ragged dress, and that I had not combed my hair in far too long. So I did comb it, and pinned it up with my bronze butterfly clips, and put on a brown dress with cream-coloured lace at cuffs and hem. Brown slippers too— and then I rushed out into the courtyard.

The air felt like storm. We had been waiting for this—for a breaking of heat, a washing-away of dust—but it felt wrong now, somehow. Even Borl seemed unsettled; he whined and panted and did not follow me, as he usually did. The purple-black really was alarming; it pressed on me and on the trees and I imagined all of us shrinking away from whatever would come from the sky.

It came quickly. By the time I reached the keep's doors the rain had started (fat, heavy droplets), and as I stepped inside, lightning turned the darkness yellow. The thunder followed me—still distant, but it seemed to shudder all the way into the stones beneath my feet.

I ran from the keep down to the Great Hall, and I did not even think to look for Bardrem. I would not have seen him, in any case; I could barely see my own feet through all the mud and water. The rain came down in warm, billowing, blinding waves.

"You will do no such thing, Cousin!" I heard Lord Derris say as the double doors were opened for me.

"I should," said the king. He was pacing in front of the dais. I had never seen him pace before; usually it was Teldaru who did this, and Haldrin who reprimanded him. Teldaru was motionless now, leaning back against the dais, his legs crossed at the ankles. But while his body showed only ease, his eyes leapt as if he were seeing everything, or nothing.

"I should," Haldrin said again, then turned and saw me. "Nola! Good. Come in. We wanted you, since you also had visions of her—of Zemiya—we wanted you here."

"Notice, Hal," Teldaru said, "that Nola has just been outside."

Haldrin scowled at him and looked back at me. I saw him take in the dripping, sodden mess of my clothing and hair. "I want to meet her," he told me. "On the road outside the city."

"Can you give him a single reason why he should?" Lord Derris had never addressed me directly before. I cleared my throat, just as Dren had done as he fidgeted in my doorway. I was far too aware of the way my dress had moulded to my body, and I thought, quite suddenly, how relieved I was that I had not chosen the one with the white bodice.

"Perhaps, my king," I said, with pretend solemnity, "if you have not yet had time to bathe today . . .?"

Haldrin laughed; Lord Derris smiled; Teldaru nodded at me as if I had pleased him unexpectedly.

"I wanted to welcome her," the king said. "I wanted the entire city to greet her. There were going to be flower petals."

"And there still can be." Teldaru straightened. "In here. Stop worrying; you're making us all nervous."

"Just think, though," Lord Derris said, "the rain will wash away the smell of the latrines—at least for awhile."

"And our grass may be green again, when it is over," Teldaru added. I could almost see his energy—restlessness, excitement, even anger, pulsing from his skin and eyes.

"Very well," the king said, and sighed. "Nothing to do but wait, then."

I heard later what happened in the city below us, while we waited—for many Sarsenayans did lean out their windows and stand shivering in the streets, despite the storm. A carriage—sent by Haldrin to meet the Belakaoan boats—halted just outside the southern gate. A woman climbed out of it and stood very still in the downpour, gazing back the way she had come. Her skin and hair were so dark that they were difficult to see until lightning forked, and even then her image was swiftly gone again. Her dress might have been a colour—one of those glorious, bright island colours for which all Sarsenayan girls yearned—but now it was dark too, wind-whipped and clinging.

Another woman alit beside her. This one was taller and slimmer. She touched the first—on the shoulder, some said; others said the back—who turned slowly to face the gate. She gestured, leaned close to the taller woman to say something. The taller woman climbed back into the carriage. And so it was that Zemiya, *moabe* of Belakao, walked alone into Sarsenay City in the rain and the wind and the thunder, her eyes only on the road, and not on the people who lined it.

⁂

"Haldrin, King of Sarsenay, I present to you Zemiya, Princess of Belakao." The Belakaoan herald's words rang, but he looked terribly uncomfortable—as wet as the rest of his party was, his hands clutching his spear as if he was afraid they might shake.

"I welcome you," King Haldrin said to Zemiya, "as *moabe* of your own land, and as future queen of this one."

He was standing at the foot of the dais. Zemiya was just inside the doors. *She already looks like a queen*, I thought from my own place beside Lord Derris. She was beautiful, and stood as if she did not notice the water dripping from her dress and fingertips, onto the flower petals on the floor.

"I thank you, Lord King," she said. Her voice was just as rich as Teldaru had said it was.

The king stepped forward and I smelled the flower petals, stirred and bruised. "Zemiya," he said, and I felt a rush of surprise and something else that I did not want to name, hearing him say this word. "You should have dried yourselves, taken more time. . . ."

"No," Zemiya said. When she shook her head the jewels in her hair sparkled. Crimson and clear, I saw. Blue and yellow and green. "I preferred to come immediately."

The herald took two paces and brought his spear down on the floor with a crack. "And I also announce—"

"Neluja," Zemiya said to Haldrin. "Yes—you remember her? My family's representative at this blessed time, for my brother the *moabu* did not see fit to come himself." I sucked in my breath at the bitterness that throbbed beneath the smoothness and the small, white smile.

Neluja walked to stand beside her sister. She was not quite as wet; I saw that her dress was orange, patterned with white circles. The cloth that hid her hair was a darker colour—green, perhaps, or brown. Her eyes were all black except for pinprick white centres. "King Haldrin," she said in a higher, cooler voice than her sister's.

"*Ispa* Neluja," he replied. "I am glad that you have come."

"I had to," Neluja said. She stepped closer to the king, but her eyes seemed to be on Teldaru. "For I had to tell you myself: this marriage should not happen."

Lord Derris gasped and the herald started and the king frowned, but it was Teldaru I looked at, my heartbeat heavy and uneven in my chest. I knew his smile; the hungry one that showed only the tips of his perfect teeth. "I was looking forward to greeting you both," he said to Neluja, "but now instead I must ask you, *Ispa*, what you mean, and why you seek to mar the joy of this occasion."

"Master Teldaru," Haldrin said, holding up a hand, "*Ispa* Neluja—let us not talk of this yet. Go and rest, and—"

"No," Zemiya said. "Haldrin, let us talk of this now."

They all waited, for a moment. I noticed, as my heart continued to thud, that there was a lizard perched on Neluja's upper arm. It was small and bright red, and its eyes looked like tiny faceted amber domes.

"The *isparra* has shown me," Neluja said at last. "I have seen images of future time."

"As have I." Teldaru's gaze slid to me. "Mistress Nola has, as well. She Othersaw for a Belakaoan merchant, months and months ago, and she saw precisely what I had before her: a shared path of abundance and joy."

"Is that so?" Neluja said. The lizard's eyes began to swivel, around and around, sickeningly fast. Its tail looped and tightened around her arm, just above the elbow. "For my own visions have been dark."

Teldaru shrugged a little. "But if, in your country, no one Path is more likely than another, such visions should not trouble you."

"In my country we speak of tides and currents, water that flows in ways we anticipate and ways we cannot. I have searched the water many times, and all I have seen is darkness." She turned again to Haldrin. "I have not come to try to stop this marriage myself. We would not have come at all, either of us, if we sought to escape it. But I hoped . . ." She swallowed, and the lizard cocked its head toward hers. "I hope that you will think on what I have seen, King Haldrin. My brother refuses to do so, but perhaps you will."

Haldrin looked from Neluja to Zemiya. The *moabe* was smiling very, very slightly; a challenge, a promise, a question—I could not tell.

"Teldaru." The king turned and faced him. "Look again, now." He turned once more, to me. "And you too, Nola. Both of you: look, and tell me what my Pattern will be."

Thunder cracked directly above us—around us, it seemed, in a great, descending wave. When its reverberations had faded, Lord Derris cried, "My lord!" His already breathy voice was strained almost to nothing.

He is happy, I realized. *Overjoyed.* I knew that the king usually asked for Otherseeing only when custom dictated; that he preferred his own ideas to sacred visions of the Otherworld—and I knew that this had always frustrated Lord Derris. So now he wheezed his delight into the Great Hall as I walked over to Teldaru, thinking, *No, no; not this . . .*

"We will," Teldaru said quietly.

"And you, Neluja—would you join them?"

She shook her head. "I know what I have seen. I have no need to look again. But he will help"—and the lizard skittered down her arm and dropped to the floor.

"An intriguing creature," said Teldaru.

Neluja nodded. "Indeed. He found me after I lost my bird, Uja—perhaps you remember her?"

"Uja bit him," Zemiya said. "Several times. I am certain he remembers her."

It was all intolerable to me, suddenly: the weight of the air and the knowledge that Bardrem was beneath it too, so close; the smiles I did not understand; the rich, clear voices and the words they were speaking. The way I knelt, cursed and helpless, and watched the lizard's legs and tail make paths in the petals while Haldrin said again, "Tell me what will come" and Teldaru touched my hand, lightly. The way the Otherworld rose to meet me. My desire and my dread.

Haldrin. Just him, kneeling on dry, cracked earth. His shoulders are trembling, and so is the long, curved line of his back. I whisper his name. He raises his head and I see that there are tears on his cheeks, and that he sees me. He smiles at me, and the ground beneath him sprouts grass and ivy and shoots that coil outward, trailing tiny flowers. He lifts his hands and takes off his circlet (which is a deep, dark red, not gold). Sets it on the ground, where the ivy loops around it until it disappears. His tears make deep green furrows in his cheeks.

I was leaning forward on my closed fists when the real world returned. I strained for breath, found it, made it slow and even. I raised my head and saw Teldaru staring up past the king. Teldaru's eyes were still and clear with Otherseeing. Haldrin glanced from him to me and back again. Everyone else was distant, to me; smudged, featureless, obscured by black spots.

Teldaru bowed his head. When he looked up his gaze was focused and bright.

"Well, Daru?" Haldrin said.

"I . . ." Teldaru began. He smiled at the king, at me, at Zemiya and Neluja. He reached out and stroked the lizard, and he chuckled when it nipped his finger. "I saw the ocean at rest. I saw new land rising from it, so gently that the waters hardly moved. It was beautiful, Haldrin. My king."

"And Nola?" Haldrin said. He spoke more lightly than he had before. "What did you see?"

You, and myself too; I don't know how I would describe it, even if I could. "Gems," I said, "spilling like fire from the mouth of a volcano. Where they land, stones grow, more and more of them, until there is a monument—like Ranior's, only taller and lovelier." I could not look at Neluja, or indeed at anyone. I bowed my head as Teldaru had.

"Thank you," Haldrin said. "*Ispa* Neluja, for telling me of your visions, and Teldaru and Nola, for telling me of yours. They will give me much to think on." He walked over to Zemiya. "And now," he said, "please, Zemiya: let me show you to your rooms."

She did not smile at him, and there was a distance in her dark eyes, but she raised her hand and laid it lightly on his arm. "Yes," she said. "It seems that it is time."

Teldaru slipped his hand into mine and stroked my palm with his thumb, and I felt his trembling and my own and could not pull away.

CHAPTER TWENTY-NINE

I wonder sometimes at the certainty of words. At how real they make the past look, and how precise. "Selera wore a white dress with ivy patterns stitched in Belakaoan gems"—and even if I'm nearly sure she did, the words, once they're written, make it true.

I'm usually fairly certain about images—both the ones from my visions and the others. Things like Selera's dresses, and whether all the eagle's talons were bloodied, or just a few. Other things are more difficult to remember. How soon after a particular event did another event happen? A week, a month? Is it true that he asked me a question and that I answered in such-and-such a way? And if I'm not sure, should I not leave that part out entirely, or write, "I cannot remember precisely, but perhaps this is how it happened"?

Except then it would not be a story. And I need to tell a story. Something whole and certain.

Sometimes it's the images that help me call up the rest; the colours and light and textures that start the words again. Times like this. For Selera's dress *was* long and white and stitched with gems. The dress she wore when she went away.

⁂

Grasni found me on a bench by the main courtyard stage. It was the bench furthest away from the performers; from it I could see the king and Zemiya, in the raised viewing area that had been erected for them, and all the other benches too, as well as the space around them. I had been sitting here for over an hour, and so far I had seen four dancers (three excellent and one so terrible that even Haldrin had looked uncomfortable), two acrobats and an actor who had attempted to transform himself into an erupting volcano using red silk scarves and an armful of very large stones. I had not seen Bardrem, though my eyes darted all the time, seeking him, expecting him.

"No wonder the princess looks so forlorn," Grasni said as she slipped into the space beside me. "Look at him, all tangled up in his scarves, trying not to cry because he's just crushed his toe with a rock. I wonder why the king was so eager to show her what fools Sarsenayans can be."

"She's not forlorn," I said, lightly enough to hide my surprise at Grasni's presence. "She's smiling a little. And maybe that's what he wanted."

"Is that a smile? I'm not sure. . . ."

But it was—I, at least, was sure of it, as I squinted into the morning sunlight.

"Let's get closer," I said. "It's crowded, but Borl will help us make a path." He craned his head up when he heard his name and I scratched him between the ears.

"No." Grasni eyed him and then me. I thought that she might ask a question I would not be able to answer; something like, "Why is he so attached to you now, when he only ever tried to bite your fingers off before?" She said nothing else, though, so I continued, "Or let's leave—we could go see if Dellena will let us taste some of the recipes she's created for the wedding. Or"—I spoke faster because Grasni was no longer looking at me, and because she was tugging at the ends of her hair in a way I recognized—"we could just go to your room, or mine, and talk about things, because we won't be able to do that for much longer. Because soon—"

"Not soon," she said quietly, and suddenly she *was* looking at me. "Now. Master Teldaru's just told us: we're to leave later on today. Selera and I."

"Today?" I said. "But he told Selera it would be after the wedding. She . . . Where is she?"

"In her room. She refuses to come out. I even offered to let her cut my hair." I stood up. "He can't do this."

"Of course he can. Apparently our new employers are growing impatient; they've written to ask for our presence immediately."

"And did he show you these letters?"

"No—Nola, what's wrong?"

He's lying again and he's plotting something again; I know—I know and I can't bear knowing, can't bear any more of anything, and now you're leaving. "You're leaving," I said, "and I can't bear it."

We walked up to our courtyard without speaking. Borl kept nudging at my hand, and I thought, *How perfect: the only one who truly understands me is a dog I brought back from the dead.*

We stood outside Selera's door and I called to her, but she did not come, and there was no sound from within. Dren brought us bread and cheese. We walked by the pool; Grasni said, "I'm excited to be going, but I'll miss everything here, even the heat and Dellena's Mysterious Hard Bits Soup." We both tried to laugh, and we both failed. I thought suddenly of the guard—Sildio, the one she loved—and I wanted to mention him, to show I remembered and was thinking of her, but I did not.

We were sitting by Selera's door when Teldaru came. "Surely she'll have to come out to use the latrine," Grasni said, and then we saw him striding out of the trees. He was smiling.

"You missed an extraordinarily talented musician," he said when he had reached us. "I've never heard the knee-harp played so well." He was speaking very quickly, bobbing a bit on the balls of his feet. I felt a familiar cold seeping into my belly and wrapped my arms around myself as if this would warm me.

"Grasni, go and fetch your things. The carriages are waiting."

I watched her rush to her room, her long, shapeless dress puffing up after her like a cloud of orange-ish dust. "What are you planning?" I said. My voice trembled a bit.

"Nola!" he exclaimed. I did not turn to him, but I could imagine his arched brows and wide, twinkling eyes. "Whatever do you mean?"

She was coming back already, stooping beneath the weight of a bag on her back and clutching a leather case in both hands. "It cannot be her," I said, very quietly. "Whatever you're planning, it cannot have anything to do with her."

"Silly, suspicious girl," he murmured, and stepped forward to take the case from her. He set it on the ground, and the bag beside it, and rapped on Selera's door. "Selera. You've been listening; you know it's time. Come out, please."

Silence.

"Selera." A little more firmly.

Mistress Ket was coming, I saw, clacking her way along the path. Dren was walking with her and the other students were behind them. A farewell procession. I swallowed sudden tears and looked back at the door.

"Dearest." A new tone, one I'd never heard before. "Come out to me."

I took Grasni's hand and pulled her away, to where the procession had halted. I watched him say something else, his forehead against the door, both hands splayed as if he would draw her out through the wood with them.

The door opened slowly, and Selera emerged slowly, and Teldaru fell back a few steps, also slowly; perhaps time itself had forgotten to breathe, seeing her.

"Oh!" a little girl beside me gasped. "She's more beautiful than *ever*!" And she was. I had never seen this white dress before—the one with the jewelled coils of ivy. I had never seen her hair done so intricately, in whorls and loops, pinned by gold and yet more jewels. Her slippers were golden too, with heels that made her taller.

"Ah," Grasni muttered, "so she would make him regret what he's done."

Perhaps he does, I thought as I watched him watch her. *Perhaps, right at this moment, he does.*

She did not look at him once. She walked over to us, bent to kiss the children and the top of Mistress Ket's head. Mistress Ket was weeping. "Child," she said, "you will make us so proud. They will love you as we do."

Selera did not glance at Grasni or me either, not even when Teldaru said, "It is too crowded for you and the children, Mistress Ket; only Nola will accompany us to the gate." It must have been difficult to avoid glancing at her only three companions, but Selera managed it. She walked slightly ahead of us, holding her dress up in her hands. She was moving quite quickly, now; the guards carrying the cases struggled to keep up. We followed her through the keep and down the steps to the main courtyard; we followed her among the tents and around the largest stage, where a girl was playing a viol. Only when Selera reached the castle gate and the two carriages waiting just inside it did she slow.

Teldaru stepped past her and turned to us. "Come here to me, you two," he said to the others. They went to stand with him; all three faced me, though only Teldaru and Grasni actually looked at me. "Nola," he said, "perhaps after you have said your farewells you would like to watch from the gatehouse tower."

"Just me?" I said. "What about you? Would you not like to wave them away, too?"

He was touching each of them: Grasni on the elbow, Selera on the smooth, pale skin of her back—just above her shoulder blade, I guessed. "I will be accompanying them," he said. Now Selera did look at him, her mouth that small, perfect "o" it always made when she was surprised.

"You're leaving?" I could hardly hear my own words above the sudden clamour of my heart.

He smiled at me. "I will escort them a very short ways. You will hardly notice I'm gone." He removed his hand from Grasni's elbow and wagged a finger at me. "Don't get into any trouble, now," he said brightly, "or there may be dire consequences."

Will there? I thought dizzily. *What happens if you leave me? Does that part of the curse stop working? If it does, you have no way of hurting Bardrem because he's here and you don't know it—I could find him and we could go together and there would be nothing you could do.*

"I'll behave," I said, as steadily as possible. "As I always do."

He gazed at me, not smiling any more, and I turned my own gaze away, to Selera. "Farewell," I said. "May you find everything you seek, in your new home: renown, fortune. Love." I did not intend to be mean—not this time—but perhaps my distraction and excitement made me sound it; she glared at me—for the last time, I thought—and walked to the nearest carriage.

"And you," I said to Grasni, and found that I could say nothing more.

"And you," she said, and smiled, though her eyes were bright with tears. We clung to each other for a moment, until she drew away. She patted her freckled cheeks and her shapeless dress and said, "Renown, fortune and love," and we laughed together—for the last time, I thought. Just before she climbed into the second carriage she looked up at the castle walls—for him, I realized. Sildio, who had so entranced her that she had come to me, that night when everything had changed between us. The night that had made our friendship more about words not spoken than ones that were.

Teldaru bent close to me, before he got into Selera's carriage. "Take care, Nola," he said. "I won't be long." He ran his finger along my jaw and quickly, quickly over my lips and then he was gone.

Gone, gone—the word circled in my head as I ran up the gatehouse tower steps. I would have to make certain that the carriages were out of sight before I made any attempt to find Bardrem. *You do not need to find him,* whispered a voice in my head. *Just try to go; try now. And then what?* my other, louder mind-voice demanded. *What will Teldaru do when he finds me gone? Whom will he hunt down right away? No—I won't endanger Bardrem that way . . .*

I lost sight of the carriages as soon as the horses drew them down the road into the city. I leaned as far over the tower's edge as I could, craning, waiting. It seemed like an age before I saw them again, out past the other, further gatehouse, already well onto the long, straight eastern road. It seemed like another age before they dwindled. The sun was behind me, and the pure, vivid light made the tiny horses and carriages very distinct and not quite real. I waited until they were just specks—flickers of light off wheel hubs and harnesses. *Gone, gone*, said my head, and I picked up my skirts and ran.

I hardly saw the guards I passed as I flew down the stairs. One of them called to me to be careful. I burst from the tower into the courtyard and would have kept going except that someone caught me by the arm and pulled me to a reeling stop. I wrenched myself around, opening my mouth to say something shrill, but instead I cried, "Bardrem!" and wrapped my hand around his arm. We stood there gripping each other like dancers who had forgotten their steps.

"I saw you," he said at last, as I tried unsuccessfully to retrieve all the ideas that had filled me only moments before. "I saw you go up there, and then I watched you. You could have fallen over, you know. I would never have caught you in time."

I made a sound that was part laugh and part sob. "Did you see the carriages?" I asked, and he nodded. "And who was in them?"

"No," he said. "Should I know who was in them?"

"No"—thinking, *Of course he didn't see Teldaru—if he had he'd be upset—furious, shocked* . . . "They were friends. Going away." I took a deep breath that steadied me. "Bardrem. I have to leave the city. Come with me."

"What?" He let go of my arm, though I kept hold of his. "Why?"

"Because," I said quickly, like an impatient mother avoiding a real explanation, "I have to."

He was not angry this time—just puzzled. "My turn at the competition is tomorrow—it's why I've been looking for you; I was wondering if you might come to listen . . . I suppose I'll go with you, as long as I'm back in time."

"You won't be." I dug my fingers into his skin and he winced. "I'm leaving for good."

He pried my hand away. "You can't mean this. Nola—be serious, don't—"

"I am." I felt more tears; when had I ever cried so much? "This is the most important thing I've ever had to do. Please, Bardrem—stay here. Wait for me. I'll be back as soon as I can."

I hardly breathed. I watched his face, which showed me nothing, not even when he said, "I don't understand. I haven't understood anything since you found me." A long pause; I tried not to reach out and clutch him again. "How do I know," he finally said, "that you won't just disappear?"

My breath escaped in a noisy rush. "I won't. I'll come back—I promise."

"*I'm* not promising anything," he said. "I'll just wait for now, if that's what you want—only Nola, I . . ."

But I was running again, waving at him over my shoulder.

I would have to remove everything I could from my room. If I left anything that had come from my body—a hair, a fingernail—Teldaru would be able to use it to Othersee, just as he had done when he had been hunting Chenn. I found an extra bag in Grasni's room and took it back to mine. I began shoving dresses, skirts and shifts inside—for although he would not be able to use the cloth itself to find me, there might be stray hairs caught in lace or bodice ribbons. Luckily I did not have too many clothes; I moved swiftly on to the hair combs and clips, the necklaces and earrings and bracelets. (The jewellery I packed simply because I loved it.) Not too many of these, either—thankfully I was not Selera, with her five cases—and I reached for the toy horses. They were too big to take with me. I looked them over carefully, found nothing but matted material and bead eyes; I held them both for one long, still moment and then I placed them back on their shelf. I would have to strip the sheets from the bed; maybe I'd claim they were crawling with ticks and have Dellena burn them. I'd have to sweep and wash the floor too—so much; too much. I was moving toward the door, intending to find a broom, when someone knocked on it.

I halted. Said nothing.

There was another knock, and another pause, and a voice. "Mistress?"

I took the final three steps to the door and opened it.

"There you are," said King Haldrin. "Thank the Pattern. Come with me, Nola; I need you."

CHAPTER THIRTY

"What has happened?" I asked the king. Blood was rising to my cheeks, singing in my ears.

"I've called a break in the competition. Zemiya still needs to rest; perhaps this *was* too much for her, though I'll never tell Derris he was right. And now there's something important that I must do, and I think you are the only one who can help me with it."

"But what . . .?"

"Come with me."

"But my king, I cannot; I—"

"Please."

He was smiling. The students were gathered around the pool, watching, whispering, their eyes very wide. King Haldrin came here with Teldaru, sometimes, but never alone.

His smile was terribly winning. I could not say no to the king, especially not in front of other people. And if we stood here for too long he might look past me into the room and see the case on my bed and the pile of sheets on the floor.

"Very well."

He took me to rooms in the keep where I had never been before—his rooms, bright with wall hangings and late afternoon sun. I looked but did not see. I saw only a window that showed the courtyard. I saw the top of the gatehouse tower, but of course I could not tell whether Bardrem were waiting at its foot.

"I am trying to choose a gift for her. I am failing. Look, Nola, and help me."

A brocade chair and a small, round table, both covered in things. A cloak draped over the chair; a pair of slippers, a pile of necklaces, a book, a tiny statue on the table. I went close, touched, thought, *Just pick, quickly*. He was entirely motionless, watching my face for clues; I could not be too quick. I considered each item and I did care, a little—a gift for the new queen, and he had come to me.

I chose the statue. It was the likeness of a girl with long, straight hair, her dainty stone hands cupped before her. "It's very old," Haldrin said as he took it from me. "My great-grandmother's, I think. I've been told the girl is her. She used to hold something, but it's long lost. Why this?"

"Because it's Sarsenayan stone," I said, and felt a brief, warm surge of truth. "And she's lovely. The girl, and Zemiya too."

"She is." He was serious, quiet. He told me I would take some food and drink with him, at a larger table by the window. I said no. He insisted. Zemiya was resting; he had some pressing tasks that he wished to put off. The sun was going down. How long had it been? I tried not to look out the window but the sky seemed to tug at me and I had to turn to it. I ate food I did not taste and drank my wine so swiftly that my cheeks flooded with heat again, as they had when I had seen him at my door. He talked to me; I responded. The light outside was bronze.

He pushed his chair back at last. "There are two more dancers to see this evening," he said, and rose. "The last two, thankfully. I will be glad to listen to poetry tomorrow."

Be there, I thought as I ran back across the courtyard. *Bardrem—be there still, please. I am coming.*

I would not worry about the sheets, or about sweeping or washing the floor. I would take my case and go.

When I was nearly at my door, already reaching for the latch, a shadow slipped out of the other, deeper shadows of walls and trees. "*Ispa* Nola," said Neluja as Borl growled at her from his place by my door. "Forgive me for disturbing you here."

I almost laughed that unfortunate, hysterical laugh of mine. Instead I said, in a tight little voice, "I am tired. Come back tomorrow, as early as you wish."

"It is about *Ispu* Teldaru."

"Oh," I said, helplessly. We went in. She stood just inside the door, which I closed. It was quite dark in my room, but I did not light a lantern. Her eyes gleamed.

"What did you see, the other day?" she said. "When *isparra* showed you the king?"

"I told you—I told everyone. A volcano of gems, and—"

"What did you truly see?"

I forgot Bardrem. I stood before her, trying to hold my head up before her black eyes. "Why do you think I saw something else?"

The lizard crept out from the sleeve of her dress. It picked its way up her arm and circled her neck and settled in the hollow of her collarbone. Its tail lay over her shoulder, curling a bit at its tip.

"I do not think. I am sure. Your words did not match your eyes." She paused. "And I saw you. When I was a girl and *isparra* showed me Teldaru. I saw you, older, different, and you were with him, and you wept tears that were words, and though people gathered close around you they could not read them."

"What else did you see?" I could barely speak.

"Things that did not seem possible. Zemiya invented something, years ago—a wild, mad vision to mock Teldaru. And then I had a real one—for any word spoken, any thought made real for another, even if it is false, causes change. He will change all the tides, all the currents. And you with him. I am Belakaoan: I seldom say 'will,' for *isparra*'s waters are seldom so clear. But I am certain of this. And I am afraid."

"Neluja," I said. "*Ispa*. I can say nothing to you, though I want to."

The lizard scampered around her neck again, twice. She put her hand gently over its head and its body sagged against her, clawed feet splayed. "Nonetheless," she said, "I will speak to you another time."

"Yes." I almost regretted that this could not be true.

She closed the door carefully behind her. For a moment I stood still. Then I seized my case and opened my door, closed it, one last time.

It was quite dark now, but the pebbles of the path still glinted a little. "Borl," I called softly, and I heard him growl again, though I did not see him. I took a few steps, and for the second time that day, fingers wrapped around my arm.

"Having a visit, were you?" Teldaru murmured. His lips stirred the hair at my neck. "And now you're going for a walk? Lovely. Let us go together, shall we?"

He was dressed as Orlo: dark tunic, dark cloak, both of them plain. It was that night again, at the brothel—his hand on the small of my back, propelling me— except that this time there was no pretence of safety, no promise of care. He draped me in a cloak, too—a rich purple, maybe; it did not look quite black. It was velvet, and hung from my shoulders like a pair of hands, dragging me down toward the earth. Sweat slicked my back and belly.

No, I thought, *not again, not this time*—but his fist was knotted in the cloth at the base of my spine, and he was scraping my skin, and I walked forward.

No one stopped us in the keep. Why would they have? He was Master Teldaru, smiling, greeting the guards and the serving girls, who blushed. I was Nola, his favoured pupil, just made Mistress. Some of the guards said my name and nodded at me as Teldaru guided me out the door and down the steps.

He pulled my hood up over my hair, when we reached the bottom. "You are no one, now," he said as he tugged his own hood up. "I am no one." His teeth gleamed; they were all I saw of him, as he turned his shadowed face away.

The cloak was long and I tripped on its folds and he was forcing me to walk too fast, so I tripped some more. I was angry, and a few stumbled paces later I was furious. The fury was cold; I felt it hardening my limbs and muscles. More steps, through the crowd, toward the gatehouse. There was no one there—no one right at the tower's base except for a guard I did not recognize. Bardrem must have left hours ago, certain of some new betrayal or carelessness on my part. Despair threaded through the rage but I twisted it, smoothed it over with strength. I glanced back at Teldaru and thought again, *Not this time.*

We were nearly at the gate. I slowed a bit and felt his hand shift on my back, seeking a tighter hold. I drew in my breath and wrenched myself around and free. I spun and righted myself in one motion and took four long, speeding-up strides toward the open gate. I did not let myself remember the last time I had tried this, years ago, when I had run but never escaped. I remembered nothing and thought about nothing except the space before me—and then a weight fell against my back and bore me to the ground with a force that took away all thought, all breath.

He was laughing. I felt it as he lay on me, pressing me into the dirt, and I heard it when he straightened away from me. I gasped and coughed and scrabbled at earth and pebbles.

"Mistress Foolish Seer," he said. He was kneeling beside me. I could see his face now, because I was looking up at it. His hood was still pulled over his head.

"What's happening here?" The guard, peering over Teldaru's shoulder. "Get up, man. And you too," he added, gesturing at me.

Teldaru rose, twitching at his hood. "My apologies," he said in a voice and accent that were not his. "It was a race, something foolish. We'll be going now."

I sat up, shaking my head free of the folds of my hood. *I'm Mistress Nola*, I tried to say, *And this is Master Teldaru.* "I'm a brothel girl," I said. "Help me find my way home."

The guard frowned. He opened his mouth to speak, but Teldaru laughed a ragged, nervous laugh. "More foolishness." He bent, gripped my arm. "Off we go, Jalys," he said, and pulled me out beneath the gate.

Enough, I thought, groping for steadiness, for focus. *Don't say anything else to anyone; don't let him make you a madwoman again. There is another way—just think. . . .*

He stopped walking a few steps beyond the gate. He gripped both my arms, just below the shoulder, and leaned in close. Anyone watching might think that he was going to kiss me, but instead he snapped, "Enough, Nola. Enough. You are making me *angry.*" And he squeezed so hard and suddenly that I cried out. Then he made a strangled, muffled noise, and one of his hands fell away.

Borl's jaws were fastened around Teldaru's ankle. I heard the dog's low, unbroken growl; abruptly I heard the water of the royal fountain, too, also constant, like a song that sometimes changed but never ended.

"Borl!" I cried, as sharply as I could. "Borl—stop!"—because it was no use; Teldaru was still clutching me, and he was too strong, not surprised enough— and anyway, even if he did let me go, I needed to think now, not run.

Borl did not hear me, or did not listen. He clung, his claws slipping in the spaces between the cobblestones. Teldaru grunted and shook his leg, and I saw him tense, felt it in the bunching of his arm muscles. A moment later he lifted his free leg and kicked. His foot hit Borl's side with a dull sound—one full sack of grain landing on another—and the dog yelped and staggered away. He shook himself and snarled, his teeth and gums glistening, and he was on Teldaru again, scrabbling and tearing at his cloak, and at the flesh beneath it. Another savage kick, and this time Borl fell onto his back. He rolled over, but Teldaru's foot caught him in the ribs, over and over. He had let go of me. I seized his arm and pulled back on it with all my strength. He kicked once more, and this time there was a sound like a branch snapping, and Borl sagged onto the stones.

Teldaru stared down at him. He was breathing hard; there was sweat running down the sides of his face (I could see this; the hood had fallen back, though not all the way). He smiled and reached for my hand. He laced his fingers with mine, quite gently, still gazing down at the dog, who was motionless except for the laboured rise and fall of his chest. Borl was whimpering—another noise like the water, though much quieter. Teldaru stroked my palm. I did not move.

He whistled. Those notes—three short and low and one long and high—

that used to call Borl to him. Borl jerked back and forth, trying to rise, but he could not. He strained his head toward Teldaru's leg and his teeth snapped, found nothing but air. Teldaru whistled again, very softly, then chuckled and turned. He picked up my fallen case and led me down the road (he limped a bit, at first, but not for long), and I let him, because I was thinking. Trying to. Because there must be something in the white ringing silence of my head that would show me what came next.

There were only a few other people about, once Teldaru and I left the castle road. We strolled—just a pair of lovers, hand-in-hand, seeking starlight instead of the smoky glow of our lamps. And there *were* stars; I tipped my head back to look at them, when the street beneath me was flat. It had been day when I had watched carriages shrinking on the eastern road. Day when I had touched a statue by the small, round table in King Haldrin's room. Day when I had begged Bardrem to wait for me and he had said *yes, all right, perhaps.* Now I walked with Teldaru's hand around mine and could not imagine sun.

We traced a winding path through the city. The houses and squares were smudges, to me. *Think,* I told myself with each footfall. *There is still a way—only* think, *idiot woman.*

We were at the city gate. The eastern one, I noted, and was not surprised; this was a path we had walked before, together, a pattern already set. Teldaru spoke to one of the guards, who called up to another, and the gate opened with a grinding of gears and chains, and I was not surprised. When we were well away from the walls Teldaru halted and turned to look back. He was frowning. I looked with him and saw nothing but the dark shape of the city and the empty road. We walked again, further and further into the countryside, with its hissing grass and tall, bending trees. When we had come this way before, in sunlight, I had felt weighed down by the sky; now it wanted to pluck me up and float me away. Only Teldaru's fingers held me to the earth.

"I'm sorry," I said at last—for now I thought I knew what to do.

He looked sidelong at me. His hood was back; his hair was silver in the starlight.

"I will not defy you again. I'm just frightened. By what might happen with the king and Zemiya. By what I might do with you. It's so . . . so big. Probably not for you, but you understand everything so much better than I do."

He pulled us both to a stop. Put his hands on my cheeks and tilted my head so that he could see my eyes. "Of course," he said slowly. "This is to be expected." His thumbs touched my lower lip and rested there. I did not move. "But," he continued, smiling a little, "you have always been strong. You will soon be at ease with my plans, and your part in them."

We walked another few steps. I hoped my hand was not sweating, giving me away.

"And Nola," he said, so lightly he almost sounded cheerful, "if you are lying to me, I will hurt you. Badly, though not irreparably. But I'm sure you know this."

I managed to smile and squeeze his hand and we walked on, toward Ranior's Tomb.

Even from a distance the hill looked higher than it had the last time; a trick of the darkness, perhaps, or just my dread. When I glanced up at its peak, the stone seemed to be falling, and I flinched. "Now, now," Teldaru said, "we've done this before."

"Of course." I laughed, as if I were embarrassed.

We had no light, but he did not falter as he led me into the hill and then beneath. *What now?* I thought. *Show me—one image, one quick vision, one hint of Pattern and Path*—but there was only the deep moist black, and his hand.

I followed him up the steps to the inner door. He turned to me at the top and stood for a moment, stroking my hair. I heard him draw in his breath and waited for him to speak, but he did not. He pulled the door open.

The same torchlight beat against my eyes, making the same blur of tears. I walked forward before I could truly see, so it was the sound that was clearest— the low, broken moaning that echoed from the painted stone. *What . . .?* I thought, and blinked the chamber into focus.

Selera's dress was not so white any more, though the jewelled ivy glinted even more brightly here than it had in sunlight. She was lying on her side by the sarcophagus. Her wrists and ankles were bound with golden rope. She must have heard our footsteps; she lifted her head and looked out from behind the tangle of her hair. Her face was streaked with blood.

"Nola," Selera whispered. "Nola . . ." She lowered her head to the floor and began to weep.

CHAPTER THIRTY-ONE

Selera did not cry for long. As I stood staring at her, she raised her head again and wrenched herself around on the stone until she was nearly upright, with her back to the sarcophagus. "Nola," she panted as she twisted, "Nola; I should have known—you were always jealous of me—and may your Path burn your flesh from your bones, you . . ." Her words were so quick and shrill that I hardly understood them. Her teeth and lips were smeared with blood.

Teldaru set my case down by the door. "Now, Selera," he said, "you mustn't blame Nola for this. And you won't, once you understand what we'll all be doing."

"And what will that be, O Great Teldaru?" I said, looking at him. "And will I understand it too?"

"Don't be insolent." A frown. "Of course you will. I was intending to save this until much later, when Haldrin and the island whore had been married for a while. I thought that patience would serve us best until we saw how their Path together began. But when I saw Zemiya again"—he licked his lips; I wondered whether he knew he had—"I needed to hurry. Needed to know if we could do this."

"Grasni." I spoke quietly, even though the thought of her had exploded into my head. "Where is she?"

He went to Selera and knelt beside her. Put two fingertips against her cheek and drew them slowly down, leaving smudges in the blood. She gazed at him and did not move. Her eyes looked as black as his.

"On her way to Narlenel," he said. "As I told you she would be. Though," he continued, holding his fingers to his mouth for a moment, then setting them back on her face, "I did consider having her help us. The decision caused me some vexation. But I concluded that you, Nola, might enjoy it more if it was Selera."

"And what is 'it?'" I said.

Selera was leaning her head against him; he turned his hand around so that he was cupping her cheek. "Laedon and Borl," he said. "Tell Selera what you did to them, Nola."

I laughed. "I can't tell—remember? No, wait—let me try, like this"—*I used the Bloodseeing on Laedon and killed him; I used it on Borl and brought him back from death*—"I was a friend to both of them." I laughed again and did not care that I sounded mad.

Selera bent so that one of her ears was against her shoulder. Teldaru pressed her head until it lifted again. "She undid Laedon's Paths," he told her. "With the Bloodseeing. I taught her to do this." Selera's eyes widened even more. "Yes," he said, as if she had asked him a question, "I know—this is a surprise to you; another forbidden thing. It was hard, my sweet, silly girl, to keep the secret from you. And then, when Borl died and Nola remade his Paths, it was even harder to be silent. But I have done it. I was waiting for this."

He rose and held out his hand to me. I stepped forward, my eyes darting. *The torches are too high*, I thought, *though I could probably reach that one, if I stood on the sarcophagus lid—if I could just reach it, and if he had his back turned . . . I would know exactly where to hit him because I hit that guard once, with Chenn's red glass bottle.*

His hand closed over mine. "Nola and I will kill you," he said to Selera. His fingers were trembling and I squeezed them savagely; he did not even flinch. He crouched in front of Selera, dragging me partway down with him. "And then Nola and I will bring you back. We will destroy you and remake you, and someday all the world will know it."

There was a moment of stillness. Teldaru and I both looked at Selera, who was looking down at her bound hands. She raised them very slowly and then she lunged at him. She struck him in the chest three times before he caught her wrists. "It should have been me," she hissed, and suddenly she was screaming, spitting blood-pink: "Why didn't you choose *me* . . . it should have been me . . . I hate you, *I hate you*—"

The noise of his fist meeting her jaw was louder than her screams. She crumpled and slid down the side of the sarcophagus. She made no more sounds.

"Nola," he said softly. "Is it your bleeding time?"

"Yes." No point denying it, and why would I? He would only make me bleed another way.

"Good. You will wound Selera—"

"But she's already wounded."

"I am aware of this. You will wound her and we will go together into the Otherworld."

"Do I not get to wound you too?" I said archly, trying to hide the tremor I felt in my throat.

He smiled. "Now why would I trust you to do that? No—luckily, I am already prepared."

He pulled his cloak back from his legs and I saw that his left calf and ankle were dark and wet. *Borl*, I thought with a rush of dismay—*of course*—*Borl bit him and he was bleeding all the way along the road, for all those hours, and I should have known. I was bleeding and so was he, and I could have slipped into his Otherworld and struck. But there's a knife. He must have one, for Selera.*

I smiled back at him. "Where is the dagger?"

He cocked his head. "Dagger? There isn't one."

"But," I said when he did not continue, "how will I hurt her, then?"

He shrugged. "I'm sure you will think of something."

I took a step backward. "No." Another step, another "no," and I spun and leapt for the door.

He caught me before I'd even managed to reach it. He seized me and threw me and I heard a crack that must have been my head against the wall. I was blind, scrabbling at his hands, which held my shoulders while the rest of him pressed my breath away.

"Remember," he said, and his own breath was sweet on my face, "we are both bleeding. I could be inside your Otherself in a moment, and I could do more damage than any dagger. Remember that, Nola, and do what I tell you to do. Now."

He stepped back and I fell to my knees. My vision returned in patches that grew and shrank and grew. I thought I might be sick but I swallowed until the feeling passed.

When I looked up he was standing by Selera. Her head was up; they were both watching me. She was smiling now—that quirk of her pretty lips that taunted and gloated and stung. *I am mad*, I thought as I lurched to my feet. *I really am; he's right again.*

I crossed the floor to them. *Mad, mad, mad*—the only word, so many times repeated, each time a stone in a wall. Something to keep me apart, even when I knelt by Selera and gazed into her eyes, which were so green again, this close.

"You won't," she whispered. "You can't."

I bit her neck. I moved quickly and my teeth closed hard and I was already pulling away when she cried out. I spat onto the flagstones.

Teldaru was laughing. "Good! Oh, very good, Nola! And now—now . . ." He held the back of my hand to his lips, which tickled me when they moved. "Now you will lead. Lead, dear heart, and I will follow."

I can try not to, I thought, but it was a faint thought and his words were much louder, laden with the power of the curse, and I believe I even wanted to, in the clear, cold madness that was upon me. I sought out her eyes, and it was the dark grey around the green that caught me—the rings that were the marks of her Othersight. They seemed to spin their own paths and I spun with them, around and around and in.

These roads look the same as Laedon's did and I pause, surprised, on the yielding silver. Those hills too, and the canyons—all crimson and breathing as his were. But as I dig my toes into the wide road upon which I stand I see that it is gold as well as silver, and that it ripples like water, while Laedon's was still, at least at first.

"Nola." Teldaru is behind me. I see his shadow and I feel his hands—real or Other, maybe both—stroking my hair and back. "Choose," he says, as he did before, and I do, because I have no choice, but also because the Bloodsight is flooding me with scarlet hunger. I pick a large road that curves off to my right. It lashes in my hands as I draw it in, thinking, as I did with Laedon's: Come to me. *It is harder to hold onto than his were, and I fumble and strain to keep my hands wrapped around it. It wriggles and falls and I drop to my knees, which sink into the moist ground.*

"She is strong," Teldaru says as he puts his arms around me and sets his hands over mine. We both grip and pull and the path slackens. It twitches once and then it loses its shape, flows over our hands and up our arms and straight into our veins. I feel Teldaru moan. I turn my head and I find his lips with mine—I do; I seek this out—and the kiss, real and Other, makes me even hungrier.

We consume the silver roads together, one by one at first and then in bunches. We are one body when we eat and when we touch. I have no mind: I am all skin and space, lengthening muscles and need. There is no more gold and soon no more silver, either, and the bone lattice thrusts through the hills until they crumble. Bones and blowing, drifting sand, and soon there is just the sand. Teldaru is as vast as I am; I cannot see his features when I twist around to find him, but I feel them beneath my fingertips and tongue.

"Nola"—his voice inside me but also far away—"we must return now; there is more to do."

"No," I say, and my own voice is like thunder. "I'm still hungry. . . ."

He laughs with his lips against my throat. "I know—and that is how you must be, if we are to bring her back. Come, now—we must make sure this part is done."

The tomb swam up around me, its walls hardening every time I blinked. The torchlight was livid green, the stones splotched black, like bruises. I was lying on my side facing the sarcophagus. Teldaru was at its foot, holding a shape that looked gold and silver, just for a moment. Then I pressed my shaking hands against my eyes, and when I looked again it was just Selera's white and her jewels, covered in the squiggling black fish of my after-vision.

I sat up and crawled to Teldaru. I felt the power of my Otherself pushing at my flesh and muscles and this was what propelled me, not any desire to know what he was holding. I was coursing with strength and numb with horror, and I crawled and knelt and saw.

Selera's eyes were open. She was staring up at his face—*dead*, I thought with relief and another surge of horror, but then she blinked. It was a slow movement, as was the rise of her chest and the fall that seemed to come much later. "Alive," I said aloud, or almost.

Teldaru lifted an arm and put it around me. He pulled me and I could not resist; he tucked me in against his side and held us both, Selera and me. "Yes," he said, "but watch . . ."

Her eyes rolled. They found me and focused. Slid back to him, where they remained. She took another breath and I heard this one; it was wet and very long. He took my hand and placed it on her cheek, which was scalding. I had expected cold; I started and tried to pull my hand away but he held it there. *The desert*, I thought, *the bones and the sand and the white-hot sky.*

He bent slowly forward and kissed her forehead, then her lips. Her breath rattled one more time. Her eyes fixed on his face. Her skin went cold so suddenly I thought it must never have been hot. I had imagined it; I was imagining all of it. Except that I still hummed with power and hunger, and her neck was ragged and oozing where the marks of my teeth were.

He kissed her once more, deeply, as if she would respond. He must have felt my shudder, for he straightened, said, "You are troubled; we must be quick. Look at her and find a way back in."

No, I thought—but how could I think this? We had to bring her back now, and I was ready; my body and vision were urging me as he was. I blinked away the black spots and focused on her face—but it was her neck that drew my gaze. The stark, wet pattern my mouth had made there. I narrowed my eyes and I was in and away, so quickly, with him laughing and warm behind me.

Selera's living Otherworld was like Laedon's; her dead one is nothing like Borl's. Of course not, I think, he's an animal—but I reel anyway. I throw my arms out—or I am fairly sure I do—but the space around me is so black that it is all I see. And there is nothing below my feet, which churn and stretch, searching or evading or maybe both.

"Be still," Teldaru says from somewhere that sounds close. I relax my limbs and he is there, pulling me against him. I thrust at him but his arms are roots wrapped around me and I am a little relieved, because the darkness feels very deep.

"It's too late," I murmur. "She's gone."

"No." He puts his hands on my face and tilts it and kisses me on my forehead, nose and chin. "Look for a colour," he says against my lips. "There will be several; just find one."

He turns me around so that he is behind me, as he was in the last vision. I close my eyes and open them and there is a difference: the Otherworld is eddying with shadows. Some look black and it is their motion I see: they bend and blow like smoke. Others, a little further away, seem lighter—grey or white—and as I concentrate on these a few begin to change. I see a glint of green and another that is bronze, and I throw myself forward. I do not expect to touch one of the flickers already, but the green one is in my hands. It is limp, and as hot as Selera's cheek was, and I nearly drop it. Teldaru's hands close over mine and we both hold tight.

"Now another," he says, and suddenly I see all sorts of colours, where the green was: a tangle of ribbons, each of them a different shade, each of them motionless. Teldaru reaches past me; I see his arm, which is impossibly long. He grasps a handful of ribbons and brings his arm carefully back. He plaits them, or that is what it looks like, and as he touches one to the other they begin to twitch and glow. With every bright, crossed strand I see an image: a baby, the sun, a necklace, a mirror. There are so many, and they change with every one of my heartbeats.

"How do you know what to do with them?" I ask.

"I feel it," he says. "They still remember. Add yours: you'll see."

I bend, holding the green strand toward the others. As soon as it touches them it jerks and snaps. My palms burn but I manage to wind it around a blue and an orange. Abruptly it slides from my grasp and finishes what I began, twining itself, weaving its own pattern. I laugh in disbelief and feel my strength again, and I reach for more, greedy and certain.

The darkness begins to brighten, or maybe it is just the dazzle of images. I can't even name them now, because they come and go so quickly. The sky—I see sky, so it is not simply the pictures that are light. There is ground beneath me, rough and splintered. A red hill in front. Teldaru throws a braid of ribbons that melt into a road when they fall: a pulsing, silver road with a sheen of gold. I toss the knotted length that is in my hand and it, too, becomes a road. It slithers its way out over the earth, which is softening beneath my bare toes.

This is easy, at first. I am still so powerful, and it feels effortless, drawing in the faint, sagging ribbons and making them breathe. Easy, easy, I think as I watch them harden and slide away from me. Easy, as canyons open and mold and the distance puckers with hills.

Only then it is not easy any more. I am holding a blue cord when I feel a tug from deep within me. I gasp at the shock of it, and at the pain, which is as sharp as the metal Teldaru uses to cut me.

"Don't worry," he says, "you'll hardly feel it if you keep going"—but I do feel it. Every time I touch a strand or see an image my insides tear. I remember how the strength flowed from my veins into Borl's dead paths, but this is nothing like that was. I cry out and claw at my own skin but the pain is too much.

"Nola! Stay with me!" He is touching me. I can hardly feel him. "Nola!" The red is flooding with black—is it mine or hers?—and all the colours are gone. His hands are on my arms. He pushes me, and I do feel this, and the rush of wind as I fall.

The stone gathered itself around and beneath me. Real stone. Ranior's Tomb. I was on my back and all my bones were broken—but they were not, because I was writhing and bending.

He will be angry, I thought. I was too tired to care. When his hands crept up over me, from knees to breasts, I expected them to gouge or twist. They did not. They lingered, and each stroke returned me to my body. His hands. My naked, aching skin.

I opened my eyes. His head was bent over my breasts. He looked very far away. *My dress?* I wondered through the thickness in my head, and then I realized that it was bunched up under my arms. Its folds were moving like waves. I wanted to close my eyes again, but the black shapes that played over Teldaru's head and arms were mesmerizing.

His tongue was cool. I saw it making wet circles on my nipples—and his teeth, after, closing hard but also gently. I moaned. *Selera?* I thought—or maybe I said it aloud, because he lifted his head, murmured, "It's all right. You did very well. You'll do better next time."

I forced myself to look for Selera. She was not where she had been—she was halfway to the door, and I wondered whether she had moved there herself or whether Teldaru had driven her there. (*Teldaru and I*, I thought, and shrank away from it.) Selera was broken, just as Laedon had been. Head and legs contorted; one arm beneath her, turned the wrong way. Not even my warped vision made me believe she was alive.

Teldaru's body was on mine. His weight was crushing; he was hardly supporting himself. He held my face between his hands and I was too weak to pull it away. His black eyes were spotted with red and flashes of silver that looked like lightning branches. They stayed open, even when he kissed me. Even when he nudged my knees open with his and leaned down more heavily yet. And then he was inside me and I was moaning again, twisting around his stillness. When he finally shifted it was just an easing away and a smooth, slow return—just this, over and over. I bit my lip to keep from making any more sounds. I squeezed my eyes shut and he forced them open with his thumbs and forefingers. He gazed at me until he gave one last, gentle thrust, and a shudder ran through us both. Then his eyes dipped shut and he sagged off me, onto the cool red stones.

I gasped for breath and it scalded my throat. I heard a noise that I discovered, moments later, was my own whimpering. There was something else, though—a low, regular grumble. I rolled over (wincing, throbbing) and he was there, his face level with my breasts. His breath was warm on my skin, and it was his breath that was so noisy. I craned so that I could see his face. His eyelids were fluttering but mostly closed. I lay back and listened to him snore once, twice, three times. Then I moved.

It seemed to take a very long time to sit, but once I succeeded the rest was easier. I was on my knees, rocking forward on my fists; I was in a crouch, my dress falling, arranging itself back over my body. I felt a warmth that I knew was blood but did not want to waste my strength finding the strips of cloth that used to be wadded between my legs. I lurched to my feet and stared down at him, through the wobbling of my after-vision.

Kill him. A torch will do, if you hit him hard enough.

Teldaru sucked in a different-sounding snore and went silent for a moment that seemed to last far too long. *He's dead* now, I thought giddily, but then he breathed again and rolled from his side to his belly.

Kill him and the curse will never break.

I stood over him, gazing at his slack lips and his cheek, with its fuzz of hair that I knew was red-gold, but that looked greenish now. His limbs were like a child's, sprawled and careless.

If you can't kill him, run.

No point—you know this. You cannot leave him: you were a fool ever to think you could.

Run anyway. Do something.

I stumbled around him and over Selera's body. I paused by the door just long enough to pick up my case; I pushed the door open and this time no one stopped me. I plunged down into the darkness and set a shaking hand to the walls.

Please, please lead me like you did before; be stronger than the curse; show me the Path that will take me away. . . . The Pattern hummed around me. I followed it even more swiftly than I had the last time, my fingers gliding along the spaces between the carvings. Each step gave me strength. I was nearly running by the time I reached the upper door. My blood pounded in my ears as I gripped the bolt and slammed it free. *It's working; I'm out, I'm away*—this time somehow, truly away. . . .

I did not close the door behind me. I took a few steps that carried me beyond the hill, to where the path was. A few more lengthening paces, and then something hit me in the chest and I toppled backward. I yelled and flailed but the weight was still on me—and it was warm and hairy, and it smelled like rotten meat.

"Borl!" I gasped, and the pain ebbed a little more as I laughed. "Off, boy— off, Borl; let me up!"

He was gone, too abruptly, deposited in a whining heap beside me by a shadow that turned swiftly to me. Hands hauled me to my feet; a face loomed, so close and speckled with dark vision-blotches that I did not recognize it. Not until I heard the voice.

"What is going on?" said Bardrem. "Tell me, Nola, before I—"

"No," I said, twisting in his grip, "not now—we must go, quickly—*we must go.*"

He held me still. He had to be seeing me—the blood on my face, and whatever was in my eyes. "Why?" he said in a low, even more urgent voice. "Tell me—I won't go anywhere until you tell me why he hurt you. I followed you—I waited all that time and I was angry and then I saw you, and I saw him catch you and then kick the dog . . . the dog made me come—I don't know if I would have, I was that angry. But he hurt you." Bardrem touched my cheeks with his palms and I flinched. "Where is he?" Bardrem asked, very quietly. "*Who* is he?"

"Ah yes," said Teldaru from behind us. "I was wearing my hood, wasn't I? You didn't see my face."

There was no hood now. He walked over to us; stopped about five paces away. Borl growled and cowered. Bardrem drew himself up—I saw this and remembered Yigranzi's thin, bare tree, and I wanted to touch him but could not.

"Orlo," Bardrem said.

Teldaru smiled. "Kitchen boy. Will you try to kill me now?"

He was holding an unlit torch. Bardrem was holding nothing.

"It is a good scar," Teldaru said, gesturing with the wood. "The one I gave you. Have you bedded many girls because of it? My own scars have been very useful that way—haven't they, Nola?"

Teldaru's teeth gleamed.

Bardrem launched himself forward—a blur, a wind that pushed me back a step. He sent Teldaru back too, and both of them fell. For a moment Bardrem was astride him, pummelling and grunting. But then Teldaru heaved Bardrem off in a single effortless thrust, and he was grinding his knees into Bardrem's chest, and the torch was rising and descending and making a sound that was louder than Bardrem's cries, or my own. I saw Bardrem's skin, pale in the starlight but dark, too, with shadows and blood. The blood spread across his face with every blow. It sprayed over my hands and arms when I wrapped them around Teldaru and pulled at him, as hard as I could. He threw me off with a grunt and stood, and now the torch's arc was higher and it landed on Bardrem's chest and his back when he tried to roll away from it. I knelt, my muscles bunched and ready for the spring that would carry me to Teldaru again. I would be stronger. I would claw at his eyes and sink my teeth into his flesh—but no. He was turning to me. Bardrem was motionless, bent wrong. His fair hair was black, where it met his neck. Teldaru's face was also streaked with black. He lifted the back of his hand and wiped it across his cheek, and the blood smeared and thinned in the shape of his knuckles.

"Go on." His breathing was ragged. His eyes looked silver, and they held me on my knees. "Try to run from me again. I won't chase you. Go."

I shook my head. I should have said, or even thought, *No—I won't leave Bardrem, even if you* have *killed him.* What I did say was, "My feet will keep leading me back here, won't they? No matter where I try to turn. You'll laugh and laugh."

He lifted the piece of wood slowly, with both his hands. "Something very much like that, yes. I'm sorry, Nola—truly."

The first blow caught me on my right side. I sprawled, straightened, crawled away from him and onto the path, as if this would be a safe place; as if I would simply pull myself home now. The numbness in my side was spreading to my legs, which dragged behind me. I saw Borl on the path, his belly pressed against the stones. I heard his whining, even though my own whimpering was high and loud. The next blow took me in the back and I crumpled flat. My mouth was full of pebbles and dirt and blood. Teldaru's footsteps crunched so close that, even with my eyes squeezed shut, I knew he was nearly touching me. I waited. The pain lapped at me, from fingers and toes inward, to my chest, and from my chest out again. I imagined the waves slipping off me, vanishing lines of darkness that left crab shells on the sand.

"Nola," he said, low and tender, and then the pain bloomed white and I was gone.

CHAPTER THIRTY-TWO

I woke to find Teldaru weeping against my chest. Later I wondered whether I had imagined it, since my eyes and head had still been swimming with fever, and since he was his calm, smiling self when I truly did wake. It's strange, but I am more certain of it now than I was immediately after. He was there. His head was lying between my breasts and he was sobbing like a child.

My jaw was broken, and my nose, and several of my ribs. The healer kept me asleep with herb concoctions for many days. When I was no longer fully asleep I dreamed (but I know I did not dream him). I dreamed of my mother and the dirty pallet I had slept on with the babies, in her house. I dreamed of the Lady's silver belt and worn blue velvet dress. I dreamed that I was awake and swinging my bare legs over the bed, ready to rise and walk out the door.

Then I did open my eyes and he was there, weeping, and the pain under my skin was too real, too sudden, and I was away again, falling into an Otherworld where I had never been before.

I tried to flee the pain but it was too big. I woke over and over, for longer and longer stretches, and lay listening to my own wordless droning. My eyes were horribly dry, and everything I saw seemed edged in blue flame. The window (not my old one) and the shutters. Someone's hands—whose? Teldaru's? Selera's?—on a bowl. I waited to see her braid swinging and thought that it would probably look beautiful with the blue around it—but as I waited I realized that she would not be beside me, ever, though I did not know how I knew.

One day the blue shimmer was fainter. I rolled my head on the pillow. The pain in my jaw was a dull throb; I did not need to moan. One of the shutters was open, and there was a wedge of sunlight on my bed. I looked at the green coverlet and the knobby shapes of my knees. At Teldaru, who was sitting on a chair near my feet, his legs in sun, his lowered head in shadow.

I remembered, as I watched him sleep. The layers of dream fell away until all that remained were true images. I did moan, then. Borl laid his muzzle on my arm; he was beside me, stretched out long and straight. *You were hurt too*, I thought. *You were hurt because I was.* He whined; Teldaru's head came up and his black eyes opened.

"Nola," he said. He smiled his tender smile—the one that made me feel safe and treasured, even as I thought, *I should have killed you.*

"I feared that I would lose you," he said. He leaned forward so that his knuckles touched the coverlet. I felt Borl stiffen and growl, so low in his throat that it was just vibration, not sound. "But the Pattern has led you back, and I thank it."

I do not, I wanted to say, and *Are you lying or are you mad?* I'll never know what words would actually have emerged, for I choked on my own voice. Teldaru clucked his tongue.

"Hush, love. You will not be able to speak yet."

I lifted one of my hands. It felt heavy, and it shook, but I managed to move it to my head. There was a piece of cloth there, looped under my jaw and up over my cheeks and ears. I could not find the knot. When I touched the cloth, the skin beneath it, which had merely been throbbing, began to burn. I could have tried to growl at him anyway, through my clenched teeth and the flesh that felt torn between them. I was silent.

He rose and crossed the room, out of my sight. I heard water being wrung from cloth and was instantly, achingly thirsty. He came up beside me and thrust the whining Borl out of his way with his foot. He set a basin on the bed and a cloth on my forehead. It was so cold that I closed my eyes again. I heard him dip the cloth and raise it, and then there were droplets on my lips, slipping between them and also down the sides of my neck.

"I will have one of Dellena's kitchen boys bring you soup later," Teldaru said. "Perhaps tomorrow you'll be able to manage something soft—some skinned fruit or bread soaked in milk. Or something a little more exotic, left over from the wedding feast."

He was watching my eyes. When they widened, he smiled. "You've been asleep for a long time, dearest."

He walked back to his chair. He pulled it closer to me and sat, leaning his forearms on the edge of the bed. His clasped hands rested on my right side, very lightly, but now I felt the bandage that was wrapped around my ribs, too. It was as if every place he or I touched woke my body to what had happened to it.

"They were married two days ago. Such loveliness—Selera would have revelled in it—shall I describe it to you?"

I hate you, I thought. *Hate you hate you.* The words sounded blurred even in my head; I was sleepy again, leaden and dizzy at the same time. I tried to keep my hot, dry eyes on him.

"The rites were held at Ranior's Hill, as they always are. But imagine, Nola, how much more meaningful it was for me than it was for any of my predecessors! To be standing beneath the earth, in the tomb of the War Hound—at the heart of our land, where you and I had so recently channelled the Pattern's might. . . . It was clean," he continued briskly. "Servants had spent days scrubbing the corridors and the tomb itself. All the stone gleamed. Torchlight filled every passage. Lord Derris was weeping with wonder before I even spoke."

I was so tired, and I did not want to listen to him—but I did listen, and thought, *How much of* this *story is a lie?*

"I suppose you will want to know what Zemiya was wearing," he said, and chuckled. If I could have, I would have curled into a ball and pulled the coverlet over my head. I felt a surge of nausea and wondered briefly what would happen if I needed to vomit.

"She wore Belakaoan gowns, both to the Hill and afterward, at the castle. I had thought she might wear a Sarsenayan one—I had hoped it, for she would have looked ridiculous, with her brown skin and thick, muscled limbs. But she wore a green and yellow island dress beneath Ranior's Hill. The cloth was covered in tiny shells. They clacked every time she moved, and the ones in her hair did too. At least her sister wore no decoration."

I tried to imagine Neluja standing tall and straight by the image of the War Hound—by the stone of his sarcophagus—and could not.

"I spoke the words of binding, over the King's Mirror."

A small one—very old, made of bronze, not gold. It was used only for marriage and birth rites, and I had never seen it; only been told of it by Mistress Ket, who also told us some of the words. "The Path you walk together will run straight and smooth through the wilderness." Teldaru had spoken these words in his deep, solemn voice. Haldrin and Zemiya had held the edge of the mirror and he had put his hands on theirs—dark and light—and said that they would walk a straight, smooth road together.

"Zemiya's fingers were clenched tight, but they trembled a bit anyway.

She was afraid. The proud, sea-born princess who lived among volcanoes was afraid of a chamber made of Sarsenayan stone, or afraid of me—of the Pattern she saw in my gaze—I do not know, but it pleased me. And then we came out into the sunlight, and the king and queen mounted the horses that had been brought for them. They rode, and Lord Derris and Neluja and I came behind in the carriage. There were people lining the road—more than had been there at dawn when we had first passed that way. People on the country road and people on the city one. Some of them threw petals and ribbons and bright strips of Belakaoan cloth. The poor ones cheered. The rich ones were silent."

I am not sure why I thought of Bardrem, just then. Perhaps Teldaru's mention of the city's rich and poor reminded me. I saw the brothel, the girls who arrived there, bruised and dirty, and the silk-robed men who paid them. Bardrem sitting on the courtyard stone, the long ends of his hair brushing the paper on his lap. Bardrem lying on his belly, broken and blood-soaked. I turned my head away from Teldaru and closed my eyes, but I was still dizzy, and I still heard him.

"The Belakaoan merchants in the upper city drummed on their balconies and doors with their palms or pieces of wood—no wonder their Sarsenayan neighbours did nothing but stare at them, and at their dark new queen. Savages, all of them, and yet they live in mansions in the city, and one of them lives in the castle. Our own rich men are right to be dismayed."

I heard his smile.

"There was feasting, of course. Queen Zemiya"—he said "Queen" as if it were profanity—"wore a red dress so heavily stitched with gems that it hardly moved. Gems in spiral shapes that reflected the lamps and torches so that she herself seemed to be aflame. Haldrin goggled at her like a besotted boy. I spoke the public words—the ones that are met with drunken cheers. And then there was drunken dancing, and I returned here. To you. And I watched you sleep."

His voice sounded fainter. I reached carefully for the darkness that was seeping in around me.

"There was one thing about the feast," he said. "A gift Neluja gave her sister, after I had spoken. A bracelet made of bones."

Such muffled words. The shadows were easing up over my ears.

"Mambura's bones, Nola. Do you hear me? The hero's bones—and we shall use them."

I did not understand, but it did not matter. *Bardrem*, I thought, and I followed his name down into the dark.

"Mambura's bones." The words circled and swam, in my sleep. They too were dreams. They were meaningless and fleeting and I would forget them when I woke.

Except that when I did wake, Zemiya was standing above me. Her dress was orange and her hair-shells were yellow, and the bracelet that coiled from her wrist to her elbow was white. It was made of polished pieces that looked like beads, but weren't. A few of them were strange and knobbly. *Knuckles*, I thought, and remembered Yigranzi. A few were long and slender and gently curved, so that they fit against the slope of her forearm. Some were absolutely smooth, while others were crisscrossed with lines that looked like hard, yellowed veins.

"Mambura's bones," I heard in my head, one more time, and then I raised my eyes to look at the queen.

"Nola. We are sorry we woke you." Not Zemiya's voice; Haldrin's. He stepped into my vision and stood beside his wife. He smiled at me. She did not.

"But we are also relieved to see you awake. And we must thank you."

Now you will tell me all the lies Teldaru has told you, I would have said, if there had been no curse, and if my jaw had not been strapped shut. I tried to raise my brows. *Go on. Tell me.*

"*Ispu* Teldaru says you saved him," Zemiya said. She did not sound thankful. *Cold*, I thought; *suspicious*—but these words did not quite describe her tone or her narrowed gaze.

Haldrin said, "He says you may not remember it clearly, or even at all. Do you?"

I shook my head. My hair scratched against the pillow. My braid was curled like a snake on the green coverlet, which was pulled up to my shoulders.

"Then we will not remind you of it," the king said. "It might be too unpleasant, and you must recover your strength. All you need to know now is that Sarsenay is grateful to you. I am grateful."

I shifted my legs and shoulders. *Grateful? No. He killed Selera. We did. He killed Bardrem, I think. He would have killed me, except he needs me to help him kill yet more people—Belakaoans, on a battlefield* you *told him of, my Queen.*

"So we will leave you, and—"

"Haldrin." The name sounded wonderfully strange, in Zemiya's voice. "She is itchy. Her skin, under the bindings that are around her chest." This was not why I had moved, but as soon as she said the words they were true: I was hot and itchy and sore, and I squirmed a little more, beneath the cloth.

"I will loosen them," the queen continued, "and check her. My mother's father taught us all such things; the *ispa* will be well attended to."

Haldrin frowned a bit. Zemiya reached out her arm—bare and brown and rounded with muscle—and laid her hand flat against his stomach, just above his belt. She smiled.

"Go on, Husband."

He smiled back at her. "Very well," he said, "but do not be too long."

Zemiya gazed at the door for a moment, after it had closed behind him. Then she turned and stepped over close to me and pulled the coverlet down to my hips. I peered down at myself and saw that I was wearing nothing but clean white cloth strips wrapped tight from my breasts to my waist.

"*Ispu* Teldaru says you did not feel you had told your friends farewell with enough warmth." She undid the knots one by one, watching my eyes, not her own fingers. "He says you took a horse from the castle stables and went after the carriages. One of them had already turned north, but the other was lying on its side by the tomb of your hero-dog."

The bone bracelet felt cold against my skin, and the air was cool too, after all the days I'd been bound. I felt my nipples pucker, and saw Zemiya's gaze flick to them.

"*Ispa* Selera was mad, Teldaru says." The queen stared at my breasts, her head tilted to one side. *She sees bruises*, I thought, and then, in a rush of new dizziness, *she sees scars. Please look longer, Zemiya; please see them and ask me why they're there. Even if my voice cannot tell you, perhaps my eyes will.*

She looked from my breasts to my face. "She had already killed the carriage driver. She was standing above the *ispu* when you arrived. He was pinned beneath one of the carriage's wheels. She was screaming. He had forced her to leave her city, and she would not have it. She would not be banished to a place so far from him. But since he had done this—since he had made her go—he would suffer. She shrieked these things, he says. She stood above him with a knife in her hand and she brought it down"—Zemiya bent so close that the folds of her dress brushed my hand—"and you took hold of a bough that was lying by the road and you hit her. One strong blow, and it sent her spinning, and the knife too, and the bough, which rolled beneath her hand and was *in* her hand when she rose to face you. She hated you, the *ispu* says. From the moment you came here to him, years ago, you and she were water and fire. So she came at you on that road like a rainmonth tide and you could not withstand her. By the time the *ispu* had freed himself from the wheel's weight, you were just a patch of blood upon the ground. He took the knife from the grass and stabbed her in the back and in the chest, when she spun to face him. And so the worm-hearted woman died and the sun-hearted woman became a hero to her people. There, now," she said, and sat down on the chair beside me in a billow of orange cloth, "does that help you remember? Or does it not, because no word of it is truth?"

I made a low sound and she smiled a wide, cold smile. "But of course— you can't speak." The smile vanished. She stared at me, up and down—at my nakedness and my eyes. "What happened by that hill? And what is he to you?"

I raised my hands and laid them beneath my breasts, where most of the marks were. As if this reminded her of what she was supposed to be doing, she rose and began retying the cloth strips, much more loosely. I touched my mottled skin (black and yellow-green, I saw, only now) and then I grasped one of her hands and held it to a scar.

"Ah yes," she said. She pushed my hand away and made another knot, right where it had been. "So it is like that." She straightened, as I made strangled noises, and tugged the neck of her own dress down until I could see the dark swell of a breast, and the purple-black rim of its nipple. She pressed a finger to her skin and I saw a bubbled scar, pink and brown, about as long and thick as my thumb. "He cut me too, once," she said. "With a broken shell. When we were young, in Belakao, and he was angry. My blood . . . excited him." She stepped even further back, rearranging her dress. "I was strong enough to resist him. You, it seems, are not. Perhaps you think you love him?"

I wanted to laugh that high, mad cackle of mine. I wanted to leap from the bed and seize her shoulders and cry, "Neluja would understand!" I did not—I did nothing at all, for the door swung open and Teldaru walked into the sunlight.

"Zemiya," he said. His mouth and eyes went wide. "Oh dear—forgive me— *Queen* Zemiya."

"Haldrin calls me *moabene*," she said. She looked very tall, just then, and very bright. She swept by him and left without another word or glance at us.

"Did you see it?" He put his hands under my arms and eased me up in the bed; I sat and gasped at the pain and relief of this. "The bracelet," he added impatiently. I wished I could scoff, *The string of white bones that takes up half her arm? No, I didn't notice.* I nodded.

"We need it, Nola. With Mambura's bones we shall remake Mambura. The Flamebird will fly again."

Of course, I thought as he reached for the cloth that wrapped my head. I did try to laugh, then, but it sounded like one of Borl's snuffles.

"And I am going to be generous. A generous fool, perhaps, but I am going to entrust you with this. You will prove your worthiness, after all your attempts at betrayal. You will steal Mambura's bones for me."

Time seemed to slow. His fingers hardly moved on the knot (which was behind my head). When he turned to me and smiled, it took minutes. His smile filled my eyes. His smooth golden cheek was almost touching mine.

Until you remake my Paths, I will not kill you, I thought. *So I will pretend, instead. I will be the woman you want, until I know as much as you do and the curse is undone—and then I will know how to break you.*

"Nola? Did you hear me?"

The cloth fell away. I closed my eyes briefly, expecting anguish, but I felt only a wonderful, bruised looseness filling my cheeks and slipping between my teeth. I opened my eyes and smiled at him. "Yes," I said.

BOOK
THREE

CHAPTER THIRTY-THREE

It was a game. It was only words and blood that soon dried (even Bardrem's). I should say that I thrust all the horrors away because I was numb with shock, or because I could not bear to live with them. That I had to concentrate on my planning; on being Teldaru's willing, grateful woman, and the Otherseer who had saved him. But it was not that, really. Because I enjoyed being that Otherseer—and being that woman was not nearly as difficult as it should have been. The blood dried, and I was a heroine, and people cheered for me and bowed to me, and handsome guards blushed when I smiled at them.

A game. And even hating myself now seems like part of it.

It was weeks before the heroic Mistress Nola could walk about the castle. Weeks of knitting bones and fading bruises and waiting.

"We must be patient," Teldaru said, several times. "Neluja cannot be here when you take the bracelet; she is too clever. We must wait for her to leave."

He himself seemed quite patient until one evening in the Great Hall, about a month after Selera's death. He hardly touched his food, and he drank more wine than he usually did, when he was with the king. I watched him, as I ate. (I could eat tougher food now, at last, like potatoes and applies with the skins and bread not soaked in milk.) He was flushed, and his eyes were bright as they darted over the people gathered below our table.

"Why does she not go?" he hissed.

I angled my head so that I could see Neluja. She was sitting beside her sister, scooping potato bits up with one of the flat-bottomed spoons Belakaoans used.

She plucked at a much smaller piece and held it for the lizard that clung to her shoulder. I watched its tiny black tongue flicker.

"Why does he permit it?" Teldaru said. "Does he not see that, while an island queen is difficult enough for his people to accept, an island Otherseer is worse?"

"You should want this," I murmured. "Tension and anger. Shouldn't you? Aren't these things part of what's to come?"

I smiled to myself as he scowled. *Fool*, I thought. *You're a child who hasn't got his way. And you're jealous of her, or nervous—it doesn't matter which. She unsettles you, and that unsettles you.*

"Perhaps she will be here on Ranior's Pathday," I said.

He turned and stared at me. I smiled a little. I had developed a new smile, this past month—an alluring yet innocent one that was more in my eyes than on my lips. It allowed me to speak impudent or bold words that did not end up sounding impudent or bold. The old Nola had not had sufficient restraint for this.

"I had hoped to have Mambura's bones by then," he said. He had leaned very close to me. His breath was warm and wine-scented. "There is something I want to show you, and I had hoped to do this directly after the rites at the Hill."

"Show me anyway." I tried to look nonchalant, but my fork shook a bit in my hand. I imagined plunging the tines into the muscle that stood out on his forearm, and this steadied me.

He chuckled. How easily I distracted him. "No. First you get me the bones. Then I will show you."

Neluja was still at the castle on Ranior's Pathday, two weeks later. The morning was heavy with fog—a close, thick, end-of-summer fog that seemed wrong, somehow. It should have dissipated by late morning, or turned into rain, but it did not: it wrapped the city and the eastern road, and deadened the music and voices that should have rung clear into the sky.

"The way is hidden," Lord Derris said as our carriage jolted over a rut in the road. It was the first time I had made the journey to Ranior's Hill in a carriage; the first time I had not walked and danced my way there surrounded by city folk, and friends. But I was a Mistress now, and Teldaru's chosen one; I rode with him, the king and Lord Derris (Zemiya and Neluja were in a carriage somewhere behind ours). I could hear the people on the road—muffled voices shouting and singing—but they seemed far away. I tried to imagine their anticipation, their eagerness to see the carriage door open and the Master descend among them, ready to lead them up. Ready to gaze into the future of their land and tell them of it. I tried to imagine this, but could not: Lord Derris' knees were knocking against mine, and the king was fumbling with his cloak pin, and Teldaru, beside me, had his head in his hands.

"The way is dim," Haldrin said, sucking on a pricked finger, "because it is foggy, cousin."

Derris scowled. "Of course. But the fog must itself be a fashioning of the Pattern, sent to confound or challenge us. Is this not so, Master Teldaru?"

Teldaru did not move.

"Master?" Lord Derris' eyes were wide. I imagined how much wider they would go if I slid my hand over Teldaru's thigh or up into his thick, red-gold hair.

Still he did not lift his head.

"Daru." Haldrin leaned forward. He was frowning. "What is it? Are you unwell?"

Teldaru sat up so quickly that both men started. "Lord Derris is right," he said quietly. "The Pattern is clouded and strange. I see this."

"Even now?" Derris whispered. "Without the great mirror?"

I wanted to roll my own eyes. I wanted to kick my heels against the seat or stretch out on the floor with my hands behind my head.

"It is close," Teldaru said. He was twisting his hands together. "The Otherworld; all the Paths, here and there. I feel them tugging at my feet, leading me toward a revelation that already shakes me, though I cannot yet see it clearly."

A revelation, I thought, and, *He means to speak of the prophecy at last.* I knew it; saw it so clearly (perhaps the Pattern was tugging at *my* feet?). I laughed. It was not loud—more of a snuffle than a guffaw—but all three men looked at me.

"Mistress Nola?" Lord Derris said, his odd, breathy voice hissing over my name. "You find something amusing?"

I turned from him to Teldaru, who was gazing at me with one brow raised. "No, my lords," I said slowly, all solemnity, now, "it is just that I feel a little of what Master Teldaru does. It fills me with excitement. At such times I am but a child before the wonder of the Pattern."

Teldaru smiled, but his eyes were cold. And it was then that I knew, in a rush that made me dizzy: I would do something to surprise him, this day. Nothing he would be able to fault me for; just enough to annoy him. Unsettle him without being disobedient. *I am so weary of your games*, I thought as I smiled back at him. *It is time I played my own.*

The fog began to lift the moment I set my feet on the ground at the foot of Ranior's Hill. This is what I heard people say afterward—that at *my* arrival the worlds stirred and changed. My heart raced, hearing this. And, even after all that has happened since, it still does. (Shame puts such a keen, nasty edge on pride.)

While this might have been a satisfying way to begin a fanciful tale, I must say that I remember it like this: the fog did not burn away until we were about halfway up the hill. I stared at my feet, since they were all I could see well. Teldaru was somewhere ahead of me and the king and his family behind. Behind them was Lord Derris, no doubt still fretting about what all the fog could *mean*, and perturbed that the masses of good Sarsenayans behind him would not be able to see as they should. Instead they were stumbling and laughing, half-blind. I heard them, from my place near the head of the procession. I heard and thought of Grasni, then Selera, and I wished us all fourteen again.

I was gasping with exertion, struggling up the steepest part of the slope, when I noticed that I could see the copper beads at the hem of Teldaru's tunic glinting at me. I glanced over my shoulder and saw Haldrin, who was holding Zemiya's hand. A few minutes later I could see the shapes of the people behind them. By the time I reached the top the fog was more like mist, and the sky seemed to throb with light. The huge golden mirror that hung by Ranior's monument was bright, though not yet blinding.

Teldaru and I stood before it, waiting for the crowd to gather. As they did, the laughter faded. The people stood—the Otherseeing students, grandparents, children—and they waited in silence for Teldaru and me to look into the mirror. It was as tall as he was, suspended from its black iron frame. It would catch all the faces, and the sky; it would show us the future of Sarsenay.

"There will be a confusion of images," Teldaru had told me. "Imagine how complex a single person's Otherworld often is—and imagine this complexity increased a hundredfold. We must look, for the people must be sure of the vision—and Lord Derris will be watching our eyes, in any case. The words, however, will be different from the images." I had arched my brows; he had shrugged. "I know—it is the most public and renowned of all Otherseeing rites, and yet the words are made up. Planned. They must be, for no matter what the vision, the people must be reassured that their land will continue strong."

Made up, I thought now, as King Haldrin stepped forward. *Planned.* I breathed deeply—cool, damp air that smelled of earth.

There were no speeches made on Ranior's Hill (these all happened later, in the castle courtyard and in the Great Hall after that). When the king spoke here, it was only seven words. I had listened to them from the hillside, on all those other years, and imagined them being spoken to me. But now I thought, *No, my king—speak them to Teldaru, only, so that the curse does not claim me and force me to see, when now I must make myself blind. . . .*

Haldrin faced Teldaru and said, "Tell us what will come, for Sarsenay."

Teldaru and I turned our faces to the mirror. The last of the mist seemed to vanish, right then. The sky opened above us, blue flooded with its own gold. In another moment Haldrin would repeat the words, and the metal would swim with images. I shifted a little so that Teldaru was between Lord Derris and me. Everyone else was behind me.

"Tell us what will come, for Sarsenay," said the king. His voice was deep and strong.

I closed my eyes.

The king's words had only just faded when I whirled away from the mirror and fell to my knees. Some people gasped; one sobbed; a child giggled. A bird called, from the gold-drenched sky. When silence had returned, King Haldrin bent close to me. I felt him doing this but did not see him, since my eyes were still closed tight. I groped for his arm and let him raise me up. When I was standing I leaned my forehead and both hands against the stone of Ranior's monument. My fingers sought out the carvings there: the spirals and jagged lines; the marks of the hero's life, its Paths shaped and shaping.

"Mistress." The king spoke quietly, but many would hear him. "What have you seen?"

I opened my eyes, just a little. I saw Teldaru stir. He too turned away from the great mirror, though he did it slowly. A few who were there spoke of it later: of how he stood blinking the golden centres back into his eyes, the Otherworld subsiding. Of how he gazed at his former student with an expression some called pride, and others anger.

"My King," I said, my voice cracking, steadying, rising high above the crowd and the hill. "I saw a mountain in the sea, breathing fire and smoke."

Queen Zemiya must have cocked her head; the gems woven into her hair rang like tiny bells. I could imagine her own eyes, narrowed and dark. I could imagine her sister, gazing at the ground.

"Beyond this mountain was a wall of red stone. It broke the waves, rose higher before my gaze, just as the flames did." I paused, as if my breath had caught in my throat. "And then a man rose from the mountain," I went on. I straightened my shoulders, my eyes still mostly closed. Now I imagined the silk of my blue dress shimmering like water, or long, sleek feathers. Those close enough said later that my eyes had rolled, beneath my lids. Some said, too, that the marks Selera had left on my arms began to glow with a steady silver light.

"He was broad and tall, and his head and shoulders were like black, polished stone. Instead of a mouth, he had the black, hooked beak of a bird. He strode out over the water, his spear cleaving a path of sparks. As he approached the red wall, another man emerged from its stones—a man as fair as the other was dark, with the long, gleaming teeth of a hunting dog. He bore a sword, and a shield with two silver hands upon a blue background. The two men met in a splintering of stone and a surging of water. Their struggle churned earth and waves, and nothing could halt it—until a third man appeared."

I opened my eyes. Even though I knew their centres were clear, people said that they had seen the darkness of the Otherworld in them yet, like the fog that had wrapped them all, before. I was still—everyone was, except for the queen, who moved her head again, to look at Teldaru—and Teldaru, who raised his to look at me. Neluja still gazed at her own feet. The slope of her neck was long and graceful, beneath the red cloth that covered her hair.

"He was taller even then the other two," I said. "Black fire streamed from his eyes. It surrounded the warriors, who stood poised, frozen upon the sea. Their eyes were fixed on him. He raised his hands and black and gold light leapt from his fingertips. The waves calmed. The orange fire turned to ash and fell away to nothing. The warriors bent their heads in obeisance. And the red stone wall grew higher and higher, toward the sun whose gold did not glow as brightly as the man's eyes." I turned. I held out my hand, palm up, fingers pointing. "This man's eyes. Teldaru's."

For a moment the silence returned. The wind rose with a long, low moan; the mirror creaked on its iron hinges. A bird cried—a different one, or the same—and then a baby, in short, breathless gasps that soon quieted. Then someone shouted, "Teldaru!" and someone else "Ranior!" and "Sarsenay!" and the sky seemed to shine brighter yet with their rejoicing.

Teldaru did not speak to me, as we watched people Pattern-dancing on the plain below. Almost everyone was there now, though there were still some children at the summit, doing their own wild dances around the stone and pausing sometimes to pant and send wide-eyed glances at the king and queen and Otherseers.

Teldaru did not speak, so I did.

"Teldaru." My voice was low, even though the others were not close enough to hear. "You are displeased. Tell me why."

"Why." He chuckled, but there was no amusement in the sound. "That should be my question, not yours. Why did you say what you did?"

"I thought only to help you. To speak words that would have more strength coming from me than they would from you. Why does this upset you?" I put my hand on his back. I felt his muscles bunch; I felt the gentle inward curve of his spine, low down. "Do you doubt the visions—mine or Neluja's, from so long ago?"

He reached a hand behind him and wrapped it over mine. "I do not."

"So you do not fear the disdain and disappointment of the people, if the visions do not turn out to be true."

"They were true. They are."

He was not looking at me; I smiled so that he would hear it. "Then you should be grateful to me, for I have only made it truer." I paused and wiggled my fingers until he loosened his grip, a bit. "Surely you are not angry because you were not the one to speak of it before all those people? Surely you are too strong a man—too strong an Otherseer—to be envious."

Someone was singing, below. One voice, then more; an ancient Pattern-song with my name woven into it. I felt myself flush, deliciously slowly.

"Teldaru!" Haldrin called. "Join me, please."

Teldaru let go of my hand. As he walked toward the king, Zemiya and Neluja walked toward me. I thought, *Look at his shoulders and neck—so stiff—he wants to turn to us but he won't let himself.*

"*Ispa* Nola," Zemiya said when they reached me. "That was a wondrous seeing you had."

My heart was pounding; I felt as if it were lodged in my throat. "Yes," I said.

The queen ran her hand up over her bracelet. I watched the bones shift. Some of the smaller ones turned completely around so that different bumps and veins were showing.

"So wondrous," Zemiya said, "and so strange, that *isparra* would bring you the same pictures as it brought my people, years ago. Pictures that—"

"There were no pictures." Neluja spoke softly but her words were jagged. "Not years ago in Belakao, Zemiya-*moabene*—you know this, and I have told Nola so. There was no vision at first—just the gift used as a plaything, by you. Deception that became truth. And there were no pictures today, either."

Her eyes were steady on me. I looked up into them, though I did not want to. Their centres were *isparra*-marked white.

"Your words were different," Neluja said to her. "You are different. There is something in you—a silence. A weight on my ears when I see you, as if I am diving. *Isparra* thick but dark."

The pounding was in my head now. *Yes*, I thought, and, *No*. But why such dread, when there should have been only hope?

"She is *his* lover," Zemiya said. "Perhaps it is his taint you see."

It was too much; I thrust away the dread. *Neluja,* I wanted to say, *your sister saw my scars but did not understand them—look at them, now, because you will— you will understand the marks of Bloodseeing. . . .* I tried to lift my hands to tug at my bodice, but they remained motionless at my sides. *Ah,* I thought, feeling the laughter in my throat again, *I see: it is my desire and will that wake the curse; Zemiya only saw my scars because I did not think to show them to her.* I imagined the curse as lengths of cloth, wrapped tight and knotted.

"No," Neluja said, and frowned. The lizard poked its scarlet head out of the neck of her dress and gazed at me without blinking. "That is not it—I—"

"Come now!" The king was walking toward us, waving his arm. "Back to the carriages!"

Teldaru and I went first down the hill. Everyone watched: the dancers, the children, the king and Lord Derris and the Belakaoan women. When we reached the bottom, Teldaru put his hand on my neck, beneath the knot of my hair.

"What did the island witch say to you?" he murmured. "What were you talking of?"

I shrugged a little and his fingers shifted. "My vision," I said.

"Mistress Nola!" a man called then, from somewhere deep within the crowd, and I lifted my hand and smiled.

Neluja left Sarsenay two weeks later. "Haldrin's just told me," Teldaru said as he pulled me behind him to the stairs that led up to the castle wall. "She spoke to no one but him—and Zemiya, of course. She wanted to walk out alone—to walk! Imagine! But Haldrin sent her with a guard; we may still be able to see. . . ."

The sun was bright and directly above us. The air felt cool and pure, as it always seemed to up here, away from stables and midden heaps and kitchen chimneys. I looked even further up, at the gatehouse tower. Haldrin and Zemiya were there. He was behind her with his arms wrapped around her shoulders. She was standing very straight. Her hands were clutching the battlement stones.

"There!" Teldaru said. "That must be them—just beyond the city gate—a carriage and two soldiers ahead and behind."

I did not look. I could not move my gaze from the king and queen. She was so stiff—her arms and neck, her jaw. I wished I could see her eyes. Haldrin bent his head; I thought that his lips must be against her neck. Perhaps he said something; perhaps he kissed her. She tilted her head toward his. His hands slipped down over her belly and stayed there, fingertips touching. She took her own hands away from the stone and placed them over his.

Beside me, Teldaru sucked in his breath. "Ah," he said. I did not glace at him, but I knew he was seeing what I was. "So it is true—an heir, already. Hal told me on Ranior's Pathday; he said she was almost certain. Nola, Nola—do you see the Pattern branching? All the Paths—and they come from us. Look at them, love. . . ."

The Flamebird's bones glinted as Zemiya tightened her grip on Haldrin's hands. "Yes," I whispered, "I see."

CHAPTER THIRTY-FOUR

It is full winter, now. I keep my shutters open while I write, since I seem to need the clouds more than I do the heat of my poor, guttering fire. Sometimes the quill falls from my fingers because they are so cold, and only then do I notice that their ends (outside my gloves' wool) are purple.

There's still so much more to write—but how much? A winter's worth? A spring's? Will the lycus trees be blooming again by the time I've finished?

Teldaru told me I had to steal the bracelet myself. He told me he didn't want to know how I planned on doing it, or when.

"Bring it to me," he said. "That is all. And do not try to trick me. You wouldn't do that, would you, Nola? You're a changed girl. A woman."

It took me ten days: three to think of a plan and seven more to set it in motion. On the fourth day Teldaru found me outside the school (for I had finally begun teaching again) and said, "Now that your lessons are done, where will you go? I won't come with you, of course—I was simply curious."

I shrugged and smiled at him, that time. Two days later, when he fell into step with me in the lower courtyard and said, "Where to now, Mistress?" I mock-scowled at him and replied, "I am secretive because you told me to be. Now off with you; I cannot have you underfoot for what I must do next."

I laughed when he scowled back at me, but I was also pressing my fingernails into my palms. For my plan was nearly ready, by then, and I was giddy with terror and anticipation.

Queen Zemiya had two serving girls: one Belakaoan and one Sarsenayan.

The Belakaoan waited on her during the day and the Sarsenayan during the night. They both helped her with her baths—one at dawn and one at dusk. The Sarsenayan servants said they had never seen anyone bathe so often; the Belakaoans informed them that if Zemiya had been at home, she would have spent half the day in the sea or in a hot pool or spring. I had a serving girl now too, named Leylen, and she told me these things. She also told me that when the queen's girls were not attending to her, they lived in two of the tiny rooms that lay below the kitchen. Leylen had a room there as well. "Take me to it," I told her one day, "so that I will know where to find you if I need you."

Leylen was thirteen. Teldaru had had the king give her to me when I was recovering from my injuries. She was the only castle servant I had yet met who was not afraid of Borl. I liked her for this, and for her chatter and her wild tangle of red hair, but there were times, when I asked her questions and she answered—so willingly—that I wished Teldaru had never brought her to me.

She took me to the servants' rooms. They were barely large enough for the straw-stuffed pallets that lay on the floors, and they had cloth doors, not wooden ones. The Belakaoan girl's had a crooked shelf with a spiral-ended shell on it. The Sarsenayan girl's did not have a shelf, but it did have a hook with an embroidered bag hanging from it. The drawstring was a ribbon—faded blue, with frayed ends that had been tied into knots.

Leylen's room had a hook too, though all that hung from it was a plain brown dress just like the one she was wearing. "I have nothing pretty," she said as we watched Borl nose at her pallet. "Nothing like the queen's girls, anyway. My mother told me not to bring anything or it'd be stolen. The queen's girls are different, though. No one would steal from them."

"What are their names?" I asked a few minutes later, as we climbed the steps to the keep. I breathed deeply; the warren of rooms had smelled of onions and meat. "The queen's girls."

Leylen said, "Jamenda's the Belakaoan one. Selvey's the Sarsenayan."

Selvey, I thought. *It must be you.*

***

Why are you doing this, Nola-girl?

My knuckles were resting on the door. I heard muffled noises behind it: words, a ringing of metal, quick, high laughter.

Why?

The planning had consumed me, these past ten days. Only now, standing still and ready, did the question come. But there was no time. Nothing would move forward if I did not do this. Nothing would end if it did not begin. I smiled when I thought this, because it sounded like Yigranzi.

I knocked, loudly. The door opened right away. Jamenda was there. She was wearing a Sarsenayan dress, which looked bright against her dark skin. I wondered, as she bowed her head to me, why she was wearing this.

"I need to see the *moabe*," I said.

"She is in her bath." Jamenda's voice was soft and low. I did not know if she had come from Belakao, or if she had been born here. I would ask Leylen.

"It is an important matter."

Selvey walked up behind Jamenda, who opened the door a little wider. I did not want to look at Selvey but I did, steadily, taking in her golden hair and her freckles, which reminded me of Grasni's. Her eyes were light, though I could not tell what colour they were because of the shadows and the lantern glow.

"Mistress Nola," Selvey said. She was only a few years younger than I was. Perhaps she was the age I'd been when Orlo had taken me from the brothel.

"The Pattern has brought me a vision," I said. "I must see the queen."

Jamenda and Selvey glanced at each other. "I will tell her," Jamenda said, and slipped off into the room.

"I am sorry to make you wait." Selvey was very solemn. I wished she were not so pretty. Yes, if she only had snaggleteeth and pockmarked skin and a goiter on her neck . . . *Stop*, I thought. *Concentrate*.

"*Ispa* Nola," Zemiya, called from a farther-off room. "Come in."

I had never been in the queen's rooms—just the king's, when he had asked me to help him choose the gift for her. I saw that gift now: the statue of Haldrin's great-grandmother, standing on a shelf above the narrow day bed in the first chamber. The bracelet was lying at the statue's feet. I told myself to keep walking, to look away from it, but this was so hard. It was close. It was not on her arm or coiled on the floor by the bathing tub. It was away from her, as I had hoped it would be.

This room was nearly bare, except for the bed and the shelf and the thick carpet that covered the floor. I wondered, as I followed Selvey across it, where all the Belakaoan things were—and then we walked into the bathing room.

The tub was in the middle. It was the biggest one I had ever seen; it was like Teldaru's mirror, glinting and vast, its facets catching lantern light. Water reflections rippled over the walls and ceiling. Things hung from the ceiling, too: crab shells, and shells of other creatures whose names I did not know. Some were tiny and others were huge; they were strung together with black, brittle stuff that might also have come from the ocean. I saw fish skeletons, stitched up whole somehow, their mouths gaping and lined with tiny teeth. A spear too, its bronze tip angled toward one of the skeletons. Everything seemed to be moving. Waves of light and air, and Zemiya lying looking up, imagining it was all sea.

"A vision," she said. Her arms were lying on the tub's sides. Her legs must have been extended all the way, because they were invisible, even her knees. The rest of her was hidden too, except for her neck and head. There were no shells or gems in her braided hair but it shone anyway, beaded with water.

"Yes." I had to look at her when I spoke, but this was not as difficult as I had feared it might be; when I looked anywhere else the undulating light made me dizzy.

"Another as grand as the one you spoke of on that hill, by the stone? Another battle between Firebird and War Hound, with your lover the master of both? It must have been grand like that for you to come here to me now."

She rolled her head toward me. I saw the scorn in her gaze and on her full, moist lips, and I wanted to say, *Zemiya, we could be friends, if you knew the truth*— but I felt the other words rising and wanted to say them, too.

"I saw your child."

She did not move. The bath water that covered her was as smooth as a sheet made of silk. My lips felt terribly dry but I did not lick them; I could not move until she did.

"What child?"

"The one you carry now, my Queen."

She was still for a moment more. Then she shrugged, and the water parted around her shoulders and breasts. I could see her scar; wet, it was a brighter shade of pink. Both smoother and more puckered. "Haldrin told your lover and he told you and you dreamed of it—maybe that is all."

"No." My voice was rough with urgency. "It was a true vision. He—Teldaru— asked me to Othersee for him after my vision at Ranior's Hill. I saw many things, but the child—your child—was the clearest."

"But you did not come to me until now."

"I did not know how . . . my Queen, I am accustomed to telling people of pain and darkness, but this was you. I did not know how to do it."

I felt sick, all of a sudden. *Why?* I thought again. *Why this reason, this story?* I swallowed over the sourness in my throat. *Because it had to be a believable reason for me to come to her here. Because it will hurt no one, in the end.*

"Haldrin esteems you," Zemiya said. I blinked at her. "He believes what you say."

"And you do not?"

"My sister does not. Me, I simply do not like you. But know that Haldrin listens to your seeings and trusts in them. And remember that this is his child."

There was sweat all along my brow. I could feel tendrils of hair clinging to my neck.

"So tell me," the queen said. "Say what you want me to believe about this child."

I swallowed as I had before: convulsively, in a way that nearly choked me. *Remember*, I thought. *You prepared these words.*

At first they came out right. "I saw a baby lying on a bed lined with bright red feathers." Obvious—too obvious—don't look at her now, or you'll falter. "A boy baby, plump and brown, with thick loose curls. Beneath the curls were the folded velvet ears of a dog." How had I thought that this would sound convincing? Too late.

"He is laughing. He is beautiful. The sun is shining on his face. But then the feathers turn into flames, and the dog ears on his head are wounds opening."

This last part was wrong. *His chin lengthens into a muzzle*, I had intended to say, *and his whiskers tangle together, and the flames singe them black. The baby is crying.* But I said none of these things. The words flowed from my mouth as if I were speaking of a true vision, and yet they were lies; was it curse or Pattern or just my own wayward mind that had made them?

"He bleeds. He burns. His flesh falls away until there is nothing but a spiral of bones on the ground. Someone is laughing—people—a man and a woman. Night falls, and even though there is no fire any more, the bones glow red."

I took a deep breath. I had not planned to say any of this, and yet I knew I was finished.

The queen's eyes were heavy-lidded, as if she were nearly asleep. "And so, *ispa*," she said slowly. "What does it mean?"

I closed my eyes. "Danger," I said. "Peril for your child and both our lands."

She rose. I heard the water surge and I opened my eyes and she was standing facing me. She was all dark, wet muscles and curves. "Such insight," she hissed. "Peril—truly? Leave me." She said this loudly, without pausing. "Go back to your teacher, your lover, and tell him I did not believe you—tell him you were glad I did not summon my husband. Jamenda! Selvey!"

Jamenda came in immediately. "I shall dress now," Zemiya said, "and *Ispa* Nola shall leave." Jamenda lifted a long, yellow robe from the floor. She did not look at me. Zemiya did not look at me. Selvey, who was hovering in the doorway, did. She was wide-eyed, and her hands were bunched in her skirt.

"I am sorry, my Queen," I said. Truth, at last. I turned away from her and walked to the door. *Move, Selvey*, I thought; *go to Zemiya*—but she followed me into the other room.

"Mistress Nola," she whispered, "I wish she had not spoken to you that way." She was twisting her skirt now. Her knuckles were white. Her eyes were blue, I noticed as they leapt from me to the bathing room door. *Please*, I thought. *Go—go*. I was not looking at the shelf but I felt Mambura's bones there, like a heat against my back.

"Mistress," the girl said, just as the queen called, "Selvey!" very loudly. Selvey bobbed her head to me and hurried back into the bathing room. She closed the double doors behind her; for a moment, as she was doing this, I saw her face clearly. Her freckles, so like Grasni's. Then I whirled. I took four paces, already reaching out and up. I swept the bracelet off the shelf and looped it around my own arm. It clung to me, beneath my loose sleeve. I opened the door to the hallway and pulled it shut behind me, as quietly as I could.

I ran. It was still very early, and the keep's corridors were empty except for a few serving boys and guards. I slowed a bit, when I saw them, and smiled. All of them smiled back, and some bowed. One boy, who was spiky-haired and sleepy-eyed, tripped and blushed furiously. When I was past them all I ran again, all the way out of the keep and down the long staircase to the courtyard, and from there into the sprawl of kitchen buildings, with all the tiny rooms beneath.

I had to stop, at the bottom of the stairs that led to this corridor. I stared at the rows of curtains, which were all the same. I heard some murmuring, but I saw no one. I walked to the door that I thought was the right one (my feet were silent; my breathing was not) and parted the curtain just enough to peer through. The embroidered bag was hanging from its hook. I glanced behind me and slipped inside.

I drew the bracelet off my arm. The bones were strung on a slender wire, which had been wound into balls at either end. It took me several minutes to pluck one of the balls apart; my sweaty fingers slipped, and I pierced the tender skin beneath my nails over and over and had to suck at the blood, because I did not want it to drip anywhere. *Leave*, I thought. *Take it and go—there is no real need for this—Teldaru will hide the bones and you will never be blamed for stealing them.* But this had been part of my plan—a clever part—and anyway, it was more than a plan, now: it was a story, and I had to keep trying. So I plucked, and I swallowed blood that tasted like metal, and at last the ball unwound.

The bits of bone slid off onto Selvey's pallet. Scattered, they no longer looked like beads; they were something dead and small, perhaps a cat. *Teldaru*, I thought, *you will never make a hero out of these.* I put the largest ones into the pouch at my belt. The smallest (I chose four) fit into my palm. I opened the embroidered bag and slipped them inside. (There were other things within but I did not pause to see what they were.) I threaded the wire so that it was half in, half out of the bag and tugged at the frayed blue ribbon. I looked at the bag for a moment. There was a shout from outside, and the sound of footsteps running past, and I turned again to the door.

Two girls were standing at the foot of the stairs, their heads bent together. They were talking, and I did not have time to wait for them to move. They were not Selvey or Jamenda or Leylen, but I stiffened anyway, as I walked toward them. They noticed me when I was a pace away, and then they straightened and gasped my name. I nodded at them. I wanted to say something that would justify my presence here, but I did not. I smiled a bit, as if I were telling them what a hurry I was in, and that I had no time to explain. Not that I would have needed to—for I was Mistress Nola, who had spoken of the Otherworld on Ranior's Hill. And if one of these girls remembered that I had been here, just before Selvey was found with the remnants of the queen's bracelet, it would not matter to the girl or to anyone else. So I smiled a bit and walked past them up the steps.

The sky above the keep was pale grey, but the corridors inside were still dark. I went by my door, to Teldaru's. It was not locked; it never was, though I had heard Haldrin scold him for this. I passed the wooden table and chairs and entered his bedchamber. His shutters were open, so I saw him very clearly. He was on his back, with his arms sprawled above his head. A sheet lay over his belly (his hips made two gentle hills in the cloth). His chest was bare. His face and arms were golden; the rest was pale.

The tiny jewelled knife was lying on the floor beside his bed, between his worn leather shoes.

Pick it up. Plunge it into his heart. He told you that the curse would live on if he died, but maybe he was lying; maybe it would *die with him.*

No. Everything he has told you about the curse has been right. And so—you kill him, and the curse does not lift. Then what? You will never speak truly, or be able to leave this place. Your Paths will be twisted beyond repair, forever.

You are a coward.

There will be another way.

I drew a deep, silent breath. I pulled up my skirts and eased myself onto the bed. I was above him, the insides of my thighs barely touching his sides, when he opened his eyes. He did not move. I lowered myself so that I was astride him. I opened my pouch and lifted it and watched his black gaze focus and still. I tipped the bag and the bones rained down onto his chest. I leaned down until my lips were brushing his.

"There," I said. "What now?"

CHAPTER THIRTY-FIVE

He made me wait three more days. "You did well," he said, still on that first day, hours after I had scattered the bones onto his naked chest. "Very, very well. Let us see what comes of your clever little plan."

"What do you mean, what comes of it?" We were standing beneath the seers' courtyard trees. I remember that I was very tired; four people had come to ask me to Othersee, right after I had stolen the bracelet. I had been very popular, since Ranior's Hill, and this was exhausting and exciting and horrible. So many true vision and false words, and the Otherworld lingering like a mist at the edges of my eyes.

"We have the bones," I said to him, beneath the trees. "That's what we wanted. What more is there?"

Teldaru put his fingers in my hair and pulled my head closer, so that he could lean his own head against it. "There is always more," he said.

He was right, of course.

"Oh, Mistress!" Leylen gasped when she came to me in my room a few hours later. "One of the queen's girls stole the bracelet her sister gave her to keep her safe! It was made of the bones of the greatest hero of Belakao—imagine us doing such a thing with Ranior's bones. . . ."

By now she was unbraiding my hair (something I had found ridiculous, when Teldaru first sent her to me, but which I now enjoyed immensely). I twisted away from her hands.

"Which girl was it?" I tried to sound innocently curious, but I spoke too harshly. Leylen blinked at me.

"Selvey. She just had time to break the thing into pieces and put it in her bag before the queen realized it was gone and went herself to search Selvey's things.

You should have seen her, Mistress, holding the pieces in her hands—Selvey, I mean—crying that she'd taken nothing, over and over, and the queen just staring down at her and saying not a word."

Blue eyes, I thought, and squirmed even further away from Leylen, as if she was the one who had upset me. "And then what did she do? The queen?"

Leylen bit at the inside of her cheek. "She told us all to go away, and she did talk to Selvey, behind her curtain, but too quietly to hear. Then two guards came and took her away. To the king, I think. And I heard"—she was leaning toward me, and I hated her whispered glee because I almost shared it—"that the queen wanted her flogged and the king said no—but Selvey will be sent back to her village and cannot ever return. And now," she said, straightening and drawing a deep breath, "all the Belakaoans in Sarsenay City have heard, and they are unhappy."

"Unhappy," I thought one night later, standing with Teldaru on the castle wall, looking at the fire-spotted darkness below. *"Unhappy" is not the right word at all.*

News of the theft had spread quickly. When the wagon carrying Selvey left the castle, at dawn, the city's streets were already lined with people. Some of the Belakaoans threw stones and rotten food. Some of the Sarsenayans simply watched; others attacked the Belakaoans—any of them, not just the ones who had thrown the stones and food.

"By Pattern and Path," said Mistress Ket, after the students told us this, "was the piece of jewellery really so precious?"

Teldaru laughed when I told him this, atop the wall. "Old fool," he said. "She does not deserve her black eyes. 'Piece of jewellery'—oh my."

"But I didn't know either," I said. The fires looked beautiful from here, and the shouting was faint. "I didn't know, or maybe I just didn't think . . ." A game. A clever little plan that would impress him. I imagined Selvey huddled in the wagon, clutching her embroidered bag. I could not sleep, later that night; she was the only thing I saw, when I closed my eyes.

The night after that the fires still burned. Soldiers patrolled the city. Some of them came back to the castle bloodied or even unconscious. The cells beneath the keep were full of Belakaoans, and a few Sarsenayans, too. Queen Zemiya urged her people to be forgiving and calm; King Haldrin urged his to be reasonable. And Teldaru told me to walk with him into the middle of it all.

"Come, Nola. You must see what you have done."

"I would rather not." I was tidying lesson books in the school, even though it was very late. He came up behind me and reached around to put his hands over mine. Borl growled at him, from his place by the door—as if he could actually see Teldaru's motions.

"It is time for me to show you what is next. And we must go down into the city, for me to do this."

And so I went with him into the streets, which smelled of burning. *Don't look*, I told myself. *You are about to find out something you can use against him— think only of this.* But my feet scuffed through ash and torn, blood-splotched cloth, and I could hear shouting, too close to us, and I had to press myself against walls whenever soldiers ran by.

The third time I shrank back from the street, trying to avoid the flailing bodies of a Sarsenayan and Belakaoan, who were pounding at each other silently, Teldaru grasped my hand and drew me on. Borl's breath was hot against my other hand. "Now, Nola," Teldaru said, as the sound of blows faded behind us, "you should not be afraid—you should relish this, as I do. But then, you are not as strong. . . . So walk close to me—like this—and listen only to my voice." He squeezed my hand; my own fingers were limp. I watched my feet, moving through the white-grey ash and the black soot.

"I'm thinking of another night," he said, as if we were strolling through the seers' courtyard. "Rain. You beside me for the first time. Nearly six years ago— do you remember?"

"Of course." I remembered my old hope, too, with a useless, stinging shame.

"I will take you to the same place we went then. We can pretend these years haven't happened. Go together as if it is the first time."

"So you still go there," I said.

"Did you imagine I did not, just because you were no longer there? For shame!"

He pulled me to a stop. Ran his hands up my arms and over my shoulders to my neck, where he laid them lightly. He stroked my throat, my jaw, my cheeks. I looked at him and thought of how I had reached for him beneath Ranior's Hill, and how I had touched him the other night, when I brought him Mambura's bones. I remembered his surprise and thought, *Would it be the same?*—and then I stepped back, so that his hands were touching nothing.

"And the other girls you keep there?" I said quickly. "Do you think they rest, while you're away?"

He laughed and took my hand again, and we walked on.

From the outside, the house looked the same. The garden seemed changed, though I could not tell how; it was too dark, and he drew me up the pebbled path too swiftly. The chain of keys was around his neck; he set one to the double doors. As he was doing this, I felt Borl's wet nose in my palm. I scratched at his head absently. "Come, Borl," I said when the doors were open, but as I stepped toward them he whined and cowered and would not go forward with me.

The smell inside was different. I could not recall exactly what it had been before, but it had certainly not been this heavy, sweet decay that stung my nose and throat and made my stomach heave. Teldaru did not appear to hear the low sound I made; he was lighting lamps as he had that first time, years ago. I watched the flames bloom, my hands clenched at my sides, waiting to see the source of the stench—but all I saw was the familiar entrance hall, with its mirrors and tapestries.

"Your bedroom first," he said when he was done.

I went ahead of him, thinking: *I forgot. All those years at the castle I never thought about this place, but now it's as if I was climbing these stairs only yesterday. . . .*

When we reached my old door he put his hand on the crystal knob, then let it fall. "Please," he said, and stepped back, gesturing at the door.

I opened it. That first time—that first morning: the tall windows, the wardrobes with their layers of soft, clean cloth. The stench was overwhelming, now. I covered my nose and mouth, bent and retched and wiped at my eyes with the back of my hand. The light of the single lamp by the door blurred. I straightened, my other hand still over my mouth. The wardrobes were there—everything was the same—the chairs and carpets and the high bed. But no: one of the chairs had been pulled up beside the bed. It was turned at an angle, away from me. I took three paces, my feet moving before I could command them not to. Another pace. Teldaru lifted the lamp behind me, and in the sudden light I saw that there was a man in the chair.

This is the Otherworld, I thought as the man's features sharpened. *Teldaru has trapped me somehow, and I only think this is real. . . .*

It was Laedon, but not—the same cap, the same straggling hair, but flesh that was so thin that I could see the web of bones beneath. The bones themselves were wrong: jaw and cheek and brow were twisted, as if I were seeing them through water. His lips sagged open. His eyes, too, were open.

Otherworld, I thought again. *He is dead.*

He blinked.

I heard a sound, as I stood looking at him: a high, sweet skirl of notes. *Uja*—the word swept everything away, even the smell—*Uja, help me. . . .*

"Is he always so lively?" I said, somehow.

Teldaru smiled at me over his shoulder as he walked to the window. "Nola. How I admire your spirit." He pulled open the curtain. I could see the shadows of the trees outside. He leaned back on the sill and looked at the dead man who was not dead, and at me.

"I dug up his body," he said. "Only the bones were left, and I used them all, and I was pleased with the results."

"Yes," I said, "he's even handsomer than he was the first time."

Teldaru pushed himself away from the window and walked back to me. Restless; something still to show. "Now to the kitchen," he said. Again he gestured for me to go before him, and again I did, down the stairs and along the hallway I felt I had never left.

I did not hesitate at the kitchen door; best to be quick about it and move before the dread held me still. I pushed the door open and stepped inside.

The fires in both great hearths were low. Teldaru went past me to the stack of wood and picked up an armful of logs. He fed them to the guttering flames, which leapt higher and brighter and spewed sparks. I blinked, looking at shelves and windowsills and the long, dark table. All of these surfaces were cluttered—with bowls and jars, trays and knives and coils of rope. I stepped up to the table. One of the coils of rope was not, in fact, rope: it was a braid of white-streaked black hair, tied at top and bottom with red ribbon. Beside it was a jar full of amber liquid; suspended in the liquid was a finger. It looked fat and pale, even in the amber, and its nail was purple. Beside the jar was a saucer piled with tiny crescents—fingernail trimmings, yellow-white. Another jar, this one holding what looked like an eye. I turned away from it, from all of it, and looked at Teldaru, who was beside me once more.

"You've been busy," I said. The words sounded firm enough.

He nodded as if he had heard me but was not really listening. "Yes, yes—now look there." He pointed at one of the hearths. There was a cauldron hanging above the newly stoked fire. I heard bubbling. "It needs stirring." He was watching my eyes.

No, I wanted to say, but my feet moved just as they had in the bedroom. When I was nearly at the hearth I thought, *Remember, Nola-girl: every new thing brings you closer to his ruin and your freedom. Remember, and be strong.*

The liquid in the pot was dark and flecked with foam. A long-handled spoon was hanging from a shelf next to the cauldron. I unhooked it and eased it into the liquid. I swirled the spoon around and then fell back a step, because the smell that rose was so horrible. I looked over my shoulder. He was watching, smiling. He nodded—*go on, love*—and I turned back to the cauldron.

I stirred in wide, deep circles. The spoon caught; I lifted it, and a chunk of something came up with it. Bones—large ones—and a web of clotted hair and maybe flesh, pale and porous. I let it fall back into the liquid. I could not swallow, and yet my voice emerged from my throat anyway.

"What is it?"

"Not what." He was right behind me. His breath was on my neck. "Who."

I drew the spoon out of the pot and hung it on its hook. It dripped blotches onto the brick.

"A brothel girl? A child from the lower city? Someone you killed."

"No," he said. "Someone *you* killed."

I stepped backward. Perhaps I would have fallen, if he had not been there. He wrapped his arms around me and brushed his lips along the curve of my neck.

"Say it," he whispered. "Say the name."

I managed one slow, dry swallow. "Selera," I said, and I laughed, harder and higher, until I bent and vomited bile onto the hearthstones.

CHAPTER THIRTY-SIX

We went to the house every night. Our cloaks were always dark and our hoods were always pulled up to hide our faces, but once the violence in the city had abated, there were hardly any people on the streets to see us.

The anger was simmering, now. Even through the fog of my exhaustion I heard things: a delegation of Belakaoan merchants had come to the king to petition for the release of their countrymen; the king had let some go, but not the ones who had wounded or killed (though the Sarsenayans who had done the same also languished in their cells). *Moabu* Bantayo wrote to King Haldrin, expressing his outrage at the sacrilege involved in the theft of the hero's bones, and at the laxity of the punishment exacted upon the thief. Bantayo told Haldrin that he hoped Ranior's bones would be seized and scattered and broken by birds, so that Haldrin might comprehend the Belakaoans' sense of violation.

Teldaru gloated as he informed me of these things. "This is the true beginning," he said, "for now my plan has its own breath, in the world."

I heard his words—and indeed everyone's—through weariness that was like a weight of water on my ears. I spent my days teaching—more than I had before, since Mistress Ket's health had begun to fail—and my evenings Otherseeing for everyone who came to me. I remember how vivid the images were—as if the only thing about me that was truly awake was my Othersight—and how dark and blurred my words were, and how I could not care. I returned to my room, once the last person had left the seers' courtyard or the Otherseeing chamber on the first floor of the school, and I slept for a few hours, and then I woke, every night, to Borl's tongue on my hand and Teldaru's knuckles against my door.

"You do not seem yourself, Mistress," Leylen said to me one morning. She left me each evening as I was going to bed and came back just after dawn, and so she had no idea that I did not actually *stay* in my bed.

"The Otherworld is with me all the time, since Ranior's Hill," I said, and she nodded as if she understood, and said nothing more about it.

Teldaru and I left the castle through a postern gate set in the southern wall—so even the night guards did not see us. We were shadows.

"I looked for you last night," Haldrin said to Teldaru at the morning meal, one day. "You weren't in any of your usual places."

"No," Teldaru said, "Nola and I—we sometimes go . . ." He trailed off and looked at me with a crooked smile that was so gentle and full of desire that I flushed what must have been a dramatic shade of pink. Haldrin glanced at me and cleared his throat.

Zemiya has spoken to him, I thought, *or Teldaru has; the king thinks we are lovers.* I imagined—fruitlessly, for the thousandth time—being able to stand up and tell the king everything. I imagined screaming curses, instead. I imagined speaking all sorts of words, but none of them—not even the true ones—could have described what Teldaru and I did, in the big, dark house in the city.

Teldaru took a knife from his belt—not Bardrem's knife, but the one with the sapphires and rubies, which I had killed Laedon with. Teldaru jabbed at the tip of his forefinger and we both watched blood bead and tremble there. He stepped so close to the bed that his thighs were touching the mattress by Laedon's head (for Laedon was lying on the bed now). The blood fell—very slowly, it seemed. It clung to the old man's misshapen brow for a moment before it eased its way down his face and onto the sheet beneath him.

Teldaru's eyes were wide and fixed. There was no gold in them any more: only black, or something deeper than that. His lips were parted. I thought, *He is still beautiful.* And then I thought, as I had before, *You could kill him, Nola, now*—because while he seemed to be holding tightly to the knife, he was also in the Otherworld, and I might be able to wrest the weapon from him and use it before he could return. But no: I might not do it right—and if I did, how would my Paths return to what they had been? I felt sick with shame. I did not move.

He bent toward Laedon, whose face was turned away from him. Laedon blinked. He blinked again, and Teldaru made a sound, deep in his throat, and Laedon's head rolled on the pillow.

I stumbled away from the bed. I was at the window, my fingernails gouging wood, my heart hammering so loudly that if Teldaru made other sounds, I did not hear them. Laedon was looking at him. He was looking, his eyes clear and focused, as I had never seen them when he lived—and as I watched, their blue flooded black. His whole body rolled, and he was facing Teldaru, and me. The sheet slipped off his chest and tangled between his thighs. His shirt was loose and unlaced, and I caught a glimpse of yellow-grey skin, pitted with tendons and muscles that looked like they were in the wrong places.

Teldaru sagged forward, and the knife fell to the floor. His forearms and elbows were on the bed, holding him up. His shoulder blades jutted behind him like blunt, unformed wings.

Laedon sat up. His muscles twisted and strained. Every slow movement was an echo of some other effortless, remembered one. His legs slid over the edge of the bed. His claw hands were upturned; his fingers twitched. His eyes were steady and still, fixed on Teldaru's bent head. And then they shifted and sought and found me.

His mouth was slack. His whole body was, now. Only his eyes lived. *It's just Teldaru behind them*, I told myself—but this did not seem right: there was still blue in the black. Laedon was here, and he saw me.

I straightened so that I was no longer leaning against the window. *When he comes toward you*, I thought, *do not run; he will be slow and ungainly and you will have time to move away*. But he did not come toward me. He sat staring at me for a moment more, and then he fell to his left, so quickly that it would have been comical, under other circumstances. At the same time Teldaru turned and eased himself down until he was sitting with his back against the bed. He licked his lips. His eyes were closed; his shoulders and arms were rigid. I had seen him like this before, in the tiny, windowless room that had been my cell, when I first came to the castle. No doubt I had looked like this before, in this very room. Spent; wrung by Bloodseeing.

"Water," Teldaru rasped, and I went to the pitcher and poured some into a thick clay mug. I wondered briefly whether it would taste the way the air smelled. My hands shook a bit as I held the mug to his mouth.

"If it costs you so much simply to make him sit up," I said, "what kind of effort will you need to make him stand? And when it is Mambura or Ranior, how will you make them hold swords—and *use* swords? Because this is how you intend these heroes to do battle, yes? You will control them."

Teldaru raised his finger—the one he had pricked—and put it in his mouth.

"We," he said slowly, around his finger. "We will control them; we will *be* them. You will be the island Bird. I will be the Hound."

He got to his feet. His strength was already returning; he moved smoothly, if more carefully than usual. He pushed Laedon onto his back and arranged him so his head was on the pillow again. Teldaru drew the sheet up over Laedon's sunken chest.

"And what will happen, after we do this?" I said—as if it were even possible. As if I wouldn't have stopped him long before then.

"I will be greater than either of them," Teldaru said. "I will rule. And you with me."

I wanted to laugh, as he reached out a hand, but instead I forced myself to step forward and take it. I held his fingers very tightly. *I will ruin you*, I thought, yet again, and I smiled into the darkness of his eyes.

<hr />

Selera's bones lay on a piece of red velvet. Teldaru arranged them, from nubby toes up to pitted ivory skull. She was hundreds of parts but also whole.

"We must choose," he said to me one night. "We do not have all of Mambura's bones, so we cannot use all of hers." He was stroking the brownish clump of stuff that was her hair, which he had laid on its own, smaller piece of velvet.

He picked an arm, and her hips. He worked his wrist into the space between the hipbones and grinned at me. "Now you," he said.

I chose quickly—three ribs—the most graceful, unhorrifying things on the red velvet. I held all three of them in one hand. They were smooth and pocked with tiny holes, neither warm nor cool. Borl whined; his eyes darted as if he could see my face, and the things in my hand.

"Good," Teldaru said, and turned.

We went upstairs. "It must happen here," he said as he pushed the door to the mirror room open. "The Otherworld is here, always."

And so is Uja, I thought. I had not seen her since he brought me back to this house; I had only heard her, singing long, lovely phrases that I was sure were for me. So now my heart pounded as I stepped into the room and looked for her—and she was there, on one of the lower branches of her cage-tree. Her amber eyes were level with mine. I expected another song, or at least a whistle, but she sat silently and very still. She did not even blink. She gazed at me as if she did not know me, and did not look at Borl at all. I waited for him to growl at her, as he always used to, but even he was quiet, though the muscles of his back were rigid beneath my hand.

Teldaru spread the red velvet out on the floor between the cabinet and the mirror. The knives were the same; the gold was the same. I wondered for a moment whether the woman whose white-streaked braid was coiled in the kitchen had ever stood here, staring at the knives and at the beauty of his face and beginning to be afraid.

He arranged the bones on the cloth and sat back on his heels. There were so few bones.

It won't work, I thought. "And now what will we do?" I sounded eager; I *was* eager, and heavy with dismay.

"I think you know." The lamplight flickered on the golden facets and on his skin—all so smooth, so bright.

I smiled, keeping my face turned to him even as I sank down into a crouch. I did not recall deciding to do this; it was the Pattern moving in me. I took hold of the knife hilt that jutted from his boot and pulled the blade free. I rose. I grasped his left hand and set it next to mine. Our palms were turned up; they looked ruddy, fleshy in the light. I drew the knife's edge across his palm and then mine in one quick, steady motion. Neither of us flinched.

"There," I said as our blood welled black, together.

The darkness is stifling and still. There are no ribbons of colour, as there were in Borl's dead Otherworld. There is nothing but Teldaru, behind me. He feels cool—his breath, and the words that prickle my skin.

"Wait. Be patient. Watch."

Time passes. Usually I do not feel this, sunk in a vision, but now I know: it has been minutes, hours, and I cannot breathe in the dark, and there is nothing to see. I am exhausted, and I have done nothing, yet.

"There." It is my voice. My hands reach, at last, for a deeper shadow. A black spark hangs somewhere in front of me. I move my hands carefully until I see the spark bob, and then I curl all my fingers around it. Cold spreads up my arms and into the space behind my eyes. I see my fingers loosen, and Teldaru's closing over them, drawing them together again. The spark warms. Light pulses—wan and white, and after yet more time, silver. Teldaru's hands open and so do mine, and the spark rises and floats away from me, trailing silver through the black. It is more and more distant, just a speck, and the path it has left is green now. I watch it, and I am holding it: it is coming from me, or it ends with me—I cannot tell which, but I am spinning slowly, clinging and gasping because I am so tired.

"I can't," I say somehow, and Teldaru slips his hands around my waist as the Otherworld falls away beneath me.

I coughed, and this hurt my chest and filled my eyes with tears. When they were gone I saw one of the ribs arcing gently about a hand's breadth away from me. The black after-splotches wriggled over the bone, so that it seemed to be wobbling. It was no different. I could tell, even with the splotches—the bone was pitted and bare and just as it had been before.

"Didn't work." My voice was a croak.

"Did." Teldaru's was the same as mine. His hand twitched on my hip. He was lying behind me, of course.

I lifted my head and his hand was there, propping it up, letting me see more clearly. The rib was bare, but it was not dry: it glistened with a sheen that looked orange, with my after-vision. And the bone was dark, not yellow. Dark red, I saw a bit later, when I was sitting up and my gaze was clear. The other bones lay around this one, and they were certainly the same as they had been.

"You see," said Teldaru, and Uja keened, long and low.

So that was how Selera began again—with dampness and deep red and a single, curving bone. Every night for two months we remade more of her. I know it was two months because my bleeding came twice. I was relieved when it did, since it kept me from needing a knife, to enter the Otherworld—and I was already covered with tiny scars. My belly, under my arms and breasts—it took many, many cuts to bring Selera back.

We tore at the darkness of her Otherworld; used our living blood to fashion scarlet sand and dull grey sky. All the bones on the cloth glistened with fat and flesh. There was always a moment of dizzy triumph as I looked down on what the old, dead Paths had become: fingernails and earlobe, a fuzz of hair and the wet glint of an eye. The moment would pass, of course, and my pulse would slow, and I would stare with horror at what we were making and think, *I will not be excited next time; I will not catch my breath when Teldaru whispers, "Ready, love?"* But I did.

I did not understand, and I could not keep from asking him questions, even though I knew that the curse would keep me from making these questions intelligible. "How does it work? How can we do all this with just these few bits of her?"

He smiled, of course—delighted to be asked, and to instruct. "Everything is in each part. Each part is whole. A man can be remade from a single hair, or a spine. An eyelash would be enough—but it is harder. The oldest, smallest Paths are well hidden. They are easier to find in the larger bones, the newer ones— and that is why we are using some of those."

"But how do they know to knit?"

"They remember."

And they did. I hoped that one night I would open my eyes and see Selera's nose embedded in her belly, or a nipple protruding from her forehead, but this did not happen. Blotches of fat adhered to bones that had not been there before. All her bones, old and new, were hidden by white and red stuff that wobbled or stretched taut, and everything was in the right place.

"Let me see it," I said one night. He had brought a pillow for her head, which by then was covered in a layer of moist yellow skin and patches of wispy hair. There was no velvet any more; just a piece of thick, folded linen, because she oozed and stained whatever was beneath or around her. "Let me watch you so that I can see how things join."

Teldaru shook his head. "I need you in the Otherworld with me. There is no time for lessons now. We must remake her, and then Mambura and Ranior, as quickly as we can—for after the queen's child is born there will be change. We must be ready for it."

"Just once," I said, as if I had not heard him. "Let me watch you once—surely that would not delay us much."

He brushed my cheek with his knuckles, which were smeared with blood— Selera's, I knew, for it was black, not crimson. "No, my love," he said, and brushed my nipple then, until it hardened beneath the undershift I wore here. "I need you with me, always."

We gathered the scarlet sand and spun it into lattice. We caught at ribbons of colour that flitted among the lattice and hills and up against the sky, and we made them into rolling green—but she was still dead. *She will stay this way*, I thought as I lay spent, staring at the fresh gleam of her lips or the arch of an eyebrow. Even as I watched her Paths stretch away from me over the greening hills I thought this—because they were black Paths, trails of soot or ashes, and the ends I held did not move. *Maybe Laedon will be the only one*, I thought; *maybe Selera and Mambura and Ranior will simply lie on the floor like meat and we will fail and there will be no battle.*

But at the end of that second month, a Path shivered between my fingers. It shivered and then it lashed, and I saw that the one Teldaru was holding was lashing too. The two roads rippled upon the green, and they flooded slowly silver, from our fingertips outward, to the farthest edge of sky. I cried out, for the silver came from me, and it tore at me as it left my veins. Teldaru laughed. He plucked up another road, and so did I, and I was laughing now, throbbing with pain and hunger. Every Path we touched turned silver. The red sky glowed brighter, and bruise-purple vines swarmed and knotted on the hills.

"Go back," I heard Teldaru say. I saw him raise his hands, which were still tangled with silver, and felt them push me, hard. I was on the wooden floor, panting and whimpering, and Uja was singing, somewhere above the pounding of my blood. Teldaru was beside me, his eyes Otherseeing black, his shoulders hunched and straining. I struggled to my knees, scrabbling at my eyes to clear away the after-vision shapes. Selera was lying as she had been: her limbs straight, her face turned to the ceiling. Her nose was sunken and her lips were black. All her skin, from forehead to toes, was mottled white and brown. Her hair was too thin and short and filthy to look blonde. As she had been—except for her eyes. They were open, as always, but they were not green: they were black. And they were blinking.

I pushed myself backward and my feet scraped along the floor. Her head moved, as if she had heard me. It rolled on the pillow and she looked at me, or Teldaru did—maybe both of them did, out of her living eyes. Her lips twitched and pulled back over her teeth. She smiled, and Teldaru smiled, and I ran from them, retching and blind.

The smell clung to me, no matter how often I bathed. I hardly noticed it at the house any more, but at the castle it wafted up at me from my own hair and skin. When winter came, the stench seemed stronger because of all the layers of clothing I wore, and the smoky dampness of the rooms. I spent as much time as I could outside, walking the snow-crusted paths beneath the trees, but I had lessons to teach, and people to Othersee for, and anyway, the cold did not seem to help. The only relief it gave me was solitude.

"Something is rotten here," the queen said one night at dinner. She leaned forward, both hands on the gentle swell of her belly. Her eyes flicked from Teldaru's face to mine.

"Your sense of smell is heightened," Haldrin said. "Perhaps the meat is old and only you can tell." He cleared his throat. I knew that he was lying, and I felt sick with shame and rage.

"No." Teldaru leaned forward too, and placed his hand lightly on mine. I stared at the piece of raisin bread I was holding. I could not lift it, now that he was touching me, and I no longer wanted to.

"I am showing Mistress Nola the deepest mysteries of our gift. I am leading her along the Paths of the dead."

There was a servant reaching over my shoulder with a ladle full of soup. He dropped the ladle, after Teldaru spoke, and the soup spilled onto my lap and over our joined hands. *Lovely*, I thought, trying not to moan at the burning. *Now I'll stink of dead chicken as well as dead people.*

"This is forbidden," Lord Derris said. I could hardly hear his voice above the din of other voices in the Hall, and yet the words seemed very clear.

"Simply walking the Paths is not," said Teldaru. "Dangerous, yes, and exhausting, but not forbidden unless you seek to change them. My own Master feared these roads and showed me nothing of them, so that when I found them on my own, the danger was even greater. So I am showing Mistress Nola. Guiding her." He stroked my knuckles with his fingertips.

"Take care." Haldrin spoke so quietly that I almost could not hear him, either.

"Of course," said Teldaru. I felt my lips twist into something like a smile, and I bowed my head.

Brilliant, I thought. *The Great Master will lead them so close to the truth that they will not see it.*

Perhaps the servant went off and told other servants; perhaps Lord Derris told some of his pious friends. However it happened, I became even more popular and revered. In the evenings, when I did not teach, I sat in the Otherseeing chamber as a succession of people came to me—mostly nobles who gave me coins, but often servants too, or soldiers, who thought I was showing them great favour when I looked into their Otherworlds and did not ask for payment.

I thought, *You poor fools; my words are as rank as my skin.* And yet even the smell of me, it seemed, was cause for awe. Most of them recoiled at first, when they sat down facing me. I watched their hands and nostrils twitch, and then I watched them lean in closer. I saw their wonder and revulsion and need, and I hated them more than I hated the lies I had to tell them.

CHAPTER THIRTY-SEVEN

We remade Mambura, that winter. As he grew, so did Zemiya's baby. I remember these things as if they had been one: a single act of creation, horrifying and exhilarating. The long bones of Mambura's fingers, bare, then wreathed in dark skin. Zemiya's dark fingers kneading her sides, finding other bones, beneath. Mambura's skull on the mirror room floor, fashioned from nothing; the curves of it, chin and cheekbones, brows and eye sockets. Zemiya's belly, round and high. Her face and breasts fuller too; Mambura's wet red muscles thickening with fat and flesh.

It took us five months. We were slow and careful, and we used every Otherseeing tool we could, because Teldaru said this would make the hero stronger. Each tool made his Otherworld look different: the sky lighter and smaller when we used wax on water; the hills dim and further away when we used grain. Though when Uja stepped through the grain—when our blood spattered the marks she left with her tail feathers and talons—the Pattern was almost unbearably vivid: the colours, the yielding ground, the sharpened edges of lattice and roads.

The only thing we did not use was the mirror. "Wait," Teldaru told me, as he had so many times before. "It will be last."

Selera lay in my old bed. She wore a silk gown—green, of course, which matched her eyes, beneath their blind white film. My own eyes were black.

I did not notice this until Teldaru took my face between his hands one night and said, "Your eyes are fully Other; you are the Pattern's now." I leaned close to the hall mirror, before we left the house, and saw that he was right. As I met my own gaze I thought of Yigranzi and Chenn and then Bardrem, and I was glad when Teldaru drew me away.

Selera in my bed and Laedon in the chair beside it; the Flamebird of Belakao taking shape on the floor by the mirror. And Zemiya—*moabe*, queen, island witch—swelling with the child who would change everything.

"An Otherseer must attend you when the babe is born." Haldrin was holding one of her hands in both of his, and yet she seemed to be far away from him. She was sitting, looking out the window of the library. Her orange dress was loose around her legs and feet but taut over her belly, where her other hand lay.

"No," she said.

Teldaru, who was standing beside me, sighed. Her eyes did not move from the snow, which danced and drifted in the partly shuttered window.

"It is our custom," said the king.

"You mean Lord Derris wishes it."

Haldrin glanced at us. "Yes—of course—but it is more than that. An Otherseer must be present at a royal birth—to witness, and to say the words of welcome. It is right."

Zemiya turned her head fully toward the window. All Teldaru and I could see was the back of her head: the tiny braids, the tiny shells. Haldrin could see more.

"I want my sister."

I thought her voice had trembled. I wondered if there were tears—or maybe I just wanted them.

"You cannot have your sister, *moabene*." He was quiet, for a moment; then he squeezed her hand, said, "Nola would be good company."

"No."

"Teldaru, then. It must be one of them."

Zemiya turned her head. She looked from me to Teldaru. There were no tears.

"Her, then," she said. She spoke to Haldrin but was still looking at Teldaru. The hand on her belly was splayed and clenched, both. I wondered how it felt: the baby, twisting and grinding within her. I thought of silver roads wrenching at my blood and breath, and I wondered.

"Mistress Nola," the king said. He smiled at me as he always had, because he had never understood. "Will you do this for us? Will you see our baby born, and welcome him?"

I bowed my chin to my chest. "Thank you both," I said. "I will."

Haldrin summoned us again the morning after we finished Mambura.

We had used the mirror, at last. Stood at the edge of it, our eyes leaping from the man-thing on the floor to the gold, and the blood that clung to it. The Otherworld rose around me like golden rain, falling up, pulling me down and away. Hills and sky were shadows behind blinding white; the snake-Paths were still black, but even darker than that. They breathed smoke, and Teldaru drew my hands into it so that it rose higher. It was cold at first, but it warmed as it flowed through our fingers, and very soon it was scalding. I cried out, and as I did the smoke turned from grey to silver and fastened itself to the roads. They shuddered, and they were silver too, and my veins coursed life into them, sending them out and out to where the white sky was deepening to red.

Mambura blinked his black eyes. His burnished chest—which was so dark that I could only see the purple blotches on it when I moved—rose and fell. His head was hairless and smooth. His arms and legs lay still. They were bunched with muscle; I expected them to flex and bend, to carry him up into a crouch or a spring.

"He is magnificent," said Teldaru. I moaned, deep in my throat. I was too weary to speak. My own muscles were water.

A few hours later I was sleeping so soundly that Leylen had to shake me awake. I flailed at her, saw her duck away from my fists before I realized that they were mine. My eyes swam with purple spots, like the ones on Mambura's body.

"Mistress," she said breathlessly. "The king is asking for you."

Teldaru was already sitting at the library table when I arrived. Lord Derris was there as well—and Zemiya, looking out at the seers' courtyard again but standing, this time. Haldrin was hunched over in his chair, his elbows on the tabletop, his forehead in his laced-together fingers.

"There has been another incident," he said when the door had shut behind me. He did not look up. "A Belakaoan merchant has been murdered by another merchant. A Sarsenayan—his neighbour. I need counsel from all of you before I decide what must be done."

"Obviously we must punish the murderer," Lord Derris said. "We must prove to King Bantayo that we do not condone such actions, no matter what the provocation may have been."

"In that case," Teldaru said, "the murderer too must die."

Lord Derris' eyes went wide. "No! Master Teldaru, that would be too much. Only the murderers of noblemen are put to death. Our people would be angry; there would only be more bloodshed."

Teldaru and Haldrin were gazing at each other. "Perhaps," the king said slowly. "But it would be more dangerous to anger Bantayo. He is already threatening to break our alliance. If we act swiftly now, he may be reassured. Zemiya, tell us—what will he think?"

For a moment she did not move. I could see her face, this time; she was looking at the trees, but her eyes were half-lidded, as if she were trying not to fall asleep. Her hands were pressed against her belly.

She licked her top lip. "It will not matter what you do. He hates Sarsenay now. Even if he forgets why, this will not change."

She closed her eyes and leaned into the windowsill with one hip. She bent forward. Her fingers went pale as they tightened.

"My Queen," I said, and took a step toward her. I was dizzy—awake but not fully; moving through space smudged with crimson and black.

Zemiya turned her head and looked at me. The others were on their feet, coming up behind me, but I saw only the gleaming whites of her eyes and teeth.

"Are they pains?" I heard Haldrin say. "How long have you been having them?"

"All night," she said. Her breath caught, and the words trembled. Her eyes did not leave mine. "And now it is time."

She did not make any sounds at first. No cries or screams, anyway, which I had heard so often from the brothel girls, and even (if I allowed myself to remember) from my own mother. Zemiya did moan, when the pains had her, and her breath was deep and ragged-edged between them, but otherwise she was quiet.

"It will be an easy birth," the midwife whispered to me while the queen moaned. She was squatting in her bathtub, her arms rigid along its lip. Jamenda was pouring more warm water in. The girl's eyes darted from me to the midwife, who lowered her voice further. "Yes—easy, because island women are made for birthing."

The midwife is too young to know this, I thought. *How many Belakaoan births can she have attended? How can she sound so certain, be so certain, as she puts her hands into the water and kneads at Zemiya's belly?*

And yet she was right. Only a few hours after the queen had left the library she finally cried out—a high, unwavering sound that brought the king to the doorway and the midwife back to the side of the tub.

"Out you get, now," the midwife said to Zemiya as her cry turned into a low, guttural grunt. "The baby's coming."

The queen raised her head. Her eyes were as black as if she had been Otherseeing. I wanted to push past Haldrin and run, but the Pattern I longed to flee held me there.

"I know," said Zemiya. "And I am staying. Here. This place has no tides, no currents . . . no waves. But my child will be born in water."

She closed her eyes. Lowered her head back down against the tub's rim and groaned again, again, pausing only to take breaths that drew her whole body up.

"My king," Lord Derris called from the other room. "Come away—leave them."

"No." The word was loud, but it shook. I saw the king's shadow leaping on the wall where all the other shadows were—the fish bones and crab shells and seaweed—but I did not look over my shoulder at him.

Zemiya threw her head back and gave a yell that became a laugh. The midwife's hands and arms were in the water; she pulled them out, and she was holding a small, limp, dripping thing. She grasped it in one hand by its ankles, and with her other hand reached for the length of ribbon she had set beside the tub hours ago. I moved forward to help, but the midwife was already looping it around the cord that joined the baby to Zemiya. The midwife grasped at the ribbon with her teeth and fingers and suddenly it was a knot, cinched tight around fleshy stuff that pulsed and then did not. She took hold of the knife that had been next to the ribbon—a little knife, just a sliver of blade. She sawed at the cord until it separated with a gout of dark blood. Zemiya was still laughing, softly now. The whites of her eyes were webbed with red.

The baby was a girl. When I saw this I felt a rush of relief, thought, *Of course that dream I told the queen of was false; that child was a boy.* But my relief ebbed as I looked at *this* child. She seemed to have no bones. She only moved because the midwife was rubbing her with a piece of cloth (soft and thick and white; it came away yellowish-green). The midwife stopped and leaned close to the baby.

She swept her finger inside the tiny mouth, pressed gently on the chest, puffed breath between the parted lips. The baby lay splayed and glistening and still did not move.

Moments passed. Haldrin was next to the tub. His hands were on Zemiya's shoulders because she was clawing at the metal, trying to rise. She was sobbing words that I did not understand; Jamenda, behind them all, was speaking the same ones. Zemiya sagged back into the water when the midwife folded the cloth over the baby's face.

"Give her to me," the queen said, as firmly as if she had never been sobbing.

"My Queen," the midwife began, and Haldrin said her name, but Zemiya snarled, *"Give her to me now,"* and the midwife did. The baby was a formless bundle until Zemiya unwrapped her and tossed the cloth on the floor. She held her just above the water. All I could see was the head, with its wet black hair, and two curled hands that rested on Zemiya's breasts.

"Leave me," the queen said.

"No." The midwife was twisting her hands in her dress, just as Jamenda might have. "There is still the afterbirth; I must attend you until it comes."

Zemiya cupped her hand over the baby's head as if she did not want her to overhear. "I will take care of myself. You have been here long enough." She looked at everyone in turn. "All of you—leave me."

The midwife backed out of the room. The king hesitated by the tub, one hand hovering, as if he could not decide where to put it. He did not notice me when I knelt on the wet floor near him. The queen did not notice me. I picked up the knife. I watched the king's face, as I did; saw his lips making silent words.

"Go, love," Zemiya said.

Haldrin whirled and walked into the other room and Jamenda went after him.

I pierced the tip of my own forefinger.

"You." The queen sounded weary, disgusted, but I rose up on my knees and leaned close to her.

"Moabe. Please give me your baby."

Another laugh, this one incredulous.

"My Queen, please. I must look at her—just for a moment, and then I'll give her back to you." Zemiya did not move. "The Patt—*isparra* will show me more than anyone else could see. Your sister would know this. You know it."

Zemiya's hands came up out of the water. They supported the baby's head and bottom, but the rest of her hung.

I took the body. It was slippery and smooth and warm, but only from the water. I arranged it on the cloth and crouched over it so that Zemiya could not see. I watched a thread of blood ooze from the stump of the cord that was attached to the baby's navel. A thin thread, barely pink, but it would be enough. I touched the baby's palms, which were lying open on either side of her head. I gazed at the bloody smudges my fingertip left on the pale, creased skin. I gazed at the rows of ribs that jutted in the swell of chest.

Princess, I thought, *we must be quick*—and then the room melted around me.

⚜

Her Otherworld is small and dim. Not dark or glaringly white, like the dead places I have already been. Just vague, shrouded in red mist that parts every time I breathe, so that I can see the little hills and the low, curved sky. I feel the seeping of my blood, and hers too, and I watch it eddy in the air before me. Two streams, mine and hers; I reach for them and fill myself with metal and wind and I breathe and weave until the mist blows away completely and the bones of the hills are covered with green.

I opened my eyes. I was kneeling exactly as I had been.

"Mistress Nola." The midwife's voice; her shadow looming, and Haldrin's behind her. I blinked at them. I looked down and blinked at the blur that was the baby.

"There is no point, Mistress—nothing can be done. Here, now. Let me take the child. And my Queen, I see that the afterbirth has come; I'll—"

The baby gurgled. Perhaps the sound was from her stomach, or perhaps her lungs, but all that mattered was that it was loud enough to silence the midwife and stop everyone moving. Everyone except Zemiya, who pulled herself out of the tub in a surge of water and fell to her knees beside me.

My vision was already nearly clear. I saw the rise and fall of the baby's chest. I saw the thick milky froth that poured from her mouth and nose. I saw my fingers wiping at the liquid and then resting on the lips, which twitched and pursed.

"Pattern protect us," hissed the midwife.

The baby's eyes opened. They were smoky grey beneath a translucent layer of white. They blinked back at me, even though I knew they could not see me.

"What have you done?" Zemiya murmured. I might have been the only one who heard her. I did not look at her, or at Teldaru when he called my name from the doorway. I did not look at the king, who was kneeling too, and sobbing.

"Welcome to your place," I said, steady and strong, as the baby began to cry. "Welcome to the Path that is yours."

Only it is not yours, I thought. *You were dead and I remade you, and the only Path you have now is mine.*

CHAPTER THIRTY-EIGHT

"You are mine." He ran his hands down my arms and rested them on my hips. I was in bed, naked; I had bathed, earlier, and had not had any clean shifts to put on afterward. So he stroked my hips and thighs and I murmured—not a word, because I was still mostly asleep. A question-sound.

"I taught you, Nola. I showed you the Pattern that can only be seen with blood—and you have disobeyed me and obeyed me, but never until today— until that baby's birth—have you used it on your own. Not like this." He dipped his head. His hair glinted red in the firelight. I felt him kiss my belly, and lower, lower, and I was awake and fever-flushed.

When he lifted his head I saw that there were tears on his cheeks.

"I am glad I have made you proud." My voice was rough. The neck of his tunic gaped. I could not look away from his collarbone, which was beautiful— gleaming, curved, smooth. I ached with the need to touch it. My mouth tasted of sickness.

"I wish I could give you something," he said.

I swallowed. "You could." I swallowed again, and tried to think—but not too much, or I would not be able to say anything more. "You could remake *me*. You could give me my words back—now, not later."

I expected him to laugh but he did not. He gazed at me for a moment and I saw no gold in his eyes; maybe the tears had drowned it. Then he eased himself off me. He put his hands on my hips again and pressed; I let him, even when the pressure turned me over and out of bed. I was lying with my cheek against the blanket and my knees on the floor. He pinned my arms straight on either side of me, along the edge of the bed. I kept my hands motionless, somehow. My fingers did not tense when he moved in behind me. His naked flesh was on mine. I felt heat, and muscles bunching; his hands stroking me and himself.

He took my ear between his teeth and moaned. His breath whooshed and tickled and I could not help it: I wriggled, which made him moan again, and thrust against me (but not in). I went still. I had to be still, no matter what he did.

He shifted, and cold air rushed over me. He was standing. I was not looking at him, but I saw his shadow on the wall. He put on a shadow-tunic and bent. I felt him one more time, breathing words, now.

"Good girl," he said. "Good, sweet Nola. I will think on your request."

And then he left me kneeling in the dark.

※

I had a few nights of peace after Princess Layibe was born. I did not know why—Teldaru had told me over and over that we would not rest until Ranior too was breathing. But I did rest; I slept, with Borl stretched out beside me, and nothing woke me until Leylen came just after dawn. I taught my lessons with a clearer mind than I had had since the summer. I noticed the taste of food again. I took a long, scalding bath, and when I was out and dry I imagined that the smell of rot had gone away.

A few nights—and then he was at my door, smiling and holding out his hand.

Ranior, I thought as we walked with our heads bent against the snow. *The War Hound's time has come*—but if this had been the case we would be going to his tomb, and instead we were weaving into the city. To the house.

"I have been thinking about what you asked for," Teldaru said as he lit the lanterns in the front hallway. "I promised I would, and I have."

"Oh?" I stepped away from Borl, who was shaking the wetness from his fur. I shook my own cloak out and hung it from a hook by the door. When I looked at Teldaru he was on the stairs, bobbing on the balls of his feet. *The excited boy*, I thought, and my throat went dry.

Selera was not in my old bed; she was sitting in a chair beside it, and Laedon's chair was beside hers. I looked past them, and past the rumpled bed, at another chair that had been placed by the windows. A rough wooden one that had not been here before, and a girl in it.

"I will give you back a little," Teldaru said to me. "You deserve this."

The girl's wrists were tied to the chair arms. There was a twisted piece of red velvet wedged between her jaws. The bodice of her dirty brown dress was unlaced; dark coils of hair—escaped from braids—were touching her small breasts. My eyes shifted back to the bed, with its strewn pillows and churned bedclothes. To Selera's eyes, and Laedon's, which blinked and stared. The girl moaned. Her fingers scrabbled at wood and her feet thrust at the floor and she stared at me too, from behind a sheen of tears.

"Let her go," I said.

Teldaru snorted. "Do you want me to remake your Paths or do you not?" He was by the window now, pulling a second wooden chair to face hers. "I will do this for you. Sit, Nola."

I sat.

He tugged four lengths of golden rope from his belt. He looped one of the strands under the chair arm. I snatched my own arm away. "You don't need to do that to me," I said. Borl was beside me, growling and bristling. Teldaru shoved at him with his foot and Borl snapped at his leg, but he fell back, and sat.

"Do I not?" Teldaru shook his head.

He bound my wrists to the chair arms. He bound my ankles to the legs. The girl was quiet, and I was quiet; he hummed a Pattern-song. When he was finished with me he went to stand behind her. He ran his thumb down her cheek. Her eyes widened a little more but she did not flinch.

"She will not bleed," he said to me, "but you must." And he walked back to me, holding the dagger—the tiny jewelled one. This time I strained toward it, against bonds and hatred. He rucked my dress up, his hands scrabbling at cloth and then skin. He cut me on my left thigh. I watched my skin open. I watched the line of blood bead and seep, and the hatred was for me—for my hunger and my joy.

He pricked his forefinger and squeezed so that his blood dripped onto mine. He bent and drew his tongue along my cut. When he lifted his head his smile was wet and smudged.

I saw the gold vanish from his eyes. I felt tugging—the tight ache that was him within me, drawing my Paths together or apart. The girl gave another groan and a panting sob, and I made a sound too, that was like one of Uja's little songs. I thought, *He is flooding my burned black Paths with silver.* He sank to his knees. I gazed at his Othersighted eyes and the space between his bloodied lips. No Selera, no Laedon, no squirming girl or whining dog. Teldaru and I were alone.

It was a very long time before he blinked. He looked at me blankly, between worlds for one more breath, and then he saw me.

"What . . . I do for you." His voice was not as weak as it had been the first time he had changed my Pattern. *He* was not as weak; he rose slowly, almost immediately, and stretched his arms above his head. *He is more powerful all the time*, I thought with a shiver. *The more he uses Bloodseeing, the more effortless it is.*

"Let's see, then." My own voice shook. "Let's see what you've done for me."

"No more blood," he said. "So choose. How will you Othersee for her?"

I wet my lips. "Wax on water."

He chuckled as he walked to the small round table by the door. "I guessed. It has always been your favourite." He picked up the goblet and the stubby stick of wax that were waiting there. Deep red wax, I saw when he brought these things to me. He wedged the goblet stem between my thighs and held the wax over a candle. One quick, delicate drop, and another, much more sluggish and round, behind it. I wrenched my gaze from it to him.

I said, clearly enough that she would hear me, "Do not hurt her."

He smiled. "Soft-hearted girl. She is a brothel brat, just as you were. We will let her go, and even if she tells someone, it will not matter. Now look, love. Look down."

Tiny dark islands joined and parted, congealing on their sea. So simple—the first way Yigranzi had shown me. I thought of her, and I thought of the other girl—Larally—the one who had died after I had told her the vision I thought I had understood. I tipped the goblet with my thighs, just a bit, so that I could see a shadow of this girl, and Teldaru's shadow moving in close to her. "Say them," he said, "the words I told you to"—and he must have taken her gag off, for she let out a piercing shriek. I heard him slap her. I saw her shadow-head snap back. I heard words—hers, mumbled and broken, and his, low and angry: "Say them, whore, or I kill you."

"Tell me." She spoke a bit louder, but the words were still broken. "Tell me what will come, for me."

Her shadow rippled and the wax scattered and so did the world around me.

The vision feels the same. The images—spinning rain with coloured facets—faces and forms in each. Time-to-come and Paths already walked. A kitten with snow melting on its fur; an arc of blue sky; a man's hairy-toed feet sliding into red leather shoes stitched with silver thread. And a wolf, turning its long, dark muzzle to wind I cannot feel. A wolf—the same, or maybe not—hunkered in a doorway spattered with mud and clumps of hair. Flames licking around its paws and up into its eyes, curling the edges of every Path, of the Pattern itself—and yet the wolf's eyes burn brighter, and do not blink.

My dress was sodden, clinging to my thighs. The goblet was on the floor. Teldaru was kneeling by me again, his hands on my calves. The after-vision was like a sheet of water, shuddering and silver.

Silver.

"What did you see?" he said.

My mouth opened as it always had, since the curse: almost without my noticing, and certainly without my caring. Why take care, when nothing was true?

"A rich man's feet in red leather shoes."

As soon as these first words were out, I should have been on my feet. I should have tried to run away from him, with this one, slender Path restored—but I did not. I sat. My body was a dead, leaden thing; only my voice moved. I laughed, but there were tears too, and I choked and gasped until there was room for more words.

"A wolf in the wind and another in a brothel doorway. Hair from the dead stuck to the brothel's stones with mud and shit"—I was Uja once more, and every word was a note, a glossy, glorious feather—"and then fire—the Pattern burning Paths to ash."

The girl's face twisted as Larally's had, years ago. Years ago, and yet I was the same: I was unbound power, and there was no Yigranzi to punish me this time; only Teldaru bending his smooth, shadowed face to kiss me.

"Thank you," I said against his lips. "Thank you—oh, thank you . . ." Burning, myself, with desire for what I used to have, and for more. For all he had promised me.

He eased himself away. I was still gibbering—the vision words, now, over and over, a Pattern-song of spittle and triumph. He walked over to the girl. I noticed that her gag was back on, and that it was soaked dark. I noticed this with my old eyes, which my voice did not care about. These eyes watched him wrench the gag out of her mouth; watched him kiss her, and her thrash her head back and forth. She screamed once, and there was an answering screech—Uja, from beyond this room. Maybe it was this sound that brought me back, even before he set the jewelled dagger against the girl's throat and cut.

"The wolf," I heard myself say. "The wind in its fur. Its ears are flat. It's brindled and hungry." I gave one more crow of a laugh.

"There we are." He was before me, pricking his finger again. "You see what I will do for you—this and more, when the battle's done."

I shuddered as he slipped back into my Otherworld, to unmake what he had so briefly remade. I looked at the open lycus blossom of the brothel girl's throat and I cried, but not for her.

When he was done, the windows were filled with a dull grey light and I was not crying any more. "Come," he said, and held out his hand to me. He finally looked weary; grey himself, except for bruised purple patches under his eyes. Both of our hands were shaking.

I saw wolves and mud, I tried to say, but what I did say was, "I saw a glade with a dry cracked fountain." I was too tired for more laughter or tears, though both of these rose in my throat.

"Hush," he said. He pulled me to my feet and I sagged against him and he staggered back to balance us. We shuffled to the door. I turned toward the stairs, when we went out into the hallway, but he said, "No—this way," and we walked to the mirror room instead.

I thought: *I cannot look at Mambura. At any of them—Selera or Laedon or the dead girl—and not at Mambura either. I want to see only my castle bed, and Leylen's plain, living face.* But I did look at him, of course. He was lying where he had been before, dark and blinking. Teldaru stepped around him. He stood by the mirror and drew me up beside him.

The mirror's bowl was covered with bones—so many that they shone from every one of the golden facets. They were very old; I knew this immediately because they were smooth and yellow, and because I had seen so many bones, by now. These belonged together. All the ribs, and the hips, and the long legs and knobby hands—they were one man's.

"Ranior," I said.

He squeezed my hand. "Touch him, Nola. Go on." But I already was. I vaguely remembered having plucked up Selera's ribs because they had been slender and small, but this time I pulled away from Teldaru's grip so that I could use both of my hands, and I picked up the skull.

Teldaru laughed.

I ran my fingers over the hinge of jaw and up around the dome. I almost expected to feel knobs—scars from the War Hound's shorn-off ears.

"You see?" Teldaru said, has hands gentle on mine. "Look how close we are—you are. Soon you too will be whole again."

CHAPTER THIRTY-NINE

I used to begin some of these sections by describing the sky, or my thoughts about the words themselves. My thoughts about where I am, not where I was. I haven't done this in a long time—partly because I no longer need to feel my way into the writing, and partly because I've been realizing something, and I'm afraid that if I let my quill stop moving across the page for too long, I'll have to write of this something, too.

I've been concentrating so intently on the before and the now, but I'm beginning to see the after. It swims up at me, wobbly as an image in a dented copper mirror, but its edges are clear enough. And I'm terrified, looking at it, and excited too, and this only makes me more terrified.

But no more—for I won't write of it. Not yet. I need to peer down at it a little longer.

So back I go, again.

Queen Zemiya, it was quickly decided, did not love her daughter.

"Jamenda says the princess cries and cries," Leylen told me, "and the queen just stares out the window. Only the king tries to soothe the baby. And Jamenda says the queen has an island woman to nurse the child—and this is never done on Belakao."

No one saw them, except for servants and the king. I heard my students muttering that the queen had gone mad, or even died, and Haldrin was so worried about Bantayo's wrath that he was hiding it. I heard them say the child had died too. I heard them say the child had strange, distant eyes that saw nothing of this world. "Stop your gossiping," I snapped at them. "They are both well. We will all see them soon."

And we did a month later, at the baby's naming feast. Winter had begun to give way to spring; on the night of the feast I smelled lycus blossoms as I was crossing the seers' courtyard. I stopped and looked up into the trees and saw nothing but branches, bare and black, but still I smelled it: petals and green, somewhere close.

The Great Hall was streaked with late afternoon light. The copper plates on the lower tables shone; the silver ones on the dais table did too, and so did the jewels in Zemiya's hair. There seemed to be hundreds of them—she was wreathed in colours that would have danced, if she had moved. She did not. She sat beside Haldrin and gazed at her plate. She did not look at him, or at the baby he held against his chest.

The baby was crying. Not crying—wailing, so piercingly that the sound rose above the clinking of metal and—later—the sonorous words of the poet, and—later yet—the music. I was glad of the noise, when I first sat down beside Zemiya, because I thought I would not have to speak to her, or to Teldaru, who was on my other side. But very quickly the squalling made me think of my own siblings, and hunger, and filth, and our mother, who had not cared for any of us. I leaned forward a bit to see past the queen. The baby was a tiny, round head whose black curls frothed beneath Haldrin's chin, and a pair of clenched and waving fists that Haldrin caught in his own huge hand and kissed. He did not seem to mind the screeching. He cradled the lace-draped bundle effortlessly in one arm and beamed—except when he looked at Zemiya.

He pushed her plate closer to her and murmured words I could not hear. She picked at a piece of Belakaoan sandfish but did not eat. It was almost all Belakaoan food, tonight: fish and crab, soup made from some sort of dark green plant and swimming with spice that made my eyes water.

"All for her," Teldaru whispered to me. "To make her smile." *He* smiled, and touched my thigh lightly, under the table.

It was the dessert that finally pleased her: an array of fruit carved into the shapes of shells. She took a tiny yellow one (melon) between her thumb and forefinger and turned to Haldrin. I could not see her face, but I saw his; the relief on it was almost as stark as pain would have been.

He rose and raised his hand. He still held his daughter; her lacy dress trailed down nearly to his knees. She was snuffling now, her head flopping back and forth, seeking milk. *Hurry, my King*, I thought; *you have only a few moments before she wails again.*

"Pelor!" he called. A man standing by the Hall doors straightened as the diners fell silent. "This meal has pleased the queen and me. We would meet the cooks who prepared it—each of them, no matter how lowly. Bring them here to us now."

The crowd began to mutter as soon as Pelor had gone. Lord Derris muttered too, on Teldaru's other side. "Folly," I heard him say. "Consorting with cooks and babies when there is work to be done with Lorselland and Belakao." He bent so close to Teldaru that I could not hear any of the words he spoke after these.

Good, I thought as Teldaru twisted away from me. *Now I will not have to speak to anyone.*

"She was dead." The queen spoke them softly, but her words brushed across my skin like fingertips. "And you brought her back."

Yes. He taught me this. "No."

"My sister has done this. I have watched her. Do not lie to me."

I have to. "I did nothing but clear more mucus from her mouth."

"The midwife did that. Why do you lie to me, *Ispa* Nola? Why do you lie all the time?"

I looked into her eyes—so dark, but not with Otherseeing. My heart thudded in my chest. I said nothing.

"If my sister was here," the queen began, and then she sucked in her breath and bit her lower lip and was quiet, though she still gazed at me.

I shifted on my seat. *Speak*, I thought, with a useless, desperate surge of need; *think of words that will be just true enough for her to hear*—but the Hall doors opened and people began filing in and the king rose again.

"Welcome!" he cried. "Come here, up to me, so that we may speak to you."

I counted them, as they approached—two short, squat men and one tall woman; two other women, also short and plump—but when I saw the sixth I stopped counting. A slender young man with light hair and a scar across his forehead, limping a ragged path through the rushes. His skin was ruddy and aglow with sweat.

The limp is from when Teldaru beat him, I thought, each word calm and clear. *The sweat is from the kitchen.* He took another shambling step, and raised his eyes, and I heard only white silence.

He looked straight at me. Not at the king or queen—at me, as if he had known exactly where I would be. He did not smile, but he looked triumphant.

"Good, good," the king was saying to the first few cooks, who were arranging themselves before the dais. Bardrem was coming up behind them. He looked at me for one more step, and then his gaze slid to the man who was sitting beside me.

"Master Teldaru!" Haldrin said. "Which dish was most appealing to you?"

Teldaru glanced over his shoulder at the king. I watched him do this, and then I watched Bardrem—his eyes widening, his mouth falling open.

Now he knows, I thought. *Orlo is not Orlo—he is the greatest Otherseer in Sarsenay—Bardrem finally knows, and he is not safe.*

Teldaru shrugged. "The fish," he said, and waved his hand at the cooks without looking at them. He bent again to Lord Derris.

"And *moabe* Zemiya—what was your preference? The fruit, yes? Who was responsible for this?"

No one spoke. The tall woman glanced behind her and cleared her throat. "Him, my King," but Bardrem was limping away, back toward the double doors.

"You, there!" Haldrin cried, but Bardrem did not pause.

"He's a strange one, sire," the woman said. "Arrived not so long ago and won't tell us where he's from. But the shells were his idea."

"And his name?"

The woman smiled. She was flushed too, from kitchen heat and probably from speaking at such length with the king.

"Bardo," she said.

The king called out the name, and Bardrem hesitated with his hands on the door handles. He looked over his shoulder at me for a moment that seemed endless, with something on his face that might have been fear or anger.

Teldaru was turning; I felt this, saw it at the edge of my vision. "Go," I said to Bardrem silently, with my mouth and also with my eyes. He pulled the doors open and went out into the courtyard, where shadows were lengthening on the muddy ground.

"What was that about?" Teldaru said as a serving girl closed the doors.

"Nothing." My voice was already trembling; I spoke only the one word.

"Hmph." He picked up a sour melon piece that had been carved into a long, slender shell banded with crystallized sugar and put it in his mouth. I watched his cheeks hollow as he sucked; then I slumped back against my chair and closed my eyes.

Ispa Nola." The queen's breath was hot on my cheek. "Why do you lie?"

The kitchens were hot, of course, but also quiet. It was morning—after the day's first meal, before the second. Grasni and I used to come at this time, when we wanted to beg Dellena for sweets or drinks or soft, steaming bread.

"It's been a long time, Mistress," said Dellena now. She was old, like Mistress Ket, but with clear, bright eyes and hair pulled into such a tight knot that none escaped. She was sitting on a bench, shelling peas into a bowl. *Too menial a task for her*, I thought, *but perhaps it calms her.* A black and white kitten scampered around her feet, batting at the pods as she dropped them.

"I am just Nola, here," I said.

"Nola used to steal from me sometimes. And she said rude things about my mutton stew. I'm pleased Mistress Nola is here instead. Though I'm not sure yet *why* she is."

I twitched the folds of my dress—a dark blue one stitched with whorls of silver thread. I had thought it would make me feel strong and beautiful, but it did not; I felt ridiculous, like a child in her mother's clothing. The hollows under my arms and along my spine were soaked with sweat.

"At the feast last night," I began, and stopped. I pressed my lips together for a moment. "There was a man—Bardo. He left the Hall before the king could speak to him. I wanted—the king wanted—to make sure that this Bardo knew of our appreciation."

There were only a few other people in this room with us; very young ones, servants, scrubbing hearthstones and tabletops and the insides of iron pots. No Bardrem, which had both disappointed and relieved me when I arrived.

Dellena frowned and smiled at the same time. "Bardo—yes—I heard of his flight from the Hall. It did not surprise me. He has little love for the company of others. He has been here since midwinter, but has made no friends that I know of."

"And he will not say where he is from—one of the other cooks told us this last night."

Dellena threw the last of the pods on the floor and clapped twice. A girl rushed over and knelt to sweep the pods into a bucket. The kitten swatted at her apron laces, rolling on its back and growling a tiny, fierce growl.

"He won't say, no. When he first came he said only that he'd been a cook's boy, once. I told him to cut potatoes and carve a duck—simple tests I give anyone who comes looking for a place here. He cut the potatoes into spirals so thin you could see through them, and arranged them on a platter with greens so that they looked like flowers." She shrugged. "So he's a cook now, not a cook's boy—a more distinguished Path, but it doesn't seem to make him happy."

Because he's a poet, I thought, *and yet the Pattern always leads him back to kitchens.*

"Could you take me to him, then?"

"He'll be sleeping now. And he'll likely not say a word, in any case."

"Please."

She narrowed her eyes at me, and opened her mouth as if she would say something. In the end, though, she simply rose—slowly, with a hand against the small of her back—and led me among the long, scarred tables to a narrow flight of stairs.

"His room's the third from the end, with the wooden door. You'll have to find your own way from here, for I can't manage the stairs and I need all my girls for the next meal. Take care walking, for though I tell them all to keep their feet dry, they hardly ever listen."

The stairs *were* slick: I imagined generations of feet coated in cooking fat or soapy water or sodden bits of vegetables and fruits. I walked slowly, even when I got to the bottom. I passed rooms like Jamenda and Selvey's, except that one of these had a slatted wood door, not a curtain. The wood was smooth and speckled with holes. I traced one with a fingertip and bent to put my eye to it.

"Come in, *Mistress* Nola."

He sounded far away, and tired. I waited for my flush to subside and then I pulled the door open.

He was standing, leaning one shoulder against the wall. His head was angled because the ceiling was too low for him. I remembered his tiny room at the brothel; the notes he'd leave for me on the pallet (like this one), when he knew I'd be looking for him; the blanket smudged with ink and snipped quill ends. This blanket had been pulled tight and straight over the pallet, and there was nothing on it, not even the marks of his body.

"You look terrible," he said. He pursed his lips in what was almost a pout; above them, his eyes burned. My own lips parted, but he laughed and held up a hand. His slender fingers shook, a bit. The littlest one was crooked and looked swollen around the knuckles.

"No," he said, "don't bother speaking. You'll only tell me why you can't speak, anyway. No—let *me*—you look terrible, I was saying. Older. Sallow. Your cheeks are sunken, and your eyes too—but your eyes! So black, with those silver centres—an Otherseer's eyes, except that yours look dead."

He was breathing hard. I thought of the tent where we had stood, the last time we found each other, the men on the other side calling, "Master Bardremzo!" when he smacked the cloth. My fear at the force of his anger; my joy at the solid, living presence of him. I felt the same things now. I wanted to touch him—wanted to smile, at least.

What I did was say, "They told me you hardly talk at all." I did not expect *him* to smile, or to unclench his other hand, but I hoped he would. He shook his head and his mouth twisted, and I said quickly, "I don't mean to make light of anything, Bardrem, but I'm so happy—I was certain you were dead." *Stupid girl*, I thought as he pushed himself away from the wall and took a limping step toward me. *You stupid, stupid girl.*

"I nearly was." He thrust the words through his teeth. "The birds were already circling. If someone hadn't found me there by the Hill, I would have been carrion. Because he—" Bardrem drew a hand across his forehead, over the wrinkle of scar. "Because of him. Because of you, somehow. It was you I came here for, of course. I didn't want to, for a long time, but I kept hearing about you: Mistress Nola had a vision on Ranior's Pathday; Mistress Nola is young and beautiful and will someday eclipse the Master himself . . . I told myself I didn't have any desire to see this Mistress Nola, but I did, and so I came back. When I was well enough. And I've been here since, not looking for you yet, because I knew I'd found you. But now I've found him too. Orlo." He laughed again. "I should have known him all those years ago, at the brothel. Should have glimpsed Master Teldaru in some procession—and I loitered outside the castle walls enough, when I was a boy. But I never did see him. Not then, and not these past few months. And when I learned the king had called for us last night, I thought only that the Pattern had arranged for me to see you at last, and for you to see me."

"And you did," I said, as he took another step. He was very close. I could have touched his cheekbone, or held his little finger and stroked its bumps and bends. "You saw me, and—"

"—I saw him, and as soon as I did, everything changed. I'm grateful. Because you aren't the reason for anything, any more. He is."

"No," I said quickly, "you don't understand—you mustn't do anything; you should go, *now*."

He frowned, and I couldn't help it: I thought of the boy, scuffing his boot in the dried mud of Yigranzi's courtyard. "You said that the last time, before the king's marriage. So you were telling me to run away because of Teldaru—warning me without telling me why. Are you so ashamed of whatever you're doing with him that you cannot tell the truth?"

"Bardrem," I said, low and harsh, "you almost have it; you are close"—I *was* holding his hand, kneading it—"but if you get any nearer I will never be as I was when I was a girl—I will be changed. . . ."

"So it's yourself you fear for, after all." He shrugged. "You are already changed. Go, Nola. Leave." He was free of my hands and I was small, shrinking away from his disgust and my own.

"No," I said, but I did leave, stumbling and slipping up the steps.

I was more composed when I walked again into the kitchen. I had learned this—to be poised, because anything else would elicit gossip or questions I could not answer, even if I wanted to.

"Well?" Dellena said as I passed. "How was Bardo? Was he gracious, at least?"

"He called me Mistress Nola," I said, smiling a rictus smile, and then I was away into the morning.

CHAPTER FORTY

The day after I spoke to Bardrem the city was in flames again. *Moabu* Bantayo had decided to trade only with Lorselland, Lord Derris told me—weeks ago, he added, glaring at me as if I should have known (which I should have). And last night the richest Belakaoan merchant in the city had been murdered by his stable boy, who had, under questioning, revealed that a group of Sarsenayan merchants had paid him gold to do it, and promised him more when it was done. The boy was now in a cell; before they could join him, several of the Sarsenayan merchants had died at the hands of their own Belakaoan servants. Hours after this, Sarsenay was burning.

"King Bantayo is a fool if he thinks our people will suffer indignity quietly," Lord Derris rasped.

"Not quietly, no," Haldrin said, leaning forward at the library table, "but with murder and fire? Surely we are more civilized than this."

Lord Derris was still frowning. "Sometimes the Pattern can make calm only from chaos—is that not right, Master Teldaru?"

"Yes," Teldaru said, though he was looking at me. "This is so."

"If only Derris were king," Teldaru said to me later, as we were walking toward the school. "The battle would be nearly upon us. But no—no—it is better this way, for we have more time, you and I. More time, though we must hurry now, even so."

He was speaking very quickly, and the words were slurred. His chin and cheeks were covered with stubble. I felt a stirring of hope, followed, as ever, by dread—*If he's too weak, how will he mend me? And if he is dead—if Bardrem gets to him, how will I go on as I am, crippled, lesser?*

"Tonight." Teldaru took my face in his hands. His own face was dappled with sun and branch shadows that trembled and bristled with buds that had not been there yesterday. The wind smelled even more strongly of spring—but now, too, of burning.

"Ranior tonight, O Seer-Who-Will-Be-Queen. Ranior tonight and every night until he breathes—for no, we do not have much time at all, in fact."

I imagined Bardrem everywhere, as I had before. Among the throngs of people in the main courtyard—the soldiers in their lines, and the servants, the stable boys, the guards. And even though there were hardly any people in the city (everyone hiding behind the walls that stood, unblackened), I imagined him there too, disappearing around corners and into alleyways, somehow, impossibly, a boy again. Night after night Teldaru and I slipped to the house, through sooty, heavy air, and I was more and more tired every time, from the War Hound's remaking, and from thinking Bardrem was nearby, even when he was not.

Only he was.

"Mistress." Leylen, one dawn a month after the fires had begun—a month of fires throughout the city, and no one ever caught setting them; a month of Bantayo raging at us in letters that went on for pages. "Mistress, I've something to give you."

Her voice was strange; I could tell this, though I was not yet fully awake. I had been asleep for maybe an hour. It was all I ever got, these days, and it was not so much sleep as it was a dizzy blur of images: gobbets of flesh and clean, sharp, red bones.

"Mistress! Here, in my hand . . ."

It was a little, folded piece of paper. I felt it in my palm and remembered, so suddenly that it made me dizzy, how Bardrem used to leave me notes just like this in the brothel, under my rug or in one of my shoes.

I sat up. Leylen was blushing, turning the end of her braid around between her fingers. "He was handsome—Bardo, the one who gave me that. Said he'd known you long ago. Said he didn't want Master Teldaru to find out—a secret longing, he said." She bit her lip and glanced at me.

"Thank you, Leylen." My voice was steady. "You may go."

"But I must help dress you soon . . . and your hair—"

"Go, Leylen. I'll dress myself today."

And then I was alone.

I unfolded the paper. My hands were not steady.

Two cloaks and two hoods
House
Fence
Lock
Every night the same
I will understand, Nola.

I touched the letters as if I would be able to feel them. His quill and ink; his marks, which I did not actually understand until minutes after I'd first read them. A note like so many others, which I had found in unexpected places.

I refolded it; I would only gaze at it foolishly otherwise, and be late for my class. I slid the paper under my wardrobe. The other one was there too—the one he had left for me the same night Orlo had lured me away from the brothel. I did not look at it again later, when I returned to my room. I could still feel the words, though—then, and after midnight, when Teldaru and I slipped out the postern gate and down into the city.

I will understand, Nola: words as rounded and urgent as veins beneath my skin.

Three months. Three months after I had met Bardrem in his room. Three months after I had lifted Ranior's skull from the mirror's golden bowl. Princess Layibe three months old. The city still burning fitfully, a night-pattern of flickering orange and rising smoke.

It was early summer, and *Moabu* Bantayo was coming to Sarsenay.

"We have no time," Teldaru said.

I had never seen him look so stricken. "You did not plan for this," I said. "You did not foresee it"—and he turned to me, his black eyes narrowed.

"Are you mocking me?"

I smiled—for him, and for the people who might be watching us from the tables below. "No, no—how could I, now that I understand so much? I am only asking; wondering. . . ."

He gazed at me a moment longer. His fingers were drumming against the underside of the table. "We will take them away tonight," he said at last. I arched one of my brows, while my chest tightened so suddenly that I feared I would gasp.

"I wanted to wait until he was finished," Teldaru continued, "but now we must move more quickly. We will take them to the Hill tonight, and hope that it will not hurt him."

He came to my room much later than usual. I was half-asleep when Borl shook himself and whined. I sat up and then the knock came, light but insistent.

He did not speak to me at all as we walked to the house. *Bardrem*, I thought, as I always did now, but it was just a word; there had been no other note or glimpse, and I had lost the sharp hope I had had before.

There was a wagon and a single, stolid horse in the street in front of the house. "Up," Teldaru said to me. The word sounded harsh, after all the silence. I climbed to the long wooden seat. Borl scrambled after me and slid, and I held him around the middle to steady him. I looked back into the wagon, which was open, and saw a jumble of sacks and garden tools.

Teldaru climbed up beside me and lifted the reins. He laughed as he flicked them. "Imagine! Two ancient heroes lying unattended in the back of a wagon, and no one the wiser!"

I wanted to look over my shoulder again but did not. I wondered, as we clattered over the cobbled street toward the east gate, how Teldaru had managed to get them down the stairs—Mambura, who was tall and bulky with muscle, and Ranior, who had only just grown a layer of skin, and whose own muscles did not yet seem solid.

I wondered too, when the gatehouse guard stepped out to meet us, whether Teldaru would fail to be convincing this time. But as soon as the man saw who was sitting with the reins in his beringed hands, he bowed and smiled nervously and I knew we were as good as out already.

"Mistress Nola and I are taking plant specimens," Teldaru said, nodding over his shoulder at the sacks, and the trowels and shovels that lay near them.

The guard peered into the back of the wagon. *Just poke at the cloth with your sword*, I thought. *Just ask him why we're plant-collecting in the middle of the night.* Except that Teldaru would probably have had an answer.

"Mistress Nola," the guard said after he had stepped down, "I . . . that is, my family was near enough to you on Ranior's Hill last Pathday to see you." *The smile is for me*, I thought then, and I smiled back at him, glad that the darkness would hide my flush. When we were out on the road beyond the city, Teldaru chuckled and said, "Nearly one year later! The legend of Nola. . . and yet there is so much more greatness to come."

When we arrived at the Hill, I saw that Mambura and Ranior were strapped onto litters. Teldaru hauled Mambura's off the wagon; I knew it was him, even though he was wrapped in cloth, because he was so big, and the lines of him so firm. I winced when the litter hit the ground, and Teldaru laughed again and reached a hand out to tug on my braid. He did not let me help him. He pulled the litter down the stairs and along the dark, damp corridors. He set it down just inside the door of the tomb and went immediately back into the corridor.

I sat by Mambura and waited. I imagined what would happen if Bardrem appeared now. I pictured Teldaru returning, and myself standing and crying, "Kill him!" I pictured Bardrem and me doing it together, with knives or fists or feet. "It was like a terrible, terrible dream that I feared would have no end," I would say when it was over. "I could not speak or act because he had cursed me." And I would gaze at Bardrem with my eyes that could see both worlds, and kiss him with my mouth that could say anything.

But no—*that* was the dream.

Teldaru dragged the second litter up into the chamber. He laid it down by Mambura's and untied the ropes that held the cloth in place. Mambura's blind eyes stared at the dome of ceiling. Ranior had no eyes yet: only two slick hollows above the fleshy wrinkle that was his new nose.

"Why have we brought them here?" I said. "It's so much farther away than the house."

Teldaru drew his fingers along Ranior's smooth, yellow brow and then rubbed them against his thumb. I could almost feel the clinging wetness myself.

"The battle will take place nearby, sooner than we may think. We will finish Ranior here, to be certain we are ready. And in any case, this place is his. He died here; it is only right that he be remade here, too."

He took his knife from his boot with one hand, and held his other hand out to me. "So come, now. We must continue."

We got back to the city at dawn—later than usual, and Leylen was waiting for me.

"Mistress, where've you been?" she asked, and I gestured vaguely, said, "Master Teldaru and I were together outside the city, gathering plants."

I noticed, through the haze of my exhaustion, that she was shifting from foot to foot. I noticed that she was holding a piece of folded paper—which I read when I had sent her away.

Not the house tonight
But the Hill—that fabled place

Death there for the Hound
Laming for the Cook
But Otherseers, at night—
What is there for them?

I slid the paper under the wardrobe. I crawled beneath my sheet but did not sleep.

A Sarsenayan boy raped a Belakaoan girl—a thing that had happened before, while the city burned, but not to the daughter of a wealthy cloth merchant whose wares were bought by castle women. One of the girl's brothers killed the Sarsenayan boy.

Bantayo's ships landed on Sarsenay's eastern shore. There were four ships. "For now," said Teldaru to me. The island men were only a few weeks away.

"This is not enough," Teldaru said. He was pacing in front of the table where I was sitting, by his window. "This violence, and the fires—there will need to be more, if Bantayo is to be sufficiently provoked."

"But if we're not ready anyway," I began, and he whirled to face me.

"This is the time, Nola. The only time. I would have waited longer, but the Pattern has led us by a swifter way." His eyes were glittering—*feverish*, I thought as I looked at them, and at his sallow, sunken cheeks. He had finally shaved, but he must have done it too quickly; his chin and throat were covered with blood-encrusted nicks.

"The Flamebird of Belakao and the War Hound of Sarsenay." He smiled. Fell to his knees before me and wrapped his hands around my waist. "They will do battle on the plain. And they will not die."

"But they will," I said slowly, finding words that would not bring the curse up into my mouth. "If you and I do."

He laughed. His whole body vibrated, even after he stopped laughing. He trembled and twitched but did not seem to notice.

"We will not, my love. They will not. Do you have no faith in your own visions?"

And then he went very still, and his eyes fixed on nothing. I almost expected to feel an aching beneath my skin—but he was not in my Otherworld this time; just somewhere else that was far away.

He smiled. His teeth were as straight as they ever were, but they were not so white; there were grey lines on some of them. I wondered if my own would soon look the same.

"So simple," he said. "The only way to ensure Bantayo's rage. I should have thought of it before."

"Tell me," I said lightly, but he shook his head. He laid his head in my lap and closed his eyes.

CHAPTER FORTY-ONE

"Tomorrow morning," Teldaru whispered to me at dinner one evening. "You should go see the queen."

It had been several days of nothing—no notes, no plan revealed. Nothing but the man-creatures beneath the Hill, and a weariness so overwhelming I could hardly sit upright at the lesson table, or here.

"Why?" I whispered back. "I can see her now—look—she's wearing a green dress and a necklace of wooden beads."

"Insouciant girl. You pester me relentlessly for information and now I am giving you some. Go to her chambers tomorrow before your lessons."

We went to the Hill that warm, rainy night. We made one blind, brown eye and five fingernails, and while we were watching, Ranior's lips parted for the first time, slack and wet. We returned to the castle and I collapsed into bed with Borl beside me, but soon I woke with a start because I remembered Zemiya. Zemiya—why?—I fumbled with bodice laces and slippers and pushed past Leylen, who was just arriving.

"Mistress? What now, Mistress—wait!" But I was running, even though the hallways seemed to melt and bend around me.

I was nearly at the queen's door when I heard the scream. One piercing note; a girl's voice.

No one was in the front room. The bathing chamber's door was open. I stumbled as I slowed, just inside it, and I slipped too—not because I was moving too fast but because the floor was wet. *She is bathing*, I thought in that first instant—*yes, of course; that is all, and perhaps Jamenda only screamed because she fell herself, on the wet floor.*

The floor was pooled with red. The walls were sprayed with it. It was like

Chenn's room at the brothel, when there had been different screams, and girls clustered around the doorway, craning to see in. Now it was only one girl— Jamenda, kneeling beside the tub, clutching Zemiya's blood-streaked hand.

The queen was lying with her head back, as I had seen her do before. But there was no water this time. She was naked, patterned with cuts and blood that looked darker than her skin. Her eyes were open, staring at the great, splayed crab's legs above her. I looked up too, then down again, toward the window—and I saw another body. A man, lying flat on his back with his arms outstretched, his wrists gaping. His own blood had darkened his clothing, but I could see he was a guard. I knew his face; somehow, in that long, still moment, I remembered him: Jareth, who had let me inside the castle years ago, when I had thought I would tell everyone the truth. Me in my pink dress, and everyone laughing but him. His beard was matted with blood now. His eyes were closed.

I knelt beside Jamenda. She was holding the princess in the crook of her arm. Even as I noticed the baby she began to cry. The sound was thin, and the flailing of her fists was weak, and her white-veiled gaze flitted over everything and nothing.

There was a shout from the outer room. Footsteps pounded away; soon there were others, much closer, and the chamber seemed full of people. Someone gripped my shoulder.

"Nola . . ." Haldrin was beside me, sagging to his knees. His fingertips ground against my bones. "What did you see? What do you know?" His voice was Lord Derris's, suddenly. His face was collapsing, spreading lines; he was old now, forever.

Teldaru did it. People will say that Jareth did—and they did, for it turned out that the Sarsenayan youth who had been killed by the Belakaoan merchant family was Jareth's nephew, and this seemed like reason enough to people already accustomed to madness—*but it was Teldaru.*

"I know nothing," I heard myself say. "I was coming to see the princess— I knew Zemiya was having trouble, still, and I couldn't sleep anyway, so I thought . . ."

I reached for Layibe then, my body confirming the lie. Jamenda let me have the baby, who quieted as soon as she was up against my shoulder. She burrowed and snuffled and clung to my dress and my braid.

"No," Haldrin said. I could feel him shaking. "Not this. *Moabene* . . ."

"Oh, Hal." It was Teldaru, behind us. His own voice broke. "Hal—my King— come away; let someone cover her."

"I will. I will wash her, too." I looked up at Teldaru as I spoke. "It is only right."

He smiled down at me sadly, but his eyes were still glittering. I wondered where he had put his bloodied clothes, and how long it had taken him to get himself clean. I wondered if she had managed to laugh at him at all, as she had long ago, by the courtyard pool with its tiny glowing fish.

They left us alone: Jamenda, Layibe and me. Jamenda fetched me buckets and buckets of water. I poured it over Zemiya's ruined skin, and Layibe listened, kicking her legs out in delight.

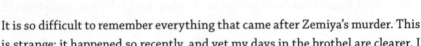

It is so difficult to remember everything that came after Zemiya's murder. This is strange; it happened so recently, and yet my days in the brothel are clearer. I want to make a list of words, only: Soldiers, Bardo, Uja, mourning, tomb. But it would not be enough. I must try harder.

I stumbled to the kitchens, the day Zemiya died. Or I intended to, but when I was only halfway down the stairs to the main courtyard, Teldaru called out from behind me. I ran a few more steps (three of my footfalls in the time it took for the gatehouse bell to toll once). Then I stopped, because he was beside me, holding my forearm.

"Where are you going?" His voice was tight. He was clawing at my bare skin.

To find Bardrem. And to find the words, somehow, that will tell him he is right: you must be stopped. I have waited too long to try to find these words, and maybe I won't—but I need to go to him. "Away," I said. "Anywhere."

"Foolish girl—you know you won't be able to leave these walls while I'm still within them. And in any case, you mustn't leave me, even for a moment. I need you close. We must be close."

I smiled into his fevered eyes. I thought, *I will find another way.*

I was alone later that evening, though I knew I would not be for long. I dipped a quill in ink and set its tip to paper. *Help me,* I tried to write. *I will help you. Trust me, even if you cannot understand me.* I tried to write very quickly; tried to hardly think about the words, since this might keep the curse at bay for a moment. But I wrote only, "I will"—and the rest flowed out, unplanned and strange, as smoothly as if I had intended it:

"I will eat mutton before dusk."

Teldaru came for me early. "Haldrin is silent," he said as his piebald mare bore us toward the gate. "He says nothing at all, so Derris is speaking for him. We will summon soldiers from other cities and even from the borderlands. We will be ready to face the islanders when they arrive."

The bell was still tolling. The streets beyond the castle were empty.

"Are we not going to the Hill?" I asked, for he had turned the horse away from the road that would have taken us toward the gate. I felt a throb of hope, though I was not yet sure why.

"No—to the house. There is a sword there that I think will be useful."

I was alone again, while he searched for the sword. I slipped into the mirror room and stood with my hands wrapped around the bars of Uja's cage.

"Uja." She blinked at me from her highest perch. "I know you understand me. I don't know why, but you do. And you have seen . . . everything."

She cocked her head. I could hear Teldaru's footsteps above me.

"You . . . open things. You've opened them for me. Now I need you to sing me to sleep." I shook my head violently and pressed my forehead against the bars for a breath. "I need more opening. Listen, Uja." *Listen, for Bardrem will follow us, or come here again alone, and you must let him in just as you once let me out.*

She bobbed her head. Her crimson neck feathers ruffled and smoothed.

"Thank you," I whispered—and that was all, because Teldaru was in the hallway, calling my name again.

What are you doing, Nola? You and Teldaru?

I've seen inside the house. I've seen the island bird and the creatures—a man, a woman, and they are dead, except they breathe. And the red book in the library—Bloodseeing—what is this? Tell me now—or is it already too late?

When I straightened from the wardrobe (this note slipped away with the others), Leylen was behind me.

"Do not look at me like that," I snapped. "And fetch me a clean dress; this one was filthy when I put it on."

She stared at me a moment longer, then turned and went to do my bidding. I sat on the bed, hunched forward. My tears were warm and clear on the backs of my hands.

Sarsenayan soldiers streamed into the city as Belakaoans streamed out. There were scuffles between them, but no real violence; both sides saving strength for whatever would happen next.

"And so the armies gather," Teldaru said as we all watched the comings and goings from the tallest tower. Haldrin was there, but his eyes seemed to be seeing nothing—not even Layibe, who was lying limply in his arms, crying her thin, tremulous cry.

"My King," Lord Derris said, his voice even higher and windier with impatience, "please give the child to Mistress Nola—she is the only one who seems to be able to soothe it."

Haldrin did. He smiled at me a little, but I did not think he knew it. "Daru," he said, "do you remember the time when you balanced Old Werwick's mirror on your head to make my sister laugh? But she cried instead, and you sulked for days—worse than any girl yourself, people said. That was just before the fever, I think. Before she died."

"*My King.*" Derris was gasping with effort and emotion. For the first time I thought that he too must know what it was like, never quite being able to make words sound right. "Think of where you are. Look there—that is an army, and it needs a leader. You must be that man—now, Cousin. We all need you *now*."

"He is right," said Teldaru. His voice wavered a bit, and Lord Derris glanced at him.

Yes! I wanted to cry. *Teldaru is even madder than the king!* I put my lips against Layibe's fine curls, instead. She was asleep, her chest making swift, shallow movements against mine.

I would go to the king now with what I know, but it isn't enough. I need to know what you and Teldaru are doing at the Hill, too. I need more proof. I am a cook. Who will believe me, let alone the king? Bloodseeing! The Paths of the dead remade! Who will believe me?

If you are committing these atrocities against your will, why do you not tell me so? And if you are committing them willingly, why have you not told Teldaru about me?

There is one thing. One thing that will make everything else plain. Why do you not help me, Nola?

There were no lessons any more. The students returned to their homes—the farther away from Sarsenay City, the better. Dren's mother cried when she saw him; he cried when he left. Mistress Ket sat in her tiny dark bedchamber and would not Othersee for anyone. "That beautiful lady," she said to me one day, when I brought her a fresh bun and some soup. "That beautiful queen, and her poor baby. Such twisting Paths; I do not know why my own has been so straight."

She would not Othersee for anyone, so I did. I could not refuse them, after all, and I could not steal away on my own: Teldaru checked on me several times a day. Sometimes he even brought them to me: "Here, Mistress Nola—Keldo the stable master—he was hesitating outside, so I have brought him in myself."

For years I had hardly noticed the lies that came after I Othersaw. Now they were mouthfuls of bile. The images were very bright, and they lingered, as the curse thrust out twisted shadows. And I felt weak, even as I reached for my mirror, or for seeds to scatter. Ranior was nearly remade because we spent almost every hour of darkness with him—and so I bled and wove my own strength into his, and then I returned to the castle and slept for an hour, and then I gazed on other people's Paths and told them lies. I was more in the Otherworld than I was in my own, and I was wrung with fear.

I thought, once or twice, that I could lose myself. Look into the mirror at my Otherself until I went mad, and be done with everything. I even started to look once, bending over the copper, watching my eyes swim into focus beneath me. But it was Grasni I saw, instead of myself—Grasni bending over too, to grasp my ear and pinch it. "All you need to know about your Path is that you will tell other people about theirs. You give; you do not take. You are too important for that." It was enough to stop me, though I did not know why.

One afternoon I was finally alone. Except for Princess Layibe, who was lying on a blanket beneath a tree. I was watching the baby: her arms and legs, which had relaxed since her nurse brought her to me an hour before; her sliding, sightless eyes, which were beautiful. There were branch shapes on her skin and her cream-coloured dress. I was alone and hoping to remain this way—so when I heard footsteps on the path I did not look up. *I am not here*, I thought. *Let him pass me by.*

The footsteps stopped. I could feel someone behind me, but I did not turn.

"Nola."

He sounded very calm. We were in another courtyard, perhaps with a wooden walkway and a scrawny tree and girls leaning on railings above, looking bored.

"You haven't come to me. Did you get my notes?"

"Yes." I should have turned then, and gripped his tunic in both hands before I pushed him off along the path, but I stared at Layibe instead. She moved her head, as if she were listening to us. Her cheeks were plump, though the rest of her was not.

"At least look at me, Nola."

I did, slowly. I was sitting cross-legged and he was standing. In the slanting light he was a giant whose face I could not see.

"I can make no sense of my Pattern or anyone else's. So look for me, and tell me what *you* see."

I could not say, *No—go now, before we both are lost.* I saw the dappled, dancing light on his face and I sank into the shadows that lay between.

His face dissolves. It oozes together again, so slowly that each pore must be taking its own turn—but soon it's done, and he's back, but he's a boy. His hair is lighter and so long that it falls over his eyes. His lips are fuller. Even as I strain to hold his face still it recedes, so swiftly that it feels as if I'm falling backward. There are stones behind him: row upon row of them, all tall, all bent into terrible, bulbous shapes. He stands among them and cries a long, raw, ragged-ended cry. Looking at me—but not at the woman-me: the Other-me, who (I see, looking down) is wearing a dirty brown tunic and no shoes. There is no braid hanging over my left shoulder. I wrench my gaze to him again and he shouts again. Maybe it's my name? His mouth twists and he rubs tears away with his palms, viciously. Just then a bird rises from the stones: a glorious scarlet bird with a blue head and a green and yellow tail. Blood is coming from his eyes now, and from mine; I feel it on my arms, warmer and thicker than tears. If I could look down and see the pattern of the drops; if I could just do this perhaps I'd be able to find a way back through the shadow-sky. I try to look, but I'm frozen, watching him bleed and weep, and suddenly a scream rises in me, as quick and bright as the bird was, but even it gets trapped—

My head was in my hands. I felt words coming, through the knot of the curse. "I saw a cottage by the sea. I saw a child."

I was crying. I did not know this until he leaned down and ran his finger along my cheek—then I felt the wetness and the warmth.

"I heard a bird calling. I saw you kneeling to touch something in the surf—a shell—lovely, the colour of ink that has only just dried. . . ."

He was squatting. His head was a little higher than mine.

"Tell me the rest. Please; tell me what you know."

Layibe whimpered. Borl whimpered. I did not look at either of them. I looked at Bardrem's eyes and mouth and the collarbone that jutted from the neck of his tunic. He was as sharp and slender as he had been as a boy. Or he was not— but I made him so because I needed to.

"No." The curse was thickening in my throat.

"Why?"

I closed my eyes.

"Nola—look at me. Help me."

"I cannot," I said, over the tears which had risen despite Orlo or Teldaru; despite Paths burned and knotted. I lurched to my knees and thrust at him— the palms of my hands against his tunic and the taut, living flesh beneath.

"No—*no*—and you must leave now—"

He put his hands on either side of my face, just as Teldaru so often did— but it was not the same; Bardrem's hands were strong and gentle, and though they held me, they did not hold me still. He kissed me, suddenly but slowly. His hands were on my braid, unwinding. My hair fell around us both.

Just as I was sagging against him he pulled back. I gasped one long, deep breath and said, "Go," even as he rose. He stumbled away from me, just as he had years before, though now his limp made him look even more headlong— and now, too, there was someone else to see him go.

Teldaru was coming through the trees. He was on a path that ran away from the one Bardrem was on, but they were close, separated only by a few tree trunks and some low-hanging branches. I watched Teldaru turn his eyes to follow Bardrem. I watched Teldaru frown and turn his eyes to me.

"Who was that?" he said when he was standing above me.

"A stable boy," I said calmly. "He was not happy with what I told him." I gave a little laugh. "Ran off without paying me. But there were many others, today. It was not worth following him."

I ran my hand over the pile that was sitting beside me on a piece of purple cloth: some copper coins, a length of green silk, a pair of silver earrings, some cherries. I smelled the cherries when I lifted my hand—their soft insides, almost too ripe. I wondered, suddenly, what Borl and Layibe smelled.

"Ah." Teldaru hunkered down and took my face in his hands, as Bardrem had. His eyes darted from my own eyes to my mouth. "Ah," he said again, as his fingers pressed and pressed.

CHAPTER FORTY-TWO

Bantayo was only days away.

Ranior was breathing.

He was not the same as Mambura or Selera or Laedon. He did not look as though he would be able to sit, let alone stand; he was looser, somehow, as if his skin had still not quite adhered to the rest of him. As if the bones themselves were wobbly and soft, beneath.

"He is magnificent," Teldaru said, on the night we finished the remaking. His voice trembled.

I watched the War Hound's chest rise and fall. Something rippled under his breastbone—a worm crawling—an end not tied down, trying to find a way out.

"He is," I said, thinking, as I looked from Mambura to Ranior: *I understand why this is forbidden. I see how strength becomes decay.* But I smiled, too—for Teldaru could not see the truth, himself, and so he would not see his own failure looming.

"We must practise." He went to the litter that had held Mambura and picked up a short spear; it must have been wedged beneath the hero's body.

"That was from Zemiya's bathing chamber," I said. Although its bronze head glinted clean, I wondered if there were blood on the metal, or maybe on the haft, which was wrapped in dark leather.

"Indeed," he said. "She was most distressed to see me holding it." He laid it across Mambura's chest, then went to Ranior's litter and lifted up a sword. This he placed on the stone beside Ranior, the pommel touching his swollen, purple-tipped fingers.

He knelt beside Ranior and I knelt beside Mambura. "What will happen?" I asked. A real question, which felt stranger than all my lies.

Teldaru smiled at me, across the bodies, and drew his palm along the sword's blade. "Let us see."

The spear tip's edge was keener than I had expected it to be; he must have honed it, after he wrested it from her ceiling. I watched the blood drip from my palm to the mottled flesh of Mambura's arm—two drops, three, and then the red sky of his Otherworld rose up around me.

The sky is not empty, as it was when we first remade him. The green hills are not bare. Mambura's Paths pulse among images that are thick as forest or cloud, and I am on my knees on this ground too, clawing, clutching for purchase. A breaking wave, and a fish gasping in mud; a naked man lying on his stomach on a beach of black rock, smiling in his sleep; a scarlet feather drifting out of a shower of sparks, in darkness. These things blur and sharpen and blur again, layer upon layer of them, and it is only me among them—no Teldaru, this time, to hold me steady.

I hear him, though. He shouts—far away but also so close that I know I could touch him, if I tried. It is a formless shout, at first, and then it is words: "Two bodies, Nola! Two at once! Look outward and find his hand. . . ."

Look outward.

I gaze through the swirl of pictures. I see another layer, beyond the sky. The surging of my blood carries me out along the Paths, and I hold my hand out to break the fall I can feel coming—and there is another hand around mine. My fingers wriggle within its fingers. My palm rubs against a larger palm. I am dizzy again, and I think I may be sick, but after a moment I flex my fingers and my arm, and the strangeness of wearing another skin is not as intense.

I remade you, Flamebird, I think, and now I am inside you.

I grope. A crab scuttles by my cheek and a woman in a blue headscarf swoops to kiss my forehead and a sheet of lava rises and ripples. I reach past all this. I feel worn leather. My fingers remember how to wrap themselves around it. My hand and arm remember how to lift wood and balance it so that the bronze head does not dip. I see the spear lift. I see a man's pale face, past the farthest hills, and a sword gleaming, and I remember rage and need.

I lunge.

"No!" someone cries, from the pale man's lips, and "No!" I cry—me, Nola, writhing within other flesh, trying to be stronger. And I am. I hold us both still, though I think I will die from the effort of it, my breath squeezed away by the weight of sky and memory.

I was coughing. There was blood in my mouth. I spat so feebly that the blood ended up on my chin. I was sprawled on my belly; I realized this slowly, as my body ached its way back. My cheek was pressed against something yielding, and I thought that I was not back; I was caught in the Otherworld, on a Path that would soon envelop me. But I lifted my head, after a time, and I opened my burning eyes—and I saw the splotched skin of a thigh. It throbbed with after-vision. I was lying across Mambura's lap. I heaved myself away, scrabbling and whimpering like Borl—because Mambura was sitting up now. He was sitting up, his left hand resting on the floor but still wrapped around the spear haft.

I crouched with the soles of my feet braced against the sarcophagus. I retched but nothing came up. I gazed through the squiggling black shapes at Teldaru, who was sitting back-to-back with Ranior.

Toys, I thought. *All of us are toys, waiting for some great, guiding hand to move us.*

"Your man," I said eventually, slowly; exhausted, but also plucking words that would not call up the curse. Teldaru swung his head around to look at me. "Did he have images? Memories?"

Teldaru blinked as ponderously as the heroes were. He licked his lips but said nothing.

"Teldaru—they are real again. They are their own men, somehow."

He fell forward onto hands and knees and pushed himself up into a crouch. "No," he said, and stood. He swayed, dropped to one knee, then both. His eyes never left me. "They are ours—*ours!*"—and he coughed until blood sprayed from his mouth and nose.

Hours later. Close to dawn.

"What will happen when they do meet? What if one wounds the other—will we be wounded too?"

"That will not happen. They will meet, yes—they will stand, and their weapons will clang together once or twice, and then I will rise up and subdue them both. Mistress Nola's vision made truth. The people will rejoice."

"And—forgive me, Master—what will you tell them when they ask how the men came to meet again? How they came to *be* again?"

"Enough questions, my love. They are far too clumsy—my own fault, I know, but they irk me."

"You will say you were blameless, won't you? You will say that it was me. . . ." I was breathless. I had not thought of this before—how had I not thought of it?

"Hush, Nola! Dearest girl. Come here, now—quietly—there. There . . ."

And so he took me again, on the floor of Ranior's Tomb. This time, afterward, I did not run.

Moabu Bantayo and *Ispa* Neluja walked into Sarsenay City at noon on a hot, clear, late summer's day. They were flanked by four Belakaoan men with spears. There were no drums. The rest of the Belakaoans—hundreds of them, our soldiers said—were encamped beyond Ranior's Hill.

"Not enough," Teldaru hissed. "Why are there not more? These hundreds might simply be the ones who left our city—where is his *army*?"

Bantayo and Neluja were led into the Great Hall, which had been cleared of everything except for one table, now a bier, draped in orange and green island cloth. Zemiya was lying on it. She had been dead for weeks, but thanks to the work of the healers, who attended to as many dead bodies as they did live ones, she looked smooth and clean—just resting, with her hands folded across her breast.

Bantayo did not even glance at her. He looked at Haldrin, who was standing next to the bier. The gems on the *moabu's* golden tunic-dress winked as he lifted his hand and pointed at the king.

"What will you do," Bantayo said in his voice of metal, "to repair the damage you have done to the honour of my land?"

"*Moabu*." Haldrin was very pale, but he sounded stronger than he had since Layibe's birth. "We will speak of this—now, if you wish. I thought, before we did, that you might want to see your sister and your niece."

I stepped forward. Layibe was lying on my shoulder. Her curls tickled the skin under my jaw, and my neck. There were shells in the curls, threaded there by Jamenda, who would not leave the castle.

"My sister is dead," Bantayo said, "thanks to Sarsenayan treachery. I have no reason to look on her. And I have no wish to see the child." I wondered how he could hold his eyes so steady. He almost did not blink.

"But I do." Neluja turned from the bier. One of Zemiya's arms was lying straight now; Neluja must have moved it, perhaps to hold her hand.

She walked to me. She seemed even thinner than she had been: her arms and neck, her cheeks. She held out her arms and I passed the baby to her, thinking: *Surely the princess will be quiet with her own aunt.* But of course this was a ridiculous hope; the princess stiffened and lifted her head, and Neluja looked down into her face. Into her rolling, grey-white eyes.

I heard Neluja suck in her breath. As she did, the scarlet lizard slipped out of the neck of her dress and onto her shoulder.

"The child is blind," she said—to Bantayo, but really, I thought, to me.

"Haldrin," Bantayo said. He managed to make the word both taunt and threat. "Here is yet more shame. Tell me—is there some other insult you have prepared?"

"*Moabu*," Haldrin said, between his teeth, "let us speak now. Privately."

Layibe was wailing. Neluja gazed at her a moment longer and handed her back to me.

"*Ispa* Nola," she said, "we should speak together also."

Yes. Yes—you understand so much more than anyone else, so I will not need perfect words.

"And with me, perhaps?" Teldaru said from behind me. "For I am Master, here."

"You." In the silence after Neluja spoke this word, Haldrin and Bantayo's footsteps sounded very loud. They fell on rushes and stone. They grew faint—out the door and into the courtyard—and died.

"You," Neluja said again, when we three were alone (we three and a dead woman and a baby), "are even less than you were as a boy—and you were nothing then."

She was taller than he was. She stared down at him with her black eyes that were edged and flecked with pearl, and I thought, She *is magnificent.* And yet she looked at Layibe and then at me, and she turned and went. Her lizard held itself up on its clawed feet and watched us, all the amber facets of its eyes reflecting sunlight and space.

"And so we are alone again." Teldaru's breath was stale with old wine and sleeplessness. I had not noticed this smell before.

I nodded. "But the king—will he not need you?"

"Oh, Nola," Teldaru murmured, "there is only you, for me"—and he laughed as he kissed me, with his hot, cracked lips.

The king did not need Teldaru. Haldrin and Bantayo shut themselves in the library, as they had before. Days passed.

Teldaru and I began to ride back and forth from the Hill in full daylight. Only soldiers were allowed on the road now—but an exception was made for us, of course.

"We must be at the place where Sarsenay's Pattern is strongest," he told the guards. "We must be close to Ranior, and to those who threaten us."

Except that no one *was* threatening us—not yet. We stood at the top of the Hill and gazed at the plain, which was patchy with fires and people and a few horses. "This is not an army!" Teldaru cried. "These are old men, women with babies, waiting to return home with their king. Bantayo has brought no *men* to defend the honour of his land!"

"You cannot possibly see that." I squinted at the tiny people-shapes and their tiny coils of smoke. They were Pattern and Paths, and everything around them was shadow, even in the sun; I shuddered because I did not know whether to feel relief or dread.

We practised, on these days. We were Mambura and Ranior, and each time we had more power over them: over their limbs and movements and the memories that only drifted, now, like coloured mist. Several times I thought that I could lose myself—run out forever along Mambura's endless, always-dying roads. But I did not. And every time I returned to the hard, painted stone of Ranior's Tomb, I wondered why.

"You are never in your bed, Mistress," said Leylen one morning.

"It is a busy time." I pushed her hands away and undid my own laces with fingers that did not falter, since they knew the motion so well.

"And Bardo has sent no more notes." Her voice was strange—clipped and shrill, as if she had expected to speak these words but had not expected to feel so awkward about it.

I pulled my dress over my head and took the clean one she held out to me. "As I just said, it is a busy time. But why should this concern you?"

"Oh, because I worry—you know I do, Mistress, too much—I think he might need me, or you might, and I want to be close by if you do."

I wrenched the clean dress on. "We do not need you, Leylen, and we will not. In fact, do you have family you could go to? It might be best."

She gaped at me. My brush hung from her hand. "You would . . . you would send me away from the castle?"

It was too much for me, all of a sudden, and she was too easy a mark. "Yes, girl, I would! I will! Go now—I do not want to see you again. *Go!*"

The brush slipped from her fingers. She whirled and ran from the room. I heard her sobs receding down the corridor, and I did not think to care.

It was late afternoon on the day I sent Leylen away. It was the fifth day since Bantayo had arrived. I was standing with Teldaru in the Tomb. He was pacing in front of the two heroes, who were sitting beside each other, almost as if they were watching him. He was talking. I heard him say something about how he should have waited to kill Zemiya until her brother arrived, for then he would surely have been shamed and enraged enough to take immediate revenge. I was not really listening, though. I was thinking: *Tonight I will get away, somehow. I will pretend I am ill, at dinner, and have Sildio escort me to my room; Sildio is much bigger than Teldaru and does not seem to like him, so he will insist, if I do, that he be the only one to go with me . . . And I will tell him to return to the Hall and whisper to Neluja to come to me—not in my room, for I will not actually go there, but in the kitchen. It will take Teldaru some time to find us. And while he's looking, Neluja will be asking questions and understanding my almost-senseless answers, and she will tell Bardrem what it means, and remake my Paths, and then I will kill Teldaru and all of this will end.*

I did not believe what I was thinking. It was a desperate jumble of words and imaginings, and I knew that none of it would come true, but for once my hope was stronger than my fear, and this seemed to matter.

"Nola."

I blinked at him. He was standing with his hands on his hips, glowering down at me. "I have said this twice already. You will listen this time."

"Yes," I said, "of course." *You twisted horror of a man—I will not have to pretend any more, once this battle of yours happens, or doesn't. Once Neluja helps me be free of your curse, and you.*

"We will take them outside now," he said.

I blinked again—as slow and mindless as the living dead across from me.

•

"We will walk them into the air, to the top of the hill. We will practise moving on earth, not floor. We will practise seeing horizon, not walls." He passed me Bardrem's little knife. My bleeding had begun the day before, but I did not mention this. I said nothing—just pricked my forefinger and slipped the knife into my belt, quickly, before Mambura's skin and sky surrounded me.

A girl walked to the king's library door. (I know this now and did not, then, but I will write it anyway.) She held herself very tall, as another girl once had, when she stood there and said, "I must speak with King Haldrin."

The four Belakaoan guards and four Sarsenayan ones glanced at each other. A few frowned; the rest smiled. It had been many days with nothing but the closed door to stare at, and nothing to hear but a muted murmur from behind it.

"And what is so important that you'd disturb the conferring of *two* kings?" one of the Sarsenayans asked.

The girl lifted her chin even higher. "Master Teldaru and Mistress Nola have been using Bloodseeing to make the dead live again. They have been doing it at a house in the city and also at Ranior's Hill. Bardo the cook will be able to take the king to the house." She held up a hand. She was clutching some pieces of folded paper. Her knuckles were white but her voice was steady. "Here is the proof of their treachery. Now let me pass."

The Sarsenayan who had spoken took the papers. He unfolded them and squinted down at the writing, then looked back at her. "I don't read. How is it possible that you do?"

The girl smiled a little, with pride and memory. "My father knew, and he taught me. Let me pass."

One of the Belakaoans reached for the pages. He lowered his head; his lips moved as he gazed at the notes. When he looked up his dark eyes were wide. "She tells the truth," he said as another Belakaoan leaned over and read, and another. They muttered and nodded.

The Sarsenayans looked at each other a moment longer. "Very well then," their leader said, and knocked on the door.

CHAPTER FORTY-THREE

I was Mambura. I was standing with my back against Ranior's monument, but I could not feel the spirals and lines pressing into my skin: I felt only Mambura's skin, inside and out. It burned. It remembered sunlight and cloud scattered by wind. It remembered moss and earth, pebbles caught between toes.

Mambura's skin remembered and so did Ranior's.

They walked around the Hill, Ranior taking long jerky strides and Mambura taking smaller steps. They walked and circled each other and walked again. This place was a memory. Ranior's eyes saw it from this height and Mambura's from below. They saw each other, Bird and Hound. Their Otherworlds crackled with slow, brightening flames.

Teldaru and I stood and sat and stood. Teldaru lay on his back and laughed; Ranior's mouth gaped, and he thrust his sword up toward the sky that was turning from blue to gold. From blue to gold to crimson, in the west, and the heroes remembered sunset.

Hours passed. It was the longest the men had stood, hefting wood and metal, and they were strong—even Ranior, whose flesh was loose around his joints and whose left foot was turned inward and dragged, a little. Teldaru and I, though, were hunched against the stone. Teldaru was panting; I hardly seemed to be breathing at all. Our sagging shoulders touched. I stirred once; I knelt, and Mambura stumbled, and Teldaru cried, "No! Stay, Nola! Longer . . ." from his mouth and Ranior's. I did. I collapsed back against the stone. Mambura threw his spear in a gentle arc. It lodged in the slope below and he walked to retrieve it. He slipped twice but did not fall.

He stepped back onto the hilltop. He stopped walking. No one else was walking, and yet pebbles slithered down a slope. Feet crunched and slid. Teldaru and I heard this and our heads turned. Mambura and Ranior's heads turned.

Haldrin and Bantayo crested the hill side by side. Bardrem was behind them, and Neluja behind him.

Teldaru and I knew these faces, even though the crimson and gold of sunset were very bright. We knew but did not move, at first. At first Mambura and Ranior did not, either. But then Borl came trotting up behind the king.

Mambura had never seen Borl—never while I had been inside him, anyway, filling him with strength and vision. Now the dog was all he saw: the hunting hound, with his lean, heaving flanks and his lolling tongue, and the teeth that had been so sharp, the last time Mambura stood upon this hill. The teeth that had torn at his flesh while his people broke and fled like a great retreating wave behind him.

Mambura's Paths lashed and bent. I tried to cling to them, and to my place upon them, but I fell. The flames were all around me, blotting out the images, but it did not matter: Mambura remembered a rage so strong that I had no strength myself.

Mambura wheeled. He was very close to Ranior, whom he had been seeing for days—but now the dog had made him recognize the man. Mambura was too close to throw his spear so he jabbed it instead, while I tried to find my hand in his, my arm in his—while I writhed and groped, trying to get out.

The spear grazed Ranior's side. It tore the white tunic Teldaru had put on him earlier that day. It made a dark, puckered line on Ranior's bruised skin. Ranior did not react. Bantayo started forward. Haldrin and Bardrem did too, each seeking a single direction, but Bantayo was ahead of them, his body low and lithe. He was just paces away from Ranior when a piercing cry came from above.

A bird wheeled among the streamers of cloud. The bird was sunset: scarlet and gold and blue. Her cry was island and blood-drenched plain, and Ranior remembered. He turned his eyes from the bird to the man who was also island, also memory. Ranior lifted his sword, and Teldaru, within him, shrieked his joy and hunger.

Bantayo had a curved knife in his hand. He charged Ranior—bore him to the ground and sank the knife into his gut. Black seeped into the white cloth. Bantayo leaned back, already relaxing. Ranior reared forward, his right fist coming up and in. It caught Bantayo on the chin with a crack and sent him sprawling. He lay on his back, twitching and gasping.

Haldrin was upon Mambura. The king had no weapon: just his hands, which he wrapped around Mambura's forearms. He was small, though, and Mambura was a dark, burnished mountain. Haldrin strained, and Mambura dropped his spear, but the Belakaoan's hands were free, and they closed around Haldrin's neck.

No, I thought, from the Otherworld. No to the rage, and my own need for it. No to the feel of skin and tendons between my hands—Haldrin's skin; Mambura's hands.

Haldrin wrenched himself away. He faced the stone, cried "Daru! Nola! What is this—*Daru* . . ." Then he lunged for Bantayo's knife, which was now lying on the ground. He hacked at Mambura's chest and slashed his arms, swift and deep. Mambura oozed black but did not fall. He struck Haldrin again and again, from face to jaw to belly, until the king stumbled to one knee. Mambura picked up his spear. Haldrin looked up into Mambura's face, his blue eyes wide and unafraid.

Mambura plunged the spear into the fleshy hollow of Haldrin's collarbone. Haldrin toppled slowly, in a shower of bright red blood.

No! I screamed—and at last, too late, I was the stronger one. I tore my fingers and arms away from Mambura's. I tore my feet away from his snake-Paths. I clawed my way through flame and foaming water and suddenly I was only myself, lying on my side beneath a tall, carved stone.

I retched and sobbed and ground my palms against my eyes to clear them. I needed to see. Mambura face-down next to Haldrin, whose blood was leaving him in streams now, not gouts. Bantayo struggling to sit. Ranior sweeping his sword in whistling arcs, at no one. Teldaru propped an arm's length away from me, his mouth dribbling spittle and blood. Bardrem crouched on my other side, his eyes darting everywhere at once—Bardrem so close that I could have touched his twisted hand or the toe of his boot. Borl lying with his muzzle in my upturned hand.

And Neluja, standing straight and still at the crest of the hill, watching the bird circling above us all.

Help us, I wanted to say. *You are the only one who can help; you are the only one who might understand any of this.*

Bardrem took a step. It was small and clumsy because he was crouching, but I could see his eyes, through the black splotches in mine. He was looking at Teldaru. He took another step. His foot was against my drawn-up knee. I moaned and uncurled my body. He gazed down at me and I moved my chin and one of my hands—*Look there, Bardrem, at my belt.* . . .

He saw my knife—his knife, really. He reached and plucked it free. He wrapped his good fingers tightly around it and smiled at me. He stepped over Borl, whose eyes rolled, following the sound or sense of him.

Teldaru's face was angled away; he was watching Ranior and his sword (though he would be seeing flames too, I thought, and ancient, Other things). He did not see Bardrem easing himself closer. Bardrem was nearly upon him. He raised the knife, and the last of the burnished light danced on its small, slender blade. Teldaru did not see the glint through his own eyes, but he did through Ranior's. Ranior blinked and sprang forward, his sword descending as Bardrem's knife did. And the sword was faster. It was heavier and so much larger—surely it should have been slow—but Ranior had been a warrior and a king, and Bardrem was just a man.

The sword sliced into Bardrem's exposed side. He hit the stone and heaved himself around so that he was facing Ranior.

I began to crawl.

Ranior pierced Bardrem's shoulder and belly. When the knife fell it struck Teldaru's thigh. Teldaru was laughing silently, watching now, through all the layers of both the worlds.

I was nearly to them.

Ranior raised his sword once more. There was a wind, just then—a sweeping of feathers and a slicing of talons. Uja was diving. She grazed Ranior's head with her talons and beat upward so that she could attack again.

I dragged myself over Bardrem's legs. I had the knife, but could not feel it in my hand. I lowered my head to draw a deep breath—and fingers grasped my braid. They pulled and pulled, and I was too weak to resist. My head was up, back; my eyes swam with tears, but I saw him anyway, staring down at me. The black and gold of him.

He tugged my hair sharply and I cried out. His other hand was around my throat, stroking, tightening. I saw bursts of white light and then darkness. I heard my heart thudding—and other sounds, too: snarling and snapping and one high, broken shout.

I was free. I coughed and sucked in air that made me cough more. The darkness flowed away.

Teldaru was on his back. Borl's front paws were on his chest; Borl's teeth were in his throat, or what was left of it. Teldaru's feet and hands twitched wildly. And that was all. He was limp and ragged, and he stared up, unblinking, into the first of the stars.

Bardrem's lips bubbled with blood. He had been lying on his side when I pulled myself up to sit beside him. I had rolled him so that his head was in my lap. Now I bent close to the slow, uneven thread of his breath. My hair was half-unbound; it dipped both our faces in shadow. There was just enough light left for me to see his eyes.

"Don't go," I said. My dress clung to my legs, sodden with his blood.

His lips moved.

"Hush," I said, even though I did not think he was trying to speak.

"Nola." It was a gurgling—a wet, uneven word—but I understood.

"Tell me," he said, as I bent even closer. Tendrils of my hair brushed his forehead.

"Yes?" No "hush" any more, because I needed to hear his voice, even as it was.

"Tell me, because you should . . . oblige me now, at least. At last." He smiled. Foam gathered and stretched at the corners of his mouth. "What has your Pattern been? What Paths . . . have brought you here?"

I thought, at first, that the shivering was all his. I thought that I was flushing only because my head was down and I was sick with weariness and grief.

I wish I could tell you. But Teldaru cursed me . . .

"Teldaru cursed me."

I was shivering. I was fever-hot.

"You will not be able to refuse a request to Othersee," Teldaru had said, so long ago, in a prison room. "If the words of command are spoken, you must answer."

Not Pattern-yet-to-be; Pattern past. Paths already walked. Questions asked that must be answered, as the swaying shadow-streaks of my hair wove my own Otherworld around me. And I could see it—I was in it because Bardrem had held a mirror up to my face and told me to look.

"He cursed me with Bloodseeing—I have been his, and mute, for eight years, but now you have returned my words to me with yours."

My head and chest were aching. My throat felt open and raw. My hair had turned to silver ribbons that rippled outward to distant hills. Many of these were cinder-black, and most stayed that way—but one, then two flooded with climbing green. The Paths looped around them and back to me, and in. My veins throbbed with change.

I could see him through my Otherworld, and my Otherworld through him. Bone lattice lay beneath him. He lifted his hand and it trailed ivy, which he twined in my unravelling braid.

"Nola," he said again. His mouth stayed open. I kissed it. I kissed his scar and I closed his wide eyes and kissed them. I wound him in silver and held him.

CHAPTER FORTY-FOUR

My arm hurt. I felt bruised and torn and wondered why it should be my arm that hurt the most—but I realized, as I straightened, that Uja was running the tip of her beak along it. I wondered then why I was sitting up. I must be in the kitchen or library; why was I not in my bedroom, where she usually woke me, when Teldaru was away?

"Careful, Uja," I said as her beak slipped up and down—a keen edge, just as sharp as metal. "Teldaru told me once that he saw you kill someone this way, on Belakao. . . ." I stopped speaking. I remembered where I was.

Bantayo and Neluja were standing together, perhaps ten paces away from me. Haldrin was crumpled closer than that, and Mambura beside him. Ranior was lying with his limbs splayed wide. *Wounded*, I thought, *and maybe irreparably, because one of the people who remade him is dead.*

Teldaru is dead. I turned the words over without saying them. His throat was as raw and meaty as Chenn's had been clean. Borl was sitting beside me. I scratched his ears and he leaned into me. I smelled blood on his breath and fur.

"Master Teldaru believed a prophecy that was not even true," I whispered. I remembered this, too—that I could speak. That there was nothing in my own throat except my voice. "Or perhaps he did not believe it. He was mad. I was mad. A brothel girl died at the house where I used to be his prisoner. He murdered Zemiya."

I looked down into Bardrem's face. There was a faint light left in the sky; I could see his eyelashes lying against his cheeks. "As pretty as a girl," Yigranzi had said, before his hair was short and his legs were long.

I could bring you back, I thought. *I'm already bleeding. You haven't been gone long; you'd be blind, but you might still speak and walk. . . .* It was just an echo of a thought, really. One I had to hear just so I could turn away from it. I laid my hands on his motionless chest and closed my eyes.

"*Ispa* Nola."

Neluja was above me. The hem of her dress was touching the sole of Bardrem's boot.

"Get away from him."

"Mistress, I could not—"

"Get away from me, *ispa*, or I will rot your Paths as Teldaru did mine."

She stepped back. She lifted her arm, and Uja dipped from the darkness and landed beside her. As she settled her wings in against her body, a new light crept up over the grass and stone. Lanterns. Torches.

Lord Derris stopped walking when he could see the hilltop, and who was on it. Four Belakaoan soldiers and four Sarsenayan ones held the flickering lights higher. Some of them dipped wildly, as the soldiers saw, too.

Lord Derris cried out. His ruined voice sounded like a child's, or a bird's. He strode to Haldrin's body and fell to his knees. He turned him over.

"You did not call for me," I heard him rasp. "How can I ever help you, Cousin, if you do not call for me?"

He lowered his head. When he raised it he looked directly at me.

"Mistress Nola," he said. "I see that one traitor is dead. Why are you not?"

I could have answered him, with words that would have been true. I looked back at him and said nothing.

"She is no traitor." Neluja's long, thin fingers waved at me. "She was his slave. She could not choose."

Lord Derris drew a shuddering breath. "Forgive me, Mistress, but this is a Sarsenayan matter."

"Forgive me, Lord, but it is not. My sister is dead. My brother stands here now, and our people wait below us on the plain. This matter belongs to all."

Bantayo walked to stand beside her. He was a small man, and he seemed smaller now. His eyes were dull in the firelight.

"Belakao's honour is restored," he said. "Though I cannot imagine speaking of what I have seen, we must do this—my victory must be known. And though I cannot imagine sitting for one more moment in that room of books or that empty hall, I must. *Isparra* has chosen me. All the tides have drawn me here, to see my people avenged. Now it is done."

Lord Derris did not move. I watched him; I knew, even from the numb, far place where I was, that he was struggling for control. His hands clenched and the bump behind his neck scar lurched as he swallowed. But he could not show his rage, or even his grief.

"Come, *moabu*," he said at last. "Let us go back to my castle. And you," he called to the soldiers, "wait here with her." A nod toward me. Nobody looked at me—not even him. "I will have wagons sent for her, and the others."

Haldrin was transported in his own wagon, hours later. I lay in the second one, beneath a canvas roof. I folded myself around Bardrem's body and waited for the horses to draw us—the dead, and me—back into our city.

King Derris spent several days with Bantayo. Many lords and even soldiers were permitted to listen to their conversations. Bantayo maintained that *isparra* had led Haldrin to his death, for injustices done to Belakao. Derris replied that the Pattern favoured no one, but that it had brought Sarsenay and Belakao to this crossroads for a purpose. They agreed that further hostilities were unnecessary, now that balance had been restored. They agreed that trade must continue. Each likely believed he was indulging a fool.

Bantayo left the city on Ranior's Pathday. There was no procession this year, and no celebration. The Belakaoans rode along empty streets and out onto the wider road. They rejoined their countrymen on the plain, and a few days later the plain, too, was empty.

Neluja stayed at the castle. I stayed at the castle—King Derris allowed me this much. I should have wanted to leave. I should have gathered my few belongings and made for the city gate the moment my shock and weakness had passed, but I did not. I had no desire to see if this part of the curse had been broken, with Teldaru's death. I wanted only to be still and small in a place I knew. Derris gave me a different room, at least: one on the lowest floor of the keep. The single, narrow slit of window looked out on the steps to the main courtyard. He took over Haldrin's rooms. He shut Teldaru's up and declared that no one would ever live there again. My old room he gave to a princess from Lorselland, who arrived a few months after the night on Ranior's Hill. The king married her, when the months of mourning had passed. Leylen became her serving girl.

Grasni's Sildio was granted leave to stand guard outside my door. "To keep certain people out," he said, in his sweet, serious way, "not to keep you in." He told me that Mistress Ket often asked for me. She did not know what had happened, and no one told her. She sat in her room, Sildio said, and did not teach or Othersee any more, nor did she seem to remember she once had. Soon the king summoned another Otherseer, from somewhere outside Sarsenay City.

Mistress Ket might not know what had happened, but everyone else did. King Derris *made* it known: the treachery of the great Teldaru; the curse he had placed upon Mistress Nola; the forbidden art pursued by both. Mistress Nola was to be pitied, for she had been but a plaything, and the victim of a monstrous man. Pitied—and yet she had used Bloodseeing. She had participated in murder. Her Paths had been tainted by Teldaru's, and she would no longer be "Mistress." Not in name, and not in nature—for King Derris tested her Otherseeing abilities on a series of servants and city folk. It was discovered that, while she was able to speak of what Teldaru had done to her, she still could not refuse a request to Othersee, and her words afterward were still lies. Now, after speaking these lies, she could say, "No. That is not what I saw at all." But it was not enough. Most of the curse remained. Her Paths were twisted beyond repair—so she was only "Nola" now.

He was a wise king, the people already said. Wise and compassionate, and stronger of will than his cousin.

So I sat in my small, bright room, and I did not miss my old one. I did not miss the seers' courtyard—the schoolrooms and the lycus trees and the pool with its green, glowing fish. I felt nothing, not even when Sildio told me, haltingly, that Mambura and Ranior had been moved into the house in the city. He did not tell me about Selera, or Laedon, who would be truly lifeless, now that Teldaru was. He did not tell me about the king, or Bardrem, and I did not ask him to, because I was too empty to care. He spoke only of my hero-creatures, who would only die if I did. He told me that people gathered at the gates of the house. They looked at the overgrown garden and the tall, barred windows, and they did not know whether they should pity me or fear me or admire me, still, maybe a little more than they had before.

I was alone for a time, except for Sildio. And Borl, too, was with me. King Derris tried to take him for himself: the hound who, though a product of Bloodseeing, had boldly attacked an enemy of Sarsenay, just as his forbears had centuries ago. But Borl howled day and night, in the royal kennels and in the king's rooms. He howled and clawed at wall hangings and doors until they brought him back to me.

And then the king himself brought someone else.

"She is sick," he said. He gestured to a nursemaid, who passed Layibe into my arms. "I thought to raise her myself, but I cannot—look at her—she is ill and miserable. And in any case, she is yours. The Pattern has seen fit to make this so."

Layibe hardly seemed to be breathing. And she was so tiny, so thin—she should have been crawling by now, and laughing, and sitting up waving plump little fists. I brushed the curls away from her forehead, where a single vein throbbed. She rolled her milky eyes at me and made a mewling noise. I thought: *This poor, poor child; she, at least, should make you feel something.*

But she did not.

Sildio rapped on my door, one morning in autumn. "Mistress," he said. He still calls me this, when there is no one else to hear. "The *ispa* is here to see you."

I sat for a moment, looking down at Layibe, who was asleep in her cradle. Then I rose and walked to the door and opened it.

"*Ispa.*" I had come to realize that my dead, flat voice sounded dignified. I stood back to let her enter. Uja waddled in behind her, her tail feathers swishing on the floor. Sildio stared at both of them.

"You must be glad to have her back," I said, gesturing at Uja. I had had no intention of being pleasant. For more than a month I had thought only about shaking Neluja and screaming up into her face—but these had just been imaginings. Now that she was here, I could not summon any sort of strength.

Neluja gazed at the bird, and at me. Her bright yellow headscarf set off the polished darkness of her face, and its hollows and edges. Her dress was orange. She and Uja were so bright that I thought even Layibe might be able to see them.

"I am," she said. "I feared for her a little, when she chose to go with him."

"She chose . . .?" I would have laughed, if I could have. "He thought he had stolen her. Of course you and she were both too clever for that." I hunkered down in front of Uja, who cocked her head at me. "Why? Why would you sit in his cage, all those years, when you could have been free?"

Neluja cupped her hand over Uja's head. "*Isparra* flows through her as it does through us. We cannot expect always to understand it—just to feel it and watch it."

I straightened. "Words!" I said, almost as I had to Yigranzi. It seemed there was strength in me, after all. "Such pretty, empty words! But no—the watching—that's true. That's something you do well."

I could feel my face flushing. I tried to breathe, to cool and calm myself; if I began to feel anything, I might never stop.

"And what would you have had me do, at that hill? *Ispas* do not hold spears. We do not hurt; sometimes this means we also cannot help."

"But before the Hill," I said. "*Isparra* has shown you only darkness for years—you told me this. You told Haldrin this. If you had been able to do something, just once—if you had drowned Teldaru when he was on Belakao—if you had poisoned his wine when you first came here—your sister would still be alive. So many people would be, if you had acted."

Her eyes were unbearably gentle. "You could not choose. And you cannot understand why others do not. But look, too," she continued, stepping over to the cradle. She bent and put her hand on the side; she tipped it a bit, so that we could both see Layibe's thin, sallow face. "See what happens when there is action, not acceptance."

"No. No—your sister was so lovely, when this baby was in her—she wanted it, Haldrin did; I was only trying to spare them grief."

My voice wobbled. Uja nibbled one of my palms; Borl licked the other. I snatched my hands away and thrust them under my arms.

"Now," I said, more steadily, "you will tell me something wise about suffering. You will say that one person's suffering is but a twig in the current of *isparra*."

Neluja smiled. She was so different from Zemiya, but something in their smiles was the same. "Now that you have said it," she said, "I will not." She was serious again, already. "You have suffered too, *Ispa* Nola. Do not think this does not matter."

I dug my fingertips into my skin. "I am no longer *Ispa* Nola," I said. "As you know."

"And would you be once more, if you could?"

I looked out my window at the strip of sky. There were no clouds in it. I could tell there was a wind, though; every few moments a strip of cloth fluttered into view. One of Haldrin's mourning flags, blue and black, flying from the gatehouse tower.

"I used to imagine it all the time." I swallowed. Sometimes my desire to speak my own words was as thick and solid in my throat as the curse used to be.

"I would imagine him remaking my Paths. I would imagine Otherseeing—all the visions, all the words—and me being deserving of people's awe and thanks and even their anger and tears. As long as it was truth."

I turned my gaze back to her. "I was fourteen when I was lost, *Ispa*. I saw butterflies and a hillside, in my last vision, and I made a brothel girl happy. It will never be like that again."

"No. But what if there were someone powerful enough to remake these last, cursed roads of yours?"

The lizard scuttled along her shoulder and upper arm, as I stared at her. I thought: *The white in her black eyes is as fluid as foam upon a wave.* It was an image Bardrem could have come up with—and I would have mocked it and he would have tossed his hair out of his eyes to glare at me, and stomped to his slanted room and slammed his crooked door. A few hours later he would have dropped sugared almonds into my lap in the kitchen while Rudicol wasn't looking.

"I used to imagine it," I said slowly. "I do not any more. And you would never do this. Why did you even ask?"

Neluja reached up and rubbed the lizard's wedge-shaped head with her forefinger. "I simply wished to know," she said, "before I left Sarsenay."

"And why did you stay in the first place, when all your countrymen were gone?"

She shrugged slightly—a Sarsenayan motion, not a Belakaoan one. It made her look younger. "Because I was not ready to leave. Now I am."

She bent once more and kissed Layibe's forehead. Then she walked to the door.

"You have to go, really," I said. If I kept talking, perhaps she would linger. I could not believe I wanted her to, but I did. "If you don't, you'll be here when the snow comes. And I think the winter will feel long, in King Derris's court."

She smiled again and lifted her hand to the latch. She looked sad, despite the smile. It was an expression I recognized, because I had worn it too, so many times. "Wait—*Ispa*—you said once that you'd seen me, in one of your visions. What was it you saw?"

She was silent for a long time. When her lips finally parted, I held up my hand. "No. I don't really want to know. Sometimes it's the knowing that brings the darkness in."

"You are wise, Nola," said Neluja, "and you are strong. These things are the rock beneath all the currents there are."

She held out her hand to Uja. "Come," she said. Uja trilled and fluffed her feathers but stayed beside me. "Uja?" Neluja said, and Uja whistled five descending notes. She still did not move.

Neluja said something to the bird in her own language—something low and tender. "It seems," she said after she was done, "that Uja is not ready to leave yet, herself."

"And you will let her stay?"

One last smile, this one wide and very, very like Zemiya's. "She is Uja. She is *moabe* and *ispa* and even more than these. And it is for the best," she added as she pulled the door open, "since birds and lizards are not friends."

I almost laughed.

Sildio knocked on my door the day after Neluja left Sarsenay City. "Yes?" I called, a little crossly. I was tired. I had not left my room in weeks and even before that I had only gone down to the courtyard once or twice, at night so that no one would see me. Layibe had been too quiet, and I was trying to summon the strength to worry. Uja and Borl had been snapping and growling at each other, and it annoyed me that they might have been enjoying themselves. And now another knock—another visitor, perhaps, to interrupt my precarious solitude.

"Mistress," Sildio called back in an odd, muffled voice, "there's someone to see you—the new Otherseer the king summoned, weeks back."

I stood up. I smoothed my skirts. *Why?* I thought. *Why would this Otherseer come to me? Surely not because King Derris commanded it. To gloat? To pity? It makes no difference—I will not be able to bear it. Black eyes that see the Otherworld, when my own no longer do.*

I pulled the door open.

"Nola," said Grasni. Grasni with short, full curls, in a dress that did not fit right. "Oh, Nola, I'm so sorry." And she held out her arms to me as I began to cry.

CHAPTER FORTY-FIVE

Grasni reminded me that I was broken. She did not mean to: she wanted only to mend me.

"You must leave this room; I insist on this now. Look at it! A dog and an enormous bird and a baby and you—come with me. Immediately. All of you."

"No." My voice shook. It seemed to have been shaking ever since she had returned, weeks ago. "Not during the day. People will know who I am—and anyway, you have lessons to teach. Otherseeing to do. So, no."

"Yes." She slipped two butterfly pins into my hair. She had cut it, two days ago—lopped the entire braid off; we both shrieked when we saw it in her hand—and now it was an unruly thatch around my ears. "People will know who you are, and they should. You are Mistress Nola. And yes, I have things to do at the school, but you can walk there with me."

"Oh, Grasni," I said, "I don't know." But I did go with her. I held Layibe on my shoulder and Borl loped behind us. Uja waddled until we reached the door to the seers' courtyard and then she took three ungainly strides and flew, high above the trees.

I hesitated. We had seen only a few guards so far, and I had managed to avoid their eyes, but the courtyard was full of students—they had almost all returned. Students who used to be mine.

"King Derris would not want me to go any further."

Grasni scowled. I remembered the way her blotches of freckles used to lengthen and blend, when she did this. They still did.

"King Derris would prefer it if there were no lycus blossoms to distract us from sober contemplation of the Pattern. He would banish kittens, if he could, and disallow tasty foods. But he cannot do these things, and he will not be able to stop you from walking in a courtyard."

"Grasni . . ."

She looked at me—not scowling, not smiling. Solemn, in a way that made me want to cry again.

"Just a few steps, Nola. Just out onto the path, where you can feel the wind."

She took my arm and we walked. *Under the trees*, I thought—*just get me there*. The leaves were russet and crimson and gold, and they would hide me a little.

But someone saw us before we reached the trees. A child—Dren—cried out my name. He ran from the patch of grass where he was playing. When he threw himself against me I staggered backward and squeezed Layibe so hard that she yelped.

"Mistress!" he gasped into the folds of my dress. "The king told us you couldn't ever come back but I knew he wasn't right, even though he's the king. . . ."

I eased his clinging arms free. Tipped his head back with my hand beneath his chin and shook it a bit, so that his black curls danced. I tried to smile, and succeeded, but I could not speak.

"Dren," Grasni said, "Mistress Nola will not visit you again if you knock her over. Step back, now. All the way—off you go, before I ask you to sort lesson books."

He grinned at me and turned and dashed away. The other students who had gathered drifted off too. Some of them—the older ones—stared at me over their shoulders. *Of course they do*, I thought. *I should be relieved that they're not screaming.*

"That's far enough," I said.

"Very well," said Grasni. "But soon you will go farther."

I did not, though—not really. A few times I went down the steps to the main courtyard, and across it to the gate. Out the gate once, but only to the fountain. The shakiness in my voice and legs did not go away.

Grasni stopped suggesting walks, but she kept coming to me. She brought me sweets and fruit from Dellena, and books I did not read. She talked to me of innocent things (the early frost, the knots that formed in her hair the instant after she combed it), and sometimes she just sat beside me and was quiet. I wanted to talk to her of other things. I wanted to tell her everything, from my mother dropping the bag of coins into the Lady's hand to me stirring a pot choked with Selera's flesh and hair and bones. I wanted to ask, "Do you still love

Sildio?" and "How is Mistress Ket?" I wanted to know the answers. But I hardly spoke, now that I was free to.

Until one cold, early morning, just as Grasni was rising to go.

"Sildio told me what happened to Mambura and Ranior. What about the rest? What happened to them, after Ranior's Hill?" This answer I needed to have, suddenly, though I was not sure why.

She frowned—with concern, not anger. "King Haldrin is in the royal catacombs, of course," she said slowly. "Bardrem was buried in the commoners' grave outside the north wall of the city. I said that he should get a finer burial than that, seeing as he'd led King Haldrin to the Hill, and others thought so too, but the new king wouldn't do it."

She stopped speaking. Looked at me almost pleadingly.

"And Teldaru?"

She cleared her throat. "King Derris had him burned on a pyre outside the city. He ordered the ashes put in a box and locked in the house with the other— with . . ."

I had only seen her struggle for words once before, on the night she came to ask me to Othersee for her. "With Mambura," I said, "and Ranior. With Selera. Laedon will be dead—really dead, this time—because Teldaru remade him alone. But the others are still there because I remade them, or helped to." I took a breath. "Derris knows they cannot die unless I do. He will not have them anywhere near the castle. So Teldaru, too, is at the house . . . yes—it's perfect— it was already a tomb."

I truly did not know why I was saying these things, and now. They had been in me, I suppose—waiting to surprise me as my lies used to do.

"I heard that he tried to burn them too," Grasni said in a rush. "It didn't work. Their skin melted a bit, but that was all. And they kept blinking. So he called for the flames to be doused and had them taken away. I shouldn't be telling you this, though—it must be terribly hard . . ."

"No." I smiled at her. "Or yes—but don't worry."

Grasni was quiet, but I could see that she wanted to say more. "Nola," she said at last, "when I first came back—when I said I was sorry—you know what I meant, don't you? That I was sorry for running from you, when I saw your Paths. For telling Mistress Ket. For not understanding anything."

I shook my head. "How could you have understood? It was a horror. Better not to understand, ever. But yes. I know what you meant."

She paused at the door and I hurried her out, murmuring that Sildio would be wondering what was taking her so long, and laughing when she blushed. I leaned against the door when she was gone. I looked at the small, guttering fire in my hearth, and the shadows it threw on the sleeping dog and the sleeping baby.

The bird, however, was awake.

"Uja," I said, "we're going out."

The northern gate was far less grand than any of the others. No banners flew from its squat guard towers, and its doors hung crookedly on their hinges. I stood with my hand on one of the door's splintered edges, looking out at winter light and hard winter ground, rising in hillocks on either side of the road. I knew what the hillocks covered. My mother was probably beneath them, and some of her babies, and Larally, whom I still saw in dreams. All of Sarsenay City's dead commoners, together and nameless.

I left the city. Part of me expected to blink and see the castle before me again—Teldaru bringing me back with the curse, even though he was dead. After all, other parts of the curse had endured. But I walked and kept walking, dizzy with space and the air that bit me every time Uja wheeled close. I stopped when I saw a patch of earth that had been recently turned. It was hard and cold under my feet, and clay-russet except for one spot, which was bright pink. I crouched close to it and saw a piece of redfruit, peeled and carved into the shape of a long, tapering shell. I touched it and felt sugar, rough beneath my nail. I curled all my nails into my palms.

Who left this for you, Bardrem? I thought, and then just, *Bardrem, Bardrem*, over and over. I tried to remember all his ages and names, all the words he'd hidden on paper and carved into roast potatoes—but the trying only made him feel more lost to me. Tears burned in my chest but I did not cry them. Uja ran her beak through my hair and cooed and I unclenched my hands and pushed her away. She waddled back onto the road and waited. After I joined her there she flew again, just ahead, marking the way back.

That night I wrenched myself around in my sheets and dreamed in searing vision-strokes that I forgot whenever I woke up. I slept and woke and slept again—until the middle of the night, when I started up with my breath caught in my throat as if I had been about to scream. Borl and Layibe were sleeping. Uja was hunkered down by the hearth, blinking at me.

"Uja," I said, "I'm so sorry about earlier. If you're angry, you don't have to come—but there's somewhere else I have to go."

I used the postern gate—of course I did, for it was night, and the hood of my cloak was pulled over my face, and my feet knew the way without my mind telling them anything. Uja took to the air as soon as we were beyond the castle walls, and I was alone (except for Borl), and *then* my mind had to say to my feet: *Go on.*

So much of the city had burned; I had not seen this clearly enough, on all the nights Teldaru and I had walked together. I passed roofless houses and shops, buildings that had collapsed to their foundations. Blackened, shattered stone and twisted metal. All of it his doing, and mine. The lantern bobbed in my hand.

The house looked the same, except that the fence was draped in strips of mourning blue and black. Uja was perched on the gate; she glided down to the cobbles when she saw me and set her beak to the lock. It opened with a click. The gate squealed a bit, and I glanced back over my shoulder, but the street was empty.

Uja gazed at me, when we were standing by the door. "Well?" I said. "What is it? Why are you waiting?" I knew why, of course; I hardly even needed to look into the gentle amber of her eyes. I did, though. I smiled at her. "This is good. This is what I must do. Please help me—you're so good at helping me."

She unlocked this door too, and we slipped inside.

The smell was so rank that my stomach heaved. It was worse than before— or perhaps the last time I was here I was simply accustomed to it. I rubbed my streaming eyes and held the lantern high. Everything was as it had been. There was a box, though—a small one made of black wood, sitting on the floor just inside the door. *They wouldn't take him any further,* I thought. *They shoved him in and slammed the door shut.*

The others, though, had been taken upstairs. I wondered whether this had happened in daylight; whether people had gathered to watch as soldiers carried Mambura and Ranior up the glass-pebbled path. They were in the mirror room now: Mambura lying beside the knife cabinet and Ranior beside the cage. Their skin was black and covered in livid pink bubbles. Ranior's hair must have burned away, for both their skulls were bare. I tried to envision this, too: the monstrous heroes on a pyre, their flesh charring and rippling but not melting; their eyes blinking from within the flames. King Derris shouting to stop—to pull them out and bring them here, where their accursed second lives began. I thought: *They die if I do, and yet when they were consumed by fire I felt nothing. It does not seem fair.*

Selera was sitting against the wall across from the door. She looked so lovely and clean, compared to the other two. Someone had arranged her green dress carefully over her legs. Her hair even looked brushed—though maybe I was just imagining this. She blinked. Her milky green eyes glittered.

Laedon was not here and he was not in the other rooms. Perhaps they had burned him too, after I told the king, in those first blurry days after Ranior's Hill, that he would truly be dead, since Teldaru was. Perhaps they had watched his skin dissolve, as skin should, in fire, and felt weak with relief and disgust.

I set the black box down on the floor. I gazed at it for a moment before I slid its lid off.

I had imagined I was only going to look, and think, *Well, there he is*, and be done with it. But when I saw the white and grey grit that had been Teldaru, looking was not enough. I sifted it through my fingers. I scraped through it so that it lodged under my nails.

Teldaru, I thought, *Teldaru*—over and over—and every time I heard his name in my head I felt a stronger surge of rage. *It should have been me who tore your throat out. Me who sank a dagger into your chest. But it could not be—and in the end I did not even get to look into your eyes as you died.*

My fingers found bone. I drew it up in a shower of ash. Just a knob—a knuckle, perhaps, because I knew such things now. I held it in my palm. I stared at it so intently that the edges of my vision smudged, as if I was entering the Otherworld.

Just a small, white, pitted piece of bone, but it would be enough.

I curled my fingers closed and smiled.

I did not tell Grasni that I was remaking Teldaru. She would not have allowed it. She would have locked me in my room until she had burned the house to the ground herself. And she would have been right to do these things. I knew this, as I walked through the sleeping city. I knew how wrong I was and it frightened me, in daylight, and as I walked in the dark. But when I was in the mirror room, and when I made those quick, small cuts on my arm or thigh or even my breast, I felt only hunger.

I took my time, with him. I was careful. Winter passed in gusts of snow and wind I hardly noticed. I heard that the queen would have a baby in the summer and for a moment I thought the queen was Zemiya, still, and that she and Haldrin would be so happy.

I was lost.

"You are nodding off again," Grasni said one afternoon—not late, but it was already getting dark.

"Mmf," I said, and straightened on the bed. She had been teaching me a game that involved different lengths of wood carved with symbols. I found the carvings beautiful but had no idea how to play the game, even after she had spent hours trying to show me.

"And you look terrible. Are you sleeping?"

I rubbed my eyes, which I was sure were bloodshot. "Not really. I'm . . . having nightmares. And Layibe is crying more, now." A little lie, a little truth. Nothing had changed; nothing ever would.

As if she had heard and understood, Layibe began to cry. She was on her belly; she drew her thin legs up under her and tried to raise herself but slumped down again.

"She is so unhappy," Grasni said as I picked the princess up. "So sick."

"And she will never be well," I said, "she will be this way all her life, because of me."

My voice was matter-of-fact but Grasni said quickly, "Oh, I didn't mean to . . . I'm sorry I mentioned it. She would be dead, if not for you."

"There are worse things than death," I said. I gazed at Layibe's face but it was Teldaru's that I saw.

I made his bones. I made his muscles and tendons and all the glistening, heavy parts they bound. I made his nose and cheeks and eyes and the red-gold stubble of his hair. I made roads and hills and sky.

Near the end I finally grew impatient. The snow was melting in air that smelled of flowers. I was so restless that several times I went to the house during the day. It was dangerous, for there were often people who might see me, at the gate. Me, and the bird whose island brightness would have told them who I was, if my own face had not. (Sildio says that tales are being told, now, of the bird and me. Tales of Ranior's Hill and castle courtyards and city streets; words to thrill or frighten children.)

Once I saw a group of girls, standing at the fence. They whispered and giggled. One of them darted forward and touched a wrought iron bar (the mourning cloth was long gone), and everyone shrieked, and they ran off down the street.

I finished him in sunlight. I tried to keep myself from going—wanted it to be night, when I was done, since this would feel more apt. But I could not keep still, in the castle. I paced my little room's length and width and I paced the corridor outside it until Sildio cried that I was making him dizzy. "Go out, Mistress!" he said. "Go for a good long walk that will calm you."

So I did. I told Borl to stay with Layibe and then I whistled to Uja and I walked straight out the castle gate.

Today, I thought with every footfall. *It will be today.*

I hauled at him until he was sitting up. I put my arms beneath his and tugged him backward across the floor and into the golden cage. I closed the door and locked it with the key that hung by the knife cabinet. I knelt. I slid the tip of the tiniest knife beneath my thumbnail. I watched the blood well beneath the nail and then into the webs in my skin: my Pattern, like ripples in a pool. I raised my eyes to his, which were closed.

I sink into the yielding ground of his Otherworld—his and mine, for I created it. There is only one Path that is still motionless. I bend and grasp it; open myself up so that my strength bleeds into it. It fills and shudders and turns from black to silver. This is all I need to do, but I linger. I lift my arms and laugh my power and my hunger into the sweep of his living sky.

I was still kneeling. I scrabbled at my eyes, trying to make the after-spots dissolve more quickly.

I saw the outline of him first: the broad shoulders, the stubbly curve of his head. Next came the shadows of his brows and the hollows of cheeks and collarbone. Next, his eyes.

They opened as I watched. They were brown, with a translucent sheen of white. They wandered, sightless and wide, and blinked. Uja sang a long, low note, behind me.

I leaned forward and wrapped my hands around the bars of the cage. "Welcome back, love," I said.

CHAPTER FORTY-SIX

I was very ill.

I went to the house night after night. I crouched by the cage and stared at Teldaru until I, too, felt blind. I walked the halls and sat in the kitchen; sometimes I clutched the dark braid that still lay upon the table, with its white streak and red ribbon. I shook so violently that I had to open my mouth to keep my teeth from clacking against each other and sinking into my tongue. I could not stop shaking, even at the castle.

"You are only feeling it now," Grasni said as she cupped her hands around mine to still them. "Everything that happened to you—it's like a slow poison, but it will soon be gone." She squeezed my hands and tried to smile.

There had been a warm fragrant rain, the last time I went to the house, but I was so cold that I could hardly walk. Uja swooped down several times, clucking and twittering. Once she tugged at a strand of my hair as she wheeled by me, and the pain made me feel steadier, but only briefly.

It had been three weeks since I finished remaking Teldaru. I had been keeping count with the fingernail clippings in the kitchen, nudging them into a line of tiny arcs on the table. It took me a very long time to get from the mirror room to the kitchen, that last day, and once there my hands did not obey me; they swept the rows of nails off the table. Uja squawked at me. "I know," I said, through my chattering teeth, "but I'll be better soon."

The rain was still falling when I left the house. It seemed thicker now; I could not see the houses around me—just the cobbles directly beneath my feet. I wished vaguely for Borl, but he stayed with Layibe, when I left the castle. I stumbled into someone, who yelled and thrust me away. I fell. The rain was so heavy; it pushed at me, until I slumped onto my side. I pulled my knees up beneath my chin. I thought: *I'll never fall asleep. I'll go find Bardrem; surely Rudicol won't still have him working.* But I did not move. I lay in the rain and disappeared.

I woke up in a bed. I was soaked in sweat. I tried to toss the covers off but my limbs would not shift at all. Someone murmured, quite close to me, but my ears were not working either. In and out, hot and cold. Once I felt Borl's nose pushing against my palm. Once I heard Uja singing. In my eyes, though, there was nothing but darkness.

"Nola. Come, now—look at me. I see you trying to."

Grasni's face leapt in and out of focus above me. Her freckles looked like inkblots in the firelight. She looked thinner. She looked afraid.

"Grasni." My voice felt as hot as my skin used to.

"Oh," she said, and bent her head. Her tears made blotches on the coverlet.

It was Sildio who had found me in the rain. He had worried when I was not in my room in the morning. When I was not back by the noon meal he took Borl outside, to the head of the courtyard stairs.

"Find her," Sildio had said. And Borl had.

King Derris declared that it was somehow meaningful that the Pattern continued to cause me suffering. He also commanded Grasni to spend less time with me. When she refused, he told her he would summon another, more appropriate Otherseer, but the students were so distressed by this news that he allowed her to stay. (A few students were children of wealthy families who were generous with their gifts to the kingdom.)

I heard all this as my body recovered. It did not recover fully, however; even months later I could not walk the length of the corridor without gasping for breath. My legs ached and my head often did too, so badly that Layibe's softest whimpers sounded like metal scraping metal. But my body was better.

Nothing else was.

"You don't laugh any more," Grasni said. It was early summer. The queen I had never seen was apparently already huge with child.

"I hadn't noticed," I said.

She frowned. "I am a very witty person. If I cannot make you laugh, nothing will."

I did not speak. I was tying ribbons into Layibe's hair—red Belakaoan ones stitched with blue shells. Her eyes followed the sounds my hands made as they picked the ribbons up and drew them tight around her curls.

"Nola," Grasni said in a lower, softer voice, "would it help you to speak to me of . . . everything? I haven't asked you to—I thought you'd do it yourself, if you needed to—but I want you to know that I'll listen. I want to, if it helps you."

"Thank you," I said. "You're a wondrous friend. But it will not help—speaking. It isn't what I need. Don't worry," I added as she opened her mouth, "I'll be sure to tell you when I know what I *do* need."

A few days later she arrived in the middle of the afternoon. Sildio knocked on my door and they both came in, and I sat up in bed.

"You should be at the school," I said.

She was smiling. She shifted the sheaf of papers she was holding from one arm to the other. "I know—I'm only here for a moment. But Sildio's had an idea, and we're here to tell you . . ."

He nodded. He was smiling too.

"What, then?" I said.

He went out into the hall and returned carrying a tall, narrow desk. He set it beneath my tall, narrow window and went back into the hall. This time he came back with a stool, which he slid under the desk.

"You are going to force me to do lessons," I said.

Grasni laughed. "Not exactly." She put the papers down on the desk. Sildio produced an inkpot and quill from his pouch and placed them beside the papers.

"It was his . . . that is, Sildio thought . . ."

"Perhaps Sildio could speak for himself," I said—and suddenly I was back in a different, smaller room, with a bucket in the corner, and King Haldrin was pulling a chair close to my filthy bed. "She will tell me herself," he was saying to Teldaru.

"I thought," Sildio said, "that since you can't speak of what's troubling you, you might to write it instead. It might be easier, and more secret, if that's what you need."

I shook my head. "I don't think—"

"Nola." Grasni was using her sternest voice, which usually made me smile. I did not, this time. "You must get it out of you. It's bile—poison, remember?

Vomit it out, then, right here. Bleed it onto paper. Promise you'll try, at least. *Promise.*"

There were patches of crimson on her face and neck. She stared at me, and Sildio did too, until I sighed and got to my feet.

"Very well," I said, "I'll try."

And so I have.

It is spring. A year since Borl found me in the rain. A year—or nearly—of sitting at this desk. Armfuls of paper and rivers and rivers of ink (all of it taken from the school).

And yet the poison is still not out. It never will be, while I live.

I have not returned to the house, this past year, but its walls rise around me anyway. When I look into Layibe's wide eyes I see Selera's too, and Mambura's, and Ranior's. Teldaru's. There are pictures, somewhere behind their eyes. There is feeling, somewhere beneath their blistered, too-thin flesh.

I have known for a long while what I have to do. I have ignored the knowledge, or denied it. Now that the story's written, though, I'm certain: it has only one true ending.

Very soon I will put down this quill. It is late afternoon. Grasni will be teaching her lesson on Otherseeing tools (the rows of grain; the sticks of coloured wax melting in warm, clutching fingers). I will put Layibe on my hip and go to the seers' courtyard. I will walk beneath the lycus blossoms and into the school and up those worn, sloping steps. Grasni will be surprised when I appear in the classroom door. She might be excited too, for a bit, because I haven't been anywhere but my room for so long.

I will smile at her, and at the students, who will also be surprised.

"When you're finished," I'll say to her, "come find me in the grove. There's something I need to tell you, and somewhere I need to take you, in the city."

I will do these things, now that my tale is done.

EPILOGUE

It was spring when Nola finished her writing. It's the end of autumn now. It's taken me too long to do this, even though I knew I'd have to. Even though I've wanted to.

Just reading what she wrote took me two months. I carried the pages with me—as many as I could without dropping any—and read them in the courtyard and in my room, which is the same one she had when we were students. King Derris tried to put me somewhere larger and grander in the keep, back when I first returned to the city, but I refused. I like this room. I always did.

I won't be able to write like she did. I had no idea how she wrote until I read this. It upset me, at first. These words of hers aren't quite as her spoken ones were. They're more like poetry—more like Bardrem's. They both might have laughed, if they heard that. But as I read more, I heard more of her that I knew, and then it was the knowing her that hurt.

She described my dress as a cloud of orange-ish dust, in these pages. I laughed out loud when I read this, and Sildio rolled over in bed and asked me why I was laughing, but by then I was crying.

I should just get to it, now that I'm finally here. She would expect me to.

I might try one thing she did: setting down a few words that will nudge me along. Mine will be:

I met her in the grove at sunset.

Dren needed to talk to me, when the class was done. I was impatient, but he thought nothing of it, as I'm often impatient. By the time I saw him off the sky was orange and red.

"I'm sorry," I said to her. She was sitting under the smallest tree. "Maybe we can go into the city tomorrow."

She smiled up at me. Her hair was full of the clips I'd put in earlier that day, but she was wearing a different dress. This one was lovely: wine-coloured, with a bit of lace along the collar. But she always knew how to choose her dresses, as she reminded me every time she saw the ones I'd chosen for myself.

"No," she said. "We'll go now. We'll need a lantern."

I didn't think to be afraid or even worried. I'd spent months trying to get her out of her room, and now that she was, all I felt was relief.

We walked out of the castle. Borl was with us, of course. Uja too, somewhere above. And Layibe, who was big enough now to sit on Nola's hip, but who still looked sickly and weak. Her hair was beautiful, though: thick and dark.

"What did you want to tell me?" I said as we walked.

"Soon," she said. "When we're there."

"Where?"

"You'll see."

"Nola!"

"Grasni!"

I hadn't seen her so happy since we were girls. I didn't care where we were going.

We stopped outside an iron fence. I peered between the bars and saw what was behind them. And even though I'd never been to this house, I knew which house it was.

I asked her why we were there. She didn't answer. Uja flew down and opened the gate, and then the door to the house. They were so practiced about it all— the bird and the dog and Nola. I started to feel sick before the door even opened.

She's described the smell better than I could. I nearly vomited. By the time we climbed the stairs I'd controlled myself. *It's like the tannery*, I thought. *The one I lived next to as a girl.*

But when she opened the next door I fell to my knees. The smell was even stronger, but it was the bodies too, that I'd heard about and thought I'd been able to imagine. I hadn't, though. The two blackened ones were hardly recognizable as men. And the woman was even more horrifying because she was Selera—a rotten, sagging Selera, wearing a dress the beautiful Selera would have adored.

These were bad enough. But then I looked at the cage and saw who was in it, and I ran out of the room and down the hall. I fell again, by a door with a blue glass knob.

Nola sat beside me.

"When did you remake him?" I asked.

"Last spring," she said.

"When you were so sick."

"Yes. I had to do it, Grasni. I wasn't done with him. But I haven't been back here in a year—not in all the time I've been writing."

"So why have you brought me here now?"

She had tears in her eyes, which looked blacker than ever. "Because I'm finished writing and I know what I have to do. And I have to tell you, because you're my wondrous friend."

"And what are you going to do, Nola? Derris already tried to burn them. You know that won't work." I wasn't sure why I was so angry. Maybe just because she'd hidden this great, terrible thing from me. Maybe because I already knew her answer would be more terrible yet.

"I know, yes. They won't die unless I do."

She took my hand and I shook it away. "I know, you know—we both do. Just tell me what you're going to *do*, since that's the thing I'm not sure of yet."

She took my hand again. "I'm going to die."

This time I didn't run. I rose and walked down the stairs and out the front door. I stood by the closed gate, where Uja was perched. It was night now, and her feathers looked much darker than they usually did.

I heard Nola's feet crunching on the glass rocks of the path but I didn't turn. "Come back in," she said. "There's much more to talk about."

"I won't go back in there."

"Then walk with me. There's somewhere else to go, anyway."

"Does it smell?" I asked.

She squeezed her eyes shut, for a moment. Then she opened them and said, "Please come with me."

We walked streets and alleys I'd never seen before. She talked a great deal, probably because I didn't. I remember only a few of the things she said, but I remember what her voice sounded like in the silent streets. She said she wished I could have known Bardrem so that I could have mocked his poetry (even though she said I would probably have loved it). She talked about a vision she'd had of Haldrin—he'd been crying, and his tears had turned the ground below him to flowers. She said that Selera's dress—the one she'd worn on her last day in the castle—was the most wonderful thing ever made of cloth and thread, and that it had made Selera even more unbearable.

Nola stopped walking in front of a jumble of stones in the lower city. As soon as I stood still my feet disappeared in mud up to my ankles.

"I thought you said this other place wouldn't smell," I said.

She laughed a clear, pure Nola laugh and began picking her way over the rubble. "It must have been destroyed during all the fighting," she said. "I didn't know, but I'm not surprised."

"Where are we?" I said.

"Just a little farther." Not answering my questions, as always. Walking ahead, holding her skirts up like a girl in a river—except that she was holding a child, as well.

We came to an open space where the moonlight was very bright. Around us were the remains of walls—stone and wood—and in front of us was a tree. One small tree with thin branches and four small leaves.

"I know where we are," I said. "You've told me about it. This is Yigranzi's tree."

Nola was already sitting with her back against its trunk. She put Layibe down, because the earth here was mossy, not muddy. Uja landed on the topmost branch and set the whole tree quivering. Borl lay down with his head in Nola's lap.

"Sit with us," she said to me. "This is the place."

She was a Mistress, suddenly, and a woman, and a friend, and yet she was already moving away from all of these, and me. I sat down with my knees touching hers.

"Don't," I said. "Let's go back to the castle. You can sleep—I'll ask Dellena for a draught for you—one of the sweet ones that she only sells for gold pieces. We'll talk more tomorrow."

"I'd rather talk now," she said.

And we did, a little. She asked me about Sildio and I blushed and she saw it, even though it was dark. "I knew you'd be happy," she said.

"But remember: we agree with the Belakaoans now—the Pattern isn't set. What you saw in that vision didn't have to be true."

She smiled at me. "I knew you'd be happy."

"We could go away," I said a bit later. "I know you're not sure if it's possible, yet—but we could try. We could go somewhere remote, if you wanted—to the eastern mountains, or maybe to a town in Lorselland—my brother could tell us where. . . ."

She just looked at me. Didn't even need to shake her head.

"All right, then, how's this: you remade the heroes and Layibe, and you say you can't make them die—but what about me? Why can't I try to unmake their Paths for good?"

"Grasni," she said, as patiently as if I had been Dren, "remember how you felt when you looked on *my* Paths? No. It would be horrible. It would change you, and it probably wouldn't even work."

I could say nothing, to this.

We were both quiet, as the sky began to lighten. I slept a little, though I didn't want to, and so did she. Both of our heads nodded and jerked up again, as they had in Mistress Ket's history class. I must have slept more deeply than that, though, because the last time my eyes flew open it was dawn, and Nola was not sitting any more.

She was standing with one hand on the tree. Her other hand was running over its bark. As I watched, she moved all the way around the tree, sometimes kneeling and sometimes standing on the tips of her toes. And then she stopped. She dug about where two branches met and when she pulled her hand away she was holding something. A piece of paper, folded into a tiny, thick, lopsided shape. I watched her unfold it and look down at it. I watched her cry.

When she came back to me her eyes were dry and the paper was nowhere to be seen.

"It's time," she said.

"No." A useless word, but I needed it.

She knelt in front of me. "I don't know what they'll all look like, after I'm gone. It could be quite horrible. You'll have to be gentle with King Derris, when you take him to them."

"I'll try. But I might have to hit him once or twice, too."

She leaned forward and wrapped her arms around me. We held each other very tightly. A bird began to sing (not Uja, who was still sitting on the top branch with her head under her wing).

Nola stood up, after we had pulled apart. She walked around the tree and out along a wooden pathway that I hadn't seen, in the dark. She walked along it to where the stones had fallen and crushed it, and then she came back. She picked Layibe up and set her in my lap.

"Hold her," she said, and bit her lip. It was this motion, more than all her words, that made me believe her.

She whistled. Uja shook her head free of her wing and glided to the ground.

Nola sat where she had during the night. She laid her fingers on Uja's blue head and the bird made a thrumming sound deep in her throat.

Nola raised her arms so that the sleeves of her dress fell away from them. Borl whined and wagged his tail and she lowered one hand to scratch around his ears and under his jaw.

She smiled at me as she held her arms straight again. Then she closed her eyes.

Uja drew her beak along the inside of Nola's right forearm, all the way down to her wrist. Her skin parted. Blood ran in rivulets that thickened into streams. Uja walked very gracefully to Nola's left arm. She gasped this time, and her fingers twitched. Her eyes opened and looked up at the leaves, which were a bright, new green in the light. And that was how she stayed.

I didn't notice that Layibe had stopped breathing until I bent down to her. Borl was quiet too, stretched out long with his muzzle on his paws. I touched his side when I went to kneel by Nola, just to make sure he wasn't merely sleeping. And he wasn't, of course.

Her eyes were wide and brown. I pressed my thumbs against their lids until they closed. I knelt there with her—with all of them—until the sun was high. Then I rose and walked back over the stones until I came to the street. The castle's flags led me home again.

There is more I could write. About Mistress Nola's belated fame, especially. The stories! She'd laugh at some of them, which are ridiculously grand. About bodies laid to rest in earth, and an island bird who flew away from a stone city. But I won't.

I don't even wish the last words on these pages to be mine. They should be Bardrem's. He must have scrawled them when he was a boy, on a piece of paper that he folded into a lopsided shape and wedged deep into the branches of a tree. The paper is yellow now, stained with brown blotches—like the rings deep within the bark, Nola might say. The words are blurred but still readable. I've already spoken them aloud to Sildio, and to the baby who has just started to kick inside me. I know these words without looking, but I hold the paper in my hands anyway.

THE PATTERN SCARS

Nola, o Nola, so lovely, so bold
When will your eyes fall on me?
I am cook, I am poet
And you will yet know it
And then our tale, too, shall be told.

ABOUT THE AUTHOR

Caitlin Sweet's first fantasy novel, *A Telling of Stars*, was published by Penguin Canada in 2003. Her second, *The Silences of Home*, was published in 2005. Her one and only short story, "To Play the Game of Men," was included in Daw's *Ages of Wonder* anthology in 2009. She lives with her family in a magic bungalow in Toronto. On the Web, you'll find her at: www.caitlinsweet.com.

ABOUT THE ILLUSTRATOR

Martin Springett has been an illustrator of fantasy book covers and children's books since 1984 when he illustrated the covers for Guy Gavriel Kay's classic fantasy trilogy *The Fionavar Tapestry*. Caitlin Sweet's first novel, *A Telling of Stars*, featured Martin's cover art. He has won the Aurora Award for fantasy illustration, and the Ruth Schwartz Award in the children's picture book field. He is also a musician, and has recorded a CD of music inspired by Guy Kay's works called *Bright Weaving*. Martin created his first authored and illustrated book, *Jousting with Jesters* in 2006, and in 2011, Fitzhenry and Whiteside released *Breakfast on a Dragon's Tail*. You can find him at www.martinspringett.com.

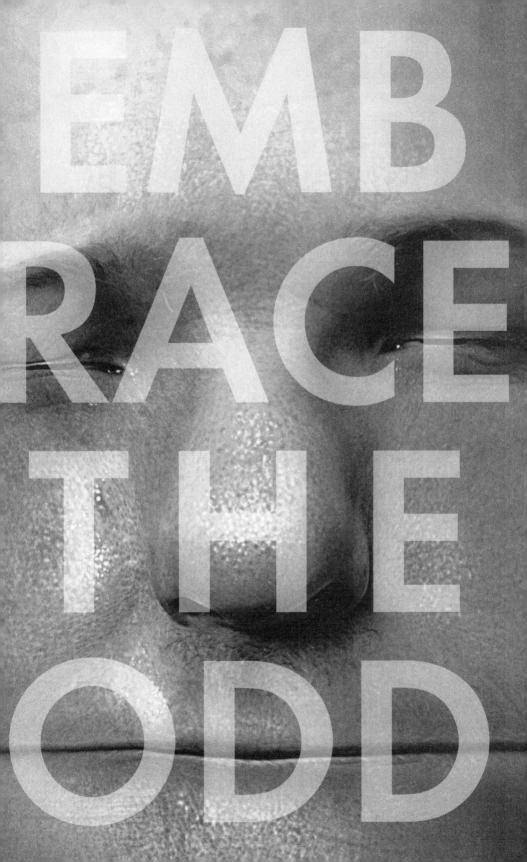

PICKING UP THE GHOST
TONE MILAZZO

AVAILABLE AUGUST 15, 2011
FROM CHIZINE PUBLICATIONS

978-1-926851-35-8

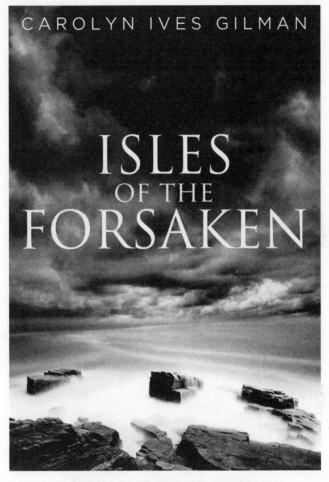

ISLES OF THE FORSAKEN
CAROLYN IVES GILMAN

AVAILABLE AUGUST 15, 2011
FROM CHIZINE PUBLICATIONS

978-1-926851-43-3

BRIARPATCH
TIM PRATT

AVAILABLE SEPTEMBER 15, 2011
FROM CHIZINE PUBLICATIONS

978-1-926851-44-0

BEARDED WOMEN: *STORIES*
TERESA MILBRODT

AVAILABLE OCTOBER 15, 2011
FROM CHIZINE PUBLICATIONS

978-1-926851-46-4

ENTER, NIGHT
MICHAEL ROWE

AVAILABLE OCTOBER 15, 2011
FROM CHIZINE PUBLICATIONS

978-1-926851-45-7